Ransom

Raena Rood

One Foundation Publishing

ISBN: 978-1-952431-25-8 (paperback)

ISBN: 978-1-952431-22-7 (e-book)

ISBN: 978-1-952431-24-1 (hardback)

Edited by Kimberly Murphree and Lori Werni

http://raenarood.com

Ransom

Raena Rood

"Rescue those who are being taken away to death; hold back those who are stumbling to the slaughter."

— Proverbs 24:11 (ESV)

Somewhere along the way, these books became about fathers. So I'm dedicating Ransom to the two wonderful fathers in my life— my dad, Larry Kissinger, and my father-in-law, Kenneth Rood. Two strong men who protected, provided for, and loved their families well. I love you both.

And to my Father in heaven—every word I write, every story I tell, is because of You.
May these books honor You.

Chapter One

"Wake up, traitor. You're home."

Kira lifted her head and stared through the bars separating her from the front of the Guard vehicle. She hadn't been asleep—she wasn't sure if she would ever sleep again. The handcuffs bit into her wrists, the sharp metal growing more painful with each passing minute. Her shoulders throbbed from the awkward position of her hands behind her back, and her stomach churned with nausea that even closing her eyes hadn't kept at bay.

The dashboard cast a pale green glow over the faces of the two Guards transporting her to the Confines. The female driver—one of the Guards she'd encountered on the bridge— kept her hands clamped around the steering wheel, her expression unreadable. Her partner twisted around in his seat to flash Kira a predatory grin.

"You're going to love it here," he said as the vehicle climbed the steep hill toward the grounds of the former Harrisburg State Hospital. "You've heard the stories about the Confines, right? Most of them are true, but hey, the food isn't half-bad.

Probably better than the rats and snakes you were eating in the Unregulated Zone."

His grin faded, hardening into something meaner. "Is it true what they say? That the Lawless have gone cannibal? One of my buddies on the Patrols swears they eat their own kids."

Kira clenched her jaw. She thought of Haven, that fragile sanctuary in the wilderness where the children had always been fed first, even when there wasn't enough. "That's a lie," she said. "They don't murder their children. Not like here."

"What's that supposed to mean?"

"Shut up, Jackson," the driver snapped. She held out her hand. "Give me the orders."

Jackson glared at her but handed over a folded set of papers.

The vehicle slowed to a stop beside a battered Guard shack, its paint peeling in long, grimy streaks. The perimeter fence beyond it told a different story—coils of razor wire gleamed under the harsh floodlights, unbroken and new.

Two Guards emerged from the shack, rifles in hand. One of them, his uniform shirt stretched tight over his gut, leaned into the driver's window and squinted at Kira.

"What do you have for us tonight, Donna?"

"New detainee," the woman explained. "The one who defected to the Unregulated Zone with the kid a few weeks ago."

The man nodded, flipping through the paperwork. "Patrols catch her?"

Donna's eyes briefly caught Kira's in the rearview mirror. "She came back on her own."

The man snorted. "Of course she did. What's wrong, young lady? Didn't find what you were looking for out there?"

No, Kira thought, swallowing hard. *I found so much more.*

A memory broke through before she could stop it: Will's

arms wrapped around her waist, his breath stirring loose strands of her hair.

"I love you, Kira. Did I tell you that yet?"

The words rang in her mind, raw and perfect. It had only been yesterday. It felt like a lifetime ago. Like a fading dream she'd been forced to wake from.

She pressed her palms against her knees, fingers digging into the fabric of her pants, trying to ground herself. She would give anything for one more moment with him. One more chance to say she loved him. How meeting him had changed everything. He'd walked into her life planning to deceive her, to kidnap her—and somehow, he had fallen for her instead. Even now, heading toward what was likely her execution, she didn't regret a second of it.

She shoved the memory of Will down and locked it away. She couldn't afford to hold on to anything now—not hope, not love, and not the foolish belief that she might see him again. She needed to accept the truth: Will was gone from her life. Forever.

And Ghost. Her chest ached at the thought of Haven's scarred and broken leader. A man who had once loved her mother enough to give up everything for her. She would never see him again either.

Kira had left him a note, scrawled with shaking hands and tucked into the pocket of Render's Patrol uniform. Render, who had slaughtered Aunt Reeva and paid the price for it. In the note, she'd begged Ghost to stop Will from following her— no matter what it took.

She'd ended the note with words meant only for him: *In a better world, you would've been my father.*

But she wouldn't tell any of that to the Guards. She'd already decided not to say anything about what she'd seen or done in the Unregulated Zone until Victor Devlin agreed to meet with her.

What if he refuses? What if he leaves you to rot here for weeks or months, letting the punishment break you before signing your death warrant as a Compulsory?

After all, making his secret daughter disappear would solve a lot of problems for him.

The older Guard handed the papers back through the window. "Go on through. Head up to the Main Building for intake."

Their headlights cut through the darkness as Donna drove past the gate. Kira pressed her forehead against the cool glass, watching shadows take shape in the beams of light. Row after row of abandoned outbuildings emerged from the gloom, their roofs caved in like broken backs, doors hanging from rusted hinges. Bright floodlights lit up the hilltop, turning the night into a harsh, artificial day.

A cracked sign caught the glare: *Harrisburg State Hospital.*

Kira knew its history. Once called the Pennsylvania State Lunatic Hospital and Union Asylum for the Insane—a name that said everything about the era that built it—it had confined those society deemed unwell until its closing in the early twenty-first century. After that, some buildings were converted into government offices, while others were left to decay.

According to her best friend Emma, whose father oversaw city construction, the old therapy rooms and patient wards had been stripped and converted into cells. The asylum had found a new purpose: containing anyone who challenged Vita Nova's elite.

The Confines.

The main building loomed ahead, its Victorian architecture standing like a monument to suffering. Vines snaked up the facade like swollen veins. Many windows were shattered or crudely boarded up, the gaps between planks like black, empty eyes. This was where the unwanted disappeared. Where hope came to die.

Donna pulled the vehicle up to the front entrance and shifted into park. She looked at Kira in the rearview mirror. "Don't try anything stupid. Just do what they tell you, and you'll be okay."

"No, you won't," Jackson said, throwing open his door. "Donna's lying. This place... it gets inside you. I don't care how tough you are or what you saw across the river. A few days here and you'll be begging for death."

His words seemed to thicken the already stale air inside the car. Even so, she felt the chill of the facility pressing in from beyond the glass, the promise of what waited for her inside tightening around her like a noose.

The rear door opened, and Donna leaned close to Kira. "They won't break you," she whispered, her eyes following Jackson as he circled the car like a shark. "Not if you don't let them."

"Okay."

It was all she could think to say.

Jackson appeared at her side. "What are you waiting for? Get out."

Her legs trembled as she maneuvered out of the vehicle, whether from the uncomfortable ride, from fear, or both. She drew a deep breath, fighting back another wave of nausea.

You can do this, she told herself. *You don't have a choice.*

Two Guards flanked the entrance, rifles across their chests. The ancient wooden doors behind them were warped and stained with age.

One of them stepped forward. "Let's go," he said, gesturing toward the entrance. "Get her to in-processing."

As they led her inside, Kira's eyes darted over the faded

portraits lining the corridor. Stern, unsmiling faces from another century. Their gazes seemed to judge her slow march toward whatever fate awaited her. It was all too much—the walls pressing in around her, those eyes boring into her soul, the enormity of the building itself. She jerked against the hands on her arms in a pathetic attempt to wrench free, but Jackson and Donna only tightened their grips on her arms, dragging her forward.

She twisted at the waist, desperate for one last look at the world outside, but it was too late.

The heavy doors groaned shut behind her.

Chapter Two

In-processing took hours.

Kira sat alone in a small room where fluorescent lights buzzed overhead like wasps. Everything felt deliberately sterile: bare white walls yellowed with age, a metal chair that leached warmth from her body, a table bolted to the floor as if they expected the prisoners to use it as a weapon. Her hands remained cuffed behind her back, her mind spinning through every horror story she'd ever heard about the Confines.

She couldn't imagine Emma in this place. Render had said she'd been imprisoned in the Confines for helping Kira rescue Will from the Compulsory Clinic. But how had her best friend, who'd always been more accustomed to comfort than chaos, survived even an hour here, let alone weeks? Was she still alive somewhere in this maze of dark corridors? And if she was... would Kira even recognize the person she'd become?

And then there was Jonesy, the closest thing to a father Will had known after his own father was murdered by the Patrols. He'd risked everything to smuggle Will's drugged body out of the city in a transport van, saving him from becoming a

Compulsory. Was Jonesy still here somewhere, his mind eroding along with the building around him?

Or had they both already been executed?

The door opened, and two Guards entered. The first was a heavyset older woman, her hair cropped so close it was almost shaved, clutching a clipboard against her chest. The second, a broad-shouldered man with a gray mustache, kept his gaze fixed anywhere but on Kira.

"Stand up," the woman ordered. "Let's get this over with."

Kira's muscles protested as she rose, stiff from hours of not moving. The man stepped behind her and removed her handcuffs with the mechanical precision of someone who'd done this countless times, while the woman launched straight into questioning.

"Name, age, address, occupation."

Kira rattled off the answers as quickly as she could, afraid of provoking the woman.

"Are you pregnant?"

"No."

"Any serious medical conditions we should know about?"

She wanted to say, "If I had any serious medical conditions, Vita Nova would've killed me already."

Instead, she managed another quiet "No."

"How many potentially infected individuals did you encounter in the Unregulated Zone?"

Kira's head jerked up. "What?"

"You were out there for..." The woman flipped through the papers. "Just over two weeks, correct?"

"Yes."

"And in that time, how many Lawless and/or potentially infected individuals did you come into contact with? I need their numbers and their approximate locations."

The question hung in the air between them, with Kira

uncertain of how to answer. If they truly believed the Job virus was still rampant beyond the barricade, why had they let her approach their checkpoint? Why hadn't they shot her on sight? Why transport her without masks or protection?

And why did this woman care about where the Lawless were?

"None," Kira lied.

"You didn't encounter anyone out there?"

"That's what I said."

The corner of the woman's mouth twitched, but she seemed more interested in finishing her shift than pursuing the truth. She made a note in the file. "Even though you've denied contact with individuals outside the barricade, you'll be monitored for any signs of infection."

The mustached guard stayed silent, his eyes locked on some distant point on the wall.

"Strip," the woman said, as casually as if she'd asked Kira to take off her coat.

Kira hesitated, but there was no point in resisting. Slowly, she peeled off the dirt-crusted clothing that carried the last traces of her life in the Unregulated Zone. Shame burned in her cheeks as she surrendered each garment, the room's cold air raising goosebumps on her exposed skin. She forced her spine straight, staring at the wall as the guards conducted their visual inspection, their eyes moving over her body like a pair of butchers appraising meat.

"Time for decontamination."

The woman's fingers clamped around Kira's elbow, steering her into a small chamber. The floor was steel grating, dark red with rust or worse, and a single industrial nozzle protruded from the ceiling.

Kira knew what was coming—she'd heard rumors about this part—but nothing could have prepared her.

The water hit her like a wall of ice, so cold it felt as if her skin were splitting open. A gasp escaped her lips before she could stop it, her whole body shaking as the chill carved its way through flesh and muscle to her bones.

The female Guard watched from the doorway, clipboard pressed to her chest. She had the look of someone who'd witnessed this process countless times before and had learned to turn off whatever part of her that might have once felt sympathy.

Something caustic had been added to the water—some industrial-grade disinfectant that burned her nose and throat. Each choking breath seared her lungs, making her eyes water and her chest constrict. The acrid chemical stench seemed designed to burn away more than grime. It felt like an assault on her soul, meant to erase who she'd been before entering this place. She squeezed her eyes shut and tried to pray, but the words burned away like the chemicals on her skin.

Finally, the water shut off. Kira stood in the center of the chamber, arms wrapped around herself, shivering so hard she could barely stay upright. The cold air hit her wet skin, leaving her teeth chattering.

"Turn," the woman ordered.

Kira forced her frozen muscles to obey. Water dripped from her hair, her chin, her fingertips. Tears burned at the back of her eyes, but she refused to let them fall.

She thought of Will, imagined him standing here instead of her, his jaw set with defiance even as ice water ran down his face. He would never give them the satisfaction of seeing him break.

Neither would she.

A thin rectangle of cloth landed at her feet.

"Dry off. You've got five seconds."

Kira snatched up the scrap of towel, which was barely more

substantial than tissue paper. Her numb fingers fumbled with the cloth as she dragged it over her skin, the rough material leaving angry red streaks in its wake. She had barely finished drying herself when the woman's voice echoed through the room.

"Time's up."

The Guard shoved a bundle of prison clothes and battered rubber flip-flops into her chest. Kira fumbled with the clothing, the coarse material dragging over her damp skin. The pants sagged on her hips, and the shirt hung off her shoulders like a potato sack, but she didn't dare ask for anything smaller. However flimsy, the uniform was armor she couldn't afford to lose.

Next came the medical exam.

They led her down a narrow hallway and into an exam room that smelled of cheap antiseptic and stale coffee. A nurse with deep shadows under her eyes barely glanced up from her clipboard as Kira entered the room. Her scrubs were stained and wrinkled, as if she'd been wearing them for days.

She grabbed Kira's arm and snapped a rubber tourniquet tight around her bicep, forcing the veins to rise. Without a word, she pressed a thumb against the crook of Kira's elbow and drove the needle in. Dark blood filled one vial, then another.

Kira watched, too numb to care.

The questions came in an endless stream: childhood illnesses, broken bones, allergies, vaccinations. Kira's answers came slowly, her thoughts thick and uncooperative.

Why do you care? She wanted to ask. *Why do you care about me breaking an arm at age five? Aren't you just going to kill me?*

When it was over, the female Guard reappeared and led Kira down a corridor so narrow her shoulders nearly brushed the walls. They emerged into the prison's central hub, with corridors branching off like spokes on a wheel. Overhead, fluorescent tubes sputtered, casting their sickly yellow light on what appeared to be a small command center. A bank of monitors showed grainy security feeds of every corridor and every cell, each screen a window into another pocket of misery. The equipment looked old, probably scavenged from old security systems.

Two armed Guards manned the main desk, their eyes following Kira's progress across the room. She avoided looking directly at them, instead focusing her attention on a half-eaten sandwich abandoned on a chipped plate on the desk. Her stomach clenched at the sight. When had she last eaten?

The memory surfaced: a single granola bar shared with Will on their journey back to Emmitsburg.

Would the Guards feed her tonight? Tomorrow?

The uncertainty was worse than the hunger.

The woman yawned, her grip on Kira's arm not loosening. "Where are we headed?"

One of the Guards glanced at the monitors. "Block A, cell number 8."

"Copy that."

The Guard pushed her down another hall lined with cell doors that seemed to stretch on forever. Each door had a small window, a portal into individual hells. Through the smudged glass, Kira caught glimpses of other prisoners: bodies curled on mattresses, others pacing like caged animals. The air reeked of despair, the quiet interrupted only by the occasional sob or cry.

She looked away.

They stopped at a cell near the corridor's end, where the flickering lights barely reached.

The woman used a keycard to unlock the door, revealing a narrow concrete box with a metal-framed bed bolted to the wall and a stainless steel toilet-sink combination in the corner. A thin, stained mattress slumped crookedly on the frame. The only window was a slit near the ceiling, showing a tiny slice of starry sky.

Kira stepped inside the cell, her rubber sandals squeaking against the concrete floor.

No instructions followed. No explanation of what came next. Instead, the door closed behind her with a final, hollow clang, and the lock engaged.

She stood in the center of the room, arms wrapped around herself, still shivering from the ice-cold shower. Then she stumbled to the cot, sinking onto the mattress. The metal frame creaked under her weight as she curled in on herself, pressing her knees tight to her chest.

Somewhere down the hall, a scream rose and broke into sobs.

Through the narrow window, the moon disappeared behind a cloud, leaving her in darkness.

Chapter Three

The metallic clunk of the lock disengaging jolted Kira awake. Her eyes snapped open, and she pushed herself upright on the bed, heart pounding in her chest.

Every instinct screamed at her to run, but there was nowhere to go. The cell was barely eight feet square.

She was trapped.

The door swung inward, and a tall figure stepped inside. It closed behind him with a quiet click.

"Daughter."

Somehow, the sound of Victor Devlin's voice brought an awful kind of relief. She'd never taken comfort in hearing him before, but in this terrible place, anything familiar felt comforting.

He moved closer, his perfectly tailored suit jarringly clean against the cracked tiles and stained walls. In the dim light filtering through the window, his silver hair gleamed like polished steel. He paused, studying her with those gunmetal gray eyes—cold, appraising, and utterly devoid of fatherly warmth.

"You look terrible," he said at last. "How much weight have you lost?"

Her throat was raw, her voice raspy from the chemicals that had burned her lungs during decontamination. "I can't believe you sent me here."

"Sent you here?" He shook his head slowly, hands clasped at his waist in that statesman's pose. "I didn't send you here, Kira. You did this to yourself. Actions have consequences. Didn't your mother ever teach you about owning up to your mistakes?"

A flare of anger burned through her chest. "Don't you dare talk about my mother."

Devlin's shoes squeaked on the floor as he closed the distance between them. "Why did you come back to the city?" His tone was almost curious. "You made it to the other side of the river. You were free. You got the little boy out, along with that Lawless boyfriend of yours. So why return?"

Kira forced herself to stand despite the stiffness in her limbs. She needed to face him at eye level, or as close as possible.

"You know why." Her voice trembled only slightly. "Where is he?"

Devlin raised his eyebrows, feigning confusion. "Who?"

"Teddy. Your men kidnapped him last night."

She stepped closer, trying to appear stronger than she was.

"Theodore Easton is safe. Confused, perhaps. Traumatized by his little adventure beyond the barricade, most certainly. But physically unharmed. He is preparing for his Reverence Ceremony tomorrow night. His previous Final Week was…interrupted."

"I want to see him."

Devlin broke eye contact and began to pace the cramped cell. "You know that's not possible, Kira. Besides, you don't need to worry about him. He'll be spending his Final Week safe in his mother's arms."

"Safe? That horrible woman is the one trying to kill him."

Devlin turned, cocking an eyebrow. "A little dramatic, don't you think? Both you and your mother always had a flair for it." He paused under the window. "Theodore is quite remarkable, actually. When we explained what happened—how his first Volunteer Week was interrupted, and how his Sacrifice had been delayed—he seemed downtrodden. Such a sweet, pure heart he has."

The fake warmth in his voice made her stomach turn. He used it in speeches and public ceremonies. Now he was using it on her in this place, when there was no reason for anything to remain hidden between them.

"Teddy's mother pushed him to Volunteer," Kira said, trying to keep her voice calm. "He's six. He didn't come up with the idea on his own. She made him think dying was some kind of hero's quest."

"And that's exactly what he—"

"Meanwhile," Kira cut him off, "she was busy flirting and doing who knows what else with another Volunteer's husband at Rolling Meadows. She's after the money and the fame, but she's too much of a coward to Volunteer herself. So she's going to get what she wants by letting the city murder her child."

Devlin waved a dismissive hand. "Why are you telling me this? Do you think it really matters? Do you think I care about the motivations of some twiggy little gold digger? All I care about is keeping this city safe and disease-free. You never understood that. You spent too long listening to your mother's lies and not enough time considering the life I've given you."

Kira couldn't believe what she was hearing. "The life

you've given me? I barely know you. You've never been a father to me."

"Judge me all you want. You're just like your mother, so I expect that. But real fathers protect their children's futures. That's what I've done. I've built something that will last, that will keep them alive—even if it costs lives along the way."

Kira stared at him. "Real fathers protect their kids from men like you."

A flicker of rage lit his eyes.

"You blame me for everything," he said. "But you never once thought about the cost of keeping this city from falling apart like everything beyond the river."

"What cost?" She spat the words at him. "You live in a mansion. You convince people to sacrifice themselves so you and your rich friends can throw parties every week. I was at the Volunteer Ball. Half of those people were over sixty."

Devlin squared his shoulders as he approached her. "You want to talk about the Ball? Fine. Those people earned their exemptions. They contribute more to this city in a day than most citizens do in their entire lives. They're the reason this city still exists."

He leaned in close. She could smell the expensive cologne, could see the artificial whiteness of his front tooth—the one Ghost had knocked out years ago.

"Do you know what happens without an elite class, Kira? Society collapses. It eats itself alive. Look outside the walls. Is that what you want? To live like animals, scrounging for scraps? Fighting over resources until there's nothing left?" He straightened, adjusting his tie. "No. I won't let that happen. Not to my city. In a perfect world, Compulsories and Volunteers would not be necessary, but this is far from a perfect world. In Vita Nova, the weak must die so the strong can live. That's not murder, Kira. That's survival."

Kira felt bile rise in her throat. "You want to talk about survival? Let's talk about the Unregulated Zone. I've lived out there, Devlin. I've lived with the people you call animals. They take care of each other. They heal the sick. They don't throw them away—they heal them. They don't murder their own children. And they're still surviving."

He smiled, but it didn't quite reach his cold eyes. "Not all of them."

Rage surged through her. The image of Avery's lifeless face flashed through her mind. Her wedding gown ruined, stained with mud and blood. "You mean the massacre you ordered? Your Patrols murdered dozens of innocent people that night."

Devlin laughed. "Innocent? That's what you call the dirty? The diseased? The Lawless? You forget I send soldiers into the Unregulated Zone every day. I know what kind of evil festers there."

The faces of the three men from the dollar store rose in her mind—hungry, violent, stripped of anything human.

She pushed the image away.

"Not all of them are sick," she shot back. "Not all of them are monsters. You've been lying to everyone in this city for years. There are normal people out there. Families just struggling to survive. But you wouldn't know anything about family, would you?"

Devlin's expression didn't even falter. "You've never let me forget how much I've failed you as a father, Kira. But don't worry—this will all be over soon. Teddy will make his Sacrifice, and you will make your own."

"Please," she whispered. "I'm begging you. He's only six. He doesn't understand any of this."

Devlin's expression hardened to stone. "Oh, he understands. Better than you ever will."

Kira felt sick. The thought of Teddy standing alone underneath the lights of the Stadium again, in his too-big suit, his mother's hand gripping his, made her physically ill. She knew she couldn't hold his hand, but if he could see her, he would at least know that she hadn't abandoned him.

"Let me go," she whispered. "Please. Let me be there for him."

"Go where? To the Reverence Ceremony?"

"Yes. I want him to see me. So he knows he's not alone."

Devlin shook his head. "Impossible. Besides, he won't be alone. The entire city will be there to witness his Sacrifice. And he'll have his mother, of course."

"His mother doesn't deserve to be there," Kira snapped. "She should be the one wearing a blue rose."

He seemed to consider her request for a moment, one finger tapping his pockmarked cheek. Then he shook his head. "No, I'm sorry. You'll stay here, where you—"

"Please, Dad."

She forced the word out, her voice cracking under the weight of it. She knew what she was doing—playing the only card she had left, hoping the title would appeal to whatever conscience he still possessed.

Devlin froze. "Strange that you'd call me that now, when the word always seemed to get stuck on your tongue in the past. Are you really going to allow desperation to steal away the last of your dignity?"

"That's not what I'm doing," she said, softening her tone as much as she could. "But you *are* my father. This is when it matters. This is when I need you."

He tilted his head to the side, studying her. "You've always wanted me to be something I'm not, Kira. It didn't matter how well I treated you or how often I came around. It was never enough for you because I couldn't be the perfect father you'd imagined in your mind. Tell me, Kira, have you ever considered that perhaps you're looking for a kind of fatherly perfection that doesn't exist in this city?"

"I'm not looking for perfection." She hoped the words sounded more sincere than they felt. "I'm looking for you. You're my father. Don't leave me in here. Let me see him one more time. Please, Dad."

Something shifted in his eyes. His right hand moved to the hem of his suit jacket, fingers picking at the edge of the fabric in an unconscious gesture Kira recognized. She did the same thing when she was nervous, though usually with the frayed edges of her sweaters or jacket sleeves.

But then it was gone.

He shook his head. "I'm not your father in here, Kira. In here, you're just another prisoner awaiting her punishment."

Before she could protest, he stepped into the hallway and closed the door behind him.

Kira's knees gave way, and she sank to the floor. Only then did the tears come, hot against her skin. The only warmth left in her world.

She'd tried to save Teddy. Risked everything. And in the end, she'd only bought him a few extra weeks. Now he would die anyway.

And she could do nothing to stop it.

Chapter Four

Ghost sat in the darkness of the ruined church, his back pressed against the wall, the familiar weight of his shotgun balanced across his knees.

Moonlight streamed through the cracked stained-glass windows, breaking into jagged, fractured patterns across the floor. Shadows crept along the warped wooden pews, twisting into unsettling shapes. Even the withered dahlias lining the aisles seemed to strain in the gloom, as if reaching for a sun that had died long ago.

He shouldn't be here.

The church was too exposed, too obvious. The Patrols would return to Emmitsburg soon. If not tonight, then by morning. He knew that. He'd fought in enough battles to recognize a losing position.

But a dark part of him hoped they'd come.

His scarred cheek throbbed with phantom pain. It was the smallest thing Devlin had taken from him. The biggest thing had a name.

Madison.

His fingers tightened around the stock of the shotgun. He pictured the door to the church bursting open, soldiers flooding in with their pressed uniforms and polished boots. He imagined them illuminated by the moonlight, lined up in his sights.

He imagined them falling, one by one.

Ghost blinked slowly, rage simmering in his stomach. Maybe this was what he'd been waiting for. Maybe this was why God had kept him alive all these years. Not to build cabins or rescue people, but to exact judgment on his enemies.

Psalm 18 filled his mind, and he whispered his favorite verses like a prayer. "I pursued my enemies and overtook them; I did not turn back till they were destroyed. I crushed them so that they could not rise; they fell beneath my feet."

Yes, if the soldiers came, he would greet them.

With buckshot.

No sooner had the thought crossed his mind than the heavy church door eased open, slowly and deliberately.

A Patrol soldier stepped into the doorway, his dark uniform blending with the shadows, weapon drawn.

Ghost's breath caught. Had God answered his prayer so quickly? He raised the shotgun to his shoulder in one silent motion, his pulse hammering in his ears. His finger tightened on the trigger.

The image wavered and fell away.

Will stood in the doorway, the hunting rifle dangling limp over one shoulder, his posture crumpled with exhaustion.

Ghost blinked hard, the breath shuddering out of him. He'd nearly killed the kid. His arms trembled as he lowered the rifle.

"Anything?"

Will shook his head and limped across the aisle. "I checked everywhere I could think of. Aunt Reeva's attic. Almost every store or apartment in town that's still standing." He lowered himself onto a pew and scrubbed a hand over his face. "I don't know where else she would've gone."

Nodding, Ghost slipped a hand into his coat pocket, fingers finding the folded note he'd taken from the Patrol soldier's corpse. He hadn't said a word about either to Will.

The note felt as if it burned his palm.

Kira's words had been meant for him alone.

I'm going back. Keep Will away from the city. No matter what.

He flexed his fingers around the paper until they hurt.

He'd lied to Will. Or at least *omitted* pertinent information. He'd said nothing about the note and watched as the kid wore himself out searching for a girl Ghost knew wasn't coming back.

Will's voice broke the silence. "You don't think..." He hesitated, as if he couldn't quite bring himself to say the words. "You don't think she went back into the city for Teddy?"

Ghost's jaw tensed. That's exactly what she had done.

But she hadn't wanted Will to know. If he knew, he'd follow her. And if he followed her, he'd be captured—just as Kira surely had been.

Ghost wasn't certain Devlin would kill Kira, but he knew the man would kill Will.

He forced out a weak, evasive answer. "I don't know."

Will kept talking, his voice growing desperate. "My gut keeps telling me that's what happened, but that doesn't make any sense. She wouldn't just leave without telling me. She wouldn't just leave Aunt Reeva."

Ghost closed his eyes for a moment and pictured the grave outside. The fresh dirt was marked with a makeshift wooden cross and a few wilting dahlias.

Will had insisted on burying the old woman himself, refusing Ghost's offer to help. He'd worked long after sundown, sweat dripping from his face. Maybe it was grief. Maybe it was penance. Maybe he just needed to keep his hands busy so his mind wouldn't start conjuring up dark thoughts of what had happened to Kira.

While Will worked, Ghost had dragged the dead soldier's body out of the church and dumped it in the basement of an abandoned house three streets over.

It was more burial than the pig deserved.

"Get some rest," Ghost said, eager to get off the topic of Kira, if only for a few minutes. He didn't enjoy lying to the kid.

"I can't sleep. Not until I know where she is. I just…" Will rubbed his face again. "I'm just going to sit here for a minute. Think of where else she might've gone. Then I'm going back out."

"No." Ghost switched to his command voice, the one he'd used in the Army. "You need to rest. Even for an hour. You've been running all night. You'll burn yourself out. When she comes back, we'll need to be ready to move, to regroup, to figure out what to do about Teddy. But we can't do any of that if you're too wiped out to stand."

Will shook his head. "What if she comes back and I'm sleeping?

"Then don't sleep. But you won't do her any good like this. One hour. That's all I'm asking."

Will's shoulders slumped, the fight bleeding out of him. "Okay. One hour." He leaned back against the pew, eyelids already fluttering. "But I'm not going to sleep."

"Sounds good to me."

Ghost watched as Will's head dipped, then jerked back up. He fought it, blinking furiously, trying to shake off the exhaustion clouding his eyes. Another few seconds passed before his chin dropped to his chest again, his breathing growing slower and heavier, sleep dragging at him no matter how hard he resisted.

This time, his head didn't come back up.

Ghost listened as the young man's breathing settled into a slow, even rhythm. He adjusted the shotgun across his lap, his eyes sweeping the sanctuary, and let out a long breath.

Kira had walked back into the city alone. Back to the checkpoint on the bridge. Back to her father.

The man who had stolen everything from Ghost.

His hand drifted once more to the precious note in his pocket. The last words from the young woman who had crashed into his life and thrown it into chaos.

In a better world, you would've been my father.

His throat tightened, heat stinging behind his eyes. He didn't deserve those words. Didn't deserve her trust. God knew he hadn't protected her mother the way he should have, hadn't saved Kira from the brutal world that had chewed them both up.

All he could do for her now was keep his promise.

And watch over the boy she'd loved enough to leave behind.

Chapter Five

Kira woke to hushed whispers.

Her eyes felt raw and swollen from the tears she'd shed after her father left—tears she hadn't been able to stop until there was nothing left in her. But none of it had been for herself.

It had been for Teddy.

For the way he'd trusted her without question. For how completely she had failed to save him.

Exhaustion had finally dragged her under like a riptide, pulling her into a heavy, choking sleep filled with shapeless nightmares she couldn't remember. Even now, awake, the guilt gnawed at her. A hollow emptiness, like the abandoned buildings across the river, their roofs caved in and open to the rain.

Pale light spilled through the narrow window high in the cell wall. A single sharp beam cut across the concrete floor, almost painful to look at. For the first time in days, the sun had finally broken through the clouds.

She blinked hard against it. Was it morning? Afternoon? She couldn't tell. The concept of time had dissolved here.

Her stomach cramped and let out a sharp growl. Last night she'd felt too sick to eat—not that she'd been offered any food—but now hunger clawed at her with a vengeance. She closed her eyes for a moment and imagined a plate of scrambled eggs from the mess hall in Haven, the scent of coffee, and the sound of off-key hymns being sung in the background.

Eggs and Christian hymns.

Home.

A sound dragged her back to the present: slow, deliberate footsteps in the corridor outside.

She recognized the heavy tread of Guard boots. Normally they passed her door without pause. But not this time.

The steps slowed. Stopped.

Two faces appeared in the tiny square window in the cell door.

Instinctively, she snapped her eyes shut and pretended to be asleep. She didn't want to give them any reason to come inside.

"Look at her face," one Guard muttered, voice muffled through the door. "What did I tell you?"

"Same eyes. Same chin." Another voice, female, sharper. "It's so obvious. Makes me sick."

The steps resumed, but more followed soon after—another pair, then another.

Eventually, she opened her eyes and sat up. She used the toilet, then leaned over the tiny, stained sink, cupping her hands to drink the brackish water. It tasted of rust and chlorine, but it filled her stomach enough to dull the ache.

Finally, she sat on the edge of her narrow bed, scratchy blanket bunched around her waist, waiting.

They kept coming.

Faces appeared in the small window—some pressing close, their eyes scanning every inch of her features like a puzzle they were trying to solve. Others tried and failed to be subtle, flicking glances as they passed, only to circle back for another look.

Their voices drifted through the cracks in the door.

"…looks so much like him…"

"…why would he lie about her…"

"…what else is he hiding…"

She sat still, watching them.

And despite herself, she almost smiled.

Her father's carefully guarded secret was unraveling.

SOME TIME LATER, THE PATTERN CHANGED. A SINGLE FACE appeared at the window. Female. Someone she recognized.

A keycard beeped, followed by the soft thunk of the unlocking mechanism, and the door swung open.

Donna, the Guard from the bridge, stood in the doorway, a neatly folded bundle of clothes in her arms. "Get dressed," she said, tossing the clothes onto the mattress. "I've got orders to transfer you."

The clothes weren't prison-issue gray—no rough fabric or loose threads. Instead, Donna had brought dark slacks with crisp creases, a cream-colored blouse that felt like silk, and a pair of low, elegant black heels. Clothes meant to transform a prisoner into something else entirely.

"Where?" she asked, though she already suspected the answer.

Donna's lips pulled into a thin line. "The Executive Mansion."

Something in the woman's eyes had changed. The way she looked at Kira was different now. Not the way a Guard would look at a prisoner, but something closer to awe. Or wariness.

Like someone who had realized they'd been guarding royalty without knowing it.

"Your father wants to see you."

THE VEHICLE CAME TO A STOP IN FRONT OF THE Executive Mansion. Kira stared out the tinted window at the Georgian facade. The red brick glowed in the afternoon sun, making the place look almost welcoming. Flowers lined the circular driveway in carefully tended beds, with no stray weeds or dying blooms in sight. The grounds were immaculate and welcoming.

Nothing like the Confines.

Through the windows, Kira caught flashes of motion: Guards in crisp uniforms patrolling the corridors and staff moving briskly, going about their daily duties.

This was her father's world, the beating heart of Vita Nova's empire.

Donna opened the rear door for her, and Kira stepped out of the car. Her wrists were bare. She had not been cuffed for the ride, which she took as a good sign. She ran her hands over the sleek fabric of her slacks, struck by the contrast to the scratchy gray rags of the Confines.

Just hours ago she'd been another prisoner, using the toilet in front of strangers and drinking metallic-tasting water from her hands. Now she wore an outfit that cost more than most of Vita Nova's citizens made in a month.

Part of her wanted to laugh at the absurdity of it.

How quickly Victor Devlin could change the narrative to suit his needs. Even her transport from the prison had been carefully choreographed. No battered Guard van, no armed escort for the mayor's secret daughter. Instead, she'd arrived in

a sleek black car with tinted windows, like any government official being shuttled to a meeting.

The interior of the mansion was as elegant as she remembered. Polished floors that reflected the chandeliers above.
White walls decorated with artwork her father appreciated.
Expensive furniture fit for royalty, not a family. She had to
remind herself that children lived in this house.

Her siblings.

As they walked through the Grand Hall, Kira couldn't help
but remember the Volunteer Ball. The rich taste of perfectly
seared duck breast on her tongue. The mingling scents of
expensive perfumes and colognes that had hung thick in the air.
The chime of crystal glasses clinking in toasts as the city's elite
celebrated their chosen martyrs.

The feeling of Will's arms around her as they danced.

He'd worn a tailored black tuxedo that turned him from a
rugged sanitation worker into a prince. Even his hair had been
styled, the usual tousled golden-brown waves slicked back until
they gleamed almost black under the chandeliers.

When the song ended, they had kissed in front of everyone
—the young Volunteer and his advocate, putting on their
doomed little show.

She squeezed her eyes shut, forcing the memory away.

That night was over.

Will was gone.

Donna led her across the Grand Hall's marble floor and up
the broad staircase, past the gallery of oil portraits of past
mayors who had guided the city through one crisis or another.
At the top of the stairs hung the largest portrait of them all:
Victor Devlin himself, captured mid-speech, his eyes sharp and
commanding even in paint.

Two Guards snapped to attention outside his study. They

stared at Kira as she approached, their eyes lingering on her face, studying every feature.

Even here, in her father's domain, the rumors had taken root.

Donna paused at the open door and knocked lightly on the frame.

"Sir? Ms. Liebert is here."

"Come in, Ms. Liebert. Close the door behind you."

Donna's eyes met Kira's. There was something almost apologetic in them. "I'll be right out here."

Kira nodded once, then turned. She took a deep breath, pushed the door all the way open, and stepped inside.

VICTOR DEVLIN STOOD BY THE WINDOW OVERLOOKING HIS city.

He didn't turn when she entered. Didn't so much as glance in her direction. Instead, he swirled the amber liquid in his crystal tumbler, the ice clinking softly in the unnatural quiet of the room.

Kira closed the door behind her and waited.

She recognized this tactic. Her father had always enjoyed wielding silence like a weapon. He'd used it on her when she was a child. Back then it had worked, filling her with anxiety and guilt until she cracked and apologized for whatever awful sin she'd committed, such as calling him Victor instead of Dad.

But she wasn't afraid of him. Not anymore.

"Victor?" she said, raising her voice just loud enough that the Guards outside would hear. "Why did you bring me here?"

Devlin took a long sip from his tumbler, then set the glass on the table beside him. Only then did he turn to face her, his jaw working side to side, grinding his teeth.

"Once again, dear daughter, you've really made a mess of things."

She fought back a smile, taking some satisfaction in seeing him this unsettled. "Really? How so?"

"The whole city is talking," he said, his voice tight with the effort to remain calm. "Apparently, the Guards you ran into on the bridge noticed the resemblance. And they have very loose lips. It wasn't very thoughtful of you to publicly claim to be my daughter."

Kira let out a quick breath that was almost a laugh. "It wasn't very thoughtful of you to abandon my mother." Her tone was icy and controlled. "Or to stand by while the city killed her."

Devlin's expression twitched—just for an instant—then he forced his face back into its usual calm mask. "Back in your cell, you asked if I would allow you to attend tonight's Reverence Ceremony. Do you still want to see Theodore Easton again?"

Her mouth went dry. She knew this was a trap.

But it was Teddy.

"Of course."

Devlin smiled at her, the red splotches on his cheeks hinting that he'd consumed more than one drink before her arrival. His collar sat slightly askew, something the perfectly groomed Victor Devlin would never allow during public hours.

"Good. Then you'll be my guest tonight." He picked up his glass again but didn't drink, rolling it slowly between his fingers. "Before the roses are distributed, I'll introduce you to the city as my daughter."

She frowned, not understanding. "Why would you do that?"

He walked to his desk, tracing its polished surface with one finger. "Because we're going to tell them a little story. A beautiful, little story they're going to love."

"What kind of story?"

He leaned back against the desk. "The story of a heroic mayor, forced to make impossible choices to protect his city. And his brave, loyal daughter, secretly working with him all along. She agrees to play the role of a suspected defector's advocate to gain intelligence on his criminal network."

Kira could only stare at him, not believing what she was hearing.

"And when things escalate—when he and his traitor friends are suspected of bombing the Tenements and kidnapping Vita Nova's most precious Volunteer—she infiltrates their group at her father's command, risking her own safety to recover the lost boy and bring him home."

She felt sick. Her real choices, twisted into propaganda, with Devlin as the selfless savior and Will recast as a murderer. Every truth she had lived through carefully reshaped to make Devlin the hero and her the obedient daughter.

And she knew the city would believe it.

"You're completely insane," she muttered when he finished speaking. "Everything you just said is a lie."

Devlin's smile widened as he turned to the window, straightening his collar in its reflection. "It's a wonderful story, isn't it? It gives you a chance at life outside the Confines, and it gives the city what they need."

She folded her arms across her chest. "And what's that?"

He turned to face her. "People need to believe in heroes, Kira. Especially in dark times such as these."

She shook her head, not wanting to believe he could rewrite her narrative that easily. "But people saw me. The Guards chased me through the city."

Devlin gave her a patient sigh, as if explaining something to a stubborn child. "They didn't see your face. They only saw the Porsche—*Emma's* Porsche. She was the one driving it. She's the one who jumped into the river with the boy. She was recovered and imprisoned. But the Lawless pulled the boy from the water before we could reach him. That's when you agreed to follow your Volunteer into the Unregulated Zone, to gather the intel we needed to bring him home."

"What about Rolling Meadows? Kimber—"

She caught herself too late.

Kimber Worley had gone to school with Kira. She had also worked at Rolling Meadows, the resort where the Volunteers stayed during their Final Week. She was the one who had allowed Kira to visit Teddy on the day of his Sacrifice.

Right before Kira stole him away.

Devlin's smile didn't falter. "Don't worry. Kimber Worley has already been dealt with."

Kira swallowed. "Dealt with" meant rotting in the Confines.

Or dead.

She forced her breathing to steady. She had to think. There had to be gaps in his perfect story. Something he hadn't accounted for.

And then she remembered.

"You sent your Patrols into Emmitsburg," she said, that awful last night in Aunt Reeva's attic resurfacing in her mind. "They knew the truth. They were looking for me. One of them found me."

"Some of them did. A few of my best soldiers—the ones I would trust with my life—knew the truth about you, but they didn't know you were my daughter."

Kira felt her heart freeze.

A few of my best soldiers.

Render.

My father sent that killer after me.

"Stop trying to pick this apart, Kira. I'm offering you a chance you don't deserve."

Devlin moved across the room and lifted a garment bag from behind his desk. He unzipped it slowly, revealing a flash of deep blue fabric. He pulled out a simple but elegant dress that perfectly matched the color of the roses that were distributed at the Reverence Ceremony.

She stared at the dress, not understanding. "What is that?"

"It's for you. I want you to look perfect when you stand next to me on that field tonight."

"What are you talking about?"

"I know Sienna Graves usually handles the Reverence Ceremonies. But I think it's important for the city to see me tonight. And they need to see you, too. They need to see you standing in the middle of the field, with the full support of the city's leadership. They need to believe you're a hero, not a traitor. That won't be easy."

Kira stared at him. "You're insane."

He smiled at her. "You asked to be near the boy. I'm granting your request. You should thank me. We can make any necessary alterations to the dress, though I suspect it will fit perfectly. You have your mother's build—slight enough to be forgettable."

Kira's hands clamped shut, her nails digging into her palms. She wanted to attack him. To launch herself across the desk and claw at his face until it was as scarred as Ghost's. To make him feel even a fraction of the pain he'd inflicted on others.

But she didn't move.

Instead, she forced herself to nod. Resigned herself to playing the role he'd cast for her.

Because Teddy was waiting. She was closer to him now than she'd been in days. She needed to see him again. To look into his eyes one more time, even if it were just to say goodbye.

Even if it meant becoming Victor Devlin's daughter.

Chapter Six

Ghost knelt in the old church's infirmary, the stale scent of antiseptic and mildew lingering in the air. He worked methodically, sorting bottles of antibiotics and vials of morphine into neat piles. Some labels were so faded they were barely legible, so he twisted the caps and inspected the crumbling tablets inside before wrapping the salvageable ones in towels for transport.

Twelve years ago, he wouldn't have bothered with medicine this old. Wouldn't have trusted it. But the world was different now.

Expired medicine was better than no medicine at all.

A quiet rustle of movement came from somewhere behind him. Ghost didn't need to turn to know who it was. He knew the sound of those boots and the way they dragged when the kid was exhausted or angry.

"Those are Reeva's supplies," Will said from the doorway.

Ghost didn't look up. He wrapped another bottle in a towel and folded the corners.

"She doesn't need them anymore."

"So you're just going to take them?"

"Yes." Ghost set aside another bottle of antibiotics. "We can use them in Haven. Might save someone's life. We need to leave soon if we want to get back before dark."

He heard Will's boots scuff against the floor as he stepped into the room. "We can't leave. Not without Kira."

Ghost forced himself to his feet, his joints popping after crouching too long. He turned to face the kid, who stood just inside the doorway, the hunting rifle slung over his shoulder.

"Will, the Patrols are going to find this church. We've stayed here too long already."

"Then let them come." Will tapped the barrel of his rifle. "I think I'd really like that."

The kid's eyes were glassy and wild. It was like looking in a mirror, twelve years younger.

"You're not thinking clearly. Your mind—"

"My mind is fine. Kira's still out there. She's just hiding. Waiting until it's safe. Say what you want, but I'm not leaving without her."

Ghost kept his expression blank. It wasn't fair of Kira to ask this of him. He knew exactly what Will was feeling. That raw, desperate need to protect someone, even if that person didn't want protection.

"She's not hiding."

"You don't know that."

"We need to get back to Haven." Ghost's tone left no room for argument. "That's what she would want."

Will stepped closer, eyes blazing. "Don't pretend you know what she would want. You barely know her."

Ghost almost smiled at the irony of it. If the kid only knew.

In a better world, you would've been my father.

His hand moved to his pocket, his fingers brushing the folded note that had haunted him since the moment he'd discovered it on the soldier's body. He wanted to honor Kira's request, but Will would not leave Emmitsburg without her. And the longer they remained this close to Vita Nova, the more likely they were to be discovered.

And then what would happen to Haven?

Slowly, he withdrew the note from his pocket and held it out to Will.

The kid took it and unfolded it with jerky movements, his eyes racing over Kira's loopy handwriting. There were only a few sentences, but he read them multiple times, his eyes tracing the lines again and again. When he finished reading, he folded the note and tucked it into his pocket.

"She went back for Teddy," he said, rubbing the back of his neck.

Ghost nodded. "Yes."

"How long have you had this?"

"Since we found the dead soldier."

Will's gaze shot to him, his eyes bulging. "All this time? While I was searching for her? You knew she was gone?"

"I was trying to respect her wishes."

Will shook his head and laughed, a dry, humorless sound. "She's dead. You realize that, right? You killed her."

"She made her choice."

"Her choice?"

"You read the note. You saw what she asked me to do."

Will dropped the rifle and surged forward. He shoved Ghost hard in the chest. "She doesn't understand what she's asking!"

Ghost didn't react at first. But when Will tried to shove him again, Ghost's hands shot out, closing around the boy's wrists.

"Don't."

Will ripped his hands from Ghost's grip, but only because

Ghost allowed it to happen. "Don't what? Don't make you feel guilty? You're just going to let Devlin kill her!"

Will rushed forward, barreling into him, and they crashed to the floor, scattering bottles and bandages. The old cart of medication Ghost had been sorting tipped over and fell with a loud clatter.

The kid fought like an animal—wild, uncoordinated, all adrenaline and no technique. Ghost saw himself in that rage. He knew better than anyone how quickly grief could morph into violence, how badly it burned when there was nowhere to put it.

He could have ended the fight in seconds. His body remembered every brutal lesson the military had ever drilled into him.

But he didn't.

He let Will hit him. Took the kid's knuckles on his cheek. Let him unleash all of that hopelessness and anger in a flurry of blind, clumsy swings.

Then Will landed one solid punch that surprised them both—his fist slamming into Ghost's kidney, the pain sharp enough to make him grunt.

Anger flared white-hot.

Before he could stop himself, his fist connected with Will's face, sending the kid sprawling, blood blooming on his lip.

Ghost froze, guilt surging through his veins like ice water. He hadn't meant to hit him that hard.

But Will wasn't done. Wiping blood from his mouth with the back of his hand, he lurched forward again—slower now but stubborn to the end.

Ghost let him come. Then he grabbed the kid and flipped him over, pinning him flat on the floor with one forearm braced across his chest. Holding him steady as he struggled and gasped beneath him.

"Are you done?"

Will went limp, the fight draining out of him all at once. "I know ways into the city," he said, still breathing heavily. "We can get her back."

Ghost released him and sank back onto his heels. "And then what? If she's still alive, she's in the Confines. Do you want them to put you both to death together? Is that your plan?"

"I don't care." Will pushed himself up, wiping blood from his lip. "I'd rather die trying to save her than live knowing I did nothing."

Ghost sucked in a breath. The words hit him like a hammer to his already sore kidney. How many nights had he lain awake underneath the same blanket of stars as the woman he loved, plotting ways to sneak back into Vita Nova? How much time had he spent imagining heroic rescues that had never happened?

He swallowed hard and climbed to his feet. "I'm leaving for Haven within the hour. I've got a lot of medicine here. Let's gather whatever other supplies we can carry and take them with us."

Will didn't move. His eyes were fixed on the floor, blank with something worse than rage.

Determination.

"I'm not going back."

Ghost stared at him, remembering how it had felt to be young and desperate and so certain that love could conquer anything. Remembering how it felt when that certainty had been shattered.

"You're going to get yourself killed."

Will climbed to his feet. He reached down and picked up his rifle. "It's Sunday. The entire city will be at the Reverence Ceremony in a few hours. That's when I'll cross over. I'll stay underneath the Market Street Bridge the whole time. Use the logs and debris as cover. The Patrol boats won't see me. Others have done it."

Ghost briefly considered knocking Will out. Tying him up. Dragging him back to Haven. But what was the point? The kid would bolt back to the city the first chance he got.

He let out a slow breath. "Wait until the Guards on the bridge are distracted."

Will nodded, already understanding exactly what was coming next.

"Wait for the fireworks."

Chapter Seven

The SUV glided through the empty streets of Vita Nova. Kira sat in the back seat, the blue dress cool against her skin. The Governmental Sector rose around them in orderly lines of brick and glass.

As they passed rows of imposing office buildings, her eyes lingered on the Volunteer Support Center, her old workplace. She remembered the countless hours spent meeting with Volunteers in her office, helping them plan every aspect of their Final Week. She'd granted their final wishes, arranged their goodbyes, and reassured them of the nobility of their Sacrifice, all while believing in the importance and righteousness of her job.

How blind she'd been.

Across from her, Sienna Graves crossed one long leg over the other. The deputy mayor's gray pantsuit clung perfectly to her curves, the tailored fabric emphasizing a body she was clearly proud of. Her blouse was lower cut than usual, flashing plenty of cleavage, and her makeup was professionally applied, but not enough to hide the faint freckles dusting her nose.

Even sitting, Graves maintained perfect posture, never slouching or showing weakness, her chin lifted like a swan.

Kira deliberately slouched lower in her seat, refusing to mirror that unnatural poise.

Graves's green eyes flicked toward her—sharp and assessing, as if she could hear the thoughts in Kira's head—then back to Devlin.

"Expect the crowd to be enthusiastic tonight, Victor," she said, inspecting her long, blood-red nails. "From what I've heard, everyone is eager to celebrate young Theodore's triumphant return to the city."

Devlin nodded. "Good. Vita Nova has endured a difficult few weeks. Tragedy after tragedy. A little hope will do everyone good."

Kira gaped at him. "Hope?"

One of Graves's perfectly shaped eyebrows arched. "You disagree with our assessment of the situation?"

Kira's hands twisted in her lap. She could feel her father's eyes boring holes in her skull. "I agree Vita Nova needs hope," she said carefully. "But it's not ethical to let a child make this kind of decision. He doesn't understand."

Graves leaned forward, red curls spilling over her shoulder to briefly hide her cleavage. Her smile was all teeth, slightly yellowed with age. "On the contrary. Theodore is remarkably perceptive for his age. You spent a great deal of time with him— you should know. Children often see truths more clearly than adults, and Theodore is eager to give this city what it needs." She looked at Devlin, her lips curling in that intimate, possessive way that made Kira's skin crawl. "Isn't that right, Victor?"

"Indeed, it is, Sienna."

Kira stared at them, disgusted. There was clearly something between them. Something Kira had never noticed before but probably should have suspected.

Graves was married. So was Devlin.

But nothing was beneath her father.

Devlin gazed out the window. "Unfortunately, some people refuse to see the beauty in our Volunteers' Sacrifices. They forget those Sacrifices have made their privileged lives possible."

Graves let out a breathy laugh. "How right you are, Victor." Her eyes trailed over Kira's new dress. "Speaking of beauty, you clean up remarkably well for someone who's been cavorting with the Lawless. Tell me... how revolting were their living conditions?"

Kira forced her spine straight. "Not nearly as revolting as the living conditions of the people in our Confines."

Graves's eyes narrowed, and the fine lines at their corners deepened, betraying her true age beneath the layers of makeup.

"Victor, your offspring is a firecracker. I should have expected as much. But she's easily also swayed. She spent a few weeks living among the Lawless, and now she thinks they're saints. She spent one night in the Confines and suddenly she's a champion of prison reform."

"Enough," Devlin said, his voice carrying an edge sharp enough to cut metal. "None of that matters anymore. Tonight isn't about rehashing the past. It's about the future. About rebuilding what's been broken. Isn't that right, daughter?"

The word felt wrong in her mouth, twisted and perverted, like everything else in this city. But Kira forced herself to say it. To play the role he'd written for her, because it was the only way to get close to Teddy.

"Yes, Dad."

Graves watched this exchange with interest, her expression giving nothing away. But there was calculation behind those green eyes—wheels turning, possibilities being weighed. She knew that Devlin's sudden announcement of a long-lost daughter was politically motivated, but she seemed content to play along.

For now.

The SUV turned onto the long, arched bridge leading to City Island. The orange glow of the sunset burned on the water below them, painting the river in fiery hues. Ahead, the Stadium rose from the trees, its bright floodlights flickering. Thousands of citizens had already gathered inside to witness the evening's Reverence Ceremony.

She remembered sitting with Will on the ruined western span of the bridge, watching the ceremony from a safe distance. The fireworks had seemed beautiful then, like something out of a fairy tale. It was the only time she'd ever found a Reverence Ceremony bearable. She'd been far enough away to almost forget what it meant.

Kira wore no watch, but she knew that Devlin's SUV never arrived at the ceremony until a quarter past seven. The mayor and deputy mayor were always late on purpose, timing their arrival to the minute so the citizens would be in their seats and the Volunteers already lined up on the field.

But tonight there would be no row of Volunteers. No trays of blue roses.

Just one.

For Teddy.

Kira looked out the window at the river flowing beneath them. Somewhere on the far bank, Will and Ghost were probably moving through the trees, on their way back to Haven.

She hoped.

She had no idea how Ghost would convince Will to leave Emmitsburg without her, but she knew if anyone could do it, it was him.

Would they return to the village and start to rebuild the fence? Or would Ghost lead his people far away, beyond the reach of Devlin's Patrols? Maybe north to find his friend, Brannigan, and his sick daughter?

Would Brack and Grace go with them?

She would never know those answers.

Graves's voice cut into Kira's thoughts. "I know this must be difficult for you, Kira. You care about Teddy—that's clear."

Kira shifted uncomfortably in her seat. She wished the woman would just ignore her and let the ride pass in silence. "Thank you."

Graves leaned forward. "And that's exactly why you're the right person for what comes next."

What comes next?

She looked from the deputy mayor to her father and back again. "I don't understand," she said. "What comes next?"

Graves's smile spread wider. She didn't bother hiding her excitement. "Didn't you hear? You're going to pin the rose on Teddy's chest."

Kira's throat worked as she swallowed hard. So they weren't just making her watch Teddy's death sentence—they wanted her to bless it, to help them sell their lie to the city.

Her voice came out ragged, barely above a whisper. "I can't…" she whispered, shaking her head. "No. I won't do it."

"You can, and you will." Devlin's voice took on the same sharp edge she remembered from her childhood. "This isn't a request, Kira. This is the price of your freedom. The city needs its story, and you're going to help us tell it."

She held his gaze, fury and horror clawing at her insides. Hoping he'd flinch or relent. But he didn't. When it came to silence, her father always won. She looked away, her anger curdling into something cold and hollow.

Ahead, the Stadium grew massive in the windshield.

As the SUV pulled to a stop and the door opened, Kira stared at the floodlights gleaming on the field. Once, those same lights had illuminated baseball games. Tonight, they would shine on a small child awaiting his death.

A game was still being played on this field.

Just not baseball.

The chants. The Memoriam. The fireworks. All of it was theater. A ritual designed to make murder look like sacrifice.

And her father was the master of that stage.

Even now, he was reshaping her story, turning her from defector to hero. He wanted the entire city to watch as she pinned a blue rose to Teddy's chest and condemned a little boy to death with her own hands.

Something stirred in the back of her mind. Not quite a plan, but a shadow of one. A possible next move in this twisted game that her father had created.

One he would never see coming.

Chapter Eight

Kira stood beside her father in the dugout and watched as Sienna Graves glided onto the field. Her towering heels carved small, perfect divots in the grass with each step, the muscles in her calves working over-time to maintain a steady, measured pace. The Stadium lights caught her red hair, setting it ablaze.

Viewed from the stands, Graves appeared regal and stat-uesque—like a queen ascending to her throne. But Kira had been close enough to the woman to see her many imperfec-tions: the varicose veins peeking out the bottom of her pantsuit, the slight yellow tinge to her teeth, the crow's feet she desper-ately tried to conceal with makeup.

Tiny chinks in her armor.

Kira craned her neck, trying to see around her father's broad frame for any glimpse of Teddy. What had they done to him since dragging him away from Haven? Had he been injured during the attack on the village? Had the soldiers terrorized him on their way back to the city?

She spotted him at last, standing at the center of the field, looking impossibly small in his pale blue suit. He looked like himself—sweet, young, innocent Teddy—but diminished, somehow. Hollowed out. There was no lollipop in his hand tonight. No Pandy, the stuffed panda, tucked under one arm. Instead of gazing in childish awe at the crowd like he'd done at his first ceremony, his head drooped forward, his eyes fixed on the ground. He kept reaching up to tug at his bow tie, like it was choking him.

Kira's heart broke at the sight of him.

This wasn't the little boy who'd ridden on Brack's shoulders through the woods, squealing and pointing at every squirrel and chipmunk along the way.

This was that boy's shadow.

His ghost.

His mother, Trinity Easton, clutched his shoulders with bony fingers, her jet-black hair severe against her pale skin. She swatted his hand away from the tie again and again, her bright smile frozen for the crowd. An ivory dress hung loose on her narrow frame, making her look more like a bride-to-be than a mother preparing to sacrifice her son.

Kira wondered if Trinity was still sneaking around with Tucker Morley, the older man from Rolling Meadows whose wife had Volunteered the same week as Will and Teddy. Morley wasn't on the field, of course. He'd be in the stands, playing the grieving husband in public while squeezing every last drop of sympathy out of his wife's Sacrifice.

A microphone crackled to life.

"Good evening, citizens of Vita Nova!" Graves's voice reverberated throughout the Stadium. "Thank you for attending tonight's Reverence Ceremony!"

Scattered applause trickled through the stadium. It

sounded wrong. Weak. Nothing like the unified roar Kira remembered from past ceremonies. Even the few cheers that broke through seemed forced.

It was the sound of a city beginning to doubt.

No wonder Devlin is doing damage control, she thought.

If Graves noticed the lackluster applause, she didn't let it show.

"Thank you all, truly," she purred, waving her hands as if the people in the bleachers weren't already falling silent without her permission. "Before we begin, I must warn you—tonight's ceremony will differ greatly from anything you've witnessed before."

In the dugout, Devlin shifted behind Kira, lowering his voice so only she could hear. "Your time in the Confines was mercifully short, daughter. Don't fool yourself into thinking you're strong enough to survive there for long. Last night was just a taste of what awaits if you embarrass or undermine me tonight."

Kira nodded, biting the inside of her cheek. Her father's threat made her angry—furious, even—but beneath that anger lay something worse: a deep, aching hurt. It was astounding, really, how deeply Victor Devlin could still wound her. That he could threaten her so easily. That she mattered so little to her own father that he would throw her back into that hell without blinking.

"I won't embarrass you."

"Excellent."

On the field, Graves turned her attention to the dugout. "Before we distribute tonight's only rose, I have the great honor of welcoming two very special guests." She let the words hang in the air, savoring the moment. "Please do me the honor of welcoming Mayor Victor Devlin... and his daughter, Kira."

Devlin's hand pressed into the small of her back, steering her out of the dugout and into the glare of the Stadium lights. To the crowd, it would look like a proud father guiding his nervous daughter. But Kira felt the pressure behind the touch. The implied threat.

But she kept walking.

Each step carried her closer to Teddy.

As they headed for the center of the field, some in the crowd rose to applaud while others stayed seated, their confusion obvious. The rumors hadn't reached every corner of the city yet. Most still believed Mayor Devlin's only children were his ten-year-old twins, Vance and Violet.

Teddy looked up as Kira approached, the sadness in his eyes shifting to a mix of confusion and hope. For an instant, she saw a flicker of the little boy she remembered in those warm brown eyes.

She smiled and mouthed, "It's okay."

Trinity Easton's grip on her son's shoulders visibly tightened as Kira approached, her nails digging into his suit jacket. She scowled at Kira, her heavily lined eyes narrowing with distrust. Whatever story Devlin had told her, she clearly didn't buy it.

Devlin took the microphone from Sienna Graves and paused, waiting for the crowd to fall silent before he spoke.

"My fellow citizens, I can imagine how confused you all must be. These last few weeks have been difficult and violent. Full of unanswered questions. Tonight, I stand before you not only as your mayor but also as a father. A father who has carried a burden for far too long."

The crowd hung on his every word, leaning forward in their seats.

"The rumors you've heard are true. The young woman standing beside me is my daughter, Kira. Some of you may know her from her work as a volunteer advocate for the city. Her mother and I were together for a time before I met my wife, Chandra. Kira was the result of our love."

Kira strained to keep her expression neutral.

Love?

After Kira's mother became pregnant, Devlin had walked away without a second thought, leaving her to raise their infant daughter alone while he crafted a perfect life with his perfect family.

What kind of love was that?

"When our relationship ended," he continued, "Kira's mother and I agreed to shield her from the difficulties that come with being the child of a public figure. That's why she didn't take my name, and that's why she did not live with me. But she and I spent much time together throughout her childhood. I'd like to think I helped shape her into the wonderful woman she is today."

Murmurs rippled through the stadium. Some people shifted in their seats, while others leaned close together, whispering.

These people had spent the last few weeks seeing her as a traitor—a young woman who'd kidnapped the city's youngest Volunteer and dragged him into the wilderness. No matter how convincing her father's story was, it wouldn't be enough to erase those doubts.

But Devlin wasn't finished.

"Many of you have heard rumors of my daughter's betrayal. What you don't know is that her defection was part of a carefully orchestrated plan to bring our beloved Theodore home."

He paused for effect, letting the words sink in.

"As a volunteer advocate, Kira built a connection with the leader of a network of defectors, Will Foster. He trusted her. So when young Theodore was kidnapped from Rolling Meadows and taken to City Island by Emma Castile—who, as many of you know, is another member of that network who has since been captured and imprisoned in the Confines—I realized we needed someone on the inside. Someone who could get close enough to the defectors to find the boy and bring him home."

Kira's fingernails dug crescents into her palms.

Emma hadn't tried to escape. Her only crime had been helping Kira save Teddy. Now she was trapped in the Confines, likely being tortured for answers she didn't have, while Devlin fed lies about her to the entire city.

"So I asked my daughter to do something unthinkable. I asked her to risk her life by joining the defectors. To venture into the Unregulated Zone in order to save the life of an innocent child."

He turned to Kira, his eyes glistening with tears.

Apparently he could also cry on command.

"Kira didn't hesitate, not even for a moment. Even knowing she would be wrongly labeled a traitor, even knowing she might not survive, she agreed to help bring Theodore home."

The stadium had grown so quiet that Kira could hear the American flag snapping in the wind above the upper deck.

"After Emma Castile was captured, she gave us valuable intelligence about the Lawless camps. Combined with my daughter's brave infiltration, we were able to rescue Theodore and return him home where he belongs."

The crowd was nodding along now, beginning to accept this new version of events. It was easier to believe the mayor's daughter was a hero rather than a traitor. Easier to cling to the idea that their perfect city had not faced a true rebellion.

Devlin smiled, knowing he had them. "Tonight, we don't just celebrate Theodore's return. We also honor my daughter's dedication to this city. Her willingness to sacrifice her reputation, her safety, and even her life to protect our youngest and most beloved Volunteer."

The Stadium roared with applause.

This was the story the crowd wanted—not one of betrayal or rebellion, but of heroism and sacrifice. A story that left everything they believed comfortably intact.

Devlin waited for the cheers to fade before he continued. "Now, my daughter has something she would like to do."

Kira's heart pounded as she remembered Sienna Graves's words.

You're going to pin the rose on his chest.

Graves appeared at her side with the blue rose in her hand. The thorns had been removed—of course they had. The city couldn't risk their precious Volunteers being pricked. In Vita Nova, everything was orchestrated, right down to the smallest detail.

Everything but her.

Kira didn't reach for the rose.

Instead, she reached for the microphone.

"Could I say a few words first?"

Devlin's smile remained fixed in place—he was too skilled a performer to let it slip—but his nostrils flared, and something cold and dangerous flickered in his eyes.

This wasn't part of his script.

"Of course," he said, passing her the microphone.

Don't you dare, his eyes warned.

She stepped forward. The lights were blinding, turning the crowd into a sea of shifting shadows.

"Citizens of Vita Nova." Her voice trembled at first, then steadied. "My father is right. His influence has shaped me into the woman I am today. My father has taught me many things, but the most important thing he's taught me is the true meaning of sacrifice. That the strongest among us must be willing to give up everything for the good of all."

She turned to face Devlin.

"When I was young, I didn't understand what that meant. But working as a volunteer advocate changed me. I saw men and women give their lives on a weekly basis. I've watched countless parents leave their children behind. I've seen grandparents say their final goodbyes to their grandchildren."

She closed her eyes, and there in the darkness was Lizzy Currant's face.

"But none of those sacrifices," she said, opening her eyes, "can compare to what my father is going to do tonight."

Behind her, she heard Graves's sharp intake of breath.

Kira let the silence stretch, forcing herself to keep breathing, to keep going. "You see, a leader can't just talk about sacrifice. He must be willing to make one. He must prove that nothing—no one—is too precious to give up."

Devlin remained perfectly still, every inch the calm leader. But she saw the tells: the slight tightening at the corner of his mouth, the slow grind of his jaw.

She turned away from him to address the rows upon rows of faces watching her. "Tonight, my father will show us all what true heroism looks like... by letting his eldest daughter die in Teddy's place."

For a moment, there was nothing. The entire stadium seemed to hold its collective breath. Then a rustle swept through the crowd like wind through dry grass, building into a rising sea of gasps and whispers.

Devlin's face had gone chalk-pale except for the red blotches burning high on his cheeks. But he didn't move. He didn't grab the microphone from her hand. He couldn't contradict her without destroying his web of lies.

Then the audience surged to its feet, clapping, cheering,

and roaring their approval at the grand tragedy she'd just given them. This was the theater they craved. The blood sacrifice they could believe in.

Kira felt the microphone trembling in her hands. Her heart hammered against her ribs as she stood beneath the searing lights, knowing she had just burned her father's perfect script to ashes.

Chapter Nine

Ghost knelt at the river's edge, where the water mirrored the glowing lights of Vita Nova in the distance. He cupped his hands and dipped them into the shimmering reflection, sending ripples across the city's perfect, fragile symmetry.

He wished destroying the real thing were as easy.

He lifted the cold water to his face, rinsing away the sweat and grime. It dripped down his neck, soaking into his collar, but he didn't shiver. He just stared across the black water, thinking—as he so often did—of Madison.

Two years.

Two years she'd been gone, and he hadn't even known. He'd always told himself there would be time—that one day the city walls would fall, or Devlin's grip on it would weaken, and he'd walk back into her life. He imagined walking down her street, seeing her look up and run to him. He would apologize for leaving her, and she would touch the scar on his face and kiss his lips and tell him it didn't matter.

He'd replayed that fantasy a thousand sleepless nights.

But Devlin had signed her death warrant two years earlier with a click of a pen. Somewhere in that city, a piece of paper still bore the name of his love, her fate sealed in black ink.

Where was I when she died? Did I stop whatever I was doing? Did some part of me know?

Water lapped at his knees, soaking through his pants, but he hardly noticed. Everything felt off-kilter, as if the world itself were tilting. It shouldn't keep turning. Not without her in it.

"Lord," he whispered.

Prayer hadn't come easy lately, but he still went to his knees before the Lord every night.

"I've tried to be useful to You. Tried to save who I could. But I couldn't save the one who mattered the most."

How many nights had he knelt on this bank, in this same spot, looking at the city lights and praying for a sign that he was right to stay away?

Just a little while longer, he'd told himself.

"And now her daughter... I let Madison's daughter walk right back into that city. Maybe I could've caught up with her, stopped her, but I didn't even try." He drew in a ragged breath, his fists tightening against his thighs. "I don't have much left to give. But whatever's left—my life, my soul—it's Yours. Just please show me how to help her."

He remained on his knees by the riverbank, waiting, but no answer came. No divine revelation sent from heaven. Just the endless rush of water sliding past in the dark, headed for an ocean he'd never see again.

"Okay," he whispered, relaxing his fists. "Okay, then."

He bent forward to splash more water on his face. As he did, the old two-way radio Kira had left near the dead soldier's body fell from his coat pocket and clattered onto the rocks.

His hand froze mid-reach, his fingers suspended over the device.

He remembered the last time they'd used the radio, tuning into the city's broadcast when they first returned to Emmitsburg. Maybe he was close enough to pick up a signal now. Maybe he could hear something about Kira. Her escape from Vita Nova had likely been big news. There was no reason to think her return wouldn't be as big.

He switched the radio on and adjusted the frequency dial. A harsh burst of static filled the air. Then, cutting through the white noise... a voice.

"Citizens of Vita Nova..."

Ghost froze.

It was Kira's voice.

"My father is right."

Father?

Devlin had finally acknowledged her? No, that didn't make sense. He wouldn't have acknowledged Kira unless forced. Her return to the city must have been too visible to bury, too public to spin any other way.

Devlin must've been cornered into claiming her.

Ghost's fingers tightened around the radio, his knuckles turning white as he listened to Kira speak with forced reverence about Devlin. Praising him. The man who had abandoned her. Who had likely ordered the death of her mother. Each careful word felt like a dagger being driven a little deeper into Ghost's chest.

"You see, a leader can't just talk about sacrifice," she said, her voice drifting to him from across the river. *"He must be willing to make one."*

Ghost felt something inside him twist painfully tight. This wasn't going anywhere good.

"Tonight, my father will show us all what true heroism looks like... by letting his eldest daughter die in Teddy's place."

He almost dropped the radio.

Kira was going to sacrifice herself for Teddy.

It made an awful, twisted kind of sense. It was exactly the sort of move she'd make—the only card she had left to play. The only way to keep the boy alive.

And worse, it would make Devlin look like an even greater hero in the eyes of Vita Nova's citizens. He could sell it as proof of their family's devotion, their willingness to give everything for the city.

It was a perfect plan.

Except it would end with Kira dead.

Ghost forced himself to breathe, to think past the surge of helpless anger threatening to blind him. He had to find a way to stop this.

Devlin's voice sliced through the applause from the crowd, oozing false warmth. He commended Kira's loyalty to the city, acting as if her plan had always been part of his design. But Ghost knew him too well; he heard the hard edge beneath the words.

Devlin hadn't known.

She'd caught him off guard with this one.

"My daughter's Final Week begins to—"

Ghost snapped off the radio, silencing Devlin mid-sentence, and slipped it back into his pocket.

How long until the fireworks started?

He pictured Will crouched in the shadows beneath the Market Street Bridge, waiting for his chance to cross the river. The kid didn't know he had time. *They* had time.

Five days. Starting now.

Ghost pushed himself to his feet, breaking into a run before he was fully upright. His boots slammed against the ruined asphalt, and his lungs burned, but he forced himself to go harder. Faster.

This time he'd get it right.

Hang on, Kira. We're coming for you.

Chapter Ten

A crystal pitcher shattered against the wall, sending water and shards of glass cascading across the plush carpet of the hospitality suite.

Kira flinched at the sound but didn't turn from the window. She stood with the fingers of her right hand in a V-shape over her heart. Outside, the Jumbotron cycled solemnly through the faces of the previous week's Volunteers. Their faces faded into one another, merging into a single portrait of sacrifice.

Lilly Chen. Age 42. Mother of three.

Desmond Williams. Age 38. Artist.

Ashley Mahoney. Age 25. Loving daughter and sister.

Only three faces. Three names.

There were usually more. Once, she'd seen nineteen in a single week. Why so few this time?

The hospitality suite overlooking the baseball field had once entertained team owners and wealthy sponsors. Now it was a private viewing box reserved for Vita Nova's elite during Reverence Ceremonies. The wood-paneled walls gleamed with fresh polish, and two dozen leather chairs were carefully arranged to offer an unobstructed view of the field below.

Tonight it only housed two people: Kira and Devlin.

Her father's reflection stalked the glass like a caged animal. "What were you thinking? You had one job to do. One simple task. Pin the rose on the boy's chest and keep your mouth shut."

Kira didn't respond. She watched the field below, where Teddy and his mother were being escorted off the field. The little boy kept glancing over his shoulder, as if searching the crowd for her. She pressed her fingertips to the cold glass, wishing she could tell him everything was going to be okay.

You saved him, she reminded herself. *He'll live. He'll grow up. Maybe one day he'll even understand why you did this.*

Devlin stopped his pacing abruptly. "Do you have any idea what you've done? The political fallout alone—" He stared at her reflection. "Are you planning something? Is that what this is?"

"No, I—"

"Let me remind you of something, daughter," he said, cutting her off. "Two of your friends are guests in my Confines. And I know exactly where your little village in the wilderness is located. So think very carefully before you defy me again."

Kira turned to face her father. His perfect hair was a mess, his face red and blotchy with rage. She'd never seen him so disheveled, so completely out of control. "I'm not planning anything. Despite what you think, this isn't some kind of rebellion or uprising. All I wanted was to save Teddy."

Devlin let out a humorless laugh. "You wanted to *save* him? Do you think that makes you a hero? Dying for some little brat you barely know?"

"He's a little boy!" she shouted. "You were going to murder a six-year-old. Do you realize that?"

"Murder?" Devlin grabbed a crystal tumbler from the bar

and splashed amber liquid into it. "We don't murder anyone in this city. People volunteer to die so the rest of us can live. They do something noble, and we reward them for it. Is that really so difficult to understand? But you took that choice away from the boy. Decided he was too young and stupid to contribute."

"That's not why I—"

He cut her off again. "Spare me. You stand there judging me, but tonight has shown which one of us truly craves the spotlight, dear daughter."

The door to the suite swung open. Sienna Graves glided into the room and closed the door behind her, the usual click of her heels muffled on the thick carpet.

Devlin fell silent, his hands going up to smooth his hair back into place.

"Well," Graves drawled, her eyes darting between them. "That certainly was an interesting turn of events, wasn't it?"

Devlin drained his glass in one swallow. "Tell me about it."

The deputy mayor moved to the bar and poured herself a drink. "I've been listening to the crowd. Would you like to know what they're saying about you, Victor?"

"Not particularly."

"Too bad. I'm going to tell you." She took a slow sip of the liquor, her lipstick leaving a perfect crimson crescent on the rim. "They loved it. The mayor's secret daughter—a loyal spy, fighting for the city. On its own, they would've eaten that story up like cake. But the mayor offering to sacrifice his own daughter in place of a child? My goodness, Victor. It's better than anything we could have scripted."

Her gaze slid to Kira, her smile fading just enough to show a glint of warning. "However, next time, dear, you might want to run these big ideas of yours by us first."

Kira watched as Graves closed the distance between herself

and Devlin. She rested a hand on his arm, and something unspoken passed between them.

"The timing couldn't be better," Graves continued. "After the Tenement bombings, the kidnapping, the escape... people were questioning your leadership. That's why the Volunteer numbers were so low last week. These people need to be reminded of why they believe in you. They need to see that you are willing to sacrifice as they have sacrificed."

Devlin's eyes sharpened. "The optics are... interesting."

"The optics are *fantastic*." Graves's fingernails lightly traced down his arm before resting on his wrist. "This doesn't just silence the critics of the Volunteer Program. It sells it better than anything else ever could. If the mayor sacrifices his own daughter to the program, who could question it?"

"Yes, I suppose you're right, Sienna."

Kira felt sick watching the ease with which Graves manipulated him. The way he leaned toward her, drinking in every word.

"As for you," Graves said, turning her attention to Kira. "Look on the bright side. You're getting what you want. You saved the boy. And you're about to have the greatest week of your life."

A firework burst outside the window. Blue light spilled through the room, staining the walls and reflecting on the crystal shards still scattered on the floor.

Kira turned back to the glass. The last time she'd watched this fireworks display, she'd been on the broken western span of the Walnut Street Bridge. Wrapped in Will's arms, his lips against hers. Scared and nervous but dreaming of freedom.

Now?

Each explosion of light made her reflection in the glass flare and vanish.

Five days. That's all she had left. Her father would make

sure of it. She'd seen it in his eyes when she made her offer on the field. Underneath the rage had been something else. Something worse.

Relief.

Relief that she'd solved his problem for him… and that he would finally be rid of her.

Behind her, she heard Graves murmur something low that made Devlin laugh. She saw their reflections leaning into one another, her father's mouth lingering near the woman's ear. They weren't even bothering to hide their relationship from her anymore. Why should they?

She would be dead soon.

Another firework exploded, this one red, painting the suite in bloody light. For a moment, Kira's reflection in the glass looked like a ghost. Pale. Translucent. Already half gone.

Five more days.

Chapter Eleven

The volley of fireworks exploded over the river, bathing the night in electric blue. Ghost pressed himself against a crumbling pillar of the Walnut Street Bridge's western span, the cold from the concrete seeping into his jacket. The brief light illuminated the world around him—twisted rebar jutting like broken bones, chunks of missing foundation that revealed the bridge's slow decay.

A few feet away from his boots, the Susquehanna River was a slick black ribbon hiding currents strong enough to drag a man under before he had time to scream.

A searchlight from a Patrol boat swept across the water, its beam slicing the darkness. Ghost held his breath and melted deeper into the shadows. Even at this distance, he couldn't risk being careless. Years of survival had taught him the cost of taking chances. He watched the searchlight ripple over the river before vanishing around the north end of City Island, taking its glare with it.

He edged forward and peered around the pillar. Four Guards stood at the checkpoint on the neighboring Market

Street Bridge. Their silhouettes were black cutouts against the city's glow, rifles slung casually across their chests.

More fireworks bloomed overhead—cascades of gold and silver against the night sky. Ghost used the light to study the Guards' positions. Too far apart. Heads tilted skyward, mouths slightly open, entranced. Blind spots everywhere. Sloppy. The kind of complacency bred by boredom and routine. He'd watched men die from mistakes like that in the desert, back when his uniform was clean and his face unscarred.

He seized the moment, slipping into a crouch and sprinting for the Market Street Bridge. His knees protested the sudden movement, but he forced them to cooperate, every motion controlled and silent. His eyes darted between the large checkpoint anchoring the middle of the bridge and the walkway leading to City Island, alert for even the faintest motion, any indication he'd been spotted.

But no one noticed.

Of course they didn't. They were too busy staring at the sky, faces lit with awe and something close to reverence. Ghost never understood it. Every Sunday night, these people watched the same ritual of light and death and still found it beautiful.

Maybe it was easier that way. Easier to pretend these fireworks were just fireworks and not the scattered remains of neighbors and friends. Maybe that was the only way they could sleep at night.

Or maybe they watched so intently because they couldn't help but picture their own eventual ends, painted in the same violent colors, raining down on the city they'd died to preserve.

Ghost's eyes swept the shoreline.

Where are you, kid?

Will was out there somewhere, getting ready to cross. He was reckless when it came to Kira, and one day that recklessness was going to get him killed.

Movement caught his eye. A shadow peeled away from the darkness under the bridge, about fifty yards south. Even in the stuttering light of the fireworks, Ghost recognized Will's form. The kid crept forward and crouched at the water's edge, stripping off his jacket.

Getting ready to swim.

The Patrol boat had likely held him back until now. Ghost offered a silent prayer of thanks for that delay; without it, he might have been too late.

Another explosion rocked the sky.

Ghost used the noise as cover, his boots landing on the loose gravel without a sound, every step precise—a silent dance drilled into him long ago. He felt the old training take over, steadying his breath and slowing his pulse, as he slipped through the darkness unseen.

Will had one foot in the river when Ghost's hand closed around his arm.

"Don't."

Will spun, swinging wildly.

Ghost deflected the blow, and they both stumbled on the slick rocks. "It's me, Will," he hissed. "Knock it off."

The kid stiffened as recognition hit, then immediately tried to yank his arm away. "Let go of me. I need to go *now*."

"No, you don't." Ghost tightened his grip, feeling the desperate energy pulsing beneath his fingers. "Not tonight, at least. Listen to me. She's okay."

Will stared at him. "You're lying. How could you know that? You're just trying to—"

"Because she volunteered."

The kid went rigid. "What?"

"She offered herself in Teddy's place at the ceremony. I heard her voice on the radio. I also heard Devlin claim her as his daughter."

"What? No, he wouldn't have done that."

"He must've had no choice." Ghost released Will slowly, ready to grab him again if he lunged. "This buys us some time."

"Time?" Will's voice cracked. "Time for what? To watch her die on Friday?"

"To make a plan." Ghost craned his neck to scan the bridge checkpoint again, but the Guards were huddled and talking, oblivious to what was happening beneath them. "If you go back now, you'll be dead before you make it to the other side. If you're not spotted by the Guards or the Patrol boats, you'll be pulled under by the current. You and I both know that. And then who saves her?"

Will shook his head. "I'm not leaving her."

"We're not leaving her. I give you my word, son. We'll come back here together, and we'll find her. Just not tonight."

The kid was quiet for a long moment, watching as another firework exploded and dissolved into brilliant streams of gold.

"Five days?"

Ghost squeezed his shoulder. "Five days to get ready. To plan. To do this right."

The kid stared across the river at the city lights, eyes fixed and unblinking. "You know, I spent the last hour imagining what I'd do to anyone who hurt her. All these terrible thoughts kept looping through my head. But when I pray about it, I get the same answer: that vengeance belongs to God." He looked up at Ghost. "Do you believe that?"

Something shifted inside him. Ghost knew the Scripture. He believed it. But believing it and feeling it were two different things.

I pursued my enemies and overtook them; and did not turn back till they were consumed. I thrust them through, so that they were not able to rise; they fell under my feet.

After twelve years spent imagining and planning Devlin's death, he wasn't about to leave justice in God's hands.

He didn't answer.

They retreated from the riverbank, using the rusted hunks of vehicles for cover, and slipped through the shadows of Emmitsburg. Past busted storefronts and rows of hollow houses with red numbers painted on their front doors. Overhead, the fireworks reached their finale—vibrant bursts of blue and gold that illuminated their path north.

Back to Haven.

As the last echoes of color faded from the sky, Ghost lowered his head, knowing full well his prayer was wrong even as he whispered it.

"Lord, forgive me for what I'm about to ask. Make my hands ready for war. Steady my aim. Let my enemies fall before me, their power broken and their city in flames."

He turned to look at the distant glow of the city, the night sky streaked with smoke from the fireworks.

"Give me five days to bring judgment on them all."

Chapter Twelve

The Volunteer bus wound its way through the city's streets, heading away from the Stadium. Kira sat alone in the center of the vehicle, surrounded by rows of empty seats. She'd never actually ridden this bus before. As a volunteer advocate, she'd only watched it depart—imagining the ride would be silent and heavy, with the week's Volunteers and their families speaking in quiet voices about their Sacrifices, if they spoke at all.

But tonight, she was the only passenger.

The only Volunteer.

The rose corsage on her wrist felt impossibly heavy.

Her father had insisted that she take the bus to Rolling Meadows. The same journey every Volunteer made after receiving their blue rose.

"The city needs to see this done properly," he'd said. "No shortcuts. No special treatment."

What surprised her most was the absence of any Guards on the bus. Instead, there was only the driver up front—a middle-aged man with thinning hair—humming softly to himself as he navigated the empty streets.

Either Devlin was confident she wouldn't try to run, or he knew there was nowhere left for her to go.

As the bus left the city behind, the streetlights gave way to darkness, the trees closing in tight on both sides. Branches formed a tunnel that the bus headlights cut through in thin, bright beams. She knew this road by heart. She'd traveled it so many times before, going to visit Volunteers during their Final Week—always returning afterward to her little townhouse, her carefully managed life.

But there would be no return trip this time.

They turned onto the gravel road, the bus's headlights illuminating a wooden sign dangling from rusted chains:

Welcome to Rolling Meadows.

Home to Our Brave Volunteers!

The bus rumbled through the dense grouping of trees that walled off Rolling Meadows from the rest of the city. Their long, bare branches arched overhead in twisted tangles, some of them scraping lightly against the bus's metal sides. It felt like they were clawing at the bus itself.

Reaching for her.

When the trees finally fell away, the lodge appeared ahead, its windows putting off a warm glow in the dark. It looked exactly as she remembered: the same rustic-elegant architecture, the same meticulously maintained grounds, the same carefully crafted illusion of escape from city life.

But it wasn't an escape.

It was just another kind of prison, wrapped in comfort and false promises.

The Confines in prettier clothes.

The bus rolled to a stop at the main entrance. An older woman stood beneath the porch lights, her dark hair streaked with silver and pulled back into a flawless bun. Not a strand was out of place. Her black uniform, trimmed with blue accents—the uniform of all Rolling Meadows staff—was immaculate.

Kira rose on shaking legs, whispered a quick thank you to the driver, and stepped off the bus.

The woman's face softened into a genuine smile that crinkled the corners of her eyes. "Welcome, dear," she said in a comforting voice that reminded Kira of Mrs. Walker, her first-grade teacher. "I'm Adeline Fleming. I'll be taking care of you this week."

"Thank you. I'm sorry to keep you up so late."

"Nonsense." Adeline rested a warm hand on Kira's back, guiding her into the lodge. "You don't need to worry about a thing, honey. Let's get you all settled, shall we? You must be exhausted after such an... eventful evening."

The lobby was quiet and still, shadows pooling in the corners. The overhead lights were dim, leaving the space subdued and somber. The air smelled of leather and furniture polish, with an underlying floral sweetness that reminded Kira of a funeral home.

It was less welcoming than she remembered.

"I've worked here nearly ten years," Adeline said as they climbed the staircase to the second floor. "I've seen thousands of Volunteers come through these doors. My goal is always the same: to make them as comfortable and happy as I can. And since you're my only Volunteer this week... well, I warn you, I intend to spoil you rotten. Is that alright with you?"

Despite the circumstances, Kira felt herself smile. "That sounds good to me."

The upstairs hallway was wide, carpeted in soft blue that muffled their footsteps. Framed paintings lined the walls—peaceful hillsides, a tiny sailboat on the ocean, even a bowl of fruit. The kind of mediocre hotel room artwork you don't even notice. Nothing that might cause the Volunteers to think too deeply or reflect on their final days.

They stopped at a pair of double doors. Adeline unlocked them and gestured for Kira to enter.

The suite was massive. Floor-to-ceiling windows dominated one wall, with heavy curtains drawn back to reveal the grounds. A sitting area with a leather loveseat and recliner faced a stone fireplace. A massive bed waited across from it, the duvet dyed the same deep blue as the rose on Kira's wrist.

There were small touches, too. A vase of fresh wildflowers on the bedside table. A handmade quilt folded at the foot of the bed. A small stack of books resting on the mantel.

"I know it's not home," Adeline said, watching Kira with a hopeful expression. "But I tried to make it feel a little less... institutional. You'll find the bathroom fully stocked with toiletries. And I'm told the clothes from your apartment will be sent over sometime tomorrow. Until then, there are pajamas and some of my daughter's old clothes in the closet. I think you're about her size."

"It's wonderful. Thank you, Mrs. Fleming."

"Adeline. And you're welcome, dear. Do you like to read?"

"Yes. I love books."

"Good. I picked out a few of my favorites and left them on the mantel. The kitchen's open all night. If you're hungry or can't sleep, just use the house phone and order something. We don't bother with menus around here. Tell me what sounds good, and I'll bring it to you."

Adeline crossed to the windows and closed the curtains. "Would you like anything before bed? Some tea perhaps? Or a sandwich?"

Kira shook her head, though her stomach felt painfully empty. "I just... I think I want to sleep."

"Of course, dear. Let me get out of your hair." Adeline turned and crossed the room, but she hesitated at the doorway, one hand resting on the frame. She glanced back at Kira, seemingly debating whether to speak. Finally, she drew a careful breath. "I know it's not my place, but what you did out there tonight... that was the bravest thing I've ever seen."

The woman disappeared into the hallway before Kira could answer.

She stood alone in the middle of the vast suite, arms wrapped around herself, the blue dress cold and heavy against her skin. The silence pressed in on her, broken only by the quiet tick of an antique clock on the mantel. Each tick sounded monumental, another reminder of how quickly time was slipping away from her.

Her gaze settled on the small stack of books Adeline had left behind. She let out a slow breath as she read the titles—two she recognized and one she didn't. Adeline hadn't spoken a word against the city, but she didn't need to.

The books spoke for her.

Les Misérables sat on top, the story of a city that built its own barricades in revolt against a corrupt government. Beneath it was *1984*, its corners scuffed from countless readings, its twisted world all too familiar. And at the bottom lay a slender volume she'd never heard of—*The Pilgrim's Progress*—its title embossed in faded gold letters.

She slipped off her heels and let her bare feet sink into the plush carpet. Crossing to the windows, she pulled aside the curtain and gazed outside. Rolling Meadows lay bathed in moonlight. Perfect lawns. Sculpted hedges. Beyond the trees was the city. Beyond that—the river. The line between life and death, freedom and imprisonment.

Will.

The thought of never seeing him again—well, she might as

well imagine never breathing again. The pain of it was just as immediate and physical. She pressed her hand to the glass, imagining him standing on the other side, his palm aligned with hers. Those strong hands of his—calloused but so gentle when they touched her face. She remembered his eyes that first day in her office, before either of them knew how hopelessly entangled their stories would become.

If she tried hard enough, she could almost hear his voice whispering her name.

Stop, she scolded herself. *That's over now.*

She let the curtain fall shut and turned back to the bed. A small card lay on the pillow, welcoming her to Rolling Meadows and thanking her for her "noble Sacrifice for the good of all."

She crushed it inside her fist.

Then she crawled into bed and curled up on her side, still wearing the dress she couldn't be bothered to take off.

Her Final Week had begun.

She would be pampered. Fed. Celebrated. All while being prepared for slaughter.

She'd chosen this. She had walked onto that field knowing exactly what this decision would cost her. All she could hope was that the price had been worth it.

That somewhere out there in the dark, a little boy would live because she'd been willing to die.

Chapter Thirteen

Kira woke to sunlight streaming through a gap in the curtains. She blinked at the high ceiling, disoriented for a moment. The unfamiliar softness of Egyptian cotton sheets against her legs, the gentle hum of the heating system—it was all too comfortable. Too foreign. None of it felt like hers.

Then it all came flooding back: the Reverence Ceremony. The mountain lodge. The suite reserved for Volunteers. And the cold, relentless countdown ticking in her head, marking the hours left until she died.

Outside her window, birds were singing, and for a moment she let herself slip back to mornings in Haven. Roosters crowing. Children laughing in the field by her thin-walled cabin. The scent of wood smoke and fresh bread drifting from the mess hall. Brack splitting logs in his steady, comforting rhythm. The memory felt close enough to touch, yet impossibly far away.

She pushed the covers aside and climbed out of bed, dragging the wrinkled silk dress over her head. She unclasped the corsage from her wrist and dropped it onto the bedside table. It had left an angry indentation on her skin that she massaged away.

She wouldn't wear it again.

The bathroom was bigger than her old kitchen. Marble counters gleamed under the bright vanity lights. The shower was a cavern of glass and silver fixtures. She stepped under the rainfall head and let the steaming water pour over her for nearly twenty minutes, standing there until it ran cold, trying to wash away the memory of the ceremony, the watching crowd, and her father's hand pressing into her back.

Finally, she shut off the water and wrapped herself in a thick blue robe.

The walk-in closet surprised her. Instead of the stiff Volunteer blue, it was stocked with soft sweaters in earthy colors, well-worn black denim, and simple cotton dresses.

She paused, realizing Adeline had deliberately banished Volunteer blue.

Kira chose a cream cashmere sweater so soft it felt like clouds against her skin, pairing it with jeans and black ballet flats. The clothes felt comfortable. Familiar.

She caught sight of herself in the full-length mirror. The sweater was lovely, but it couldn't hide the dark hollows beneath her eyes or the sharpness of her cheeks from the weight she'd lost beyond the wall.

A knock at the door startled her.

"Come in."

Adeline entered with a silver tray, the smell of fresh pastries drifting across the room. "Good morning, dear. I thought you might like breakfast in bed." She paused, taking in Kira's outfit. "But I see you're already dressed."

"Yes, thank you so much for the clothes. They're exactly what I would have picked."

"Of course." Adeline's gaze lingered on the cream sweater, and a brief flicker of pain crossed her expression. "Breakfast is served until ten in the main dining room, if you'd rather eat downstairs."

Kira thought about asking Adeline about her daughter—the one whose clothes she now wore. But the words caught in her throat. Something told her it wasn't a story with a happy ending.

She nodded instead. "The dining room sounds good. I wouldn't mind getting out of here for a bit."

"Wonderful." The sadness in Adeline's eyes faded, replaced by a warm smile. "Our chef has prepared something special for you this morning."

THE MAIN DINING ROOM OCCUPIED THE WHOLE SOUTHERN wing of the lodge, enclosed on three sides by large arched windows. Beyond the glass, manicured lawns rolled away toward a golf course and stables where horses grazed in their paddocks. A gravel path wound between tidy flower beds, leading to a fishing pond that glittered in the morning sunlight.

A single massive table dominated the room, its surface polished to a mirror shine. It could have seated thirty people easily, but only one place was set: fine bone china, a crystal water glass, and polished silverware. A towering arrangement of blue roses occupied the center of the table.

As Kira approached her seat, a young woman in a black and blue uniform hurried forward to pull out her chair. "Good morning, Ms. Liebert. Would you like some tea? A glass of milk? Or perhaps some apple juice?"

"Tea, please."

"Of course."

Staff moved quietly along the edges of the room, dusting surfaces that were already spotless, polishing silver that already gleamed, and fussing over curtain folds that were already perfect. Finding excuses to linger. Kira could feel their eyes on her whenever they thought she wasn't looking. Two women pretended to inspect a decorative vase on a table, whispering to each other as they stole repeated glances her way. A young man nearly tripped over a potted plant because he couldn't stop staring at her.

Adeline glided up with a cup of tea and leaned in close. "Ignore them," she whispered in a conspiratorial tone. "We're used to more Volunteers. They don't know what to do with themselves. Plus, they're all little gossips. Not to worry—I'll find more work for them to do."

Kira gave her a tired smile. "It's fine. They'll get bored of me eventually. I'm not very interesting."

Adeline shook her head. "On the contrary, you're all anyone wants to talk about this morning." She gave Kira's shoulder a reassuring squeeze before retreating to the kitchen.

Another young staff member arrived with a covered silver tray, her hands shaking a little as she lifted the dome. "Chef Thomas prepared this meal especially for you, ma'am."

Beneath the lid lay a perfectly plated eggs Benedict. Golden hollandaise pooled around crisp muffins. Fresh blueberries circled the plate, dotted with delicate edible flowers—all blue.

They couldn't even let her eat breakfast without reminding her of the real reason she was here.

To die.

She took small bites. The eggs were perfectly poached, the muffin crisp, and the bacon thick and smoky. In Haven, breakfast had been simple—oatmeal or eggs served on metal trays, eaten on wooden benches. But the food had tasted better there, with Grace by her side and Will's knee pressed against hers under the table.

"Would you like more food, dear?"

She hadn't even heard Adeline approach, but the woman was standing over her again, hands clasped behind her back.

Kira's plate wasn't even half empty, but she felt uncomfortably full.

"No, thank you." She pushed her chair back, overwhelmed by the sudden need to escape. There were too many faces. Too many people hovering around her. "I think I'll just go back to my room. Maybe I'll read one of the books you left for me or take a nap."

Adeline looked nervous. "Actually, dear, there's someone waiting for you in the lobby."

"In the lobby?"

Was it her father? Had he come to apologize for his anger the previous night? Had he come to spend time with her before—

"It's a young man," Adeline added quickly, as if reading her thoughts. "Follow me, dear."

Kira followed Adeline down the hall and into the lobby. A man stood near the front entrance, his back to her, staring through the sliding doors at the parking lot.

"That's him," Adeline whispered.

He turned at the sound of their approach. Lean and poised, he wore tailored charcoal slacks and a pale blue button-down. His blond hair curled slightly at the nape of his neck, framing high cheekbones and a strong jaw softened by full lips. He was handsome; there was no denying it.

"Ms. Liebert," he said, flashing a smile that had no doubt broken more than a few hearts in Vita Nova. "I've been looking forward to meeting you. How are you doing today?"

Kira shot a quick glance at Adeline, who offered her a small, apologetic shrug.

Don't ask me.

She turned back to the stranger. "I'm sorry... but who are you?"

"Lucas Pine," he said, extending his hand. "Your volunteer advocate."

Chapter Fourteen

A pair of ducks drifted across the fishing pond, their paddling feet sending the water rippling outward. The stone path encircling the pond had recently been swept clean, not a leaf or blade of grass out of place, as if even nature itself wasn't allowed to disrupt the estate's perfection.

"Beautiful fall morning, isn't it?" Lucas said, keeping pace beside her as they circled the pond. "This place is incredible. Have you walked the entire grounds yet?"

"Not yet. But I bet it's lovely." Kira crossed her arms over her chest, wishing she were anywhere but making small talk with a complete stranger. "All of this beauty makes suicide much more pleasant."

Lucas's perfect smile faltered briefly before snapping back into place. "I can only imagine how difficult this must be for you, Ms. Liebert. But I really am here to help."

Kira hesitated, biting back the first sharp reply that came to mind. She remembered all the times she'd sat across from difficult Volunteers, trying desperately to soothe or appease them, especially as their Final Weeks came to an end. She didn't want to be like them now, pushing away the only person offering to help.

"You're right. I'm sorry."

"No worries."

As they continued along the path, Lucas asked, "Have you given any thought to what you'd like to do this week? Any requests? Places you want to visit?"

"No."

"Really? Nothing at all?"

"I plan to stay here until Friday."

"Here? At the lodge?"

"That's right."

Lucas frowned. "But there must be something we could do. A dinner somewhere nice. Or I could arrange a shopping trip. We could go pick out your dress for the Volunteer Ball on Thursday."

Kira laughed, forgetting any promise she'd made to be cooperative. "There's not going to be a Ball, Lucas."

"Of course there is."

"There's no point in hosting a huge party for one person."

"True, but we could arrange something smaller, perhaps. An exclusive dinner at the Executive Mansion for the city's el—"

"No dinners," she said, spinning on him. "No elite. No fancy dresses. I'm not interested in doing anything beyond the Sacrifice I'm required to make on Friday morning."

Lucas shifted his weight, the discomfort evident on his face. This meeting was clearly not going the way he'd planned. "Ms. Liebert."

"Kira."

"Right. Kira. Part of my job is to help you find some peace with your decision."

"You think shopping and a big party will give me peace with dying?"

Kira turned away from him and continued down the path away from the pond. Ahead, the stables loomed, and a sleek black horse grazed inside the enclosure. She wondered if it ever tried to jump the fence or if it had been penned so long it no longer remembered what freedom felt like.

Lucas hurried to catch up with her. "Kira, I get how ridiculous this all seems. Personally? I never understood the whole *Revere the Volunteer* thing. If I were you, I wouldn't want to parade around with a rose pinned to my chest all week either. But the city wants to honor you—"

She stopped so abruptly he nearly collided with her. "The city doesn't want to honor anyone. They want to feel better about letting someone else die so they can live. There's no meaning behind any of this. It's all just for show."

Stop. Stop talking.

But she couldn't.

"All this death—it's for nothing. If we knocked down the barricade tomorrow, do you know what would happen?" She didn't wait for his answer. "Nothing. No hordes of Lawless would overrun us. No plague would wipe us out. Some people would stay. Some would leave. We'd go on living and dying, exactly the way we're supposed to."

Something shifted in Lucas's expression—frustration, maybe. He was probably wondering why he'd drawn the short straw and been assigned such a difficult Volunteer.

"I appreciate everything you're saying, Kira. And just between us? I agree with much of it. But as your advocate, I can't let you sit in your room for five days."

"Yes, you can. You're supposed to give me what I want, and that's the only thing I want."

He exhaled. "What about your loved ones? Can I facilitate visits or dinners with anyone?"

"Sure." She gestured at the distant concrete barrier barely visible through the trees. "My loved ones are on the other side of that wall. Can you arrange for me to see them again?"

"You know I can't do that."

"Fine. Then I don't want any visits or dinners."

Lucas fell silent, studying her with eyes that were unnervingly green. He nodded toward a wooden bench nestled beneath two cherry trees. "Would you like to sit?"

"Not really."

But he sat anyway, running a hand through his carefully styled hair—a gesture that, painfully, reminded her of Will. "Look. Can I be truthful with you for a moment?"

"Go for it. Truth is in short supply in this city."

"You're my first client. I just started last week."

Kira blinked at him, surprised by this admission. "I'm your first Volunteer?"

"Yes." He let out a dry, self-deprecating laugh. "I just transferred over from the Agricultural Sector. Spent most of my life watching my father work himself into the ground out in the fields. His arthritis is so bad now that he can barely stand, but he refuses to stop. My mom's gone, and he still has three daughters to take care of."

He reached for his polished shoes and used his thumb to massage away twin smudges on their tips. "When this job opened up, I figured there was no way they'd take me. But I submitted my name anyway, crossed my fingers, and hoped for the best. I owed it to my father to try, you know? And now here I am. Doing everything wrong with my first Volunteer and trying not to show her how completely terrified I am of messing up."

Kira lowered herself on the bench beside him. "Why are you telling me this, Lucas?"

He looked at her. "Because I want you to know I'm not here to sell you anything or force you to do anything you don't want. I truly just want to help. To make this week a little easier on you, if I can. And yeah... I'm also hoping to make my dad's life better in the process."

She studied him and saw the same desperate hope she'd seen in so many faces at Haven. People just trying to survive, trying to take care of the ones they loved.

"You're not doing *everything* wrong," she said in a soft voice. "You're actually better than most of the advocates I worked with. You're honest, and you care. That's rare. Dangerous in this job, but rare."

A genuine smile crossed Lucas's face. "Thanks. Though I should probably be more professional. Less sharing of personal family problems. You don't need to hear those, especially now."

"Professional is overrated. Sometimes your clients just want someone real."

He nodded. "Was it difficult for you? Being an advocate?"

Kira's gaze drifted to the distant wall as she thought of her first meeting with Will. How carefully she'd tried to keep things professional, only to fall helplessly in love.

"Most of the time I could handle it," she finally answered. "I told myself I was helping them find meaning in their Sacrifice. Making their last days easier. The work felt important." She picked up a fallen leaf, its edges dry and brown. "But my last client changed my perspective on everything."

She knew she shouldn't talk about Will. Not with anyone. But what did it matter now? Will was safe outside the city, and she was going to die soon. Besides, there was something disarming about Lucas Pine. He wasn't part of the elite. He felt different. Safer.

Lucas watched her carefully. "Will Foster, right?"

She closed her hand around the leaf, crushing it. "Yes."

"At the Reverence Ceremony, your father said you formed a connection with him. But it was more than that, wasn't it?"

Kira nodded once.

"You loved him."

It wasn't a question, but she answered anyway. "I still do."

"Do you think he'll come back for you?"

"I told him not to."

He sighed, looking almost regretful. "I'm sorry. That must make this all so much harder. Here you are, facing all of this alone, while he's..."

He let the sentence drift away, unfinished.

She glared at him. "While he's what?"

He shook his head. "Nothing. I shouldn't have said anything."

While he's safe.

The unspoken words pulsed in her mind. She opened her fist, letting the crushed leaf fall from her fingers.

That's what he's thinking. While Will is safe and free, I'm here preparing to die. Taking the bullet for Teddy on my own.

"You know," Lucas said, "as your advocate, I can take you anywhere you want to go. No cameras. No ceremonies. Anywhere. We can even go incognito, if you want. Just you and me."

She started to say no. But something on his face stopped her. The earnestness there. The vulnerability he'd shown. He wanted so badly to give her something. Wasn't there anything at all she wanted?

A thought tugged at her. A desire she'd been trying to suppress since stepping off the bus at Rolling Meadows last night.

"There might be one thing."

His eyes brightened. "Anything. Name it."

"Can you take me home?" she asked. "Where I lived with my mother. That's the only place I want to go."

He nodded without hesitation. "Of course. I'll get us a car, and we'll go there this morning."

"Thank you, Lucas."

She turned away, overcome by the sudden desire to cry.

She was going home. One last time.

Chapter Fifteen

Lucas eased the black sedan to a stop in the narrow alley behind Kira's townhouse.

"Hopefully, no one notices us back here," he said, scanning the neighboring backyards. "Doesn't seem like anyone's around. That's good."

Lucas had left her alone on the bench after their walk, vanishing briefly to secure a vehicle. He'd returned thirty minutes later with a sleek, government-issued sedan reserved for Volunteers. It felt absurdly luxurious in the Residential Sector, where private cars didn't exist and everyone crowded onto buses or walked to work.

Most Volunteers spent their Final Week riding public transportation, soaking up attention and gifts from strangers. Kira had always found that distasteful. There were a few Volunteers like her who preferred to slip quietly through the city, avoiding adoration and pity. For them, these tinted sedans were a way to remain unseen.

"You're a good driver," Kira said as Lucas shut off the

engine. "I didn't think anyone had cars in the Agricultural Sector."

"We don't." He shot her a sideways grin. "But we've got tractors. You learn to drive them young out of necessity. Once you get the basics, you can drive anything." He patted the leather steering wheel. "Didn't think I'd ever get behind the wheel of something this nice, though."

Kira smiled and turned to look at the townhouse through her window. She could see the small patch of earth her mother had called a garden. In the warmer months, they'd grown tomatoes and herbs there, spending long mornings pulling weeds and talking about nothing.

She'd tried to keep it alive after her mother died, but she had no gift for it. Even the easiest plants refused to grow for her. Now, the entire patch was choked with weeds. The tomato cage her mother had painted bright yellow still stood in one corner, its paint peeling, rust spreading like a disease on its metal frame.

Although it was just a few square feet of dirt, that little garden held the weight of countless quiet mornings spent nurturing fragile life in a city that wanted to stamp it out.

"Ready?" Lucas asked.

She nodded, though she wasn't ready at all. How could you ever be ready to visit your home for the last time?

They left the car behind and circled to the front of the townhouse. Kira's eyes darted to the street and the nearby houses, checking for any sign of movement. But it was empty. By now, most people were at work, crammed into office buildings, probably gossiping about the previous night's Reverence Ceremony and the mayor's secret daughter.

As they reached the porch, Lucas paused at the top step, glancing at the door. "I hate to ask, but are you okay with me kicking it in? I don't have a key."

"It's not locked."

He reached for the knob. "Really? Why not?"

She shook her head. "I never planned on coming back here."

The memory of that Friday morning felt like it belonged to someone else. Pulling on her clothes in a rush, eating an apple over the kitchen sink, and then sprinting out the door into the pouring rain. She'd been on her way to the sanitation lot to find Jonesy, determined to convince him to help her break Will out of the Compulsory Clinic.

Her entire life had changed that day.

Lucas pushed the door open and stepped aside, letting her enter first.

The townhouse looked smaller than she remembered, but it was untouched. Her sneakers still waited by the door. A towel hung over the edge of the sink. An empty water glass sat on the counter beside it. She'd expected the Guards to have torn the place apart by now. They'd done it before—rooting through defectors' homes to uncover treason. That's how they'd found the note about her being the mayor's daughter. The note Devlin himself had confronted her about after giving her that ride home.

The same day she'd met Will.

But Devlin hadn't needed his Guards to find out who she was. He already knew. Besides, he wouldn't have wanted them snooping around her house, potentially uncovering evidence identifying her as his illegitimate child.

Lucas remained by the door, arms behind his back, like a soldier standing guard. "So, you lived here with your mother?"

"Yes," she said, scanning the room. "Until the city murdered her."

Her eyes settled on the kitchen table... and the single, wilted blue rose petal.

That night seemed so far away now. The disastrous double date with Emma and the two Patrol soldiers. Afterward, Will had been waiting for her outside the Grotto. They'd wandered along the island's edge and shared their first kiss on the bridge.

Later that same night, the Tenements were bombed, and they'd huddled together in her apartment, watching the news in silence. When she'd pleaded with Will to leave the city before his Sacrifice, he'd insisted that God wanted him to see his Final Week through to the end. In a fury, she'd hurled his blue rose across the kitchen.

This single petal was all that remained now.

Lucas's voice broke through her thoughts. "Did you want to grab some clothes? Or I can get them for you if you tell me where."

She tore her eyes from the rose petal. "No. I'll do it. Just wait here. I'll be fast."

Upstairs, her bedroom appeared frozen in time. The covers were still thrown back from when she crawled out of bed that morning, and several pairs of jeans lay scattered across the floor. She grabbed a duffel from the closet and began stuffing clothes inside without looking. She didn't care what she grabbed. She just needed something familiar.

Something that was hers.

The duffle bag was almost full when she noticed it—the blue ballgown lying crumpled on the floor, half-hidden under the bed where she'd carelessly stepped over it that morning.

The sight of it broke something inside her.

That dress and the blue rose petal belonged to another life —a life where she'd danced with Will at his Volunteer Ball, and where he'd looked at her like she was the only thing that mattered. That night had been the only time she'd felt truly loved by anyone since her mother's death.

But it was over now.

It was all over.

Her knees buckled. She sank beside the dress and pressed it to her face. It still smelled faintly of Will. She imagined his arms around her again. His breath on her cheek. Those rough, gentle hands intertwined with hers.

Every memory of Will felt like a shard of glass lodged inside her chest. It hurt to breathe without him.

"Kira?" Lucas appeared in the doorway. He crossed the room and knelt beside her. "Hey. What is it? What happened?"

"I miss him," she sobbed into the dress, knowing how ridiculous she must look and not caring. "I miss him so much, Lucas."

He wrapped his arm around her and let her sob against his shoulder. He didn't lie to her and say it would be okay, because it wouldn't. He didn't tell her that she would see Will again. He just held her, allowing her the space to mourn everything she'd lost.

When her sobs finally subsided, she pulled away from him, scrubbing at her eyes with the back of her hand. "I'm sorry. I don't usually let myself break down in front of people."

"Don't apologize." He produced a neatly folded white handkerchief from his pocket and handed it to her. "You're allowed to break down in front of me. That's why I'm here. Honestly, considering everything, you're doing better than I would be."

"Thanks."

"Except for... uh... that thing in your nose. Whatever it is, I don't think it's supposed to be there."

She covered her nose, mortified. "Are you serious?"

He laughed. "Kidding. Just trying to lighten the mood. You see, I hate this kind of thing."

"What kind of thing?"

"When a beautiful girl cries in front of me. I'll do or say anything to make her smile."

Had he really just called her beautiful? It was meant as a compliment, but it landed wrong, feeling like a line he'd delivered a hundred times before. Or was that unfair?

Maybe it only sounded false because he wasn't Will.

Lucas stood and offered his hand. "Come on. Let's get you out of this place before anything else comes sliding out of your nose."

Kira let him pull her off the floor. "If we could never talk about this again, that would be great."

"Look at you, making lots of requests."

"Only two so far."

"Well, that's two more than you were willing to give me this morning."

Before they left the townhouse, Kira went to the coat closet near the front door. Her mother's old leather jacket still hung there. It was the same one she'd worn on the blind date with Emma. The one that had made her feel tougher than she was. The leather was soft from years of wear. Even now it smelled of Madison Liebert's favorite perfume—a subtle mix of vanilla and lavender.

Kira slipped the jacket on over her sweater.

At the front door, she paused for one last look at her home. The kitchen counters where she had made and shared meals with her mother. The window seat where she'd once read books for hours, lost in her favorite stories about heroes and villains and happily-ever-afters. The couch where she'd curled up and cried for weeks after her mother's death.

"Goodbye, Mom," she whispered. "I'll see you soon."

Then she turned away from it all and stepped onto the porch, pulling the door shut behind her.

She wouldn't be back.

Chapter Sixteen

The city blurred past them as Lucas drove the sedan back to Rolling Meadows. Kira sat in the passenger seat, her body canted away from him, her mother's leather jacket pulled tight around her shoulders like armor.

Outside, the familiar streets and buildings slid by in a dull, dreamlike haze. Places she'd walked a hundred times but would never see again. Workers streamed along the sidewalks of the Governmental Sector with their heads down, rushing either to lunch or back to their offices. None of them looked twice at the black sedan with its official plates and tinted windows. None of them had any idea that the woman inside was counting down the final hours of her life.

Her stomach churned with a combination of hunger and anxiety. She wanted food, but nothing sounded good. She wanted sleep but knew if it came at all, it would only bring nightmares.

Four days.

The words skipped in her head like a record.

Four days.

"The leaves are really starting to turn," Lucas said, breaking the uncomfortable silence. He stopped at a red light, drumming his fingers lightly on the wheel. "Bet the view from the stables is incredible right now. Maybe we could get a quick lunch and go riding this afternoon?"

Kira's gaze followed a city bus as it lumbered through the intersection, its brakes squealing in protest. Inside, commuters stood shoulder to shoulder, staring blankly out the grimy windows. Just weeks ago, she had been one of them—clutching the overhead rail, watching the city slide by, unaware how completely her life was about to change.

"I'd rather just go back to my room."

Lucas's mouth tightened. "Kira, you can't spend your whole Final Week hiding."

"Why not?"

He sighed, tapping the steering wheel harder. "We could have dinner tonight. Just the two of us. Or we could watch a movie in the theater room."

"I appreciate what you're trying to do," Kira said, though she wasn't sure she meant it. The idea of spending extra time with Lucas felt wrong—like a betrayal of Will. "But I would rather not watch movies or go riding or have dinner."

The light changed, and he accelerated through the intersection. "Tell me something. When you were an advocate, did you let your clients lock themselves away?"

She continued to stare out the passenger window, ignoring the question. Of course, she hadn't let her clients lock themselves away. She'd urged every one of her Volunteers to spend time with family and make memories with their loved ones. But that wasn't an option for her. All of her loved ones were dead or on the other side of the wall. The only family she had left in the city was the father who had denied her existence for nineteen years.

And Emma.

Somewhere in the dark corridors of the Confines, her best friend was still imprisoned for helping her save Will's life. What would happen to Emma after Kira died? How long before they killed her too?

Ten minutes later, the car rolled to a stop in front of the lodge.

"What do you want, Kira?" Lucas asked, putting his arm on the back of her seat. "Tell me how I can help you."

She watched as two Rolling Meadows staff members methodically raked fallen leaves into neat, symmetrical piles along the path. A memory flashed through her mind—she and Emma as children, clasping hands and racing toward a mound of leaves, disappearing into it with a burst of laughter—then it was gone. A breeze picked up, tugging at the smaller leaves and scattering them across the walkway, undoing the careful work in seconds.

She spoke before the thought had fully formed. "Take me to see Emma Castile."

"Who?"

She turned to face him. "She's a friend of mine. She's being held in the Confines."

"Isn't she the one who—?"

"Yes, she's the one who kidnapped Teddy." Kira hated playing into her father's lie, but what choice did she have? "I want to say goodbye to her. It's not an unreasonable request, given the circumstances."

"Kira..." Lucas shook his head. "You know I can't do that."

"Why not? I'm a Volunteer. You're an advocate. It's your job to grant my requests."

"Yes, but the Confines are different. There are rules. Security measures."

"There aren't *really* any rules for Final Week requests." Kira knew that better than anyone. When she'd been Will's advocate, his only request had been to spend his last week with her, and she'd obliged even though it had technically been against the rules. "Please, Lucas. I haven't seen her in weeks. I just need to know she's okay."

"She's in the Confines. She's not okay. And even if I wanted to get you in, I don't have that kind of authority."

"But you could try," she insisted. "Talk to my father if you have to. Tell him this is my only request."

Lucas kept his eyes fixed on the windshield, fingers tapping on the wheel. His jaw shifted, like he was wrestling with the right words. Trying to figure out how to let her down gently.

Finally, he let out a slow breath. "I'll contact some people. See what I can do. But I'm not promising you anything."

"Thank you."

"Don't thank me yet."

Kira opened the door and stepped out, grabbing her duffle bag of clothes from the backseat before he could offer to help. She was halfway to the lodge entrance when he called out to her.

"Kira?"

She turned.

Lucas leaned toward the open window, one arm draped over the passenger seat. "I'm getting the impression that trust doesn't come easy for you. And I don't blame you, not after everything you've been through. But these next few days... maybe it's worth the risk to trust me."

She opened her mouth to respond, but he was already shifting the sedan into gear. The engine rumbled as the car pulled away, gravel crunching under the tires.

She stayed rooted to the spot, arms folded tight over her chest, watching his taillights vanish into the trees and wondering if trusting Lucas Pine might be the biggest risk of all.

Chapter Seventeen

Ghost didn't like this stretch of highway.

The sun was low enough to cast long, slanting shadows between the abandoned vehicles, creating too many blind spots, too many places for threats to hide. Years of exposure had reduced most of the cars to rusted skeletons—shattered windshields, tires long rotted away, frames sinking on bare axles.

Nature was reclaiming the vehicles little by little. Vines wound through empty engine compartments. Saplings jutted up through crumbling floorboards. Thick grass grew in the dirt that collected in truck beds. In another decade, the highway might swallow them completely, leaving nothing but scattered mounds of earth like forgotten burial sites.

The thought made him shudder.

Normally, he'd have stayed in the woods, where the thick undergrowth provided better cover and fewer chances of running into Patrols or anyone else who might be in the area. But they needed to get back to Haven quickly, and while the highway was more exposed, it would cut hours off the journey.

He glanced back at Will. "How you doing, kid?"

"Great."

Another angry, muttered response.

The kid hadn't said anything that wasn't angry or muttered since they'd turned back from the bridge. Ghost didn't need to ask to know what was going through Will's head. Each step away from the city felt like sealing Kira's fate, proof he was leaving her to face it alone.

They'd holed up for the night in the gutted shell of an old farmhouse a few miles north of Emmitsburg. Will had pushed to keep moving, but Ghost wouldn't risk traveling these roads after dark. It wasn't just the animals he feared—the ones with teeth and claws—but the other predators who woke at sundown. The human kind that slept by day and hunted by night.

They'd taken turns keeping watch, though Ghost doubted that Will had slept at all. Whenever he'd checked, the kid had just been sitting there in the darkness, elbows on his knees, staring at the floor, probably replaying his last moments with Kira over and over in his mind. Wondering what he could've done differently.

Up ahead, metal scraped against metal.

Ghost stopped dead in the middle of the road, his hand moving to the barrel of the shotgun slung across his back.

The sound hadn't been a natural one—a branch snapping or a bird taking flight from the tall grass—but a single note, like a car door being eased shut.

The tiny hairs on the back of his neck stood on end. Something was wrong. The air felt different somehow. Too still. Even the rustling of small animals in the grass had gone quiet, the whole world seeming to hold its breath, waiting for whatever came next.

Years of surviving in the wilderness had taught Ghost to

trust his instincts, and right now, every one of them was screaming at him to run.

"Will."

He heard the kid come to a stop behind him. "What?"

"Did you hear that?"

"Hear what?"

Ghost didn't answer. His eyes scanned the maze of rusted cars blocking their path. "I don't know, but I think we need to get off this..."

His voice trailed off as movement caught his eye. A figure slipped out from behind a pile of metal that had once been a floral delivery van, peeling itself from the shadows like a snake shedding its skin. Dark, greasy hair hung in tangled strands across his face, partially obscuring sharp, watchful eyes.

Ghost recognized him instantly.

The dollar store.

The three men.

This one was the leader.

The man walked toward him, slipping between the abandoned vehicles, making no sound as he moved. Two knives hung from his belt, but his hands were empty.

"Howdy, friend!" The man's cheerful voice carried across the empty highway. "If it isn't the man in black. Thought I recognized you. Not so mysterious in the daylight, are you?"

Will's hand moved to his rifle strap, but Ghost caught his wrist and held it tight. He could feel the kid's pulse racing. They needed to remain calm. Fear would get them killed.

The man smiled, showing yellow, tobacco-stained teeth. "Name's Rufus. Don't think we were properly introduced last time, before you ran me out of my home and stole everything I owned. What brings you back through my neck of the woods?"

"Just passing through," Ghost called out, maintaining his iron grip on Will's wrist. "We're not looking for any trouble."

"Oh, I bet." Rufus tilted his head. "Hey, where's your pretty little friend? The blonde one. Been thinking about her, you know? Hoping I might run into her again. Get a chance to finish what we started."

Ghost felt Will's muscles coil under his grip, so he squeezed the kid's wrist even tighter, trying to communicate what he could not say out loud: *Stay calm.*

Rufus was baiting them, which meant that he wasn't alone. Dogs always hunted in packs.

"She's in the city," Ghost called back. "But you already knew that, didn't you? You've been tracking us for days."

"What makes you say that?"

"Because the Patrols knew exactly where to find us. They knew about our village. They knew where to find the boy." Ghost released Will's wrist but kept his other hand on his shotgun. "Did the Patrols feed you well for that intel?"

Rufus shrugged. "The Patrols have been good to us. They give us supplies, and we give them information. Survival ain't easy out here. We all do what we gotta do."

"Not all of us."

Rufus's eyes locked onto Ghost's scarred face, studying him. "Don't pretend you're better than me, friend. I can see it in you. That same darkness that lives inside me. I bet you've done things to survive that you wouldn't tell your innocent little villagers about, haven't you?" His lips curled into a knowing smile. "Yeah, that's right. Way I figure it, the only real difference between us is that I'm honest about what I am."

Ghost's mind flashed to two moments he'd buried deep. The teenager in Afghanistan who'd turned out to be unarmed. The sick mother in Haven who'd cursed him with her last breath when he chose to save the antibiotics for those who had a better chance of survival.

Each death justified. Each death necessary.

Each death another weight he'd carry forever.

Ghost lowered his chin, his eyes boring into Rufus's. "Nineteen innocent people are dead because of you."

Rufus barked out a brittle laugh. "Innocent people? There's no 'innocent people' anymore. There's only two kinds of people left—survivors and corpses." His hand moved to one of his knives, tapping the hilt with a dirty index finger. "Ain't that right, boys?"

Two more figures emerged from the shadows—one from behind a rusted minivan, another sliding out from beneath an overturned pickup. The bald one with the snake tattoo carried a hunting rifle, while the man with stringy blond hair had an assortment of knives strapped to his belt. The three men had positioned themselves in a loose semicircle around Ghost and Will.

"You boys remember Frank and Chet?"

Ghost's eyes swept over the two men as they closed in, noting the rifle, the knives. Calculating angles, distances, the odds stacked against them.

He kept his voice level. "Yeah. We remember them."

Rufus's smile grew wider. "Good. Remember what I said about survivors and corpses?"

"Yes."

"Well, Frank and Chet and I are survivors. Now, we're going to figure out which kind you are."

Chapter Eighteen

Ghost counted six knives between the three men, not including whatever might be hidden beneath their ratty clothes. The bald one's rifle looked military-grade—an M24, if he had to guess. Likely a gift from the Patrols for services rendered.

Rufus caught the glance. "Better weaponry than last time," he said, as if reading Ghost's thoughts. "Better odds, too. Right, Frankie?"

Frank—the bald one—raised his rifle but didn't aim. "Yup. Three against two."

"Two and a half," Will muttered, glaring at the blond one.

Frank spat into the dirt, his lip curling. "Your girlfriend got lucky when she shot Chet. Won't happen again."

Chet didn't answer. He didn't look like he could. His face was pale, sweat beading on his forehead despite the cool air, his left arm hanging dead at his side. Apparently Kira's bullet had done real damage. Ghost noted the angry red wound at his shoulder where torn and bloodstained cloth clung to infected flesh. It wasn't just a bad wound anymore—it was a death sentence.

Without antibiotics, Chet was a walking corpse.

Ghost subtly shifted his weight, keeping all three in his line of sight with the ditch at his back. One quick step and he'd have cover, but he needed to time it perfectly. Frank might have military hardware, but he wasn't a soldier. Amateurs always telegraphed their shots—a slight tightening of the jaw, a shift in stance. You just had to know how to see it.

"You boys sure you want to do this?" Ghost asked, though he could see the answer in their eyes. The desperation of men who'd long since traded away whatever shreds of decency they once had. "After I embarrassed you last time?"

"Last time you had the element of surprise," Rufus replied, drawing a knife from his belt. The blade flashed in the sun, its edges clean and sharp. "Not today."

Ghost let his gaze slide to Chet but kept Frank's rifle in his peripheral vision. "Speaking of last time—how's that wound, Chet? Infection's already set in, hasn't it? Fever? Chills? Hurts so bad you can't sleep?"

Chet's good hand rose reflexively to his shoulder. Even that light touch made him flinch.

"Yeah, that's what I thought. You need antibiotics, buddy. Real ones, not the diluted garbage the Patrols are giving you. The kind we have at Haven." He paused, letting the offer hang in the air. "Assuming your friends even want you to get better. Might be easier on them if you didn't. One less mouth to feed."

It was just a guess, but an educated one. He'd seen men like them before—sticking together out of need, not loyalty. He'd bet his life the other two had already had conversations about Chet while he slept, weighing his usefulness against the resources he consumed.

"Shut up," Rufus snapped.

"How long do you think he's got?" Ghost continued, talking as if Chet weren't even there. "A few days? Maybe less? The fever's probably already scrambling his head. Soon that wound's going to stink so bad you won't be able to sit downwind of it. After that..." He shook his head. "Well, it's not a pretty way to die."

"I said shut up!"

In the corner of his vision, Ghost saw it—the flicker of doubt in Chet's eyes. The fear beginning to creep in.

"We can help him," Ghost said. "We have medicine in Haven. I'm not offering to let you boys in, obviously, but I can bring some antibiotics to the dollar store. But only if you walk away right now."

"He's lying," Rufus muttered. "Don't listen to him. He'd never share anything with us."

"Infection's a nasty way to die," Ghost pressed on, turning to Chet. "The fever will make you see things. Hear things. You won't know what's real. You'll start to wonder who you can trust."

Chet's eyes darted between Frank and Rufus, the fear in his eyes giving way to suspicion.

"Have they started yet? The hallucinations? If not, give it another day or two. Then they'll have to decide what to do with you. Can't have a sick man slowing them down and consuming precious resources." Ghost shifted his attention to Rufus. "Or have you and Frank already had that talk?"

Something passed between Rufus and Frank—a look that lasted a beat too long—but Ghost saw it.

Chet saw it, too.

"What's he talking about, Frank?" Chet's voice trembled, his good hand hovering over his shoulder. "What talk?"

"He's just messing with you," Rufus muttered. "Don't listen to him."

"Am I going to die?" Chet's face had gone even paler. "You said I wasn't, Frank. You said it looked better this morning."

The barrel of Frank's rifle edged toward the ground. "Chet—"

"I heard you whispering when you thought I was asleep," Chet continued, growing angry now. "Didn't know what you was saying. Didn't want to get up. You and me been together eight years, Frank. You ain't gonna leave me behind, right?"

Rufus's voice cut through the air. "So what if we are? Survivors and corpses, Chet. You're already a corpse. You're just too dumb to admit it."

Chet's feverish eyes locked on the bald man. "Frank?"

The snake tattoo on Frank's neck seemed to shift with his uncomfortable swallow. "The wound ain't lookin' good, Chet. What do you expect us to—?"

Chet's hand moved from his shoulder like a striking snake, snatching the knife from his belt and whipping it through the air.

The blade buried itself in the meat of Frank's thigh.

Frank howled. The rifle jerked upward.

A shot cracked the air.

Ghost didn't wait to see who it hit. He lunged, shoving Will into the ditch and dropping in after him. They crashed through waist-high grass and loose gravel. Ghost hit the ground hard, rolling onto his stomach and swinging the shotgun around.

He scanned the bloody scene.

Frank was down, screaming and clutching his leg, blood spurting between his fingers.

A few yards away, Chet had another knife in hand but was slumped against a rusted car, his entire body shaking. He tried to throw the knife, but his strength was gone, and the blade clattered to the pavement.

But what happened to—?

Two more shots rang out.

One bullet sparked off the pavement near Chet. The other shattered the rear window of the car he was leaning against.

Ghost couldn't see the shooter, but it had to be Rufus. He stole a quick glance back at Will, just to make sure he was still breathing. The kid stared back at him, eyes wide, his rifle ready, waiting for a command.

Ghost motioned sharply for him to stay down, then rolled left, poking his head up through the tall grass to get a new angle.

He spotted Rufus aiming the rifle one-handed while trying to drag Frank's limp body behind a rusted pickup. Frank was nearly dead weight, face gray, blood pulsing from the knife wound with every heartbeat. Each step Rufus took caused more blood to well up around the blade.

"You traitor!" Rufus screamed at Chet. "After everything we've been through, you knifed him!"

Chet's hand fumbled for another knife. Ghost saw how pale he'd gone, the fever hollowing out his face. "Frank lied to me." His fingers scraped the handle uselessly. "You were gonna leave me. Leave me to die alone."

The rifle cracked again.

Chet jerked as the bullet slammed into his chest, the impact snapping him back like a rag doll. He blinked, the shock draining from his face, replaced by a strange tranquility. It was the look of a man who had finally grasped a truth he had long been avoiding. His eyes found Frank's across the highway, and he managed a small, sad smile as blood dribbled from his lips. Then he slid down the car door, leaving a smear of red blood on the sun-bleached metal.

"Your turn," Rufus shouted toward the ditch. "Come on, boys. No need to drag this out."

A bullet kicked up dirt inches from Ghost's cheek. He

pressed himself deeper into the ditch, the earth cool and gritty beneath him. He couldn't stay pinned down forever. Sooner or later, Rufus would maneuver his way around to a better angle.

Staying on his belly, he crawled to Will's side. "Listen to me. I need you to move down that way." He pointed in the direction he meant. "Stay low. Keep your head down. Crawl until you reach those tree roots over there—the ones that extend into the ditch. You see what I mean?"

"Yeah? Then what?"

"Then you stand up and surrender."

Will's eyes went wide. "What?"

"I need you to distract him. Make him focus on you. That's my shot."

"Hopefully before he shoots me."

"Fingers crossed, kid."

"What about Frank?"

"Frank's not doing anything except bleeding out." Ghost slipped the shotgun off his shoulder. "You ready?"

"No," Will grumbled, but inched away, keeping low.

Ghost kept him in his sights, forcing his own breathing to steady, the weight of the shotgun grounding him.

Rufus's voice rang out, coming from a different location than last time. "Last chance! Maybe we can work something out? You take us back to your little village. Fix us up real nice. Or maybe we kill you both and go there ourselves, seeing as we know exactly where it is."

Ghost checked the angle. Rufus and Frank had moved to the edge of the highway, a few meters away. He adjusted his aim, calculating spread and distance in his head.

One shot. That was all he'd get.

He met Will's eyes through the tall grass and gave a nod.

The kid took a breath, left his rifle in the ditch, and rose slowly with his hands up.

Rufus barked out a laugh. "Well, look at that! Frankie, this one's gonna die a coward!"

But it was Frank who saw the grass move. Frank who saw Ghost rise out of the ditch, a double-barrel shotgun clutched in his hands. Frank whose tortured scream of warning came a millisecond too late.

"RU—!"

The blast caught Rufus full in the ribs, tearing through cloth and flesh with a wet, concussive thump. The force lifted him off his feet and slammed him hard against the side of the truck. He slid down the metal and crumpled onto the cracked asphalt, blood pooling beneath him in dark, spreading rivulets.

Ghost's ears rang. The world felt muted and far away. He smelled blood and powder and saw Rufus's body twitching in that awful way the almost-dead sometimes did. For a second he was somewhere else entirely—a dusty alley in Kandahar. A dead teenager clutching a radio instead of a bomb.

Some sins can never be forgiven.

The crack of a rifle split the air.

Frank's body jerked, arms flailing as the impact spun him sideways. The rifle he'd been aiming at Ghost slipped through his fingers as he collapsed across Rufus's body, a bloom of red spreading over his filthy shirt and that stupid snake tattoo.

Ghost blinked, forcing himself back to the present. As he stared at Frank's body, he realized how close he'd just come to dying, distracted by his own ghosts.

He turned.

Will stood at the edge of the ditch, slowly lowering the rifle. His face was different. He looked older than he had an hour ago. "I killed him," he whispered, as if just realizing it. "He was going to shoot you."

Ghost cleared his throat, searching for words that he knew

would bring little comfort. "You did what you had to do. They weren't going to let us walk away from here. You know that."

Will nodded once, but Ghost could see the weight settle onto his shoulders. That heavy knowledge. The same weight Ghost had carried home with him from Afghanistan.

He remembered every man he'd killed. Two in the desert. Eight in these woods. Ten total. All necessary. All justified.

Yet each death had left another scar on his soul.

Now Will had a scar of his own.

"Come on," he said to the kid. "Let's get out of here."

As they left the bodies cooling in the dirt and headed for Haven, Ghost heard Will mumbling under his breath. He couldn't make out the words, but he knew it was a prayer. He'd whispered those same words himself once, just after the Afghani teenager bled out in his arms in Kandahar.

Back when he still believed he could be forgiven.

Chapter Nineteen

Kira sat cross-legged on the bed, picking at the dinner Adeline had brought up from the kitchen. The food was beautiful—herb-crusted trout fresh from the river, tender vegetables, warm bread still fragrant from the oven—but she couldn't taste any of it.

It all tasted like ash in her mouth.

Another day gone.

She pushed the plate away and drew her knees to her chest. Beyond the massive windows of her suite, workers moved methodically through the manicured gardens, pulling weeds and tossing them into wheelbarrows. They felt distant and unreal, like figures in a diorama behind glass—an exhibit of a world that would go on without her.

A gentle knock broke the silence.

"Come in."

Adeline entered carrying a polished silver tray with a teapot and a plate of oatmeal cookies. "I thought you might be in the mood for something sweet," she said, setting the tray on the bedside table. She took in Kira's barely touched plate. "Is there something wrong with the trout, honey?"

"No, I'm sure it's delicious. I just..." Kira gestured helplessly. "Everything tastes wrong. My mom used to joke that I'd eat anything that wasn't nailed down—and a few things that were. Now I don't seem to have much of an appetite at all."

"That's normal." Adeline hovered near the edge of the bed, smoothing her black skirt. "A lot of Volunteers can't eat during their Final Week. It's one of the cruelties no one mentions. You're finally allowed all the good food you could ever want, but you can't bring yourself to swallow it. Rebecca was exactly the same way."

"Rebecca?"

"My daughter. She died as a Volunteer. Three years ago."

Kira's gaze dropped to the clothes she wore—Rebecca's clothes—and her heart twisted. "I'm so sorry. I didn't realize."

"No reason you would." Adeline busied herself with the teapot, pouring steaming tea into delicate china cups. "Would you like some honey in your tea?"

"Yes, please." Kira watched as Adeline stirred a spoonful into her cup, trying to put the pieces together in her mind. "Is that why you work here? Because of your daughter?"

"Yes." Adeline handed over the cup before settling into the armchair. "Though most people assume I've worked here forever, probably because I'm so old." She tried for a smile, taking a quick sip of tea. "Rebecca was nineteen when she Volunteered. Same age as you. So much life ahead of her. She was quite beautiful. I haven't been able to watch the fireworks since. I close my eyes when they start."

Kira cradled the warm cup between her palms, choosing her next words carefully. She didn't want to hurt Adeline, who'd shown her nothing but kindness. "Do you know why Rebecca chose to Volunteer?"

Something hardened in Adeline's expression. She spoke with effort, each word scraped out. "Love, of course." Her voice turned brittle. "Isn't it always love that ends us?"

Kira heard Will's whispered voice in her head.

I love you, Kira. Did I tell you that yet?

His confession had been followed by her own desperate plea: *Please don't ever leave me.*

"Are you feeling okay, honey?"

Kira nodded. "What was his name?"

Adeline let out a long, controlled breath. "Xander. Grew up in the Tenements with his mother. No father in the picture, or at least none that Rebecca told me about. She didn't share much about his past or his family. Just that they met on a city bus. He gave her his seat. They both missed their stops. Ended up riding around the city all afternoon."

Kira couldn't imagine romance blooming on those grimy, smelly, overcrowded buses. Then again, her own love story had started with a kidnapping attempt and betrayal.

"They dated through summer, autumn, and into winter," Adeline continued. "I met him once at Thanksgiving. He was polite. Well-mannered and respectful. Pulled me aside after dinner and asked for my blessing to propose. I could see how much he loved her, so I gave it." She stared into her cup. "He planned to ask on Christmas. But he got sick right before."

Kira set her cup down carefully on the tray. The tea felt too heavy in her grip. She didn't want to hear the rest—she wanted this love story to have a happy ending—but Adeline needed to finish.

"It wasn't the Job virus. Just the ordinary old flu. But it dug into his lungs and wouldn't let go. The hospital turned them away for lack of payment. His mother did her best at home, but it wasn't enough. He died on New Year's Day. Rebecca was with him when he went."

Adeline's hand shook as she lifted the cup but didn't drink. "I think he took most of her with him when he died."

A familiar ache spread through Kira's chest. She remembered watching her mother die in the Compulsory Clinic. But as awful as that day had been, she knew that watching Will die would somehow be even worse. Because his death would mean hope itself had died. Without Will, there was no reason to go on.

His death would be her death.

Silence fell between them. Outside, the workers' laughter drifted through the window. They sounded cheerful and relaxed, as if tending the grounds was just another ordinary chore in an ordinary world.

It felt wrong.

The polished wood, the plush furnishings, and the fresh flowers in glass vases were all meant to comfort, to distract from what Rolling Meadows really was. A place that pretended to be alive while it quietly, efficiently prepared people for death.

"I'm sorry to be so maudlin." Adeline dabbed her leaking eyes with a white handkerchief. "I meant to cheer you up, not drag you down in the dumps with me."

Kira reached out and laid her hand over Adeline's. "I would rather not be cheered up. Honestly, most of the time, I feel like throwing a tantrum. I want to just stomp my feet and scream like a toddler until I lose my voice."

"Oh, honey, that sounds wonderful. You should do it. I'd join in, but if I stomped my feet, this whole place might collapse. Although the dusty china in the cupboards downstairs could benefit from a good shaking."

Kira couldn't help it. She laughed, the sound cracking something open inside her. It felt good. Rebellious.

Adeline smiled and refilled their cups. They sat for a while in silence, nibbling cookies, watching the staff rake the gardens below as the last light died away.

"Mr. Pine seems fond of you."

Kira nearly choked on her cookie. "What?"

"I saw you two in the gardens this morning. Then you drove off together. Gone quite a while. Did he take you somewhere special?"

Kira shook her head. "I asked him to take me to my old townhouse in the Residential Sector. It's where I lived with my mom. I told him I needed to get a few things, but... I think I just needed to see it one last time."

Adeline's voice softened. "That was kind of him."

"He was just doing his job, Adeline."

Adeline picked up another cookie, broke it in half, and handed a piece to Kira. "Well, he's very handsome, though a bit too pretty for my tastes." She raised an eyebrow. "But any fool can see your heart is already spoken for."

Kira stared at her. "What do you mean?"

"You keep looking out the window, toward the river. There's someone out there, isn't there? Someone you left behind in the Unregulated Zone?"

The ache surged back, sharp as broken glass. She placed the cookie back on the plate. "Yes."

"Tell me about him."

"Why?"

"Because it helps."

So Kira let the words tumble out, knowing in some deep, instinctive way that she could trust Adeline. She spoke of Will's lopsided dimples. The stupid jokes he told to make her smile. The quiet bravery that had saved her life more than once. The way she could still feel his arms around her, even now, whenever she closed her eyes.

She didn't say his name. She hadn't forgotten the role she

was supposed to be playing: the mayor's secret daughter who'd fooled a defector. But Will was real. He wasn't just a lie her father invented.

He was real... and she loved him.

When she fell silent, Adeline sighed. "This might help. Or it might not. But for what it's worth—I'm certain Will loved you too."

Kira glanced at the woman. "How did you know his name? I didn't say who he was."

Adeline's expression was gentle. "Oh, honey. I remember Will from his time here as a Volunteer. You described him perfectly. And everyone could see the love you two shared that night on the dance floor. How you looked into each other's eyes."

Kira bit her lip, struggling to hold back tears. Here was someone else who had known Will. Someone else remembered him as he truly was. Not as a traitor but as a Volunteer.

"Did you spend much time with him? While he was here?"

"Not much, unfortunately. There were too many Volunteers that week. Most of my attention was on Teddy. But I saw enough of Will to know he was a good-hearted young man. Nothing like the man your father described last night."

Kira stared at her hands, remembering the first time Will had sat in her office. How her carefully ordered world had tilted on its axis the second their eyes met. "I was comfortable before I met him, Adeline. Everything was predictable. Not perfect, but safe. And then he came along and ruined all of that."

"I know, honey." Adeline gave her a sad smile as she gathered the empty cups and turned toward the door. "But sometimes the messy parts are the best parts of life. Even when they hurt. Maybe especially then." She paused on the threshold, her hand resting on the frame. "Thank you for the company, honey.

I didn't realize how much I missed talking about my daughter until tonight."

She hurried out of the room before Kira could respond.

Rising from the bed, Kira walked to the window. Beyond the rolling lawns and carefully tended hedges, she could just make out the concrete wall dividing Vita Nova from the wilderness beyond.

From Will.

She didn't regret coming back to the city. Teddy's life was worth hers a hundred times over. She only wished she'd had more time with Will. More dances. More kisses. More quiet mornings. More of everything.

Soon, the pain of losing him would be over. Not much longer now.

Three days to go.

It felt like forever. And no time at all.

Chapter Twenty

Kira was pulling back the covers to climb into bed when someone knocked on her door.

She froze, glancing at the clock on the mantel. Almost eleven.

She hesitated, blankets still clutched in her hand, feeling strangely exposed in her cotton pajamas and bare feet. No one should be visiting her this late—not even Adeline, whose uncanny sense for when Kira needed company did not extend past dinner. She reached for her mother's leather jacket, draped over the foot of the bed, and pulled it on.

She would look strange wearing the jacket over her pajamas, but at least she felt less vulnerable.

"Come in," she called.

The woman who entered looked about Kira's age, with limp brown hair that fell halfway down her back. Her Rolling Meadows uniform was a size too big, making her seem smaller than she actually was.

"I'm sorry to disturb you so late," she whispered, her voice tight and nervous. "But I was asked to deliver this."

She thrust a plain white envelope at Kira.

"I don't understand. Who asked you to—"

But the girl was already backing away, eager to be rid of it. "Good night, Ms. Liebert. Sleep well."

"Wait—"

The door clicked shut before Kira could finish.

She stared at the envelope in her hands, turning it over. No name. No markings of any kind. She slid a nail under the flap, breaking the seal. Inside was a single sheet of paper with a few handwritten sentences.

Two a.m. Intersection of Elmerton Avenue.

No one can see you.

And at the bottom, as if added as an afterthought:

Only if you think it's worth the risk.

THE CLOCK ON THE MANTEL HAD JUST STRUCK ONE-THIRTY when Kira cracked her door open and peered into the hall.

Empty.

Of course, it was empty.

She was the only Volunteer in the building.

After reading the note multiple times, she'd realized that sleep was no longer a possibility. She'd changed out of her pajamas and into jeans, boots, and a sweater.

And her mother's leather jacket.

Then she'd just sat on the edge of her bed, staring at the clock.

Waiting.

Trying not to lose her nerve.

The note was from Lucas. The last line had given him away: *Only if you think it's worth the risk.* His words from that afternoon. Maybe he'd found out something about Emma.

Or—she dared to hope—he was taking Kira to see her.

Her heart thudded as she crept down the grand staircase. She kept close to the wall, fingers brushing the cool plaster, knowing these older steps were likely to groan under her weight. Each creak felt unbearably loud in the vast, silent house.

What would she do if someone saw her? She ran through different lies in her head, testing them for believability. Just going for some food. Feeling sick. Couldn't sleep.

None of them felt convincing enough.

No one is going to see you. It's two a.m. They're all asleep.

But Rolling Meadows was built on hospitality. Adeline had mentioned that food could be ordered at any hour, no matter how late. That meant there were people awake around the clock, moving quietly through these halls.

When she reached the bottom, she pressed herself flat against the wall, letting her eyes adjust to the dimness of the main floor. She held her breath and listened for any sound—footsteps, a cough, voices whispering in the dark.

Nothing.

She wiped her damp palms on her jeans and forced her feet to keep moving. As she passed the darkened dining room, her eyes caught on the single place setting at the far end of the long table—plate, cup, and silverware already laid out for tomorrow's breakfast, waiting for her.

She tore her gaze away and headed for the lobby, moving faster now. She could see the double doors that led outside.

Almost there...

And then a young woman in a Rolling Meadows uniform emerged from a side door a few paces in front of her, balancing a stack of fresh towels in her arms. It was the same girl who had delivered the letter to her room.

Kira backed into a small alcove behind a potted plant and

held her breath. The girl passed within inches of her hiding spot, close enough that Kira could smell her floral perfume. She hummed a tune under her breath as she walked by, the song fading along with her footsteps.

Only after the sound disappeared entirely did Kira exhale.

She slipped from her hiding spot and hurried to the double doors, eager to get out of the lodge before someone else appeared and there wasn't a plant nearby to hide behind. But she hesitated before stepping close enough to trigger the automatic doors to open.

Part of her still wondered if this was all a trap—a test arranged by her father to catch her sneaking out and send her back to the Confines. She could almost see the floodlights blazing to life as she stepped outside, their beams sweeping the lawn before landing on her frozen in the doorway. Guards would pour from the shadows with their rifles raised, screaming at her to get on the ground.

But she'd come this far.

She inched forward.

The doors slid open on quiet motors, letting in a rush of cool air that carried the scent of wet grass. Crickets sang in the darkness, a sound she hadn't heard since leaving Haven.

There was no alarm. No floodlights. No Guards.

The doors closed behind her.

A gravel path wound toward the main parking area. Beyond that was the long driveway that led to Elmerton Avenue, half a mile away.

She knew better than to jog along an open driveway. Even at this hour, staff might be coming and going, either finishing their shifts or arriving to start a new one. So she slipped through the shadows of the grounds, using the massive trees and ornamental shrubs for cover. She kept low and moved slowly, pausing to scan for movement before running from one narrow patch of darkness to the next.

The journey to the edge of the property took her nearly twenty minutes. When she reached Elmerton Avenue, she checked her watch.

1:58 a.m.

The road was empty.

Maybe she'd misread everything. Maybe Lucas hadn't sent the note at all. Or worse—maybe her father had sent it. It was precisely the kind of trap Devlin would devise, a test to catch her breaking the rules. She could see it clearly: being dragged back to the Confines while her father looked on, smug and satisfied, knowing he'd won.

And Teddy would die in her place.

She shoved her hands deep into the pockets of her mother's jacket, uncertain of what to do. Part of her wanted to run back to Rolling Meadows, back to the safety of her room. If she were quick enough, maybe she could make it before anyone realized she was gone.

But another part of her—the part that had jumped off a bridge with Teddy, the part that had fallen in love with Will— knew she had to wait a few more minutes. She had to be certain.

Only if you think it's worth the risk.

Emma was worth the risk.

To her left, a pair of headlights appeared in the distance.

Kira moved behind the *Welcome to Rolling Meadows* sign as the car drew closer. It was moving too slowly to just be passing by. The vehicle was black, but in the darkness she couldn't be sure if it was Lucas's government sedan or some- thing else. She sank lower behind the sign, every instinct screaming at her to run. But she forced herself to stay still, watching, waiting for any sign of who was inside.

It rolled to a stop exactly where she hid.

For a moment, nothing happened. The only sounds were the idling engine, the crickets, and her own ragged breathing.

Then the passenger-side window lowered with a quiet electric whir.

Lucas leaned across the seat, his perfect smile emerging from the darkness. He was looking right at the sign—right at her.

"Ready to see your friend?"

Chapter Twenty-One

Kira slumped low in the backseat as the sedan crept along the dark road toward the Confines. To her left, the old asylum buildings loomed on the hilltop, hulking shapes of black stone and boarded-up windows, lit by floodlights that made them look like monsters caught in a spotlight.

She waited for Lucas to veer off onto some hidden service lane or unguarded entrance that would let them slip in unseen. But instead, he flicked on the turn signal and steered them straight toward the Confines's main gate.

Panic flared in her chest. "Lucas? What are you—?"

"Stay down," he whispered, pressing the button to roll down his window.

She ducked, pressing her face into the leather seat. Through the gap between the front seats, she watched a Guard step out of the shack—an older man, the same one from two nights ago with the too-tight uniform shirt. The Guard lifted one hand into the air, not to stop them but to wave them through.

As the shack disappeared behind them, Kira let out a breath. "You could've warned me."

"Sorry," Lucas said, steering the car up the winding driveway. "You don't know how many favors I had to call in to make this happen. How many people I had to bribe. Just know that we're in this together now, Kira. If this goes bad, it's both of our heads on the chopping block."

"Thank you," she said, reaching forward to rest a hand on his shoulder. "I know I'm asking a lot of you."

He flashed her a nervous smile in the mirror. "Yeah, just remember that when you're filling out my comment card. 'Extremely satisfied' in all categories, okay?"

"Of course."

Lucas guided the sedan around the back of the main building. He killed the headlights and engine near an ancient loading dock, the concrete crumbling into large piles on the road. Rusted metal rails surrounded a frozen hydraulic lift. Overgrown hedges pressed close to the walls, the untamed branches partially concealing the entrance. Even the security light above the door struggled to stay lit, flickering and buzzing as if ready to die.

"You're sure you want to do this?" Lucas turned toward her, his expression serious. "I don't know what kind of shape your friend will be in."

Kira nodded. "I'm sure. I need to see her one more time."

He checked his watch. "Okay. We've got thirty minutes. A friend of mine is a Guard here. He'll sneak us in through the kitchen entrance, but after that, we're on borrowed time. The next shift comes on at three a.m., so we need to be out of here by two forty-five. Once we're inside, stay next to me. Don't speak to anyone. Don't look around. Just keep your eyes down and act like you belong."

"Okay."

A figure emerged from the door at the base of the loading dock. Even in the darkness, Kira recognized the Guard uniform. The man said something into his radio, then gestured for them to approach.

"Let's move," Lucas said.

The Guard filled the doorway, his broad frame blocking out most of the light behind him. He looked young but was built like a wall, with thick shoulders and a bull neck that suggested he spent his spare time lifting weights and not doing much else. His shaved head caught the glow of the security light, giving him a hard, almost sculpted look, like a marble statue.

As Kira drew closer, he gave her only a cursory glance. "Revere the Volunteer," he muttered, skipping the formal salute entirely.

"Thank you," she said.

He turned his attention to Lucas. "You remember the rules?"

"Thirty minutes," Lucas replied. "Just like we agreed."

The Guard checked his watch. "Stick to the route we discussed. Don't start exploring."

He swiped a keycard, and the lock responded with a heavy click. The door opened with a screech of old hinges, releasing a stale, sour draft of air—that same institutional smell Kira remembered from her brief stay in the Confines. It made her feel half-sick.

As they stepped inside, the Guard grabbed Lucas by the arm, leaning in close. "If this goes south," he said, shoving the keycard into Lucas's palm, "do *not* say my name. I had no part in this."

Lucas pocketed the key. "Relax, man. You're good. I already told you."

The Guard didn't look convinced. He gave Lucas a flat

stare before glancing at Kira, then turned and pulled the door open wider to let them in.

Something about the way the Guard spoke made Kira uneasy. He wasn't just breaking the rules—he was afraid. It felt less like a favor and more like blackmail, or like he was being pushed into something he didn't want to be part of.

Stop. Lucas is helping you see Emma. That's all that matters.

The door groaned shut, sealing them in darkness broken only by the red glow of the exit signs.

"This way."

She followed Lucas into the kitchen. The cavernous room held a row of appliances, industrial ovens, and stovetops streaked with grease. A row of metal refrigerators hummed against the far wall, the doors dented and stained. The air was thick with the smell of old food and mildew.

A scream tore through the silence. It sounded distant, but not distant enough.

Kira stopped cold.

"Ignore it," Lucas whispered. "We don't have much time."

They exited the kitchen and wove through a maze of corridors, each one indistinguishable from the last—narrow, dimly lit, and lined with peeling walls and heavy doors. Lucas moved quickly, avoiding certain hallways altogether, steering her left, then right, then up a flight of stairs.

How big is this place? she wondered. *And how many people are being held in here?*

Twice Lucas dragged her into narrow alcoves just in time, pressing her back against the cold concrete as pairs of Guards trudged past, their boots thudding against the concrete. She held her breath both times, heart pounding so loud she was certain the Guards could hear it, praying the shadows would hide them.

"Almost there," he said, taking her hand and pulling her into a new corridor. "This is the low-security wing."

Rows of cell doors stretched into the darkness, each with a narrow window and a slot for meal trays. From behind one came the muffled sobs of a woman—heartbroken and endless. The sound cut straight through Kira's soul. She felt an almost overwhelming urge to rip open every door, to drag every prisoner out into the light. But where would they even go? There was no freedom waiting on the other side.

The whole city was a prison.

They kept moving.

Lucas slowed as he read the numbers. Finally, he stopped. "Here," he whispered. "Two thirty-three."

Kira stepped closer and peered through the window, her breath fogging the glass. She wiped it with her sleeve for a clearer view.

The cell was small and grim, the walls a patchwork of chipped paint and what appeared to be greenish-black mold. The only light came from a single overhead bulb.

A figure lay curled on a narrow cot, wrapped in a thin, stained blanket. Even from behind, Kira could see how Emma's spine bowed and how much weight she'd lost in the few weeks she'd been a prisoner in this awful place.

Lucas pulled the keycard from his pocket and used it to open the door. "Remember, you only have ten minutes. Then we leave—no matter what."

She nodded. "Okay."

The lock clicked, and Lucas pushed the door open just enough for Kira to squeeze inside.

The smell hit her immediately—old sweat, urine, and stale air that felt thick enough to choke on. The door thudded shut behind her, sealing her in.

Emma stirred at the sound, the blanket shifting with a slow, scraping rustle. She rolled over stiffly, her movements sluggish, like every joint ached. Her face was gaunt, eyes sunken into dark hollows that looked almost bruised.

And then those eyes locked onto Kira's.

For a heartbeat they were empty, her eyelids heavy with exhaustion and defeat. She looked as if she might fall right back asleep.

But then a flare of recognition—dull but unmistakable. For a long moment she just stared at Kira, as if trying to figure out whether she was real or just another hallucination.

Kira took a hesitant step forward. "Emma?"

Her best friend's muscles tensed, her lips pulling back from her teeth in something that resembled a cross between a grimace and a snarl. Her fingers twisted into the thin blanket, bunching it together like she meant to tear it apart.

The recognition in her eyes burned away, replaced by something hard and unyielding.

Hatred.

Chapter Twenty-Two

"What are you doing here?"

With effort, Emma pushed herself upright. The blanket fell to the floor, revealing a painfully thin frame, bruises staining her legs like dark fingerprints.

She looked so much smaller than Kira remembered. Her face was gaunt, her lips cracked and dry. Her eyes—once bright and full of wicked humor—were almost colorless now, rimmed red from crying. Her dark curls were matted and limp, pressed flat on one side from hours spent lying on that mattress.

If Kira hadn't known this was Emma's cell, she might not have recognized her at all. This woman was a shell of the person she'd known—the beautiful, feisty friend who had dragged her on double dates, who loved to dance, and who would order a piece of cake and only eat the frosting.

Kira moved into the cell, stepping closer to the bed. Her gaze shifted from the bruises on her legs to the oversized prison shirt sliding off one narrow shoulder, revealing even more dark, ugly marks. "I needed to see you," she said. "To know you were okay."

Emma let out a sound that might once have been a laugh. Now it was a cold, dead sound. "Do I look okay, Kira? Does any of this look okay?"

She flung a trembling hand at the cell—its walls littered with faint scratch marks, the soiled mattress, and the stained metal toilet in the corner. "They keep me in here all day. I never see the sun except through that tiny window. And the screaming..." She shuddered. "The screaming never stops."

Kira's hands balled into fists at her sides. "Oh, Emma. I'm so sorry—"

"Sorry?" Emma's voice cracked, rising into something darker than anger. "Why should you be sorry? You got to play the hero, right? You got to save that little boy. You got to run off and play house with your Volunteer boyfriend. And you left me in here to rot. I risked everything for you, Kira. I trusted you. And you left me."

"I didn't mean to—"

But Kira's voice broke on the words. What had Emma said that wasn't true?

Her friend wrapped her frail arms around herself. "They interrogated me for hours. Days. I don't even know how long. They wanted to know everything about the Unregulated Zone. About those people over there. About Will. They thought I knew where you'd gone."

"Did they...?" She couldn't bring herself to finish the sentence.

"Hurt me? Yes, Kira. They hurt me. They beat me. Locked me in a tiny cell with no bed, no toilet, nothing. No windows. No light. Just darkness and silence so deep you start hearing things that aren't there. Seeing things, too. I thought you came to see me once. We had a whole conversation. That's how bad it got. I'm not even sure you're real now." She pressed her hands against her temples as if trying to hold back the memories. "When they finally realized I didn't know anything, they moved me in here. It's not silent here. There's always someone screaming."

Kira took another step forward, reaching for her friend. "Emma, please."

"Don't." Emma jerked away as if Kira's touch might burn her. "You know what the worst part is? I actually thought you'd come. I thought, *Her father's the mayor; she'll get me out of here.* I truly believed you would save me. But you're no different than him, are you? You both use people. And when you're done, you throw them away."

The words cut Kira deeper than any knife. She opened her mouth to deny it—to say, *I'm not like him, Emma, you know that*—but nothing came out. Because wasn't that exactly what she'd done? Used Emma to help rescue Will and Teddy, then left her behind to face the consequences?

"So tell me. What were you doing while I was being tortured for information I didn't have?" Emma demanded. "Were you out there living it up with your boyfriend? Enjoying your romantic wilderness honeymoon?"

"It wasn't like that, Emma. It wasn't easy or fun. There are good people out there, but there are bad ones, too. Very bad." She swallowed, the memory of those three men in the storage room creeping back in. "A group of men tried to attack me. I would've been..." She stopped, unable to say the word. "But someone stopped them. A man. He saved me."

Emma blinked, leaning forward slightly. "A man? Who?"

The story tumbled out of her. She hadn't realized how much she'd needed to talk to her best friend. To tell her about Ghost. "His name is Noah Hale. He's been living out there for years, leading a settlement in the woods. And the craziest part?

He knew my mother. But he didn't just know her—he loved her. My father found out and had him exiled. But not before beating him and giving him this awful scar across his face."

Emma stared at her for a moment, clearly processing this new information. "So what are you doing back here?"

"The Patrols found Teddy and brought him back, so I followed him. They locked me up in here. The only way I could get my father to let Teddy live was to Volunteer to die in his place."

Emma's anger faltered. Just for a moment. Just enough to reveal the ghost of the friend she used to be. "But your father—?"

"Is using it to his advantage, of course." Kira sank onto the edge of the cot, leaving space between them she knew she couldn't cross. "He gets to look like the noble mayor. The man who sacrificed his daughter for the good of the city."

"And you're willing to die for those lies?"

"No." Kira met Emma's eyes. "I'm willing to die for Teddy."

"And what about Will?"

"He didn't come back. He's safe. He's outside of the wall."

Emma laughed. "So now you're going to die, too? I suppose that makes me feel a little better. Although it doesn't seem fair, does it? We're both going to die while your Volunteer boyfriend gets to live."

"Emma..."

"I just wish they wouldn't make me suffer so much first." She pulled her knees to her chest, making herself look even smaller. "I wish they'd just get it over with already."

Before Kira could respond, three quiet knocks rattled the cell door. It was Lucas's signal.

Her time was up.

Kira stood, her legs unsteady. "I have to go now. But I'll find a way to come back to see you again."

Tears spilled down Emma's pale cheeks. "Don't bother. Just leave. Leave and don't ever come back."

She wasn't in any position to make promises—she knew that—but she heard herself making one anyway. "You're not going to die in here, Emma. That won't happen. I promise."

Her friend barked out another broken laugh. "Yes, I am. We both know it." She wiped her tears; the skin of her hand was nearly translucent. "But at least you're going to die before me. I guess that's some kind of justice."

Two more knocks, urgent this time.

Kira stared at her best friend, at the damage this place had carved into her in just a few weeks. She wanted to say something meaningful, to give her a small measure of hope, but Emma was already dying, piece by piece, and they both knew it.

"I'm so sorry," she whispered.

Then she pulled the door open and slipped out.

The last thing she saw before the door closed behind her was Emma curling back onto the cot, turning to face the wall, as if she'd already given up.

Chapter Twenty-Three

They drove in silence back to Rolling Meadows, Kira rigid in the passenger seat, her hands clenched so tightly in her lap that her knuckles hurt. She could not shake the image of Emma, bruised and broken, huddled on that filthy cot. Every time she blinked, she saw the hatred in her friend's eyes.

Just leave. Leave and don't ever come back.

Lucas made the turn onto Elmerton Avenue, the car's headlights cutting tunnels through the pre-dawn fog. "You want to talk about it?"

"No."

He drummed his fingers on the steering wheel. "She's been locked up for weeks, Kira. She's hurt. Whatever she said to you in there... she didn't mean it. People say things they don't mean when they're hurting."

Kira didn't respond. She turned her face toward the window. The trees lining Rolling Meadows' driveway emerged one by one from the fog, their branches creating strange shadows in the headlights.

You're no different than him, are you? You both use people. And when you're done, you throw them away.

The words rang in her ears. The worst part of all was that Emma wasn't wrong.

Lucas brought the car to a stop at the end of Rolling Meadows' driveway and turned off the engine. He didn't speak at first, just rested both hands on the wheel for a moment, staring out at the dark. His thumb tapped a quiet rhythm against the leather.

"I'm sorry about your friend," he finally said. "No one deserves to end up like that. But this is your Final Week. You can't let what you saw tonight ruin the last few days you have left."

She shook her head. "Don't."

"Don't what?"

"You didn't see her in there, Lucas. You didn't see what they did to her."

Because of me.

But she couldn't say that part.

Lucas shifted in his seat to face her better, draping an arm along the back of her headrest. His eyes searched her face. "Did you tell her you're going to die on Friday? That you volunteered to give up your life for some little kid?"

Kira's chest tightened. "She didn't care about that," she said, omitting the part where Emma had accused her of being just like her father. "But she said it didn't seem fair that I have to die while Will gets to live."

One corner of Lucas's mouth twitched, though it was impossible to tell if it was sympathy or something else. "What do you think about that?"

She didn't have to think. "I don't want him to die. If it means he gets to live a long life far away from here, I'd die a thousand times."

Lucas leaned back a little, studying her. "That's noble. But... do you really think he'd do the same for you?"

She turned away, leaning closer to the window. Fog pressed against the glass as if trying to crawl inside. She drew a line in the condensation with her finger. "He would if he could," she said. "But I'm so glad he's safe out there."

Lucas reached out and rested a hand on her wrist, his fingers warm against her cold skin. She didn't pull away, but she didn't look at him either.

"Tell me about it."

"About what?"

"The other side of the wall." His thumb brushed the inside of her wrist. "What was it like out there? What were the people like?"

Kira stiffened at the question. She *shouldn't* talk about it. She needed to protect Haven at all costs. But the memories of that place pressed so hard against her chest that it hurt to hold them in. She felt like she might suffocate if she didn't let them out.

Besides, Lucas had risked so much tonight. He'd shown her she could trust him. Or at least, she wanted to believe she could. She *needed* to trust someone.

"It was different. Hard, but good. Everything was dirty and overgrown and wild, but also alive." Once she started talking, it was impossible to stop. "And it was so quiet out there. I had a hard time sleeping at night. Eventually, we found this little village. Everyone works so hard there. They have to work hard if they want to eat. But at the same time, they were really happy."

Lucas gave a little chuckle. "Sounds like the Agricultural Sector, except for the happy part. How many people lived there?"

"I don't know for sure. A few hundred, maybe? They didn't turn anyone away."

"Was it safe there?"

"Safer than here. They don't kill their own people. The only thing they were really afraid of was us. This city, I mean. And the Patrols."

Lucas's thumb stopped moving on her wrist. "But they had defenses, right? Some way to protect themselves."

Kira nodded, remembering the fence and the Watchers with their rifles. "Yeah. They had a perimeter fence. Watchers who took shifts patrolling the fence. Most people knew how to shoot." She drew a shaky breath as memories of the wedding night rose up. "In the end, it didn't matter. People died anyway."

Lucas drew his hand away from her wrist and let it rest on the console between them. "Were you scared?"

She glanced at him then, noticing a tightness around his eyes that hadn't been there before. The look disappeared the moment she focused on it. "All the time. But not the same way I'm scared here."

"I'm sorry, Kira." He reached out again, this time brushing her cheek with the back of his fingers. "I didn't mean to make you relive all of that. I just want to understand you better."

For a second, she wanted to lean into his hand. But the thought of Will's touch stopped her cold.

Not him. Not Will.

Kira pulled away from him, his hand falling away from her face. Cool air rushed into the car as she pushed the door open.

"I should get back to the lodge."

"Kira—wait—"

She didn't. She closed the door and started across the damp grass. The early morning air was cold and heavy with moisture that seemed to seep straight through her clothes. Kira pulled her mother's jacket tighter around herself, already shivering.

She heard the car door open behind her. The sounds of footsteps coming after her.

"Kira, wait."

She didn't turn around.

"I'm fine, Lucas. I promise. I just need to get some sleep."

He caught up with her in a few long strides, grabbing her arm gently to stop her. "Kira, wait. I keep telling myself not to say anything, but I have to get this out."

"What is it?"

He hesitated, his eyes searching hers. "You're still thinking about him. About Will. And I get it. This might sound harsh, but it's the truth. You need to forget him. Your time is..." He shook his head, seeming to reconsider his words. "You can't spend your Final Week pining over someone who doesn't deserve you."

"What?" Her anger flared, an undeniable urge to defend Will. "You don't know anything about him."

"I know enough," he shot back. "I know he's not coming back for you. I know he's not here. I know he left you to face this alone."

Kira shook her head. "I *told* him to stay away," she protested. "If he comes back, he'll be killed. You don't understand."

"That might be true." Lucas hesitated before continuing. "But if it were me... I wouldn't be able to stay away from you. Not for anything. Even if you begged me to." He shook his head and let out a little laugh. "Man, that probably sounds crazy. We only just met yesterday. But it's the truth."

Kira didn't know how to respond. The words felt too personal, too wrong after everything that had happened tonight. She shifted her weight, uncomfortable with the way he was looking at her, like he expected her to say something back.

"I'm sorry." He lowered his eyes to the ground. "I shouldn't have said that."

"It's fine." She pulled her arm gently from his grip. "Goodnight, Lucas."

"Goodnight, Kira."

She turned and kept walking into the fog. Behind her, she heard the distant sound of his car door closing and the low rumble of the engine starting up again.

She made it back to her room without being spotted, adrenaline buzzing through her body, certain with every step that someone would stop her before she got there.

Once inside, she locked the door and sagged against it, her thoughts churning with everything Lucas had said. It wasn't just his awkward confession that had unsettled her. Worse were the doubts he'd planted in her mind—dark questions about Will, about whether his love for her had ever truly been real.

She crossed the room and opened the door to her private balcony. The metal chair was cold and slightly damp, but she didn't mind. She sat and watched the stars until the horizon began to lighten—a thin line of pearl gray where the wall met the sky, gradually giving way to streaks of rose and gold.

Kira had seen hundreds of sunrises in her life, but they had always been background noise to her morning routine—showering, dressing, rushing to meet Emma for coffee.

But now she couldn't look away.

She watched as the clouds caught fire along their edges, glowing the same coppery hue as Grace's hair. A jagged streak of gold tore through the horizon, sharp and unyielding, like the scar slashed across Ghost's face. The deepening blues reminded her of Will's eyes that day at the market, when they'd sat sharing food and he'd looked at her in a way that made her feel alive for the first time.

And when the light finally broke free—sunrise spilling over the earth—the morning dewdrops on the grass sparkled like Teddy's smile.

A tear slipped free before she even realized she was crying.

Three more sunrises.

That was all she had left.

She clasped her hands in her lap, fingers twisting together. "God... if You're there. Please. I don't know who to trust anymore." She swiped at her damp cheeks with the sleeve of her jacket. "I'm going to go through with this. Teddy deserves to live. But whatever happens, I only have one request. Please don't let me be alone on Friday. Please don't let me die alone."

No voice came out of the darkness. No rush of warmth filled the hollow ache in her chest.

But the sun kept rising anyway, as it always had. As it always would, even after she was gone. Kira watched it climb higher, the tears cooling on her cheeks.

And she let herself believe—just for a moment—that maybe that was her answer. That even if there were no words in return, she hadn't gone unheard.

Chapter Twenty-Four

"Brannigan? Come in. Over."

Ghost hunched over the desk, fingers adjusting the ham radio's dials with surgical precision. Static crackled through the speaker. He'd been at this since dawn with no luck. Typically, Brannigan would break through the noise within an hour or two, opening with his usual *Good copy, Ghost.*

But this morning, there was nothing.

The man on the other end of these conversations—whose first name he didn't even know—had never stayed silent this long.

He needed that voice. It wasn't the friendship he craved, exactly, but rather proof that the world held something other than ruin. That somewhere, people were rebuilding, refusing to give up.

He needed hope.

His eyes drifted to the photograph beside the radio. Madison's smile lit up the battered old image, hair whipped around her face on the deck of the Millersburg Ferry. It was the only photograph he had of her—his sole tangible connection to a love that had shaped his entire adult life. Fresh creases marred it where Ghost had crushed it in his fist after Kira told him her mother was dead. Lines crisscrossed Madison's face like scars, breaking that perfect smile into fragments. He'd tried pressing the photo flat under his Bible, but some damage couldn't be undone.

"Brannigan? This is Ghost. How copy? Over."

Outside, he heard the sounds of Haven's recovery—the hammering of nails, the low bark of orders being shouted, and the distant buzz of a chainsaw. The fence was the top priority, according to the group of men who'd greeted him upon his return from Emmitsburg, and repairs were nearly complete. Next came the church. Work had already begun, and with any luck, they'd said, it would be finished in a few weeks. For now, they would worship in the mess hall.

He leaned back in his chair, rubbing a finger over the scar on his cheek. His people were treating the attack as if it were just a setback, not the warning it truly was. Either they didn't grasp how fragile their safety had become now that the Patrols knew where to find them... or they simply refused to face it.

Ghost knew better. The Patrols weren't finished with them. They'd be back. Not for Teddy this time, but for all of them. And they wouldn't be satisfied with just torching the church.

The next attack would be an extermination.

He was going to have to crush their hope. Tell them to stop rebuilding. To leave behind the cabins they'd built with their own hands, the gardens where their children played, and the church where they worshipped. He would have to stand before them and tell them to pack only what they could carry and prepare for a journey he couldn't promise they'd survive.

They'd head north to Brannigan's settlement—the only other community he knew for certain still existed. But the stretch of country between Haven and Brannigan was a mystery, and he suspected those three corpses rotting on the highway wouldn't be the worst thing they'd find along the way.

A knock at the cabin door pulled him from his dark thoughts. He tucked Madison's photograph into his pocket and rose. Only a handful of people in Haven knew about the radio, and he wanted to keep it that way.

Hope was precious, but it was also dangerous.

Come in," he called, shutting the office door behind him.

Brack entered the cabin first, followed by Grace. Neither looked like they'd slept in days. Dark circles shadowed Grace's eyes, and she kept one hand pressed against the swell of her belly like she was drawing strength from the life growing there.

Her husband seemed diminished somehow, his broad shoulders sagging beneath his worn jacket. Ghost guessed he'd lost ten pounds since the attack. Not much for a man his size, but still noticeable.

Ghost motioned for Brack to close the door, but then Will appeared in the doorway.

He looked worse than either of them. His clothes were wrinkled and disheveled, like he'd spent the night in them—though Ghost doubted he'd slept at all. His eyes carried that empty, haunted stare Ghost had seen too many times before. It was the look of someone who'd killed for the first time and no longer recognized himself. Yet there was a restless energy in the way he held himself, every muscle taut, as if he might bolt back toward the city at any second.

It almost shamed him—Will's raw devotion. Ghost had walked away from Madison, convinced it was the only way to keep her safe. But Will wasn't like him.

Will would crawl through fire to get back to Kira.

"You don't look so good," Ghost remarked, watching Will

pace the cabin like a caged animal. "You need to take care of yourself."

Grace slipped an arm around her husband's back. "He needs to rest. We all do."

"We can rest when she's safe," Will muttered, his voice hoarse from lack of sleep. "It's Tuesday. We have three days. You told me we were going back for her. So what's your plan?"

Grace gave Ghost an exasperated look: *See what I've been dealing with all night?*

"We're only going to get one shot at this," Ghost said. "We have to be smart about it. Think it through."

"Think it through?" Will spun so he was facing Ghost. "I came back to Haven so we could regroup and go back for her. But you haven't even brought up the possibility of a rescue attempt with anyone here. I know you haven't, because no one is talking about her. No one even cares about her. It's like she never existed. They're just rebuilding that stupid fence."

Grace settled onto the corner of Ghost's bed. "Will, it's not like—"

"Not like what?" Will cut her off. "All these people care about is rebuilding their village. When are you going to tell them they're wasting their time? That the Patrols know where we are? That we're all going to die here? If you won't tell them, maybe I should."

Ghost crossed the room in two long strides. He seized Will by the collar and slammed him against the wall so hard the windows rattled. The old soldier came out in his voice, deadly quiet, controlled, and sharp as a blade.

"You're not going to tell them anything. Do you understand me? This isn't your village—it's mine. You're not in charge here. You and your friends are only staying here because I allow it. And if you do or say anything that puts my people at risk, I'll toss all three of you outside the fence and forget you ever existed."

Ghost wasn't angry at the kid. He saw in Will an echo of himself from years ago. That same fierce, unrelenting love and that desperate need to keep someone safe no matter the cost. The kind of love that didn't just hurt—it left marks you carried forever. Will's scars might not be etched across his face like Ghost's, but they were there all the same.

Will sagged in Ghost's grip, the anger leaving his eyes. "We have to do something," he whispered. "We can't just... let her..."

"We won't." Ghost released him and stepped back. "But if we're going to do this, we're going to do it right."

Brack made a rough sound in his throat. "What about the river? We could swim it north of the city. It's shallow in certain spots, and there's no wall. They can't be watching every square inch of riverfront."

"I can swim across," Will spoke up. "I would've done it yesterday if he hadn't stopped me."

Ghost shook his head. "They've got boats on the river day and night. And they're not sticking close to the city anymore. Yesterday, on our way back, we saw Patrol boats all the way up near Wagner. Even if you managed to cross without being spotted, you'd still have the wall to deal with." He turned to Brack. "What about workers moving in and out of the city? I saw that checkpoint on the bridge. Who's actually crossing every day?"

Brack folded his arms. "Not anyone who's going to help us. The only regular traffic we've seen is Patrol soldiers." He paused, his voice dropping lower. "And the corpses."

Something sparked in Will's eyes. "The vans."

Ghost frowned. "What vans?"

"The disposal vans. They're always going back and forth from the Compulsory Clinic, hauling bodies out to the burial pits. I know the routes. The schedules."

For a moment, Ghost couldn't see the room. Madison's body in a van, dumped into a pit like refuse. The image hit him so hard he had to brace himself on the wall.

Baby, I'm so sorry.

"Ghost?" Grace's voice cut through the fog. "Are you okay?"

The room swam back into view. He forced the image down before it consumed him entirely and straightened his spine. "The vans," he said, trying to keep his voice even. "If we get our hands on one, how do we get through the checkpoint on the bridge?"

"I'm not sure." Will leaned against the wall and ran a hand through his unwashed hair. "I need to think."

Brack lowered himself next to Grace on the bed. "Even if you're able to get through the checkpoint, you'd still have to make it through the city without being spotted, find Kira, and get back out again. How are you going to do that?"

"And what if she doesn't want to go?" Grace added. "Won't her leaving mean they'll execute Teddy in her place?"

"I'm going back for Teddy, too," Will said, jamming his hands into his pockets. "I'm not leaving either of them behind."

The room fell silent. Even the hammers outside seemed to pause.

Ghost moved to the window, gazing out at the village slowly being rebuilt around him. His people had been working since dawn—and soon he would have to ask them to leave it all behind. He took a long, steadying breath and let it out.

"Will is right. I need to tell them the truth."

Grace leaned forward, her long, red curls falling around her face. "The truth?"

"The Patrols know we're here. They'll be back." He turned away from the window. "There's a settlement north of here, just across the border into New York. A man named Brannigan. I've been talking to him for months on a ham radio. They've got medicine, crops, real defenses."

"And they'll take us?" Grace's hand went to her belly. "All of us?"

"I think so."

Ghost's thoughts drifted back to his last brief conversation with Brannigan—the morning of Avery and Nic's wedding. Just hours before the Patrol attack that left so many of his people dead.

Brannigan's voice had been rough that day, cracking with fatigue and the strain of deep, rattling coughs. Ghost had tried to ask about Maisie, knowing she'd been sick, but Brannigan had shut him down with a clipped, "Don't want to talk about that now." Then he'd paused, let out a long sigh, and said, "Not sure what's going to happen to me, brother. Things aren't too good here. But if you ever get up this way, feel free to stop by and say hello. I know we said we wouldn't do this, but I think we can trust each other, don't you?"

Then he'd rattled off the exact coordinates of his settlement, repeating them twice to be certain Ghost copied them down correctly.

"You should come," Brannigan had said, the words followed by another bout of heavy coughing. "You and all those with you. We sure could use some help around here."

Someone had knocked on his cabin door then. A minor problem that had seemed important at the time. When he returned to the radio, Brannigan was gone.

And now he didn't even know if the man was still alive.

"I'll call a meeting," Ghost said. "As soon as I reach Brannigan. Hopefully within the next day or so. We need to tell everyone what's coming. Get them ready to pack up."

Brack's face had gone pale. "How soon do we leave?"

"As soon as possible. If I can convince them to go, you'll lead them north."

Brack stiffened. "Why me? You and Will are going to need help going after Kira."

"What I need," Ghost stared at him, his gaze unwavering, "is someone I trust. Someone strong who can lead my people—including your wife and unborn child—somewhere safe. Can you think of anyone better for the job?"

Brack stared at him, mouth agape, but said nothing.

Grace's fingers intertwined with her husband's. "He's right, baby. You know he's right. These people love you. They will follow you."

"Just think about it." Ghost turned toward his office door. "Give me a few hours to try the radio again. Once I hear from Brannigan, we'll call everyone to the mess hall."

He didn't wait for an answer. He slipped inside, closing the door quietly behind him. The office felt stiflingly hot and small. He crossed to his chair and sank into it, eyes fixed on the battered radio. What if Brannigan never answered? Was he really going to send his people into the wilderness blind? What if Brannigan was dead? What if the settlement was gone? What if they'd been attacked and overrun?

He leaned forward and adjusted the frequency dial, listening to the static hiss and pop through the speakers. Closing his eyes, he whispered a brief prayer—that somewhere beyond that wall of white noise, his friend was still out there, ready to answer.

But if Brannigan stayed silent, Ghost knew he'd have to make an impossible choice:

Send his people into the unknown without him. Or go with them.

And abandon Kira just as he'd once abandoned her mother.

Chapter Twenty-Five

The bus's air brakes hissed as it lurched to a stop a few blocks from the Volunteer Memorial Walkway. Kira rose from her seat in the middle of the mostly empty bus, tugging the hood of her rain jacket lower over her face. No one would recognize her as a Volunteer in these clothes. No silk dresses or blue rose corsages today. Just worn jeans, scuffed boots, and a shapeless jacket she'd found in the back of her closet.

Reaching out to Lucas for a ride would have been smarter and safer. But he wouldn't just drop her off and leave. He would insist on staying with her.

And she needed to do this alone.

She shuffled toward the door, her gaze fixed on the bus floor, its rubber matting ground with decades of city grime. The only other passengers were an older woman dozing in the back with her purse clutched to her chest and two maintenance workers in grease-stained uniforms arguing about a burst water main in the Residential Sector.

"Excuse me," she said as she squeezed past them.

They didn't even look at her.

A gust of autumn wind hit her the moment she stepped off the bus, almost ripping the hood off her head. She clutched it tighter under her chin, her cold fingers fumbling with the zipper.

The Volunteer Memorial Bridge loomed just ahead, its rusted iron trusses darkened by decades of rain, stretching across the river to City Island. A sliver of land that had once been the city's playground but now served as its altar.

She headed toward it.

When she reached the island, she found it deserted, just as she'd hoped. She followed the winding path along the river's edge, taking the long way to her destination. The wind blew colder off the water, cutting through her jacket, and heavy clouds hung low overhead, threatening rain. Although it was only three o'clock, the thick gray sky created an illusion of twilight. The old lamps lining the walkway flickered to life ahead of schedule, casting their dim glow over abandoned picnic tables and weeds pushing through the cracked concrete.

She shoved her hands deep in her pockets as she passed the Grotto. The faded blue-and-white building hadn't changed much since she'd last seen it, but the sight of it brought back memories of her double date with Emma and the two Patrol soldiers, Alaric Render and Dayton Cowell. Even back then, before she'd known what Render was capable of, something about him had made her uncomfortable. She'd stayed on the date longer than she'd intended for Emma's sake, trying to watch out for her friend, until she couldn't take it anymore.

Then she'd fled outside.

And Will had been waiting for her.

She quickened her steps, needing to leave those memories behind. The path curved away from the Grotto and led into a darker stretch on the western end of the island, where the city was out of sight. Here the lamps were broken or dying, their glass covers missing, leaving vast pools of darkness between weak circles of yellow light.

She'd only ever walked this part with Will.

The roar of the river grew louder as she neared the western tip of the island. This was where he had taken her that night, over the fence, onto the decaying span of the Walnut Street Bridge. She remembered freezing at the top of the fence, too frightened to swing her other leg over. Until he'd climbed up beside her, calm and patient, and guided her over, promising not to let her fall.

And he hadn't.

Beyond the fence, the bridge's remains jutted out over the water before ending in midair, the far span on the west bank just as ruined. As she stared through the gaps in the fence, she wasn't thinking about plunging into the river with Teddy. Instead, she remembered that night when she'd sat on the edge of the bridge with Will, listening as he told her about trusting in God.

That night, she had let herself fall in love with him.

Before she could change her mind, she grabbed ahold of the fence. She climbed without hesitation, swinging both legs over the top, moving fast and confidently—so different from that first terrified ascent with Will.

She landed in a crouch, boots thudding softly on the cracked pavement. She waited, listening for any voices or movement, but there was nothing. Only the river churning below and the wind hissing through rusted trusses.

This, she thought, *is where I belong.*

On the wrong side of barricades.

She walked to the edge and sat down, pushing her hood back and letting the wind lash her hair around her face. The air smelled of mud and fish and rain, but underneath it all was something stronger—freedom. That same scent had filled her lungs on the day she jumped with Teddy, when she'd chosen death over surrender.

Being here felt like being closer to Will. As if the distance between them had narrowed somehow. This was as close as she could get now. To him, to Ghost and Grace, to all of Haven.

If only she could reach across the river, across the dark water, and touch that other life. The one where she'd been free and loved.

But that life was gone, swept downstream with the autumn leaves, drowned in the current. Just one more thing Vita Nova had stolen from her. Along with her mother. Her best friend. And her one chance at love.

Soon it would take her life.

"I miss you," she whispered, the wind catching her words and blowing them away. "I miss you so much it hurts to breathe."

She closed her eyes and let the memories come. The feel of his arms around her. His rough hands, somehow always gentle when they held hers. His steady heartbeat against her back as they watched the fireworks over the river.

I love you, Kira. Did I tell you that yet?

A sob rose in her chest, and she forced it down. At least she would die knowing she'd been loved. Even if it had only been for a little while. Even if it ended like this.

Metal rattled behind her—the jarring scrape of someone clumsily climbing the fence—followed by the sound of boots hitting the pavement.

"Kira."

Her blood turned ice-cold, her heart thundering in her chest. The voice sounded so much like Render's—soft, chiding, the same tone he'd used in the church basement before trying to kill her.

But Render was dead. She had killed him herself.

Hadn't she?

She scrambled to her feet, head whipping around, preparing to run. But her boot caught on a chunk of broken concrete near the edge of the bridge. She threw out her arms for balance, but there was nothing. Nothing but air and the river roaring below and the sound of running footsteps closing in behind her.

As she pitched backward into empty air, her last thought was bitterly comforting:

At least they won't get to kill me on Friday.

Chapter Twenty-Six

A hand closed around her wrist, yanking her back from the edge. The world tilted wildly as she was pulled forward, away from the drop, slamming into something solid. She grabbed hold instinctively, relief flooding her body.

So close.

She'd been seconds from going over the edge. She had survived that jump once, holding Teddy against her chest, but this time would have been different. A fall, not a choice. She wouldn't have survived it twice.

Her fingers dug into the soft fabric of her rescuer's jacket, her legs threatening to give out beneath her. "Thank you..." she started to say.

Then she remembered the voice.

Render's voice.

The memories came roaring back—the church basement, the gunshot, the way Render's eyes had gone wide in surprise as he fell—and she shoved hard against his chest, twisting to break free, prepared to run or fight or scream.

Or kill him again if she had to.

"Hey, hey... it's me! It's Lucas."

Lucas?

She froze, forcing herself to look up. She half-expected to see the Patrol soldier's dead, glassy eyes staring back at her. Instead, she found the familiar high cheekbones, full lips, and green eyes of her volunteer advocate. His blond hair had been whipped into chaos by the wind, falling across his forehead, making him look messy and real for the first time since they'd met.

"I'm sorry," he said. "I thought you heard me coming. I wasn't exactly trying to be sneaky."

She wrenched free from his arms and staggered back a step, legs trembling so badly she could barely stand. She bent at the waist, her hands on her knees, trying to make sense of what had just happened. How close she'd come to falling. The river seemed louder, darker, and hungrier than before, as if furious it had been cheated.

"Are you alright?" Lucas took a step closer, his eyes darting to the edge of the bridge. "Maybe you should sit down?"

"Did you follow me here?"

"Of course I did. You're my Volunteer. It's my job to know where you are."

"Actually, it's not." She worked to slow her breathing, trying to calm down. "I used to have your job, remember? I didn't stalk my Volunteers around the city."

He shrugged and gave her a crooked smile. "Maybe I'm just a better advocate than you."

Kira didn't crack a smile. She wasn't in the mood for joking. She looked back toward the river, vertigo washing over her.

"I almost fell," she whispered.

"Yes, but I would have jumped in after you," Lucas said,

somehow managing to sound completely sincere. "But I'm glad I didn't have to. What are you doing out here?"

"I needed some fresh air."

"Clearly." His eyes swept over the crumbling edge of the bridge. "Any reason in particular why you picked this spot?"

She said nothing at first. She couldn't tell him the real reason. From here she could see both sides of her life—the controlled city behind her and the freedom of the Unregulated Zone ahead.

"Best view in the city," she finally said.

Lucas rocked back on his heels. "Eh, that's debatable. Personally, I prefer to stay far away from the Unregulated Zone. But I have to admit something to you."

"What?"

"I wasn't tracking you down out of professional dedication. I was actually coming to see you when I spotted you getting on that bus. Even in that rain jacket, you're hard to miss."

She chose to ignore what was clearly meant as a compliment. "Why were you coming to see me?"

"Because I heard from your father this morning."

She blinked. "My father?"

Lucas nodded. "He called me at the office. He said he wants to invite you to dinner tomorrow night at the Executive Mansion. He asked me to drop you off there at six."

She stared at him. "The Volunteer Ball is always on Thursday night, and I already told you I'm not going."

"This isn't the Ball. It's just going to be Mayor Devlin, his wife, and his kids. He described it as a private family dinner."

"Family?"

The word felt wrong on her tongue. What was Devlin doing now? The last time she'd seen him, he'd been furious with her for Volunteering and changing his carefully orchestrated plan in front of the whole city. Now he wanted to invite her over for dinner? And introduce her to his family?

"Is this little dinner my father's attempt to convince me to show up at the Ball?"

"He didn't mention the Ball," Lucas said. "And I don't know much about your father, Kira, but I would venture to guess that this week has been really hard on him, even if he's not showing it. And I get it... the guy is hard as a rock. But he's never lost a child before."

Kira turned back toward the river, her mind racing. She didn't trust her father's motives, but what other option did she have? She couldn't refuse the dinner. She'd agreed to play the role of brave Volunteer until the end, and any deviations could result in her father throwing her back into the Confines and condemning Teddy to die in her place.

Drizzle began to fall in thin, cold needles, stinging her cheeks. She'd wanted this for so long. Acceptance. A seat at her father's table. She'd spent so many nights imagining what it would be like to be part of his perfect family, even if only for a moment. And now that she only had days left to live, he was finally offering it.

"You don't have to go," Lucas spoke up from behind her. "He told me to tell you that. He's not going to force you if you don't want to go."

But she *did* want to go. Even after all of the hurts, all of the betrayals, some small, broken part of her still wanted to be her father's daughter. To be included in his family. To be loved. Even if it was all just pretend. Even if it was only for one night.

"I'll go."

"Are you sure?"

She nodded as the drizzle gave way to steady rain, drumming against her hood and shoulders. Agreeing to attend the dinner felt like surrender. Like letting go of something vital she'd tried to hold on to. But wasn't that the point? That's what all Volunteers were meant to do—give themselves up for the good of all.

Lucas appeared at her side, his blond hair plastered to his face. He extended a hand. "Come on, Kira. Let's get you home."

Rolling Meadows wasn't home. It was just the waiting room before the end. But she took his hand anyway.

They jogged back to the fence together. The rain came harder, a dull roar on the iron trusses above them. She climbed over the top, her boots slipping on the slick metal. Lucas caught her arm when she nearly lost her grip.

When they reached his car, he stood in the rain and opened the door for her. She hesitated, turning for one last look at the bridge and the island beyond.

Just like her townhouse, she would never visit this place again.

If her Final Week was teaching her anything, it was how to let go. First, her love. Then the home she'd shared with her mother. Now this bridge and this island, with all of its memories, both good and bad.

And soon, very soon, she would have to let go of everything else.

Chapter Twenty-Seven

Kira stood beside the idling sedan, smoothing her hands over the long-sleeved green dress she'd chosen for her first dinner with her father's family. She'd found it hanging in her closet at Rolling Meadows—soft, well-made, with delicate stitching along the hem. It fell just below her knees and seemed appropriate for a family dinner. She suspected it—like everything else in her closet—had belonged to Adeline's dead daughter.

It was Wednesday evening, which meant there were less than two days left in her Final Week, and she'd wasted most of the day agonizing over pointless decisions. Which dress would make the best impression? Heels, ballet flats, or boots? Should she pin her hair back or leave it down? And her nails—should she even bother painting them? If so, what color was appropriate for meeting her siblings for the first time?

In the end, she'd chosen the green dress paired with ballet flats, settled on wearing her hair half-up, half-down, and brushed on a pale gray polish that felt safe and understated.

Lucas leaned against the driver's door of the sedan, arms

crossed, watching her. "Don't take this the wrong way, but you look like you're about to throw up. Are you sure you're ready for this?"

Of course she wasn't ready. Her palms were slick with sweat, and heat crawled across her skin, making her feel flushed and more than a little nauseous. She couldn't imagine actually sitting down to eat a meal right now, but that was exactly what she was about to do.

She swallowed hard and lifted her chin. "Not really. But I'm going to do it anyway."

"That's the spirit." He pushed off the door and climbed into the driver's seat. "I'll be back to pick you up at nine. Good luck. You've got this."

"Thanks."

As Lucas's sedan pulled away, Kira began to walk toward the mansion. She tried not to think about the last time she'd walked down this driveway, a night that seemed so long ago now. She hadn't been alone then. Will had been with her, his presence like a shield against her father. Now she had no shield. Everything had been stripped away.

She was alone.

The massive oak door swung open before she could knock. A woman in a simple black dress stood there, her silver hair twisted into an elegant knot at the nape of her neck.

"Ms. Liebert, welcome," she said, stepping aside. "The family is waiting for you."

The woman led her down a narrow corridor that opened into the dining room. Not the opulent Grand Hall where the Volunteer Ball was held each week, but a smaller, more inti-mate space clearly meant for family meals. A polished mahogany table dominated the center of the room, set neatly for five with polished silverware and folded linen napkins. Framed family portraits lined the room on all sides, showing her father with his perfect family at birthdays and holidays and various city events.

None of the photos included her.

"Mr. Devlin will be with you in a moment."

The woman slipped through a door at the far end of the dining room, leaving Kira alone.

She hesitated next to the table, her fingers brushing against the wood. Should she sit down? Wait for the others to arrive first? She had no idea what the proper etiquette was in a place like this. She'd only been there for a few minutes, but she already felt terribly awkward and out of place inside her father's world. The borrowed dress suddenly felt a little too snug around her hips, a little too short, a little too informal.

Voices approached from a connecting hallway. A child's question, followed by a woman's laughter. Although she knew it was irrational, Kira couldn't help but wonder if the laughter had been at her expense.

What am I even doing here? Why did I agree to this?

Leaving suddenly felt like the only sensible option. If she were quick, she could slip out quietly, back through the hallway, out the front door, and into the night before anyone even saw her. She felt her muscles tense, ready to turn, ready to run—

But before she could move, Victor Devlin and his family appeared in the doorway, and any chance of escape vanished.

Her father's eyes found her immediately, skimming over her hair, her dress, her shoes. His smile dimmed just enough to be noticeable, but he said nothing, only stepped aside to usher in his wife.

Chandra Devlin was even more striking in person than she appeared on city broadcasts. She was taller and thinner than Kira had expected, her blonde hair falling well past her shoulders, her black dress clinging to perfect curves that spoke of hours spent in the gym.

Behind her were the twins, Vance and Violet, both sporting heads of blond hair and matching curious expressions.

For a moment, no one spoke.

The family seemed frozen, uncertain of what to do. Vance and Violet stared at Kira like they'd discovered some strange new animal, while Chandra's face remained carefully neutral.

It was Devlin who finally broke the silence. He crossed the room with his hand extended as if greeting a visiting dignitary instead of his own daughter.

"Kira." There was a warmth in his voice she'd never heard before. He took her hand and then startled her by pressing a kiss to her cheek. "Welcome to our home. I'm so glad you came."

The kiss left her momentarily speechless. She'd prepared herself for Devlin's typical coldness, for the formality that had always characterized their interactions. She hadn't been prepared for anything resembling fatherly affection.

"Thank you for inviting me." Kira's voice came out weak and gravelly. She cleared her throat. "You have a beautiful home."

Chandra glided toward her with the graceful elegance of a dancer. Had she been an actress in New York City before the virus, before the barricade? Kira vaguely remembered her father mentioning that on one of their lunch dates, proudly boasting about his wife's theatrical accomplishments in a way he never had about Kira's mother.

"It's wonderful to finally meet you," Chandra said, skipping the handshake entirely. She pulled Kira into a hug and whispered, "You're even more beautiful in person."

Kira hadn't been expecting such a genuine and warm welcome from her father's wife. "Thank you, Mrs. Devlin."

"Please. Call me Chandra."

After the woman released her, Vance stepped forward, extending his hand with a formality that made him look even more like his father. "Good evening. I'm Vance Dev—"

Violet shoved her brother aside and grabbed Kira's hand instead. "And I'm Violet."

"Vi!" Vance slugged her in the arm, then looked up at Chandra for help. "Mom!"

"It's okay, honey."

The little girl rubbed her arm but otherwise seemed unfazed. "Do you think we look alike, Kira? Because I don't think we do."

Kira smiled at her. "You and your brother?"

"No, you and me. Momma says we're sisters, but I don't think we look like sisters."

Sisters.

Kira stared at the little girl with her blonde hair and bright blue eyes. In another life, she might have watched this child grow up. Might have held her as a baby, read her bedtime stories, and helped change her diapers. They would have known each other's favorite colors, foods, and fears. But that life had been stolen from both of them, and now it was too late to get it back.

Before she could think of a response, Vance chimed in. "Yeah. How can you be related to us if we've never met you?"

"Children," Chandra interrupted, her voice gentle but firm. "Let's not interrogate your poor sister before she's even had dinner. We have all evening to get acquainted." She gestured to the table. "Shall we sit?"

They moved to the table, and Kira found herself seated at her father's right hand, across from the twins. The children continued to study her with a mixture of interest and suspicion as the gray-haired housekeeper returned with dishes of rainbow trout, new potatoes, salad, and warm bread.

As the others picked up their silverware, Kira felt the urge to bow her head. In Haven, they prayed before every meal, genuinely thankful for whatever food they had. She remembered the first time she'd been asked to pray—how flustered she'd been—and how Will had gently stepped in when she froze.

She closed her eyes and uttered a brief prayer of thanks in her head, followed by, *Please, God, give me the strength to get through this dinner.*

"So are you really going to die on Friday?" Vance asked through a mouthful of bread.

"Vance!" Chandra's hand flew to her throat. "That is *not* appropriate!"

"But Daddy said—"

"Listen to your mother," Devlin interrupted, his eyebrows raised in warning. "We will not discuss that at this table."

Several awkward beats passed before Chandra spoke up. "So, Kira," she said, spearing a small potato with her fork, "Victor tells me you were quite brave in the Unregulated Zone. Rescuing that little boy. Theodore. I can't imagine facing the Lawless myself, much less living among them for any amount of time. That took remarkable courage."

Kira set her water glass down and folded her hands in her lap. She glanced at her father, searching his face for any reaction, but he was busy cutting Violet's fish.

But he was listening. Kira knew he was listening.

"I don't see myself as brave." *Quite the opposite, actually.* "I just wanted to get Teddy home safely."

Chandra smiled. "Of course you did. That sweet boy has stolen the hearts of everyone in this city, including my own." She looked at her children, her gaze softening as it shifted from one to the other. "I think of his mother often. Of the sacrifice she's making. I cannot fathom it."

Kira bit the inside of her lip to keep from speaking the words she desperately wanted to say. How Trinity Easton's "sacrifice" was nothing but self-serving. How the woman had spent most of her son's Final Week entertaining the husband of another Volunteer.

Chandra's voice interrupted her thoughts. "Kira, may I ask you about the traitor you were with? Will Foster?"

Kira kept her eyes on her plate, pushing a bite of fish around but not quite able to bring it to her mouth. This time, she could feel the heat of her father's gaze on her face, a silent warning to tread carefully. "What about him?"

"Well, you were over there in the Unregulated Zone for weeks. I suppose you were forced to become close to him, despite knowing it wasn't in your best interest. Your very survival—and Teddy's—depended on it. Lines can blur in situations like those."

Something in Chandra's tone made Kira look up from her plate. Though the woman's words had condemned Will as a traitor, her eyes told a different story. Something passed between them—a flicker of understanding—and then it was gone.

Kira glanced at her father, but Violet had drawn his attention away by tugging on his sleeve and gesturing to a piece of fish that wasn't cut small enough.

"Some things felt real," Kira said in a quiet voice. "I suppose that makes me a fool."

Chandra's fingers tightened around her fork. "Not at all. I'm certain he was quite convincing. Evil men usually are."

"Were you scared out there?" Violet asked. "Daddy says there are monsters beyond the wall."

"Monsters who want to hurt us," Vance added gravely.

Kira took a bite of her fish, chewing slowly, considering her response. "I didn't see any monsters. I saw a few scary people who'd survived out there by doing bad things, but I got away from them." She lifted her eyes to meet Chandra's. "Real monsters don't always look like you'd expect."

"Enough," Devlin said, waving a hand over his plate. "Let's change the subject. This one is spoiling my appetite."

The twins continued to pepper Kira with questions for the rest of the meal. Vance wanted to know about her life, her job as a volunteer advocate, and her townhouse in the Residential Sector.

"Was it a lot smaller than our house?"

"Did you have a bathroom?"

Violet wanted to know everything about Kira—her favorite color, her favorite food, even her favorite books. It was as if Kira's life were some elaborate puzzle, and the little girl was trying to collect the pieces to put them together.

Devlin watched his children interact with Kira, saying very little.

By the time dessert arrived, Kira felt the tightness in her chest loosen. She laughed at Violet's animated story about her school classroom's pet hamster, Nibbles, and his elaborate but ill-fated escape attempt. Later, she listened as Vance described an astronomy project he was working on, his love for the stars lighting up his entire face.

As she ate and laughed with her father's family, she had not forgotten that this fleeting moment of belonging was nothing more than another beautiful lie. The man grinning at her from the other side of the table was still the mastermind behind a plot to murder her on Friday morning.

But she chose for now to let it go. To let herself pretend she belonged here, with them, in this warm, inviting home.

To imagine that somewhere, in another life, this family could have been hers.

Chapter Twenty-Eight

Victor Devlin sat on the plush sofa in the living room, sandwiched between the twins, who had claimed their places beside him. Despite being the center of his children's world, he seemed strangely subdued, his expression distant. Every so often, his gaze wandered toward the windows, and he took slow, measured sips from the bourbon in his glass tumbler.

"Every Saturday, we have a family game night," Violet was saying, gesturing to the antique table in the corner. "Sometimes Daddy lets me win at checkers."

"I do not," Devlin protested, the first words he'd spoken since they'd moved into the living room. "I don't let anyone win. You're simply getting better."

"He absolutely lets her win," Vance whispered to Kira. "She's terrible. She hasn't gotten any better."

Kira sat perched on the edge of an armchair across from them, watching the family scene unfold like an anthropologist studying a newly discovered tribe. She took in their gestures, their inside jokes, the casual way they shared old memories, cataloging the rituals of a family that had lived perfectly well without her for ten years... and would keep on living without her long after she was gone.

"Daddy, tell Kira about the time we took the boat out on the river," Violet commanded, tugging on his sleeve. "Tell her about the train cars we saw in the water."

Kira's breath caught, her mind flashing back to her journey with Will and the others in the Unregulated Zone. She remembered seeing those same haunting containers, covered in graffiti and half-submerged in the river.

"Perhaps another time," he said, glancing at the clock on the mantel. "You two need to change into your pajamas and get to bed. You have school in the morning. And Kira should be getting back to Rolling Meadows."

Kira nodded. "That's right. Lucas will be here soon."

Chandra leaned forward in her armchair, uncrossing her legs and interlacing her hands around her knees. She'd been quiet after dinner, observing more than participating in the conversation. "Lucas?"

"Lucas Pine. He's my volunteer advocate."

A look passed between Chandra and Victor—there and gone in an instant. It made Kira feel uneasy, though she couldn't have explained why. It was the look of two people sharing a thought they had no intention of voicing aloud.

Chandra turned back to her. "Must you go so soon, Kira? I feel like you only just got here."

"I really should," she replied. "It's been a long day—a long week, actually. But I truly appreciate your hospitality tonight. This has been a wonderful evening."

"But you can't go," Violet protested, even as she rubbed her eyes. "We just met you, and you're our sister."

"Half-sister," Vance corrected, earning a glare from his twin.

"She's our sister," Violet insisted. "We should get more time with her."

"Violet," Devlin's voice carried a hint of a warning, but it was enough. The little girl quieted down. He turned to his wife. "Sweetheart, would you mind putting the children to bed? I'll escort Kira back to her advocate."

"You, Daddy," Vance whined. "You promised to put us to bed tonight, remember?"

"You did. You promised last night," Violet said, grabbing his arm and clinging to it. "Besides, you do the best monster checks. Mommy always forgets to look under the bed."

Devlin's eyes shifted from the twins to Chandra, then settled briefly on Kira, clearly weighing the risk of leaving the two women alone together. Finally, he gave a thin smile. "I'm sure your mother can handle things tonight."

"Please," both children whined in unison. "Please, Daddy."

Chandra rose from the armchair. "It's okay, dear. You deal with the monsters, and I'll see Kira out."

Devlin exhaled slowly, clearly not wanting to give in but knowing he had no choice. "Very well," he said, gently extricating himself from his children and pushing himself off the couch. "Let's go deal with those monsters, shall we? But first say goodnight to Kira."

In an instant, both twins were on their feet and hugging her goodbye—Vance with a quick squeeze, and Violet with a fierce hug that left her breathless, as if the little girl were trying to make up for a decade of missed embraces.

"Will you come back tomorrow?" Violet whispered. "For the Volunteer Ball? We usually aren't allowed to attend, but Daddy might let us go since it's for you."

Only a day earlier, Kira had insisted to Lucas that she had no intention of attending the Ball. The thought of being paraded around the Grand Hall like a prize animal about to be slaughtered seemed unimaginable. But now, she found herself reconsidering. One more evening. Wouldn't it be worth enduring a night of false pageantry with the city elites just to have one more evening with her siblings?

She realized she had no other choice. "I'll see you guys tomorrow night."

Violet's eyes lit up, and she squeezed Kira one more time for good measure before racing her brother up the stairs.

Instead of following the twins, Devlin paused and turned toward Kira. For a moment, his usual commanding presence seemed to falter, replaced by an uncertain hesitation as he searched her face. Then he bent down and slipped one arm around her shoulders in an awkward half-hug.

"Goodnight, Kira."

The unexpected gesture left her speechless, unable to even say a basic 'goodnight' in return. The scent of his cologne enveloped her, reminding her of those rare childhood visits that had always left her feeling more empty than she had before. She realized that in nineteen years her father had never hugged her. The clumsy attempt at affection had come both too little and too late, yet she leaned into it anyway, starved for even the smallest crumb of love from her father.

And then Devlin disappeared upstairs, leaving Kira standing in the middle of the living room in stunned silence.

Chandra moved to a small sideboard and poured two glasses of amber liquid. "Bourbon," she said, offering one to Kira. "It helps me sometimes."

"Helps you with what?"

"Everything." The woman winked at her, but there was

something beneath her smile. A pain Kira recognized, having seen it many times in the eyes of her own mother. "Walk with me, Kira. It's a beautiful night outside."

They exited the house through a set of French doors that opened onto a stone terrace, the night air carrying the scent of roses and damp earth. The stars overhead seemed dim compared to the brilliant constellations she'd seen during her time in the Unregulated Zone. Beyond the wall, the darkness had been complete and overwhelming, making the stars appear close enough to touch.

She remembered lying on the grass in Aunt Reeva's backyard with Will just a few nights before they'd left Emmitsburg. The stars had seemed so close that night. Impossibly close. She had reached out and tried to capture one in her fingers, and then Will had taken her hand in his own and pulled her back to earth with a kiss.

Chandra leaned against the stone balustrade, her perfect posture softening as she stared out at the gardens. "Bourbon is Victor's drink of choice. As you can imagine, I've developed quite a taste for it over the years."

Kira wasn't a drinker, and she hated the taste of hard liquor, but if there was ever a time to try drowning her feelings in bourbon, it was three days before her scheduled execution. She took a careful sip, the liquid burning all the way down her throat.

"You have a wonderful family," she managed, wincing at the aftertaste. "I'm really glad I finally got to meet Vance and Violet."

Chandra turned back to her. "My children are the best thing I've ever done. Maybe the only good thing I've ever done. I wish you could have gotten to know them before now."

"Me too."

"Keeping you from them wasn't my decision. You should

know that. Victor was adamant about keeping you separate from our life. He's always building walls, isn't he? One way or another."

Kira had never thought of it that way before. "My mother never pushed him to be a part of my life. She said it was better if he wasn't."

Chandra's eyes met hers over the rim of her glass. "Your mother was a smart woman, Kira. Being in Victor's orbit can be both a blessing and a curse. Lots of women have discovered that." Her lips formed a delicate line. "Including our illustrious deputy mayor."

Kira tried to keep her expression neutral, even as her father's wife stared her down, clearly waiting for some kind of response.

"I'm not sure what you mean," she said.

Chandra laughed, a sound entirely devoid of humor. "Of course you do. You've seen them together. You don't need to spare my feelings. The affair has been going on for a long time. I believe it started a few years after the twins were born."

Kira remembered the way Sienna Graves had spoken to her father in the hospitality suite after her declaration on the field. The casual intimacy of their interactions. The way the woman had touched his arm and instantly defused his anger.

"But Sienna Graves is married?"

"So is Victor, darling. Besides, I've heard rumors that her husband, Elton, has several women on the side as well. It's a sick arrangement." She drained the rest of her glass in one large swallow. "He won't leave me for her. I suppose that should give me some level of comfort, but it doesn't. Part of me wishes they would run off together, but where would they even go?"

Kira searched her mind for a response, something to make the woman feel better, something that wasn't a lie. But there was nothing to say. "I'm so sorry."

"Don't be. It's a common thing in politics. The devoted wife at home, the exciting mistress at work. I've made my peace with it. Or told myself I have, at least. We have children together. And there are worse prisons than this one."

Kira watched Chandra's face as she spoke, struck by the strange parallels between them. Both women had been deeply wounded by their relationships with Victor Devlin. The revelation about Sienna Graves should have shocked her, but somehow it didn't. Of course her father would have a mistress that he wouldn't even bother to hide from his wife. It was the same pattern of selfishness and entitlement that had shaped Kira's entire life—the man who took what he wanted and discarded what no longer served him.

Chandra set her glass on the balustrade and approached Kira, placing her hands on her shoulders. "We're all locked away in prisons of our own making. Even those of us who mistakenly believe we're free." She released Kira's shoulders and took a step backward. "But I suppose you already know that, don't you? Otherwise you wouldn't have jumped off that bridge."

Kira stiffened. Hadn't the whole city been told it was Emma who had stolen Teddy? Emma who had jumped into the river? "That wasn't me..." She tried to lie, but the words got stuck in her throat. She wasn't a liar like Devlin. "Didn't my father tell you—?"

"Your father tells me many things, dear. I've learned which ones to believe." Chandra crossed her arms over her chest. "What I really want to know is why you came back to the city."

The space between them seemed to shrink, the air growing heavy. Kira lifted her glass and took another small sip. It didn't burn as badly this time.

"It was the only way I could stop him from killing Teddy."

The woman's posture relaxed, an expression of satisfaction crossing her features. "Thank you for being honest. And this Will Foster—the one who was with you in the Unregulated Zone? He was more than just an ally to you, is that right?"

"Yes," she admitted, setting her half-empty glass next to Chandra's on the balustrade. "Much more."

"And he's still out there?"

"Yes. I left a note for a friend asking him to keep Will from following me back. If he comes back, they'll kill him, too."

Chandra nodded and picked up Kira's glass, taking another long swallow of bourbon. "I applaud you for trying to protect him, but a man who truly loves you will not stay away because of a few words on a piece of paper."

A soft knock sounded behind them, and the housekeeper appeared in the doorway. "Mr. Pine has arrived, ma'am. He's parked around front."

"Thank you, Clara." Chandra straightened her shoulders and grabbed her empty glass, instantly transforming back into the mayor's perfect wife. "I've so enjoyed your company tonight, Kira. I look forward to seeing you again tomorrow evening."

"Yes, thank you, Mrs. Devlin."

As the housekeeper escorted her through the house to the front door, Kira found herself looking back one last time at Chandra, standing alone near the French doors. In the gleaming mansion that was both her home and her prison, the woman looked small and fragile.

A beautiful bird in a gilded cage.

Kira had come to the Executive Mansion hoping to feel like part of a family, even just for a few hours. She wanted to take back something that had been denied to her before she was even born and maybe even find it in herself to forgive the man whose selfish choices had defined her life. But what she found instead was a world just as broken as the one outside the wall, only dressed up to look better.

And she learned that even someone condemned to death could still find new things to fear. Not the injection waiting for her in a few days, but the awful possibility that Will might still try to save her.

And that he might die trying.

Chapter Twenty-Nine

Ghost stood at the far end of the mess hall, watching as the villagers of Haven slowly filed into the room and took their seats at the long tables. The space that usually buzzed with mealtime conversations was unnaturally quiet, filled only with the sound of boots on floorboards and the occasional hushed whispers between parents and children. The air smelled of bread and coffee, the lingering aromas of breakfast.

His people were quiet because they knew something was wrong. If they couldn't tell by his expression, they could certainly tell by the fact that they were attending a meeting. Meetings weren't commonplace in Haven. They didn't have time for meetings. They were too busy planting and farming and caring for the animals to waste their time congregating together to discuss trivial matters.

Only the most serious situations warranted pulling everyone away from their work. Especially now, when every moment counted in their effort to rebuild after the attack. The half-repaired fence, the charred remains of the church, the fresh graves still missing their markers—all of it stood as a testament to how much remained unfinished. Which meant that whatever Ghost had to say, it would not be good news.

And they were right. He had spent years building this place for them—creating something from nothing in a world that had lost almost everything.

Now he had to tell them it was over.

"Thank you all for coming," he began once everyone had taken their seats. "I know many of you are eager to get back to work, but there's something we need to talk about."

At the far end of the room, Will stood with his back to the wall, arms crossed tight over his chest. The dark circles under his eyes looked even worse than the last time Ghost had seen him, giving him a grim, almost dangerous edge.

"We're still recovering from last week's attack," Ghost continued, his gaze sweeping the room before settling briefly on Nic Hernandez, who sat alone at the back, staring at the floor. The young man had lost his bride, Avery, on their wedding night. She hadn't been the only casualty, but her death lingered in Ghost's mind the hardest. Even now, he could still picture her lying in the mud, her wedding dress stained with blood and dirt.

He cleared his throat, pushing the image away. "The last thing I want is to add to anyone's stress, but I have genuine concerns about the safety of this community going forward."

One of the older men, Phil Jeffries, spoke up. "What kind of concerns?"

Ghost swallowed hard before answering. "I don't think the Patrol soldiers who attacked us last week were only after the boy. He was their primary target, yes, but I also think it was a reconnaissance mission. They were testing us, figuring out our defenses. And now that they know where we are and how we're protected, I believe it's only a matter of time before they come back."

A murmur rippled through the crowd. Lyle Thomas, one of the younger men who'd been working on rebuilding the church since the day after the attack, rose to his feet. He was barely twenty-five, with a patchy beard and eyes that always seemed narrowed in suspicion. Though he'd only been in Haven for a year, he'd quickly made himself known as the community's loudest agitator. What he lacked in experience he made up for in sheer volume.

"Let them come," he said, his voice loud and defiant. "They caught us off guard last time, like cowards. If they show their faces again, we'll be ready."

"No." Ghost shook his head. "No, we won't. You don't understand, Lyle. If they come back, it won't be like before. It won't be a handful of soldiers. It'll be dozens. Maybe more. There won't be a fight—we won't stand a chance. It'll be an extermination."

"How can you possibly know that?" asked Maggie Prescott, a heavyset redhead in her late fifties who'd been with Haven since the beginning. "We've always been safe here. No one has bothered us before."

"They bothered us last week," Ghost snapped, unable to hide his frustration. People never seemed to get it. Old and young alike, they never seemed to understand that they weren't invincible. Even after a massacre that had left nineteen of their people dead, they still couldn't accept their own mortality. "And they *will* bother us again. I guarantee it."

"So what are you saying?" Lyle demanded. "You want us to... what? Abandon Haven? Leave everything we've built behind?"

Ghost nodded. "That's exactly what I'm saying."

The mess hall erupted in voices—some angry, some frightened, all trying to speak over one another. Ghost let it go for a moment, giving them space to react, then slowly raised his hand. Gradually, the room quieted. "Staying here means death. Not for a few of us, but for all of us. You don't need to like that fact, but you need to accept it."

Maggie raised her hand and dropped it when Ghost looked at her. "Where would we go? The wilderness is no place for children or the elderly. You know that better than anyone."

This was the part he'd been dreading. Not only did he have to convince them to leave, but he also had to convince them to travel.

Far.

"There's a settlement north of here. Just over the border, in New York."

"*New York?*" Maggie gasped. "You want us to walk all the way from Pennsylvania to New York?"

Dozens of angry voices filled the air.

"You can't expect us to walk that far."

"What about Dave Syble?"

"Exactly! He's eighty-nine! He can barely walk. How is he supposed to make that trip?"

"We have little children here! Babies!"

"I'm not taking my children into the woods!"

Ghost raised his voice, cutting through the rising swell of protest. "I'm not asking you to cross the entire continent. I'm asking you to travel to a settlement one state away. We take our time, make camp each night, hunt as we go. It won't be easy, but it's not impossible."

Lyle stepped forward, his lanky frame pushing through the crowd until he stood directly in front of Ghost. "How do you know there's a settlement?"

Ghost hesitated, considering how to answer, then decided on the truth. What choice did he have? "I've been in contact with a man there for some time now. We speak over ham radio. His name is Brannigan."

"A radio?" Maggie's eyebrows shot up. "You've been communicating with someone over the radio, and you never thought to mention this to us before?"

"It wasn't relevant before." But the truth was more complicated than that. The radio had been his personal lifeline. His way of convincing himself there was something beyond Haven, beyond Vita Nova. Something worth fighting for. Worth staying alive for. "What matters is that we have somewhere safe to go."

"But how do we know it's safe?" Lyle demanded. "I think some of us need to speak to this Brannigan person before we even consider abandoning our home."

Ghost stared at the young man. This was the moment he'd been dreading. It was a question he couldn't answer honestly without undermining everything he'd just revealed. His gaze drifted to Brack, who sat on a nearby bench with his arm wrapped around Grace. Brack met his eyes and gave him a nod, as if to say: *Might as well put it all on the table.*

"I haven't been able to reach Brannigan in over a week," Ghost admitted. "I've tried every day, multiple times a day. The signal's gone quiet."

The silence held for only a few heartbeats before it shattered. Angry, panicked voices erupted all around the room. Chairs scraped against the floor as people leapt to their feet, shouting and gesturing wildly.

"A week? You want us to travel to a settlement you haven't confirmed still exists?"

"What if they've been overrun?"

"What if there's nothing left when we get there?"

Lyle seized the moment, whipping around to face the crowd. "You hear that? He wants us to abandon everything we've worked for because the Patrols *might* come back. And then he wants us to head for someplace that might not even be there, if it ever existed at all."

Ghost raised his voice to be heard over the crowd. "It exists. Brannigan's community has over five hundred people, along with plenty of crops and livestock. Everything we have and more. Most importantly, it's far away from Vita Nova."

"Then why the silence?" Maggie asked. "What explanation do you have for that?"

"He doesn't have any explanation," Lyle said. "Face it—they're probably already dead. Just like we'll be if we're stupid enough to follow his ridiculous—"

Ghost didn't think. He just surged forward and seized a fistful of Lyle's jacket, yanking him so hard their faces nearly collided. Their noses were inches apart as Ghost glared into the younger man's wide eyes.

The room went silent around them.

"Listen to me, you little punk," he growled. "I've buried more friends this past week than you've made in your entire life. So you'd do well to watch your mouth when you open it in my presence." He gave Lyle a hard shove, sending him stumbling backward into one of the tables. "You've been here what—ten months? Don't forget your place. Or I'll be more than happy to send you right back where you came from."

Lyle's face flushed red, but he did not argue. Instead, he lowered his head, his courage evaporating.

Ghost turned his back on Lyle and faced the room. "The Patrols could return any day. To be honest, I'm surprised they haven't come already. We need to go—and soon. Two days at most. I know that's not enough time. I know it's not fair. Nothing that's happened to this village in the past week has been fair. But you know what's even less fair? Dying because we waited too long to act."

There was no argument this time. All around the room, parents pulled their children closer, and friends exchanged worried glances. A few people were crying. The reality was sinking in.

"Devan Brack will lead you." Ghost nodded at the man, whose face flushed with embarrassment as every eye turned toward him. "He's a good man. Strong and capable. He'll keep you safe out there."

Phil Jeffries shook his head, seemingly unable to comprehend what Ghost couldn't bring himself to say. "I don't understand. Why aren't you the one leading us?"

Ghost exchanged a look with Will. "Because I'm going back to Vita Nova."

"Vita Nova? Why would you go back there?"

"Because of *her*."

The voice came from the back of the room.

Nic Hernandez stood up slowly, then shouldered his way through the crowd, heading for the front of the room. He looked nothing like the tidy young man he'd once been. His shirt was rumpled and untucked, his face dark with several days' worth of stubble. He stopped a few feet from Ghost.

"You're going back there for Kira."

Ghost said nothing, which was answer enough.

"You're going to abandon us for *her*." Nic spat the words at him. "For the person who brought this curse down on us. The Patrols never bothered us until she and her friends showed up. Avery died because of her."

Will surged forward. "That's not true."

Ghost moved into the aisle between the two men, trying to diffuse the situation. "I will come with you to New York. I'm not leaving you on your own. But Kira needs my help first. She's going to be executed in Vita Nova tomorrow morning if we don't do something."

"Who cares?" Nic muttered. "We'll all be safer when she's dead."

Will cursed and tried to lunge past Ghost, but Brack was ready for it. He shot off the bench and intercepted him, his massive arms locking around Will's chest, pinning him in place. "Don't do it, brother," he whispered. "He's not worth it."

Nic seemed to crumble in slow motion, his shoulders slumping, the anger seeping out of him bit by bit. He lowered his head, his jaw shifting as he fought to hold himself together. Tears welled in his eyes, spilling over as he gave a small, helpless shake of his head.

"She shouldn't be dead," he wept. "She can't be dead."

Ghost stepped closer to Nic, putting a hand on his shoulder and squeezing. He could feel the young man's body trembling beneath his grip. "This isn't just about Kira," he said. "It's about doing what's right. It's about facing down evil instead of turning away from it. If we stop doing what's right, we're no better than the people in that city."

He lowered his head and recited the verse from Proverbs he'd read a dozen times that morning. "Rescue those who are being taken away to death; hold back those who are stumbling to the slaughter."

No one argued with him after that. There was nothing left to say—no defense, no protest against the weight of Scripture—and they all knew it. The mess hall was silent but for the shifting of chairs and the creak of the floorboards. Everyone inside understood the brutal truth of their situation.

In this world, there were no easy choices.

One by one, they filed out, whispering among themselves. Ghost watched them go, knowing they would spend the next two days packing what little they could carry, saying goodbye to homes they'd built with their own hands, and preparing themselves for a journey that might only end in more heartache.

When the room was finally empty, only Will remained behind. He sank onto a bench, his eyes locked on some distant point Ghost couldn't see.

"When?" he asked.

Ghost exhaled slowly. "We'll leave in a few hours. Just the two of us."

Will nodded, the look in his eyes reminding Ghost of the men he'd served with years ago. Good men who walked into battles knowing they might never walk out but who did it anyway because some things were worth dying for.

Ghost reached into his pocket and touched the worn edges of the photograph hidden there.

I'm coming home, Madison, he thought, fully aware he probably wouldn't survive this mission—and not caring. *But first, I'm going to save our girl.*

Chapter Thirty

Kira sat on the balcony of her Rolling Meadows suite, bare feet tucked underneath her. She cradled a cup of tea in her hands, its fading warmth a meager comfort against the knowledge that she only had one more day to live.

She turned her head, gazing through the open balcony doors at the blue rose on her bedside table, its petals beginning to curl at the edges, slowly dying.

Had all of her Volunteers felt this way as their Final Week drew to an end? Had they felt the same painful ache in the center of their chests? The same desire to shut down early instead of living their last day to the fullest? She had always done her best to comfort them, to give them whatever they needed to make their final hours easier, but now she understood she'd been merely glossing over a terrible truth.

People were not meant to know the precise moment when they would die.

At least her Volunteers could spend their Final Weeks with their families. She'd been robbed even of that small comfort.

A knock sounded at the door, pulling her from her grim thoughts. Before she could call out or rise from the chair, Adeline entered the suite, carrying a breakfast tray laden with pastries and fresh fruit.

"I let myself in. I hope that's okay," she said, setting the tray on a small table on the balcony. She pulled her sweater tighter around herself. "You really should come back inside. It's too chilly out here. You'll catch a cold."

"Does it really matter, Adeline?"

The woman's face softened, the sadness in her eyes going well beyond professional sympathy. She placed a hand on Kira's shoulder. "Everything matters, honey. And let me remind you—you're not dead yet."

She crouched down beside the chair, her weathered hand wrapping around Kira's cold fingers. "I remember spending a week not too long ago with a little boy who was supposed to die. Nearly broke my heart every time I saw his sweet little face. But you know what? That boy is still alive today. It's not over until the proverbial fat lady sings—and I'm not singing yet."

Kira managed a faint smile. Teddy's survival had been a miracle. The one good thing she'd done with her life. But no one was coming to save her.

"Thank you," she whispered, squeezing the older woman's hand. "I truly appreciate everything you've done for me. When I woke up this morning and prayed, I thanked God for you, and I asked Him to watch over you."

"Oh honey, that's so sweet. But I haven't really done much. I wish I could've done more for you."

"You've done more than you know," Kira said. "Delivering breakfast to my room every day has been such a kindness. I can't seem to bring myself to eat in the dining room with everyone staring at me."

"Oh, I understand. I wouldn't want to eat down there either, with all those nosy lookie-loos bothering you." She gave Kira's hand one last squeeze before sighing. "Speaking of people bothering you, I don't just come bearing pastries. I'm supposed to let you know that Deputy Mayor Graves will be stopping by soon. She's bringing a tailor to get you fitted for the Ball tonight."

Kira sat up straighter, her bare feet slipping out from underneath her. "Sienna Graves is coming here? To Rolling Meadows?"

"I'm afraid so."

"Isn't that... a little unusual?"

"She's never come here before. But yours is obviously a special case. We've never quite seen anything like this before. I'm sure the city will go all-out for your Volunteer Ball."

After everything Chandra had revealed to her, Kira couldn't imagine having to share the same air with the deputy mayor, even for something as brief as a dress fitting. She considered refusing to meet with the woman—simply locking herself inside her room like a petulant child sounded like a reasonable option—but what would that accomplish beyond giving her father another reason to be angry with her?

"Fine," she said, reaching for a croissant. "I should probably eat now, since I doubt I'll have an appetite after that awful woman leaves."

Adeline's lips twitched as she fought back a smile. "Sounds good, honey," she said, heading for the door. "I'll send her up when she arrives."

Kira ate mechanically, not really tasting the food. Her mind drifted back to all the Volunteer Balls she'd watched on city broadcasts over the years—the elegant ballroom filled with the city's elite, the champagne flowing, the Volunteers whipping around the dance floor as if they could somehow outrun the death that awaited them. Even as a child, she had found the entire process unsettling—watching people celebrate what was, ultimately, their execution.

But tonight, she was going to do the same thing.

———

Twenty minutes later, Kira stood in the center of her suite, the croissant sitting like a brick in her stomach as Adeline ushered her visitors into the room. Sienna Graves stepped through the door first, her gray pantsuit immaculate, a pile of red curls perched atop her head.

Behind her came a small, wiry man with a shaved head and round glasses, flanked by two female assistants carrying garment bags the same sickening color as the body bag she'd once shoved Will's limp form into at the Compulsory Clinic.

"Good morning, Kira!" Sienna said, grabbing her hands and planting a kiss on each of her cheeks. "You look gorgeous, as always. How is our city's bravest Volunteer feeling today?"

Kira watched over Sienna's shoulder as Adeline slipped from the room, her eyes briefly locking with Kira's before she closed the door behind her.

As the door clicked shut, Kira felt trapped, like a tiny mouse in a room with a hungry red cat.

"Uh, fine... I guess. A little worn out, but—"

"Wonderful, wonderful. As you can see, I've got a special treat for you this morning. This is Maurice Cavill, Vita Nova's most sought-after designer and tailor. He's dressed nearly every Volunteer for the past decade, but most of them don't get the pleasure of meeting him in person."

Maurice stepped forward, taking Kira's hand and bowing his head in reverence. "It's an honor, Ms. Liebert." When he released her hand, he formed his fingers into a V-shape and placed them over his heart. "Revere the Volunteer."

"Thank you, Maurice."

"We've brought several options for you," Sienna continued, nodding to the assistants who began draping garment bags over the chairs. "It's going to be difficult to outdo that gorgeous blue dress you wore to the Volunteer Ball a few weeks ago, but if anyone can do it, it's Maurice."

The assistants began unzipping the bags, revealing a series of evening gowns in various shades of blue—from pale ice to deep navy. Each was more elaborate than the last, with beading, lace, and strategic cutouts designed to draw the eye. There were so many of them, each beautiful in their own way, but they all carried the same message:

You belong to the city now. You belong to death.

"Well?" Maurice prompted when Kira remained silent. "Do you see anything you like?"

Kira ran her fingers over one gown—a sapphire blue creation with a plunging neckline and crystal beading across the bodice.

"They're all so... blue."

Maurice nodded enthusiastically. "That they are, that they are! I couldn't help but notice how incredible you looked in the color of the Volunteer rose at the Ball a few weeks ago." He glanced at Sienna Graves. "Although it wasn't one of my dresses, it was still beautiful. The shade complements your skin tone and hair color perfectly."

Kira turned away from the short man, her eyes drifting to the window. In the distance, she could just make out the concrete wall that separated Vita Nova from the wilderness. From the church in Emmitsburg, its wooden pews worn smooth from generations of worshippers. Aunt Reeva had filled that sanctuary with yellow dahlias, the flowers glowing like captured sunlight against the weathered walls, transforming the place into something almost magical.

She thought of something Will had told her once, a dream he'd had about her.

You were standing in this beautiful garden filled with dahlias. Not just the yellow ones Aunt Reeva grows, but all different colors. There aren't any dahlias in this city, so I knew you were somewhere else. Somewhere better. You were wearing this beautiful yellow dress and twirling around and dancing. You just looked so happy.

She smiled and turned away from the window.

"Do you have anything in yellow?"

"Yellow?" Maurice sounded genuinely disgusted, as if Kira had just asked for a dress made of live snakes.

"Yellow. It's my favorite color."

The designer glanced at Sienna Graves for rescue, clearly uncertain how to respond. The deputy mayor's perfect features had hardened slightly, though her practiced smile remained in place.

"Kira, darling, all the dresses Maurice brought you are blue. We were hoping you could have your fitting this morning, since there are only a few hours left until the Ball. I'm certain you can find one among them that would be perfect for tonight."

"They are all so beautiful, but since this is my last night, I really want to wear something yellow." She took a deep breath before saying the words she had promised herself she would never utter. "I'd like to make this one of my final requests."

Maurice looked uncomfortable as he fiddled with the bottom of his tie. "I might be able to find something that will work, but I won't have time to return for another fitting."

"I don't need a fitting. The blue dress I wore last time is crumpled up on the floor of my bedroom back at my townhouse. Send someone over there to pick it up. You can use that to get my exact measurements."

Sienna's jaw tightened, a muscle twitching along her cheekbone. She stared at Kira for a long moment, her sharp nails dragging across her thigh. Kira pictured the varicose veins she always tried to hide, swollen and threatening to burst under the pressure.

Finally, the tense muscles in Sienna's face contorted into something that passed for a smile. "Fine. Maurice, please see what you can do about finding a suitable gown in that... particular shade. I expect you to produce something exquisite that fits our beautiful Volunteer like a glove by this evening. No excuses."

"Yes, ma'am."

"Now, would you give us a moment, please? I'll meet you downstairs. I have something I need to discuss with Kira."

"Of course." The designer snapped his fingers at his assistants, and they grabbed the dresses and garment bags and followed him into the hallway.

As the door closed behind them, the temperature in the room seemed to drop several degrees. Sienna's smile vanished, replaced by something cold and dark. She moved toward Kira until they stood only a few inches apart.

The deputy mayor towered over her. "You think you're special, don't you?" she said, her voice edged with steel. "Because you're Victor Devlin's daughter, and you're going to be wearing a yellow dress instead of a blue one?"

Kira was so caught off-guard by the sudden change in Sienna's demeanor, she wasn't sure how to respond. "I don't think I'm special."

"Of course you do. How could you not? You've been single-handedly turning this city upside down for weeks. But I'm telling you, Kira... in a few days, no one will care about you.

Yours will be just one more body among countless others. By Sunday evening, you'll be nothing more than a burst of colorful ashes in the sky, like all the other Volunteers. You'll never be special, Kira, no matter how much you try to be. Not to this city, and certainly not to your father."

Despite Sienna's height advantage and dangerous-looking nails, Kira refused to step back, refused to back down even an inch. "You don't know anything about me."

"Oh, I know exactly who you are. You're the volunteer advocate who fell for a disgusting sanitation worker—the absolute bottom of the barrel—and made a fool of herself making out with him for the whole city to see. You're the girl who jumped off a bridge with a young child in her arms, nearly killing the boy in the process. You're the traitor who somehow convinced an entire village to take her in, only to abandon them when they needed her the most. And you're the unwanted daughter who desperately craves her father's love. Love you will never, ever get."

Kira felt the words like a punch, each one striking precisely where Sienna intended. But something inside of her—the part that had survived weeks beyond the wall—refused to be diminished by this terrible woman.

"What about you, Sienna? Don't you see he's using you, just like he uses everyone? It doesn't matter how long you stay or how useful you are. He's never going to leave his wife for you. That's just not who he is." She softened her voice a bit, feigning pity. "Honestly, I feel sorry for you. At least my prison sentence ends tomorrow. Yours will go on and on—."

The deputy mayor's hand shot out, connecting solidly with Kira's face. The sound of the slap echoed through the quiet room.

For a moment, Sienna looked just as startled as Kira felt. Something flickered across her face—a crack in her carefully composed facade that offered a fleeting glimpse of the frightened woman buried beneath all that ambition and calculation.

"That," she said quietly, "was a mistake."

Kira touched her stinging cheek, wondering if the woman meant Kira's previous remarks or the slap itself. But she said nothing, only watched as Sienna straightened her jacket and headed for the door to the suite.

"I will have your yellow dress delivered later this afternoon," she said without turning around. "Goodbye, Kira."

After she left, Kira crossed to the bathroom and examined herself in the mirror. A red mark bloomed across her cheekbone, the perfect imprint of the deputy mayor's palm. She traced the outline of the mark, feeling the heat still radiating from her skin.

Sienna Graves—always perfect, always controlled—had broken her own rules. Because Kira had spoken the truth.

She turned away from the mirror, a sense of calm settling over her. Tomorrow she would die, but tonight—for the price of a slap—she would wear yellow instead of blue. Instead of wearing the color of sacrifice and submission, she would wear the color of dahlias, sunlight, and Will's dream.

The color of defiance.

And somehow, that felt like a victory.

Chapter Thirty-One

Kira spent the early hours of her last afternoon alone in her suite, alternating between pacing the floor and sitting on the balcony. She'd refused lunch when a staff member had tried to deliver it, unable to even think about eating. When she stopped her relentless pacing to check her reflection in the bathroom mirror, she saw that the handprint on her cheek had faded to a dull pink, more like a hint of rouge than evidence of a slap.

She felt nothing when she looked at it.

Maurice had sent word that he'd found a suitable gown in the shade she'd requested and would deliver it at five p.m., a few hours before the Ball. He would be accompanied by a hairstylist and likely a makeup artist to make Kira beautiful and cover up what remained of the bruise.

Halfway through her pacing, a knock drew her attention to the door. She peered through the peephole to see a young woman in a Rolling Meadows uniform standing in the hallway, her hands interlaced in front of her stomach. As Kira opened the door, the woman put her fingers in a V-shape over her heart.

"Revere the—"

"What is it?" Kira demanded, her patience growing as thin as the time she had left.

"I apologize for the interruption, Miss Liebert. But you have a visitor waiting outside."

Kira's stomach tightened. Lucas, most likely coming to cheer her up. "I just want to be alone this afternoon," she said, starting to close the door. "Can you get rid of him, please?"

"The visitor is a woman, ma'am."

Kira's hand froze on the edge of the door. "A woman? Who?"

"I'm so sorry, but she didn't give her name. She only poked her head into the lobby for a moment, and she was wearing a scarf and sunglasses. She's waiting in a car outside. If you aren't expecting a visitor, I would be happy to send her away."

Who would have any reason to visit her? The list of people she knew in the city wasn't a very long one. A former co-worker, maybe? Or someone sent by her father to prepare her for the Volunteer Ball?

"No, it's okay," she said. "I'll be right down."

The young woman nodded and retreated down the hallway.

Kira returned to the bathroom mirror, flicking on the vanity lights and examining the slap mark on her cheek. She opened the drawers beneath the marble sink, revealing an array of cosmetics that would have cost a month's salary during her time as a volunteer advocate. Foundation in various shades, concealer, bronzer, and various shades of powder. Everything a Volunteer needed to look her best.

She selected a bottle of concealer that matched her skin tone and worked quickly, dabbing it over the lingering redness on her cheek, erasing all evidence of Sienna's momentary loss of control.

When she reached the lobby ten minutes later, Kira spotted a dark sedan idling just outside the door. It looked exactly like Lucas's government car, though the tinted windows made it impossible to see who was inside.

The automatic doors whooshed open, and Kira stepped into the mild afternoon air. The heavy clouds and rain from the day before had vanished, replaced by warm sunshine and a clear blue sky. Her last full day was shaping up to be beautiful, at least on the surface. It was almost enough to loosen the knot of dread in her stomach. Almost.

The tinted passenger window rolled down.

Kira leaned into the open window, still half-expecting to see Lucas behind the wheel, despite what the receptionist had said.

But it wasn't him.

"Mrs. Devlin?"

Her father's wife wore large sunglasses and a scarf tied around her blonde hair. A weak attempt at a disguise, but it had been enough to fool the receptionist.

"Hurry," the woman said, gesturing for Kira to open the door. "Get in. Quickly."

Kira hesitated. Whatever this was, she wasn't sure she wanted any part of it. "I don't understand. What are you doing here?"

"Please, Kira. Just get in the car. We don't have much time."

Something in her tone made it clear there was no point in arguing. Kira climbed into the passenger seat and pulled the door shut.

Chandra Devlin drove them away from Rolling Meadows, the tires spitting gravel as the car sped down the long driveway. As they turned onto Elmerton Avenue, her eyes flicked between the road and the rearview mirror. She looked nervous.

"Does my father know you're here?"

Kira was fairly certain she knew the answer to that question, but she asked it anyway.

"No." Chandra was gripping the steering wheel so tightly that Kira could see the tendons straining beneath her skin. When she lifted one hand to tuck a strand of blonde hair beneath her scarf, she left a damp handprint behind on the wheel. "No one does. As far as anyone knows, I'm spending the afternoon nursing a migraine in my bedroom. But don't worry—my staff is used to me spending the entire day in bed."

Kira noticed a slight tremor in the woman's fingers as she adjusted her sunglasses. This wasn't the beautiful and composed First Lady who hosted charity events and appeared flawless at every public event. This was a woman doing something dangerous, something that terrified her.

"Where are we going?"

Chandra glanced at her. "There's something I need to show you."

They drove in silence, the familiar landscape of the city's outskirts giving way to broader streets and towering buildings. As they reached the Medical Sector, she glimpsed the Compulsory Clinic tucked away on a side street a few blocks behind the main hospital complex. The boxy brick building with its dark green awning seemed to shrink from view, as if ashamed of its purpose. Kira's stomach clenched at the sight, her throat tightening as it always did when she saw the place where her mother had drawn her final breaths.

They left the Medical Sector behind, the clinic's pale facade vanishing in the rearview mirror as the car moved deeper into the city.

Ahead, the Capitol dominated the skyline, its green dome streaked with age but still gleaming like an exotic jewel in the sunshine. Outside the main entrance, white marble statues rose on either side of the steps—naked, angelic figures carved in perfect detail. The building looked like something out of a post-card from a different time—elegant and untouched by the fear and death that now dominated the city.

The streets changed as they continued east through the Residential Sector, the buildings growing older, shorter, and packed closer together. The quaint townhomes of Kira's old neighborhood gave way to ramshackle houses and rundown apartment buildings, their windows boarded with plywood that had faded from brown to gray.

And then she saw it just ahead.

The Tenements.

And the crumbled remains of Tower 2, Will's home.

She pressed the button to lower the passenger window, struggling to comprehend the scale of the destruction before her. Massive slabs of concrete lay in jumbled heaps, crushing what was left of the lower floors of the apartment building. Exposed interior walls revealed private lives blown open and displayed for all to see: a white T-shirt tangled in twisted rebar, a couch split clean in half by the blast, and a kitchen sink still attached to a length of pipe but dangling over empty air.

Her gaze caught on a child's crib perched at the edge of the ruin, its slats shattered and splintered, the bedding inside choked with gray dust.

Weeks had passed since the bombing, but the site looked untouched. There were no cleanup crews picking through the wreckage. No bulldozers clearing debris. No construction equipment parked off to the side. The city had simply left the building as it was, a silent warning to anyone who might think about rebelling.

This is what becomes of troublemakers.

"How many?" Kira whispered. "How many people died here?"

Chandra spoke without looking at the destruction, her eyes locked on the road. "Believe me, you don't want to know."

As they passed the edge of the Tenements, Chandra brought the vehicle to a stop and shifted into reverse, carefully backing the car into a narrow alleyway strewn with broken glass. The tires crunched over the debris as she maneuvered into the shadows between two graffiti-tagged brick walls. From here, they were hidden from the main street, but the view ahead remained clear. Through the gap in the buildings, they could still see the jagged skeleton of Tower 2, its ruined floors open to the sky.

Kira glanced out her window. On the wall to her right, bold blue letters announced: *Revere the Volunteer!*

Just below it, in paint the color of blood: *How many more?*

Chandra put the sedan in park and shut off the engine.

For a long moment, she didn't speak. She just sat there with her hands folded in her lap, her head bowed as if in prayer. A single tear emerged from beneath her dark sunglasses and slid slowly down her cheek. She didn't bother to wipe it away. Didn't even seem to notice it at all.

"Mrs. Devlin? What are we doing here?"

The woman slipped off her sunglasses and set them on the console, revealing red-rimmed eyes. She wore no makeup, and without it she looked much older, fine lines radiating from the corners of her eyes and lips. The glamorous First Lady of Vita Nova was gone, and in her place was someone raw, real, and broken.

"I promised myself, Kira. Do you know how many times I promised myself I would never do this?" Chandra breathed out, a long, slow exhale. "But I suppose some promises are meant to be broken, aren't they?"

Kira suddenly felt cold, and she tucked her hands beneath her thighs to warm them. "I don't understand."

Chandra smoothed her scarf with trembling fingers. "Your father is a complicated man, Kira. And my position in his life is very... fragile. He's given me two beautiful children, a wonderful home, and a respectable status in the city. And yes, I believe he loves me, in his own way. And I still love him, despite everything he's done to hurt me." She gestured to the ruined buildings across the street. "Despite all of this."

Kira swallowed. "Despite... what?"

Chandra finally looked over at her, her eyes filled with the deepest sadness Kira had ever seen. "I think you already know what I'm talking about. Please don't make me say it out loud."

Kira shifted her gaze to the ruins of the Tenements, thinking of the conversation she'd had with her father after the Volunteer Ball. "I asked him what happened here," she said, giving voice to a conversation she had not allowed herself to think about since it had occurred. "He told me there were other forces at work in the city. People with more power than him who wanted to expand past the barricade and needed an excuse for a big military push to clear out the Lawless. He suspected they were responsible for the bombing."

"Did he now?" Chandra laughed, but there was no humor in it. "I suppose I shouldn't be surprised. Victor has always been adept at deflecting responsibility. He wasn't being entirely dishonest. There are people in this city who influence everything that happens here. You probably met some of them at the Ball a few weeks back."

Kira remembered that dinner all too well. She'd been seated beside the wife of one of the city's dignitaries and was forced to endure the woman's smug questions, most of which had been designed to embarrass her. But then Will had joined the conversation by describing the best ways to cook and eat rats. The look of disgust and horror on the woman's face had been priceless.

"Your father steers this ship," Chandra continued. "He always has. I'm sure he convinced the people behind the scenes that destroying the Tenements would be a great way to garner support for clearing out the Lawless, but the bombing was Victor's solution to an entirely different problem."

"What problem?"

The woman turned to face her fully. "Rebellion. The Tenements were becoming a hub of dissent. Small pockets of people were spreading dangerous ideas, questioning the Volunteer program, the Compulsory system, even the barricade itself. He couldn't allow that, don't you see? If people knew the truth about the world outside these walls, the power and control he wields would vanish in an instant, along with everything he's built."

"So you're saying..." Kira began, trying to put it together in her mind, "that my father ordered the killing of hundreds of innocent people... for what? To silence a few dissenters who lived in the buildings?"

"Yes. And by blaming the Lawless for the attack, Victor hoped to solidify his position as the city's protector. After all, nothing unites people like fear. Victor knows that better than anyone. He's built this entire city around it."

"But that's..."

Horrible. Evil. Monstrous.

None of the words that entered her mind seemed big enough for what her father had done, if Chandra was telling the truth.

"That's Victor," Chandra finished the sentence for her. She reached behind her seat, retrieved a slim manila folder, and handed it to Kira. "You need to see this, too."

Kira froze when she saw the name on the file.

Liebert, Madison.

"No." She didn't want to see anything else that Chandra

Devlin intended to show her, particularly if it concerned her mother. Wasn't it enough that she was going to die tomorrow? Did she really need to endure more pain before this whole thing was over?

"It's okay. Go ahead and open it."

Kira shook her head, but her hands moved on their own, opening the folder and pulling out a stack of papers. The words on the first page blurred before coming into sharp focus.

Her mother's medical records.

"How did you get these?"

"Victor keeps certain sensitive files in his private safe at home. I've known the combination for years, though he doesn't realize it." Her lips curved in a sad smile. "There are advantages to being underestimated."

Kira flipped through the pages, her heart pounding. There were results, physician notes, and prescription orders. Years of bloodwork and annual health screenings. Nothing out of the ordinary. Nothing unusual until she reached the last page in the folder.

A Compulsory Order listing her mother's terminal diagnosis as stage 4 lung cancer. Inoperable.

She looked up at Chandra. "I don't understand. Why are you showing me this?"

"Look closer, Kira." The woman tapped the papers with a manicured fingernail. "Look at her final health screening. Do you see any bloodwork or scans confirming your mother's cancer diagnosis? Do you see anything out of the ordinary at all?"

Flipping through the papers once more, she found the last screening, conducted two months prior to her mother's death. She studied the numbers closely. All of them were within the normal range. There were no markers of cancer anywhere.

The only thing in the folder that indicated her mother was sick was the Compulsory Order itself.

"You're saying my mother was healthy when she died?"

Chandra nodded, her lips pinching tightly together. "Your mother... and many others like her." She handed Kira a folded sheet of paper. "When people step out of line in this city, when they make too much trouble, they're issued a fake diagnosis and a Compulsory Order. Not all Compulsories are healthy at the time of their deaths, but many of them are."

Kira unfolded the paper with trembling hands. Names filled the page in Chandra's careful handwriting—dozens of them, each followed by their supposed diagnosis and their real crime. The list went on and on, each entry a life reduced to a few lines of text, each name a person who had died for stepping out of line.

"I've been keeping track," Chandra explained. "For years. I never really understood *why* I was doing it, especially since I didn't intend to share it with anyone. But someone needed to keep a record of what really happened to these people."

Kira's hands trembled as she refolded the paper and closed the folder. Her father had killed her mother—and so many others. Ghost had known. He'd tried to tell her. And now, hearing it from Chandra Devlin, there was no more room for doubt.

"But we weren't troublemakers," Kira whispered, staring through the windshield at the ruins of Tower 2. "We never stepped out of line. And we never asked him for anything."

"Your mother was a loose end, and Victor doesn't leave loose ends. I don't know all the details, because he doesn't tell me very much, but on several occasions he mentioned a man who had been in your mother's life. A soldier whom he had exiled from the city."

Ghost.

"That man haunted your father, Kira," Chandra continued, as if she had heard the nickname. "I always sensed that Victor was afraid of him, though he never would've admitted it. Maybe that's why he did what he did. Maybe he just wanted to make sure that man never had a reason to come back."

The manila folder felt impossibly heavy in Kira's hands, as if the truth within had added its weight to the paper.

Her father had ordered the execution of her mother. A woman whose only crime had been falling in love with the wrong man.

"Take me home," she finally said. "Please. I need to get ready for the Ball."

Chapter Thirty-Two

Maurice circled Kira like an artist admiring a masterpiece, the tip of his tongue poking out of his mouth as he made minor adjustments to the yellow gown that flowed around her. His brow furrowed in concentration as his fingers fixed the fabric here and smoothed a wrinkle there, each movement so small as to seem unimportant but somehow resulting in the dress looking even more beautiful than it had before the adjustment.

The dress was stunning—a rich, golden yellow that was the exact color of the dahlias that had grown in Aunt Reeva's church in Emmitsburg. The bodice hugged her torso before cascading into yards of flowing fabric that pooled around her feet. The dress was backless, exposing the pale curve of her skin, and adorned with a single fabric dahlia, its intricately crafted petals fashioned from the same material as the dress.

Maurice brought his fingers to his throat. "Simply magnificent. I wasn't sure about the yellow when you suggested it, but this is so unexpected, so... defiant." He stepped back to take her in fully, tilting his head to one side.

"No one will be able to tear their eyes away from you tonight, Miss Liebert."

Kira stood before the full-length mirror, barely recognizing herself. The stylists had transformed her blonde hair into a crown of loose curls that cascaded down her back like a gold waterfall. Her makeup was subtle yet elegant, highlighting the strange gray hue of her eyes. Not a hint of Sienna Graves' handprint remained on her cheek. They'd concealed it well.

"So?" Maurice asked, hands clasped before him in anticipation. "What do you think?"

What did she think? She thought she looked like a stranger. She thought she looked like someone playing dress-up, pretending to be something she wasn't. But even she had to admit that she looked beautiful. The kind of beautiful that turned heads and made people stop and stare.

She looked like a woman getting ready for her wedding, not her funeral.

"It's beautiful, Maurice," she said. "Thank you. You did a wonderful job."

"The hem is perfect," he continued, dropping to his knees to adjust a fold of material that only he could see was out of place. "Did you see it has pockets? Young ladies love pockets in dresses, don't they?"

She stuck her hands in the pockets, which were surprisingly deep and blended in perfectly with the fabric of her skirt. "They sure do."

"And the color complements your complexion—I had my doubts, I admit, but now..." He kissed his fingertips. "You're a vision, Ms. Liebert. An absolute vision."

Kira smiled mechanically, letting his words wash over her without truly hearing them. Her thoughts were elsewhere, as they had been all afternoon.

She could think of nothing but her mother's medical file

and the list of names she'd refused to read, both of which she'd stuffed beneath her mattress upon her return to Rolling Meadows.

"Are you all right, dear?" Maurice's voice cut through her thoughts. "You seem... far away."

Kira forced herself back to the present. "I'm fine. Just a little nervous about tonight."

"Oh, it's natural to be nervous. But remember that tonight is for you. The entire city is celebrating your courage and your Sacrifice."

And my murder, she thought but didn't say.

"Thank you, Maurice." She felt empty, like a ghost already haunting a life that no longer belonged to her. "Can you please give me a few moments alone to finish getting ready?"

He nodded. "Of course. Your car will be here in ten minutes. I'll send Adeline up to escort you down."

After he left the suite, Kira sank onto the edge of the bed, careful not to wrinkle her skirt or shift anything out of place. She reached underneath the mattress until her fingers found the single sheet of folded paper Chandra had given her resting on top of her mother's medical records. She pulled out the paper and unfolded it, her eyes scanning the evidence of her father's many crimes.

Henry Kaiser.

Thomas Bradshaw.

Jennifer Walsh.

Names. So many names. People with families and dreams. Lives that had been erased.

She swallowed, her throat dry, and forced her eyes to keep going.

And there it was.

Madison Liebert, age forty-seven. False diagnosis: terminal lung cancer.

The words blurred as tears filled her eyes. Her mother had never been sick. She hadn't been dying.

She'd been murdered.

Just like so many others.

"Knock, knock."

Kira jolted at the sound, scrambling off the bed and fumbling with the paper in her hands. She refolded it quickly and stuffed it into the hidden pocket sewn into the lining of her dress, patting it flat so it didn't bulge.

Adeline entered the suite, her eyes growing wide at the sight of Kira in the yellow dress. "Oh my goodness, honey. You look absolutely breathtaking."

"Thank you. It really is a beautiful dress."

"Not as beautiful as the girl wearing it."

The dress rustled around Kira as she crossed the room and stood before the mirror one last time. A stranger stared back at her. The yellow dress made her look like something from another world, radiant and untouchable.

Adeline appeared behind her, holding the delicate blue rose corsage in her palm. "Don't forget this, honey. I'm afraid you have to wear it tonight."

Kira stared at the flower—a symbol of sacrifice, of conformity, of a system built on death. For a moment, she considered refusing it entirely.

But Adeline was right. She was a Volunteer, and Volunteers wore blue roses.

She allowed Adeline to attach the corsage to her wrist.

"Listen to me, Kira." Adeline leaned in close and put a hand on her cheek. "When you're out there tonight, hold your head high. Be the person your mother raised you to be. I know why you're doing this. You think there's no other option... and you're probably right. But they're giving you a stage tonight, so make the most of it. Make sure the entire city sees you as I see you."

She stared at Adeline in the mirror, seeing not just a staff member of Rolling Meadows—a woman paid to keep her happy and obedient—but an ally. Someone who knew exactly what this night really meant. Someone who was telling her to resist. To rebel. Even if only a little.

"Okay." She nodded. "I will."

Adeline gave her a sad smile. "It's time to go downstairs now," she said, letting her hand fall away from Kira's face. "Vita Nova is expecting their next brave Volunteer."

As she emerged from her suite, she heard a collective gasp from the Rolling Meadows staff gathered in the hallway. They lined the corridor, their hands forming V-shapes over their hearts.

"Revere the Volunteer."

Each one spoke the words as she passed by.

But the words that had once filled her with pride now felt like a joke. An empty ritual performed by people who didn't grasp what they were really celebrating. When they placed their hands over their hearts, they weren't honoring her courage. They were just grateful that someone else had been marked for death instead of them. The reverence wasn't really for the Volunteers at all, but for the system itself—as if by worshipping the dying, they would be spared the same fate.

Kira paused at the top of the grand staircase that led to the lobby, gathering her skirt in one hand to avoid tripping. She could see the entire lobby below, filled with Rolling Meadows staff members, all with their fingers over their hearts.

And then she saw him.

Will.

He stood at the entrance in a black tuxedo, his back to her, head tilted as he listened to something a staff member was saying. The sight of him knocked the breath out of her lungs. The broadness of his shoulders, the way his golden-brown hair was slicked back to appear almost black—everything was exactly as it had been on the night of his Volunteer Ball.

Had Adeline done this for her? Found Will and brought him to Rolling Meadows? But how?

She pictured the moment he would turn and look up at her, his crooked dimples appearing as he smiled, his blue eyes lighting up at the sight of her.

When everyone around him grew quiet, he turned, and the illusion shattered.

It wasn't Will.

It was Lucas.

The fragile hope she'd let herself feel cracked apart inside her, leaving nothing but pain. She felt foolish for believing—even for a moment—that Will would be there, waiting. As if her father wouldn't have him detained or killed the second he crossed the river.

She forced herself to keep smiling as she descended the staircase, but she felt more alone than ever.

Lucas met her at the foot of the stairs and lightly kissed the top of her hand. "You look gorgeous, Kira."

"Thank you, Lucas. You look very handsome yourself. But what are you doing here?"

A smile played across Lucas's lips as his eyes traveled the length of her dress before returning to her face. "I thought you might prefer arriving at the Ball in my car instead of the Volunteer bus." He took a step closer, eliminating the proper distance between them. "Actually, I was hoping you'd let me escort you tonight. I couldn't stand the thought of the most beautiful woman in Vita Nova not having anyone to dance with."

The words were practiced and polished—a line he'd no doubt refined over time. Kira imagined he'd used versions of it on plenty of women. She thought about turning him down. But tonight was her last night, and she let herself accept this small, fleeting connection. Not because she wanted Lucas Pine's affection, but because what she truly wanted was forever out of reach.

"I think I'd like that," she said. "Thank you."

"Excellent." He offered his arm. "I promise you won't regret it. I'm going to make sure tonight is one you will never forget."

As they stepped outside and the automatic doors slid shut behind them, Kira made a decision. Tonight, she would not think of how much she missed Will or how broken he would be when he eventually learned of her death. She would not think of Ghost, or Grace, or Brack, or any of her other friends in Haven. She would not think of her mother or the awful things her father had done.

Tonight she would allow herself a few hours of happiness, even if it was all pretend.

Chapter Thirty-Three

Ghost stood just outside the fence, staring at the line where the cleared ground met the trees. The shadows stretched long and dark, reaching toward him like they wanted to hold him back. He was leaving again. Turning his back on the people he'd promised to keep safe. He was getting good at walking away from those who depended on him. It made him sick to realize how easy it was becoming.

But Kira was in that city, and he couldn't live with himself if he didn't bring her home. Even if it meant he'd never see Haven again. Even if it meant breaking one more promise to those he loved.

Will appeared beside him, a heavy pack slung over his shoulders, his rifle secured across his back. He offered Ghost no greeting apart from a brief nod of acknowledgement. The kid knew when to talk and when to say nothing. That was a skill most men didn't pick up until much later in life.

Ghost adjusted the straps of his pack, which was heavy with ammunition, supplies, and a few items Will wasn't meant to know about.

"You ready for this?"

Will nodded. "I've never been more ready."

"I hope that's true."

Ghost lowered his head and sent up a silent prayer for what he was about to do. The idea had been gnawing at him since he'd decided to return to Vita Nova. At first, he'd refused to even consider it, banishing it to the darkest corners of his mind. Told himself that some things were too precious to part with.

But then he'd seen Will in the mess hall, standing his ground for Kira. The kid wasn't a brawler by nature, but he'd been ready to throw punches for her. And now he was ready to die for her, if necessary. That kind of devotion deserved something. And while Ghost didn't have much left to offer anyone, he had one thing.

He reached inside his jacket pocket, his fingers closing around a small velvet box he'd purchased many years earlier but never opened. "I need to give you something before we go."

Will kept his gaze focused on the forest, as if he could already see the city lights in the distance. "It's not a death letter, is it?"

"A what?"

"A death letter. You know, when a soldier gives his buddy a letter to deliver to his family in case he dies on a mission?"

Ghost snorted and shook his head. "You've seen too many war movies, kid. And if it were a death letter, I certainly wouldn't trust you to deliver it."

Will turned to face him, his gaze dropping to the small box in Ghost's hands. "What's that?"

Ghost opened the box, revealing a simple gold band with a tiny round diamond. It wasn't much—not even half a carat. It was certainly nothing like the elaborate rings that he had seen other men give to their future wives.

"I bought this for Kira's mother years ago. I saved for months to afford it. I know it's not much, but Maddie would've loved it. She wasn't the kind of woman who cared about having lots of expensive things. She was a good woman."

Will stared at the ring. "You were going to propose to her?"

Ghost nodded. "Had it all worked out in my head. Where I'd take her, the things I'd say. I made up my mind to do it this one Saturday. I took her on a boat because she loved the water. I was going to ask when we reached the middle of the river, but I just... I don't know. I guess I lost my nerve. That was the second-biggest mistake I ever made. The first was letting Devlin get rid of me so easily."

He closed the box and held it out to Will.

Will's hands remained at his sides. "I'm not going to take that. It's yours."

"I don't need it anymore." Ghost pressed the box into Will's hands. "Now listen to me, son. I'm going to do my best to make sure you survive this mission. But I have to know—are you going to take care of Kira? No matter what happens? Or are you going to leave her when things get rough? And they *will* get rough. Things always do."

It wasn't a fair question. Ghost knew he was projecting his failures onto Will. The kid had never given him any reason to believe he would leave Kira. But Ghost needed to hear the words directly from Will's mouth. He couldn't bear the thought of Kira suffering the same abandonment as her mother.

The kid stared him down, unflinching. "I won't leave her. Not ever."

"Even if staying costs you everything?"

Will almost smiled. "I'm from the Tenements, remember? I'm used to being broke."

Ghost studied the younger man's face, searching for any

sign of doubt or hesitation and finding none. He loved Kira; that much was certain. And he was the type of man who wouldn't run away when the world fell apart around him. He'd already proven that a hundred times over.

"Good," Ghost said, satisfied. "Then hold onto this ring, and even though you didn't ask for my advice, I'm going to give it to you unsolicited. Don't wait for tomorrow because it's not guaranteed. Don't waste a single day thinking you'll have more time because you might not. Give this ring to Kira the first chance you get."

Will flipped open the box, staring at the small diamond, his thumb brushing over the stone as if trying to feel the weight of everything it meant. Then he shut the lid and slipped the box into his pocket. He lifted his eyes to Ghost, and without saying a word, stepped forward and pulled him into a rough, tight hug.

Ghost stiffened at first, caught off guard. Physical affection wasn't something he was used to anymore. But after a beat, he felt himself relax. He patted Will lightly on the back and briefly allowed himself to imagine what it might have been like to have a son. If he'd ever had one, maybe the kid would have turned out just like Will Foster—stubborn, loyal, and willing to risk everything for the ones he loved.

Behind them, Haven was settling into its evening routines, and ahead of them lay miles of dangerous territory and a city where the young woman they both loved had been condemned to death. Twelve years ago, he'd been driven from those walls with a promise never to return.

Tonight, he was going back.

Somewhere in the darkness ahead, Vita Nova waited for him, its massive concrete wall looming over everything, solid and unyielding, daring him to come closer.

A line from a children's song he'd learned in Sunday School

surfaced in his mind: *Joshua fit the battle of Jericho, and the walls came a-tumblin' down."*

Yes, the Lord had a way of bringing down walls and towers built by prideful men.

Maybe tonight He would use a broken and scarred soldier to do it.

Chapter Thirty-Four

"Ladies and gentlemen, please join me in welcoming tonight's brave Volunteer: Kira Liebert!"

Sienna Graves's voice rang through the Executive Mansion's speaker system, cutting off the boisterous conversations of Vita Nova's gathered elite class. The room grew silent, champagne glasses halting halfway to open lips. All eyes turned toward the entrance of the Grand Hall, where Kira stood frozen with Lucas by her side, her yellow gown like a single flower adrift on a vast blue ocean.

Staring at the faces before her, she saw the Volunteer Ball for what it was—a weekly theatrical production staged for the city's benefit. The elite in their blue attire were nothing but extras, while she played this week's noble sacrifice. But even she wasn't the real star of the show. That role belonged to Victor Devlin—the leading man whose performance never faltered. Week after week, year after year, the cast around him rotated while he remained constant, always at center stage.

And through the glow of their broadcast screens, the citizens of Vita Nova were the audience, watching it all unfold.

But the yellow dress wasn't in the script, and now the extras faltered, unsure how to react. They did not applaud at her introduction. Instead, whispers rippled through the room, the confusion and annoyance evident on their faces.

These were the people who controlled Vita Nova's scarce resources, who decided who lived and who died, and they weren't accustomed to any sort of rebellion, especially from someone marked for sacrifice.

Lucas's hand pressed against the small of her back, urging her forward. "You can do this," he whispered, mistaking her hesitation for fear. "I'm right beside you."

But her feet felt rooted to the floor. How could she play this part? How could she give her father—the man who had murdered her mother and ordered countless others to die—the satisfaction of her compliance? The yellow dress had been her small act of rebellion, but if she walked into the room to the stiff applause of his background players, even that gesture would mean nothing. She would still be accepting the role he had written for her.

She could not give him what he wanted.

A figure detached from the crowd. Victor Devlin strode forward in a perfectly tailored midnight-blue suit, his silver hair carefully styled. His gunmetal-gray eyes met hers as he closed the distance between them, his public smile never wavering. When he reached her, he took both of her freezing hands in his, turning them over as if admiring them.

"You look beautiful tonight, daughter," he said, pitching his voice just loud enough for most of the room to hear. "Such a vibrant color. So cheerful. So... accepting. Truly, the perfect choice."

He pulled her into an embrace, his arms closing around her with just enough pressure to appear warm rather than control-ling. Leaning in close, he whispered into her ear, "Theodore

Easton is safe at home with his mother tonight. It would be such a shame if anything that happened this evening forced me to reconsider his pardon."

Kira's resolve slipped as the truth crashed over her. Victor Devlin still held all the cards. He could still have Teddy killed if she didn't play her role exactly as he wanted. The threat hung between them like a noose. Before she could respond, Devlin let her go, stepped back, and formed his fingers into a V-shape over his heart.

"Revere the Volunteer!"

The effect was immediate. Like puppets whose strings had been pulled, the elite of Vita Nova followed their mayor's lead. Fingers found their way to chests, and the background players found their voices.

"Revere the Volunteer! Revere the Volunteer!"

The chant gave way to applause that thundered through the Grand Hall. The sound filled every corner, rattling the chandeliers and vibrating through the floor beneath her feet.

Her father extended his arm, and Kira placed her hand in his, allowing him to draw her into the room.

She felt the trap close around her.

As Devlin guided her through the crowd, dozens of hands reached for her, their fingers grazing her arms, her shoulders, and the fabric of her dress. It was as if she were some holy object rather than a teenage girl condemned to die. An elderly man with hands colder than her own touched the bare skin of her back, while a silver-haired woman clasped Kira's forearm in both palms, closed her eyes, and murmured, "Thank you," like a prayer.

Each contact sent a chill through her body, each whispered thanks making her skin crawl. She felt like an animal being blessed before slaughter, one whose death would buy these people one more week of safety.

Chandra Devlin stood at the head table, her blonde hair styled in an elegant updo, the fabric of her gown matching the deep blue of her husband's suit. On either side of her stood the twins, dressed in miniature versions of their parents' formal attire.

Standing beside Chandra was Sienna Graves. She wore a sapphire gown that mirrored Chandra's so perfectly it might have been planned. Kira felt her stomach turn, realizing that her father always placed his mistress at the head table, beside his wife, like it was the most normal thing in the world.

Although she was the one marked to die in the morning, Kira somehow felt more pity for Chandra than for herself. At least she would be free of all this by dawn. Chandra would remain right here, forced to smile through this kind of humiliation for the rest of her life.

Or however long her husband allowed her to live.

"Welcome, Kira." Chandra offered her a bright smile and pulled her into a tight embrace. Then she straightened and lifted her hand to her chest in the required salute. "Revere the Volunteer!"

Gone was the vulnerable woman who had driven her to the Tenements that afternoon. There was no hint of the confession she had made buried within her expression. Now she was Chandra Devlin, First Lady of Vita Nova. A role she had perfected long ago.

Something unreadable flickered across Chandra's face when her eyes settled on Lucas—a subtle narrowing of her eyebrows, a pause that lasted a moment too long. But it was gone so quickly, Kira wondered if she'd imagined it.

Chandra reached out to shake his hand. "What is your name, young man?"

He extended his hand. "Lucas Pine, ma'am."

"How wonderful of you to accompany Kira tonight."

"Thank you, Mrs. Devlin. It's an honor to escort her."

Victor Devlin gestured to the two remaining empty chairs at the head table. "Please, Kira, take your seat."

Kira hesitated, weighing her options. One chair would place her directly beside her father for the entire meal, while the other would place her next to Violet.

She angled toward the seat beside Violet, but before she could pull it out herself, Lucas stepped forward smoothly and drew it back for her.

"Thank you, Lucas."

"Of course."

As Kira settled into her seat, arranging the yellow fabric of her dress underneath her, Violet leaned in close, her eyes bright with excitement. "I told everyone at school about you," she whispered. "They couldn't believe that my big sister is this week's only Volunteer. They were all so jealous."

The innocence in the child's voice broke Kira's heart. This little girl had been taught to see death as something enviable, something to aspire to. That was the true horror of her father's system. Not just the lives it claimed each week, but the young minds it sought to warp and the innocence it corrupted.

Violet, and so many like her, did not know what sacrifice truly was.

Servants appeared, setting plates of food before each guest. At her previous Volunteer Ball with Will, duck had been on the menu. Tonight, the main course was braised lamb, which Kira thought fitting. Sacrificial lamb. She forced herself to take small bites of the meat, picturing little Teddy on the other side of the city in his house, curled up in his bed.

Safe. Alive.

"Your dress is beautiful, Kira," Chandra remarked, her eyes lingering on the golden fabric. She turned to her husband. "Maurice has captured her spirit perfectly, hasn't he, darling?"

"That he has." Victor's eyes locked with Kira's across the table. "Though I must admit, I would've preferred a more traditional color choice for tonight's celebration."

Kira held his gaze, refusing to look away. "Yellow is my favorite color," she said. "It reminds me of flowers... and of how beautiful and valuable life is."

A muscle twitched in Victor's jaw, the pockmarks in his cheeks deepening into craters. He reached for his crystal glass and lifted it in a toast. "To life, then... and to the necessary sacrifices that sustain it."

Kira lifted her glass and joined her father as he toasted her death. She met his eyes over the rim, holding his gaze as she took a sip, granting him this small, hollow victory.

But as the liquid slid down her throat, she closed her eyes for a moment and offered a silent prayer.

Please, God, let this be the last time Victor Devlin raises a glass to someone else's Sacrifice.

Chapter Thirty-Five

Dinner at the Volunteer Ball was as scripted as the rest of the evening. Course after course arrived at the head table while dignitaries filed up, each one hungry not for food but for a moment with Victor Devlin.

He greeted them like old friends, calling them by name, shaking hands, and laughing at jokes Kira doubted he found funny. Eventually, the dignitaries would shift their attention to her, offering thanks and a quick salute before scurrying back to their tables.

None of them looked her in the eye.

Lucas remained at her side the entire evening, refilling her water glass from the pitcher in the center of the table whenever it emptied. A flute of champagne sat before her, untouched save for the single sip she'd forced down when her father toasted her death. When her thoughts wandered and she missed a question directed her way, he would tap her hand gently beneath the linen tablecloth, drawing her back into the conversation. And when her father launched into a discussion about the need for a new burial pit, Lucas's hand settled over hers and didn't move.

After the dessert course—berries floating in cream so thick it clung to the spoon—servers materialized at every table, whisking away plates still half-filled with food. It had been the same with the lamb. Vita Nova's elite wasted more food in one evening than most citizens would eat in a week.

After the plates were cleared, the string quartet took its place in the corner of the hall. As they drew their bows across the strings, the first beautiful notes filled the air. Chairs scraped back as men stood and offered their hands to wives and girlfriends, guiding them toward the dance floor.

Victor Devlin rose to his feet and extended his hand toward Kira. "May I have this dance?"

The cameras positioned around the banquet hall shifted to capture the moment. Father and daughter, sharing one last dance before her Sacrifice. The citizens of Vita Nova who weren't lucky enough to be in attendance would watch what came next from the comfort of their homes. Some of them might even wipe away tears.

Teddy, Kira reminded herself. *This is all for him.*

She set her hand in her father's, letting him guide her to the center of the floor—almost the exact spot where she and Will had danced a few weeks earlier. The other couples moved aside, forming a neat circle around them.

Victor placed one hand on her waist and lifted her other hand into the air. "You do look beautiful tonight," he said as they danced. "Even in that terrible dress. You look so much like your mother."

"Thank you," she replied, maintaining her pleasant expression for the cameras. "I've heard that before. Usually from people who knew her."

Victor's steps didn't falter. He simply tightened his grip on her hand and continued leading her through the dance as if she hadn't spoken at all.

As they moved across the dance floor, Kira slipped into a familiar childhood fantasy. A different dance, on a different night.

A wedding.

Her wedding to Will. A day that would never happen.

At every wedding she'd attended with her mother, whenever she'd watched a bride swaying in her father's arms, Kira had tried to picture what her own father-daughter dance might be like. It was always difficult to imagine Victor Devlin in that role—holding her hands, beaming down at her with pride as she twirled in a sea of white.

But tonight, when she closed her eyes, it wasn't her father's face she saw at all.

It was Ghost's; his scarred cheek softened by a rare smile as he led her in a slow dance across the grass outside the little church in Haven.

But that day would never come.

Devlin's voice pulled her out of the fantasy. "You're far away right now."

"What?"

He spun her a little too forcefully and pulled her back in close. "Let me guess, you're thinking of your Lawless boyfriend again, aren't you? Or perhaps your little community in the wilderness?"

She said nothing, only stared at him. She wanted so badly to say Ghost's real name, just to see what kind of reaction it provoked in her father. But she had to be careful. Anything she said or did tonight could have terrible consequences for the people she loved on the other side of the barricade wall.

"Honestly, Kira," Devlin continued, "would you really prefer to be living like an animal with the Lawless in the

Unregulated Zone? Barely surviving among thieves and criminals?"

The choice wasn't even difficult. "Absolutely."

Devlin's eyes hardened, his fingers digging into her side with the clear intention of inflicting pain.

As the music ended, Kira twisted free of his grip. "Excuse me," she said. "I need to use the restroom."

Turning away from him, Kira pushed through the crowded dance floor, ignoring the curious glances that followed her. She had to get out of the Grand Hall—now. She needed air, needed space, needed to escape this suffocating performance, even if only for a few minutes.

She hurried down the hallway that led to the restrooms, her heels clicking against the marble floor as she ran away from her father. When she reached the bathroom door, she shoved it open and stepped inside, turning quickly to lock it behind her. She pressed her forehead against the wood, trying to catch her breath.

The music and conversations from the ballroom could not reach her in here. Safe behind the locked door, she let go of the tight hold she'd kept on herself all night. Grief crashed over her like a rogue wave, and she didn't stop the sob that finally tore itself free from her throat.

For the first time in her Final Week, she wanted to die.

Maybe when she died, she would go somewhere better than this place. Maybe she would see her mother again. Maybe she would see Aunt Reeva and Avery. Maybe they would all be reunited in a field of purple asters. Somewhere warm and sunny.

"Please," she whispered, lifting her eyes toward the ceiling. "Please help me through this night."

The prayer hung in the silent bathroom, simple and raw. The crushing weight on her chest didn't disappear, but it shifted somehow, becoming a little more bearable, and she found a bit of the strength she had requested.

Kira turned away from the door and approached the sink, staring at her reflection in the mirror. The mascara applied by Maurice's crew had carved black rivers down her cheeks, but thankfully the rest of her makeup had held its ground.

She grabbed a paper napkin from the dispenser, held it under the faucet, and blotted away the mascara tracks, erasing all evidence of her weakness. She couldn't break down, not now. She had to go back out there soon. She had chosen this path, had volunteered to die in Teddy's place, and that's exactly what she intended to do.

This horrible week would not have been for nothing.

When she emerged from the bathroom, she found Lucas waiting for her in the hallway, leaning against the opposite wall, arms crossed over his chest. "I was worried about you," he said, pushing away from the wall and rushing up to her. "I saw you run off the dance floor. Are you feeling alright?"

"I'm fine," she replied, hoping she'd done a decent job of fixing her makeup. "Everything just got a little overwhelming for a minute, but I'm good now. My smile's firmly locked in place, and I'm ready to face all of my adoring fans."

Lucas didn't crack a smile. "You don't have to be fake with me, Kira. I'm not like the others in that room. I'm not here to celebrate your death."

She studied his face, searching for insincerity but finding none. "Then what are you doing here, Lucas?"

A burst of laughter emanated from the Grand Hall, and Lucas glanced in that direction, chewing on his lower lip. "Can I be honest with you?"

"That would be a refreshing change of pace from everyone else tonight."

He stepped closer, his hand rising to her face. His fingers

brushed a stray curl from her cheek. "I requested to be your advocate," he whispered, his eyes never leaving hers. "After I saw what you did that night at the Reverence Ceremony, I knew I needed to be the one to help you through this week." He shook his head. "But now... it's taking every ounce of self-control I can muster not to grab your hand and drag you out of this mansion. If I could, I would take you somewhere and hide you away. Somewhere where no one could ever find you."

The tenderness of his touch caught her off guard. She shook her head, refusing to allow herself even the fantasy of running away. "Lucas... that's not possible."

His fingers ran along her jawline. "I know it isn't, but I still want more time with you, Kira. Can you please give me more time? I can't bear the thought of you going through one second of this night alone."

Before she could ask what he meant, he leaned in, his lips finding hers in a gentle kiss. And for one weak, human moment, Kira allowed herself to be held by him, to be comforted, to be wanted.

It was almost enough to make her forget...

Almost.

But as his arms encircled her waist, pulling her closer, and as the kiss deepened and grew more insistent, it was another man's face she envisioned in her mind. Another man's arms around her. Another man's lips against hers.

The only man she would ever love.

Kira pulled away, placing her palms against Lucas's chest to create some distance between them. "I can't do this, Lucas. I'm so sorry, but I can't do this with you."

What had she been thinking? Why had she let another man kiss her? Why had she allowed herself to betray Will?

Lucas stared at her, his face flushed, his expression wounded in a way she hadn't seen before. The vulnerability she saw there quickly gave way to irritation. "This is still about him, isn't it?"

Of course it was.

It would always be about him.

"I'm sorry," she whispered, not knowing what else to say. "I never meant to lead you on."

He straightened his tie, gathering himself. "The guy abandoned you, Kira. Have you forgotten that? He's a coward who left you to die, and you're still waiting for him?"

The sudden flare of heat in her face burned away the embarrassment. "He didn't abandon me. I made a choice. Don't you dare speak about him as if you know him. Will would burn down this entire city to save me if he could."

The anger in Lucas's eyes dimmed a bit but didn't disappear entirely. "You're right, and I'm sorry. I shouldn't have said anything about him. That wasn't my place. I probably shouldn't have kissed you, either. I just thought if we were together tonight, it might make things a little bit easier on you."

"I'm being executed tomorrow, Lucas. Nothing can make that any easier."

He stared at her for a long moment, as if deciding whether or not to try one more time. But whatever he was looking for in her eyes, he didn't find it. "You should probably get back to the party. People will soon wonder where you've gone."

"What about you?"

"I'll be there in a few minutes. I need to step outside for some air."

She watched him walk away, his hands stuffed inside his pockets, and disappear around the corner. She exhaled, the weight of the awkward encounter settling on her shoulders. Another burden for her to carry through her final hours.

She headed back to the Grand Hall, the music growing louder with each step. The heavy oak doors stood open, framing the scene like one of her father's paintings. Women in gowns swirled across the dance floor, while men in tailored suits stood in clusters, sipping from crystal glasses and discussing city business as if tomorrow were just another day.

Thankfully, her absence had no dulling effect on the party. The elite of Vita Nova were still laughing and dancing, still eating and drinking as they'd been doing when she'd left.

All except for one.

Victor Devlin was gone.

Chapter Thirty-Six

The stench hit Ghost first—a sickly sweet odor that permeated the air, crawling into his nostrils and coating the back of his throat with the taste of decay. He gagged and pressed his sleeve over his nose to block it out. From his vantage point behind a cluster of long-dead bushes, the pit looked less like a burial site and more like the mouth of hell itself, preparing to swallow the city's unwanted dead.

After nearly six hours of travel that had consisted mostly of running, he and Will had finally reached their destination. The burial pit lay in an abandoned limestone quarry two miles west of Vita Nova's barricade. Out of sight of the city but easily accessible by road.

According to Will, industrial operations at the site had stopped when the virus struck, leaving behind a deep wound in the earth that nature had tried and failed to reclaim. Twisted vines clung to the quarry walls, and stunted saplings jutted out at odd angles, their leaves yellowed and wilted, as if the very soil had been poisoned by what it contained.

What he saw next caused bile to rise in his throat.

White-wrapped bodies littered the edges of the pit like discarded dolls, many stacked two or three deep where they had landed. Some shrouds had come loose, exposing glimpses of the dead beneath.

A woman's tangled gray hair.

A man's legs bent at wrong angles.

And near the western edge, a small, wrapped form that could only be a child.

Will's breathing was steady beside him. The kid seemed immune to the stench and the horror before them, no doubt hardened by the time he'd spent driving bodies from the Compulsory Clinic to this very pit.

Ghost didn't think he could ever get used to it.

"See?" Will whispered, pointing. "There it is. Right on time."

Headlights swept past their hiding spot, twin beams cutting through the darkness. The white van moved slowly down the gravel access road, its engine rumbling with the low, steady growl of a diesel motor. As it pulled to a stop at the edge of the pit, the driver killed the engine but not the lights, illuminating every previously hidden detail of the horror below.

A single figure emerged from the driver's seat. A sanitation worker wearing standard protective gear. The man had a thick, muscular build that was barely contained by his coveralls. He wore a respirator mask that covered the lower half of his face, along with safety goggles and thick rubber gloves that extended past his elbows. He meandered around to the back of the van and opened the rear doors, revealing the van's cargo bay.

And the white-wrapped forms stacked within.

The worker grabbed the first body, dragging it from the van with no more care than he might've shown a sack of grain. The corpse hit the ground with a thud, the sheet partially unwrapping to reveal a glimpse of blonde hair and pale, waxy skin. He rolled the body across the uneven ground, pushed it towards the edge of the pit, and let gravity do the rest.

The body landed atop countless others who had been discarded there over the years. There was no moment of silence. No prayers. No acknowledgment that this had once been a human being with hopes and dreams and people who loved them.

Just disposal.

Madison is down there. The sudden realization caused something critical to break loose within his heart. *Somewhere in that pit, under tons of other bodies, Maddie is rotting like garbage.*

Ghost raised his shotgun, sighting down the barrel at the back of the worker's head. One squeeze of the trigger.

Clean. Simple. Done.

For Madison.

Will's hand gripped the barrel, pushing it down. "Wait," he whispered. "I know that guy."

Ghost lowered the shotgun. "So what?"

"His name is Dean Parsons," Will said, his hand still on the barrel. "He's a miserable guy to work with, but he's got two kids at home. Last I heard, his wife was sick. Some kind of autoimmune thing they're trying to keep quiet."

"We agreed to this," Ghost muttered, eyes fixed on his target. "It's our only option. You knew this part wasn't going to be easy. That's why I'm going to do it."

"We don't have to kill him, though. We can just knock him out, tie him up, and take the van. There's no reason to end his life."

The worker returned to the van for another body and disposed of it with the same lack of care as the last. How many more bodies were inside the van? How much time did they have? Ghost briefly considered putting the guy down anyway, ending the argument in the cleanest and most final way possible.

Will leaned in close. "We can't be like them. We can't treat life like they do."

Ghost didn't answer right away. He watched the worker heave another body into the pit and listened to the sound of it hitting bottom. He only realized how hard he was clenching his teeth when his jaw began to ache.

"Fine," he managed at last. "We'll try it your way. But if this thing goes sideways, I'm putting him down."

"Fair enough."

They waited until Parsons was hunched over, struggling to roll an unusually large body toward the edge of the pit. The bundle looked close to six and a half feet long and heavy enough to force the worker to stop several times to catch his breath.

Ghost and Will seized the moment. They moved fast, boots barely making a sound as they slipped from the cover of the dead bushes and descended the uneven, overgrown slope toward the pit. Stones shifted underfoot, vines snagged at their pants, but neither slowed.

Parsons was about to push the body over the edge when Ghost leveled the twin barrels of his shotgun at the back of his head.

"Don't move."

The sanitation worker froze, still hunched over, hands gripping the white-wrapped corpse. For a moment, everything went silent. Ghost held steady, his finger resting on the trigger, while Will flanked around to the left with his rifle raised.

"Drop it and turn around," Ghost commanded. "Slowly."

Parsons let go of the body and turned, his eyes wide behind scratched safety goggles. Whatever he'd been about to say died on his lips as he noticed Will standing off to the side.

"Foster," he breathed, his voice muffled by the respirator. "What are you doing here? Thought you'd taken off. Defected."

"I came back," Will said. "Couldn't stand to be away from you."

Parsons swallowed hard and backed up a step. He removed his mask, revealing a weathered face that was even uglier than Ghost had imagined. "What is this? You two gonna rob me? Shoot me and toss me in with the rest of 'em?"

"We just want the van," Will said in a level voice. "We need a ride into the city. You're going to spend the night out here. Someone will come find you in the morning."

"You ain't leaving me here," Parsons muttered, his eyes darting between the two men. He edged back another step, one hand creeping toward his belt. Ghost clocked the motion immediately, seeing the black shape clipped there.

A radio. Or maybe a sidearm.

"Don't even think about it," Ghost warned.

But Parsons kept shifting, defiance settling into his eyes. "I always knew you'd sell us out, Foster. Wasn't surprised at all when I heard you'd run off with that little blonde traitor. You think you're some kind of hero, but you're no hero, and neither is she, despite what her daddy says."

Will flinched. "Shut up, Dean."

Parsons' lips twisted into a cruel smile. "What is she to you, anyway? Your girlfriend? You think you're good enough for the mayor's daughter? Well, I've got bad news for you, brother. They're putting her down like a dog tomorrow. And when they do, I'll be there to haul her body aw—"

That was as far as he got before Will lunged forward and swung his rifle, connecting solidly with Parsons' temple. The man's eyes rolled back, his knees buckled, and he pitched sideways, out cold before he hit the ground. His body tumbled toward the pit, one leg slipping over the edge before gravity began to drag the rest of him down.

Ghost dropped his shotgun and threw himself forward, grabbing Dean's arms before he could tumble over the side. Will seized his legs, and together they hauled him back from the edge, his body deadweight in their hands.

Will stared at the sanitation worker's motionless body. "Is he...?"

Ghost pressed his fingers to the man's neck, feeling for a pulse. The rhythm was steady, if a bit weak. "He's alive. Still breathing. He's going to have a monster of a headache when he wakes up, but hey, at least you didn't kill him."

"He's lucky I didn't kill him," Will muttered.

Working together, they dragged the man away from the edge, his boots carving trenches in the loose earth. They left him sprawled behind a pile of broken limestone so he wouldn't accidentally roll into the mass grave before he regained consciousness.

Ghost moved to the back of the van, peering into the cargo bay that reeked of disinfectant and death. Four more bodies lay inside, anonymous beneath their white wrappings. They could have been anyone. And now he had to treat them as if they were nothing.

"We need to finish the job," he muttered, hating the words even as he spoke them. "We don't have any other choice."

They worked in silence, each picking up an end of the nearest body and lifting it from the van. The corpse was heavier than Ghost had expected, and they had to coordinate their movements to avoid dropping it. As they maneuvered toward the edge, the sheet slipped, exposing gray hair matted to the skull and liver-spotted hands.

They rolled the body over the edge, and it fell into the darkness, joining countless others in their unmarked graves. Two more followed without incident. The last body was smaller than the others. Lighter.

Ghost bit down on his tongue hard enough to taste blood as they lifted the small body from the van. A child, maybe ten or eleven, zipped into the same black bag as the adults. Carrying a dead child toward the pit made him physically ill. What disease had they blamed this time? What lie had they told to make it acceptable to steal decades of life from someone who hadn't even begun to live?

The body made no sound when it hit the bottom.

"God, forgive them for what they've done," Ghost said, staring into the pit. "Forgive us all."

It was the closest thing to a prayer he could muster.

The keys were still in the van's ignition. Will slid behind the wheel, and Ghost climbed into the passenger seat, his shotgun positioned between his legs. As they pulled away from the burial pit, their headlights swept across Parsons' unconscious form. The man hadn't moved an inch.

Will reached for the radio mounted on the dashboard. Static filled the van as he adjusted the frequency dial, and then a clear signal emerged. Orchestral music, elegant and refined. Music that conjured images of ballrooms, champagne toasts, and a better world that no longer existed.

"It's the Volunteer Ball," Will explained. "They always broadcast it throughout the city—probably because it makes people want to be a part of the celebration, and they get more Volunteers that way. Kira should be there. She's probably listening to this same music right now."

Through the windshield, Ghost could see the faint glow of Vita Nova's lights on the horizon, just beyond the river. Somewhere in that city, the woman they both loved was hearing one of the last songs of her life. Maybe she was even sharing a dance with her father—that was exactly Devlin's style. He would find a way to make his daughter's final evening about him.

It would be the perfect public farewell before he sent her to die in the morning.

Ghost's fingers tightened around the shotgun as one thought settled like iron in his chest: *I won't let it happen.*

Chapter Thirty-Seven

A familiar emptiness settled inside Kira's chest.

Of course her father was gone. Even on her last night, Devlin had found somewhere more important to be, something more worthy of his attention. She thought of those long-ago Saturdays when he had promised to pick her up for a father-daughter date but never showed. She recalled her mother's poorly concealed anger and futile efforts at distraction, plying Kira with ice cream and popcorn and movies, anything to get her smiling again. But even at a young age, she had known she wasn't wanted.

Why should she be surprised tonight?

A light touch on Kira's elbow pulled her back to the present.

"Your father has a tendency to disappear, doesn't he?"

Chandra Devlin stood beside her, regarding her with an expression that was part sympathy and part anger. It was the same look Kira had seen on her own mother's face countless times.

"Did he say where he was going?"

Chandra's gaze shifted toward the head table, where Vance and Violet sat huddled together, sampling various chocolate confections from crystal dishes. "Not specifically, no," she said, turning back to Kira. "But if I had to guess, I'd say he probably slipped away to his office for a few moments. Work always comes first, and he's always working on something." Her hand settled on Kira's arm. "Perhaps you should go up there and check on him."

Kira stared at her. "Why would I do that?"

Chandra offered a smile and a wave as one of the female guests slipped past them into the hallway. "Oh, I just thought you might want to check in with your father before the ball ends and see what he's been up to." Her smile remained fixed in place, but her eyes darted around the room, as if checking to see if anyone had noticed their exchange. "You know where his office is, don't you, darling? Second floor. Just remember to be quiet as you approach in case he's on an important phone call."

She wants you to go up there, Kira realized, *and to be quiet about it.*

Something was happening in Devlin's office.

Something she needed to see.

Chandra released her arm and stepped away. She approached a group of women standing nearby and seamlessly inserted herself into their conversation, their laughter echoing through the Grand Hall.

The main staircase at the front of the room was too visible, so Kira slipped back into the hallway and made her way to the rear stairwell. The last time she'd been inside Devlin's office had been during Will's Volunteer Ball, after her father had sent one of his security goons to drag them off the dance floor.

She remembered the glint of amber in her father's glass and the cold way he'd taunted Will with talk of cremation and strapping Volunteers down to die. She could still see Will's eyes when he drew the gun—years of rage and grief erupting all at once. Then her father's security detail had stormed in and slammed him to the ground.

But what she remembered most was the look Will had given her when he realized she'd unlocked the door to let them in—like she'd torn his heart out with her own hands.

The second-floor hallway was empty. She had expected a security guard or two to be hovering outside the closed double doors leading into her father's office, in which case she would have announced herself and requested to speak with him. But there was no one around. As she drew closer to the room, she noticed the doors weren't fully closed but ajar. A thin sliver of light spilled out into the hallway, along with the sound of voices. One of them unmistakably belonged to her father.

But the other voice...

Kira froze a few steps away.

The other voice was also familiar.

She crept closer to the room, claiming one precious inch of carpet at a time, mindful that something as simple as the rustling of her dress could give her away. Pressing herself against the wall beside the doors, she pressed her ear near the tiny gap between them, straining to hear the conversation.

"...is completely unacceptable," Devlin was saying, the anger clear in his voice. "You said you could handle this. You assured me you could do it. That's why I chose you in the first place. It wasn't for lack of better options."

"Sir, I've been trying—" Lucas tried to speak, but Devlin cut him off.

"You've been *trying?*" Something heavy slammed against a hard surface. "Trying to do what? You've spent all week with my daughter, and what information have you given me that I didn't already know? Absolutely nothing. Not a single piece of useful information about the Lawless group she was with, aside from an estimate on their numbers and that they're well-armed. *We already knew that, Pine!* How am I supposed to know if a full-scale attack on their encampment is necessary or even worthwhile without any solid intelligence?"

The hallway seemed to tilt beneath Kira's feet as the implications of her father's words sank in. Lucas hadn't requested to be her advocate because he believed in what she was doing. He'd been assigned the job. By her father. To get information from her.

"She doesn't like to talk about the village, sir. I've pressed her several times, but she's very careful about what she shares with me."

"Almost a week," Devlin went on, as if Lucas hadn't spoken. "You've been with her for nearly seven days and brought me nothing. I thought you could at least romance her—keep her distracted, keep her docile. But despite your good looks, you're apparently not even charming enough to convince a dying girl to spend her last night with you."

"Sir, I tried, but she's still hung up on—"

"Tell me something, Pine. What have you done to make sure this little Volunteer charade of hers isn't some elaborate plot to attack our city."

A thin sound escaped Lucas's throat. "With all due respect, sir, she's given me no indication that she's part of any plot."

"Do you expect her to skywrite it, you imbecile? Shout it from the rooftops? You were supposed to charm her, get her to trust you, open up to you, and fall in love with you. But from what I've seen, you can't even get her to kiss you. Do you realize the Lawless could be carrying out their plans right now? For all we know, they could already be inside our walls while you stand here giving me excuses."

"Sir, I'm not giving you—"

"You used to be one of my best Patrol soldiers. What

happened? Did you get PTSD after that raid on their camp? Was killing a bride on her wedding night a little too much for you?"

The hallway tilted around Kira. She reached out, gripping the wall to steady herself, fingers digging into the smooth surface as if it could hold her up.

Lucas wasn't from the Agricultural Sector. He wasn't even a real advocate.

He was in the Patrols.

He'd been there the night Haven was attacked.

He'd killed Avery.

She shut her eyes for a few seconds, waiting for the dizziness to pass. When it finally eased, she drew in a silent breath, forcing herself to stay put. She couldn't run—not now. She needed to hear every word, to know what else her father had done. There was a long pause, during which she could hear nothing but the pounding of her pulse in her ears.

Then Lucas spoke again, his voice steady.

"She's not planning anything, sir, and she hasn't tried to contact anyone outside of the city. This is all about the kid. I would bet my life on it."

"Well, you just might have to," Victor muttered. "Because if it turns out you're wrong and anything unsavory happens between now and her execution, you've punched your own ticket to the Confines."

"Yes, sir."

The sound of ice rattling in a glass. Her father must've poured himself another drink.

"What about the Stadium? Is everything in place for tonight?"

Kira leaned closer to the door. *The Stadium?*

"Yes, sir," Lucas responded. "I heard from them before I came up here. They're ready whenever you are. The prisoner has been transported and is on-site. This is going to be a game changer, sir. Exactly what this city needs."

"Let's hope so," Devlin muttered. "Assuming no one else screws up as badly as you have tonight."

Kira had heard enough. She backed away from the doors and retreated down the hallway toward the stairwell. When she tried to hold the railing to keep from tripping in her dress, her hand was shaking so badly she could hardly grip it.

Everything Lucas had told her was a lie. He was a soldier. A killer. She'd spent most of the week with him. She'd told him things about Haven. About Will.

She'd even let him kiss her, however briefly.

And her father...

Her father still looked at her and saw a traitor. He believed her return to the city and her decision to become a Volunteer were all part of some plot against him.

And now he was planning something for tonight. Something at the Stadium. Something involving a prisoner.

She descended the stairs on unsteady legs, one hand braced against the railing for support. When she reached the first floor, she paused in the empty corridor, trying to decide what to do next. What would happen if she didn't return to the Ball? What would happen if she left the mansion and walked back to Rolling Meadows? How far would she get before someone came after her?

And could she risk it?

Could she risk her father's assumption that she'd been trying to escape the city and her fate, and not just the Ball?

Not with Teddy's life hanging in the balance.

When she re-entered the Grand Hall, she moved through the crowd like a ghost, nodding and smiling when saluted, greeting the gathered dignitaries with as much enthusiasm as she could muster, and playing the role of Volunteer to the best of her ability, yet she felt completely detached from every interaction.

If only tomorrow would come more quickly. She just wanted it to be over. The waiting, the pretending, the lingering in this terrible half-state between life and death. What was the point of clinging so tightly to these final hours when they offered her nothing but more pain?

One servant approached with a silver tray and offered her a glass of champagne. Kira took it with numb fingers and lifted it to her lips. She had nearly finished the entire glass, trying to calm her racing thoughts, when a hush fell over the crowd.

All heads turned toward the front of the room.

Victor Devlin stood in the center of the dance floor.

"Distinguished guests and citizens of Vita Nova, please forgive the interruption of tonight's festivities, but there is an important matter that demands your attention. If the last twelve years have taught us anything, it's that survival comes at a substantial cost. In our great city, sacrifice is not only encouraged... it's necessary."

The crowd murmured their agreement, some raising their champagne glasses in salute.

"Although tonight is for celebrating my daughter's bravery and selflessness," Devlin continued, "I can think of no better time to remind this city why the Compulsory and Volunteer Programs were established in the first place. Ultimately, they were designed to protect Vita Nova, to preserve our way of life."

Kira felt herself being pulled forward, almost against her will. She pushed through the crowd, her shoulders and elbows bumping into others, hardly noticing the glares that followed her.

Her eyes were locked on her father.

"Tonight, I think it's fitting to give you a glimpse of what awaits those who threaten our way of life, whether from outside —or inside—the barricade." Victor gestured toward the far wall, where an enormous broadcast screen descended from the ceiling. "Those who align themselves with the Lawless, those who would betray their own city for personal gain, will no longer go unpunished."

The broadcast screen flickered to life.

Kira's champagne glass slipped from her fingers and shattered on the floor.

The Stadium loomed under the glare of the floodlights, its field scarred with muddy patches and trampled grass. At its center, a wooden platform rose from the earth, seemingly hastily assembled from rough planks and rusted nails.

And on that platform...

Jonesy.

He was almost unrecognizable. He wore tattered pants and a filthy tank top that did little to hide the purple and black bruises that covered most of his body. One eye was swollen completely shut, while the other was barely open. Blood crusted at his hairline and extended down the side of his neck.

Even through the grainy broadcast feed, Kira could see the defiance in his posture. He refused to let his body sag, forcing himself to stand tall, his back and shoulders straight despite the obvious pain written across his face.

And his chin...

It was raised as high as the noose around his neck would allow.

Chapter Thirty-Eight

The classical music broadcasting from the Volunteer Ball cut off abruptly, as if someone had yanked the radio's power cord. In the strange silence that followed, Ghost glanced at Will. The kid looked as nervous as he felt. They both knew something was coming, and it wasn't good.

And then Victor Devlin's voice filled the void.

"Distinguished guests and citizens of Vita Nova, please forgive the interruption of tonight's festivities, but there is an important matter that demands your attention. If the last twelve years have taught us anything, it's that survival comes at a substantial cost. In our great city, sacrifice is not only encouraged... it's necessary."

The van picked up speed, Will's hands tightening on the steering wheel. Ghost could feel the tension radiating off the younger man like heat from a furnace.

"What is this?" Ghost asked. "Is this normal?"

"No."

"Tonight," Devlin continued, *"I think it's fitting to give you a glimpse of what awaits those who threaten our way of life, whether from outside—or inside—the barricade. Those who align themselves with the Lawless, those who would betray their own city for personal gain, will no longer go unpunished."*

There was a pause in the broadcast—one that seemed to stretch on for hours. Ghost reached for the volume on the radio, intending to turn it up in case they were missing something. And then a single, sharp sound echoed through the van.

The sound of glass breaking.

"What's happening?" Will leaned closer to the radio as if proximity might give him a clearer picture of events unfolding miles away. "What's he doing?"

"I don't know."

An unfamiliar voice emerged from the speaker, roughened by pain and exhaustion but still carrying an unmistakable tone of defiance. The audio quality was poor and distant, as if the microphone was picking up sound from across a large space.

"Can you hear me, Devlin?" the voice called out. *"I know you can see me, but can you hear me, you scumbag?"*

Ghost lurched against the seat as the van swerved sharply to the right, his foot slamming uselessly against the floor where the brakes would've been if he were driving. They missed an abandoned car by inches.

He shot Will a sharp look. "What's your problem?"

But the kid's eyes weren't on the road anymore—they were locked on the radio.

"Oh no... oh God, please..."

"What is it?"

"That's Jonesy. He's my—" Will dragged a hand through his hair. "He's my... boss."

Ghost could sense the energy shifting in the younger man.

It felt like an electrical current building toward a dangerous discharge. He watched Will's chest rising and falling in rapid, shallow breaths and could see his hands beginning to shake on the steering wheel.

This Jonesy—whoever he was—was more to Will than a boss. And because Ghost already had a pretty good idea of what was coming next, he grabbed the kid's arm.

"Pull the van over. Right now."

But Will pressed harder on the gas, his eyes darting between the dark road and the radio, as if speed alone could get him to the city in time to stop whatever was coming.

"They're gonna find out the truth about you, Devlin." There was something in Jonesy's tone Ghost recognized instantly. It was the sound of a man who'd accepted his fate and had nothing left to lose. *"You're a murderer. And your days are numbered."*

Devlin's voice, urgent and angry, muffled in the background. *"Cut the audio."*

"They'll find out what you did," Jonesy continued, his voice growing louder. *"They'll find out about the Tenements, about all the innocent people you've murdered in this city. You know why? Because the truth always comes—"*

The old man's voice cut off abruptly, replaced by dead air.

Ghost realized Devlin had cut the audio feed. There shouldn't have been sound at all. Someone had screwed up royally, and they would probably pay for that mistake with their life.

"Will, pull over."

But the kid was beyond hearing him now. His foot pressed harder on the accelerator, pushing the van past seventy. The old vehicle protested the speed, its worn struts groaning as they hit deep ruts in the road. The van swayed alarmingly from side to side, but Will didn't seem to notice, oblivious to everything except the voices coming from the radio.

Devlin spoke again. *"The convicted, Hank Jones, has been found guilty of treason against Vita Nova. Guilty of conspiring with the Lawless to bomb the Tenements. Guilty of transporting a condemned Confines prisoner into the Unregulated Zone. Guilty of aiding and abetting the kidnapping of a young Volunteer. His sentence is death, to be carried out immediately."*

A chorus of confused voices filled the van, and Ghost realized he was listening to the reactions of the people at the Volunteer Ball. They had come for a party—to celebrate another willing sacrifice—not to witness an execution.

They had no idea what they were about to see.

The van hit a pothole hard enough to rattle Ghost's teeth. They were going to crash if Will didn't slow down.

"Pull over!" This time, Ghost used his command voice—the tone that he'd used on soldiers in combat. "Right now!"

The words finally seemed to register. Will eased his foot off the accelerator, and the van shuddered to a stop in the middle of the road, headlights illuminating a rotting deer's carcass a few hundred meters ahead.

If they'd hit that deer at full speed, the van would've flipped, for sure.

"Let this serve as a warning," Devlin continued, *"to anyone who has considered aligning themselves with our enemies."*

There was a moment of perfect, terrible silence.

Then came a sharp, collective intake of breath, followed by a scatter of panicked cries and horrified gasps from the crowd. Ghost couldn't see what they were seeing, but his mind filled in the blanks: the sudden drop, the snap of the rope, the body swinging in that awful, jerking arc.

And then, cutting through the noise, came a single, raw scream of anguish that Ghost recognized instantly.

Kira.

Will cursed and slammed his fists on the steering wheel. He doubled over in his seat, his body wracked with sobs.

Ghost reached out, resting a steady hand on Will's trembling back, but it wasn't enough. So he unbuckled and leaned across the console, pulling the kid into his arms. Will didn't resist.

"I'm so sorry, son."

Through the radio, they could hear Victor Devlin trying to regain control of his horrified audience. *"Citizens of Vita Nova, what you have witnessed tonight is justice in its truest form. We live in a beautiful city, but that beauty can be deceptive. It can cause us to forget what we're really fighting against. We cannot allow ourselves to become complacent—"*

Ghost snapped off the radio.

"We'll make him pay," he whispered, squeezing Will's shoulder. "I give you my word, son. That man will answer for what he's done. But we have to keep going now. Kira needs us."

Will lifted his head, his eyes meeting Ghost's. The grief was still there, but it was crystallizing into something harder, something more dangerous. He gave Ghost a single, silent nod, then pulled away, wiped his face with the back of his hand, and shifted the van back into drive.

The city's lights grew brighter as they approached the black ribbon of the Susquehanna. For ten years, Ghost had watched those lights from the darkness of the far bank, while Madison lived and died beneath them. He'd imagined this return countless times, dreamed of walking those streets again and facing the man who had marked his face and ruined his life.

One of his favorite verses from Proverbs came to mind: *A wise man scales the city of the mighty... and brings down the stronghold in which they trust.*

He'd never much thought of himself as wise, but he had something Devlin didn't. The Lord was on his side.

So he would scale Vita Nova's walls and bring down Devlin's stronghold.

A reckoning was coming... and it was coming tonight.

Chapter Thirty-Nine

Jonesy's body hung on the broadcast screen, unmoving.

Kira turned away, no longer able to bear the sight of his empty eyes. Someone bumped into her in their hurry to get to the door—whether to leave or to be sick, she didn't know—and she stumbled sideways. Glass crunched under her heel, and she looked down to see the broken pieces of her champagne flute scattered across the floor.

Around her, the Grand Hall had fallen into a stunned silence. The festive atmosphere of a few minutes earlier was gone. The painted, confident faces of Vita Nova's elite had gone pale, their smiles wiped away. A woman near the front was shaking so badly that her wine was sloshing over the rim of the glass and spreading across the fabric of her dress. A cluster of older men were whispering to each other, their expressions pinched and angry. And everywhere Kira looked, people seemed to be inching toward the exit, not wanting to leave but eager to get away from the image of the dead man on the screen.

And then a voice cried out, breaking the silence.

"Victor!"

All eyes turned to the head table, where Chandra Devlin stood holding her twins against her sides, their faces buried in the fabric of her dress as if trying to shield them from the screen.

But it was too late. Both children were crying.

They had seen.

The look Chandra gave her husband was pure venom, years of pent-up anger finally rising to the surface. Kira could practically see the fury radiating from the woman's every pore, shimmering like heat rising off a city street. The First Lady's composure was fracturing in real time, in front of the entire city.

Kira stared at her, waiting for the woman to unleash the truth for all to hear. To tell the entire city about the falsified Compulsory Orders. About the bombing of the Tenements. About the Patrols murdering innocent people at Devlin's command in the Unregulated Zone.

But then Chandra's eyes moved from Devlin to the broadcast screen, where her own horrified face now replaced Jonesy's hanging body. For a moment, she just stared, as if recognizing herself for the first time. Then something shifted. She seemed to remember the part she was expected to play—the part she had been playing for so long it had become a prison.

"I need to put the children to bed," she announced. "They're very tired. Please excuse me."

Kira's heart sank as the First Lady of Vita Nova headed toward the exit with her children in tow, every eye following her retreat.

Chandra's words from the other night rose up in Kira's mind: *There are worse prisons than this one.*

As his family disappeared into the hallway, Devlin cleared his throat and brought the microphone to his lips. "Ladies and gentlemen," he began. "I apologize for the unexpected nature of tonight's proceedings. But what you just witnessed was justice, plain and simple. I will not apologize for that. Anyone who threatens our way of life will face a similar fate. With that being said, perhaps it's time we return to celebrating this evening's true purpose—honoring my daughter's brave Sacrifice for our city."

But his words fell flat, the spell he usually cast so effortlessly seemingly broken. A handful of people nodded, but their eyes remained distant, still processing what they had just seen.

Before the silence could stretch too long, Sienna Graves left her husband's side and positioned herself next to Devlin. She took the microphone from his hands. "Ladies and gentlemen, we are Vita Nova. We are strong, and we will survive. Let us show the entire city our strength tonight."

She turned to the string quartet. "Play something lively, please."

The musicians exchanged uneasy glances before lifting their instruments. They struck up a jaunty waltz that sounded obscene in the wake of what had just occurred, the bright notes like forced laughter at a funeral. Nothing could have represented Vita Nova better than this desperate attempt to cover up the horror of murder with opulence and music.

Kira studied the faces around her. These were the people who had built and maintained a system rigged for their own survival, who had grown comfortable sacrificing others to preserve their way of life. But they'd forgotten what real death looked like. Despite the best efforts of the mayor and his deputy, they weren't quite ready to pick up their champagne glasses and glide onto the dance floor.

They were waiting for someone to tell them how to feel and how to react to what they'd just witnessed.

And Kira knew it had to be her.

Without thinking, she pushed her way through the crowd, her yellow dress a bright slash of color against the sea of blue formal wear. Confused faces turned toward her, but she ignored them, eyes locked on the center of the dance floor where her father stood next to Sienna Graves. The woman was still clutching the microphone like a lifeline while the quartet droned on behind her.

Devlin spotted Kira advancing. His eyes tracked her like a predator watching its prey. As she approached, he forced a smile onto his face and extended his hand. Perhaps he thought she meant to join him in his damage control, to play the role of obedient daughter one last time.

Instead, Kira strode straight up to Sienna and yanked the microphone out of her grip. The quartet faltered and fell silent, the last notes hanging awkwardly in the air.

She turned to face the crowd and the cameras. Hundreds of eyes stared back at her. Beyond the walls of the mansion, thousands more would be watching her from their broadcast screens. Kira thought of Teddy, safe in his home with his mother. Was he watching her right now?

She could not say anything that might endanger him, and she could not directly challenge her father's authority.

But she *could* honor Jonesy.

And she could reclaim this moment from her father's narrative and turn it into something else.

"Citizens of Vita Nova," she began, not knowing what she was going to say even as the words left her mouth. "We all saw what just happened. A man just died before our eyes. You don't have to care about him. Most of you didn't even know him. But when you go home tonight, please don't lie to yourselves about what you witnessed."

Her words sent a ripple of confusion through the crowd.

This wasn't the script they had expected. Not from a Volunteer on her final night.

"Because I'm a Volunteer, you think I deserve your reverence. But I don't. I'm not noble or brave. I just made a choice I could live with. But the man you all just watched die—Hank Jones—was indeed both noble *and* brave. He risked his life to rescue an orphan boy from the Unregulated Zone. He became a father to someone who had no one left. He was worthy of your reverence.... and he didn't deserve what just happened to him."

A few feet away, Sienna Graves stood rigid beside Devlin, her red lips slightly parted as if she wanted to interrupt but was struggling to find the right words.

"Hank Jones's only crime against this city," Kira continued, her voice growing stronger, "was to rescue his son who'd been condemned to die. Not because he was a terrorist or a traitor, but because he loved someone else enough to risk everything to save them. That's what a real father does. He sacrifices himself for his children. He doesn't ask his children to sacrifice themselves for him."

She turned to look directly at Devlin, meeting his cold gray eyes with her own, and saw his face flush red. The words had hit their intended target.

But she wasn't finished.

Kira's gaze swept across the crowd. "When you watch the fireworks on Sunday night, I don't want you to remember me. I want you to remember Hank Jones instead. Remember him as a loving father who died so his son could live."

She handed the microphone back to her father, her fingers brushing against his as he took it. She felt the tremor in his hands and saw the fury in his eyes—and something else, something that looked almost like fear.

Glancing down at her wrist, she saw the blue rose corsage

that had marked her as a willing sacrifice. Knowing the eyes of the city were still on her, she unclipped the corsage and held it in her palm. The ribbon had frayed, and the petals were wilting, curling at the edges in a slow, ugly death.

This was what they wanted her to be—beautiful, compliant, doomed. A symbol they could applaud and then bury.

She let the rose fall to the floor.

Then she left the Grand Hall and headed for the exit.

No one tried to stop her.

She pushed open the heavy doors of the Executive Mansion and stepped out into the night air. When she reached the end of the driveway, Front Street stretched out before her, empty and silent. Everyone in Vita Nova was either still inside the mansion or huddled around their broadcast screens, trying to process what they had just seen.

For the first time in her life, Vita Nova was hers. She could walk down the very center of the road if she wanted. She could stand beneath any streetlight without a single soul to see her. She was no longer a spectacle, no longer their offering. Tonight, she was free in a way she'd never been.

She kicked off her heels, leaving them at the end of her father's driveway like discarded shackles, and began to walk.

There was only one place she wanted to go.

Chapter Forty

Kira's bare feet pressed against the cold metal grating of the Volunteer Memorial Bridge. Soft blue lights traced the iron trusses overhead, glowing in honor of the city's fallen Volunteers, whose ranks she would soon join. Her yellow dress fluttered behind her, a bright slash of defiance against all that mournful blue light.

She didn't look at the Stadium where Jonesy undoubtedly still hung in the center of the field. Instead, she kept walking, heading for the only place in the city where she had ever felt truly alive. The place where she and Will had shared their first kiss. Where she'd first tasted the sweetness of rebellion and glimpsed the possibility of another life. A life beyond Vita Nova's concrete walls, beyond her father's reach.

Tonight she would climb the chain-link fence one last time. She wouldn't wait to be offered as a Sacrifice. She wouldn't let her father or the city dictate the terms of her death. She would choose her ending.

Kira stepped off the metal grating and onto the concrete walkway. She wrapped her fingers around the rusting railing and leaned forward to stare down into the river below. It was deep and fast-moving, its surface as black and slick as oil. She imagined herself in all of that blackness, being swallowed whole. She knew the weight of her dress would drag her down quickly, the heavy fabric pulling her under before she could change her mind.

That was the point.

Her grip on the railing tightened until the metal bit into her palms. She let her eyes drift shut for a moment, imagining the freedom of letting go. Of no longer playing the obedient daughter in a city that demanded her death.

Just one last choice. One that belonged to her.

Once she climbed the fence and made her way to the far edge of the bridge, she wouldn't hesitate. She would simply keep walking and step off the bridge's fractured ledge. She would feel the wind rush past her face and tear at her dress as she fell. And in that last breath before she hit the black water, she would picture herself somewhere else entirely.

In Haven.

Living with Will, Teddy, Grace, and Ghost.

She wasn't sure if heaven was real. But if it was, she hoped it looked a little like that village beyond the barricade.

A low rumble of an engine broke the silence.

Kira turned from the railing to see headlights cutting through the darkness, a black car driving on the pedestrian walkway. She froze, squinting against the glare as a vehicle rolled to a stop a few yards away from the fence.

The door swung open, and Lucas climbed out, his eyes locked on her. He didn't call her name or ask why she was there. He just stood there, silent and patient, as if he had all night to watch her.

Rage burned in her chest at the sight of him. Of course he would come here. Of course he had to violate the one place in the entire city where she might have found a shred of peace. His presence was like poison seeping into her last moments on earth, contaminating them.

"How did you find me?"

Lucas didn't move closer. He stayed ten feet away, hands buried in his pockets, his gaze sweeping over her bare feet and her yellow dress. He let out a disappointed sigh. "You shouldn't be out here, you know. It's not safe after what you just did."

"Go away." She tried to keep her voice calm, not wanting to provoke him. "Please just leave me alone. I'll walk back to Rolling Meadows when I'm ready."

"Why? So you can try to escape again?" He tilted his head. "Like last time. With the kid?'

In the pale blue light of the bridge, she saw Lucas clearly for the first time. There was no hint of charm to be found. The careful mask he'd worn all week had fallen away completely, revealing the real man underneath.

The one who had killed Avery.

"That wasn't me. That was Emma, remember?"

A smirk played across his lips. "Still sticking to that story? Some friend you are, letting her take the fall for your crimes."

She took a step back, trying to put more distance between them. "What about you? Pretending to care. Pretending to be my advocate while spying for my father. You lied about everything. Your job, your background, your family. You're in the Patrols, Lucas."

He reached up and loosened his tie. "Does it really matter? I did my job well, didn't I? And you certainly didn't seem to mind all the attention I was giving you. Especially tonight. I almost had you in that hallway. Don't lie. You were almost mine, at least for tonight. What would your Lawless boyfriend think of you now?"

Be careful, a voice whispered in her mind. *He's dangerous.*

"You win, alright?" she said, forcing her voice to remain steady. "I'll go back to Rolling Meadows. You can park yourself outside my door all night if that's what you want, to make sure I don't try anything." She drew in a shaky breath. "But please— just give me a few minutes alone here. At least let me walk out to the end of the bridge one last time. You can wait for me by the fence if you're worried I might try something." And then, for good measure, she added, "It's my final request."

Lucas moved closer, so close she could smell his cologne. When he spoke again, his voice was soft, almost pitying. "Oh Kira... you were never a real Volunteer. Don't you see that yet? If you hadn't volunteered, your father would've just found another way to get rid of you. That was always the plan. And after you're gone..." He gave her a little shrug. "He'll still find a reason to kill the kid."

For a moment, she felt lightheaded, like she couldn't draw a breath. Of course her father had never intended to honor their deal. Of course Teddy was probably still going to die. She'd been a fool to believe even for a second that Victor Devlin could keep his word about anything.

Kira turned away from Lucas and gripped the railing. She thought about hauling her body over the side right then, fast enough that he wouldn't have time to grab her.

But her eyes caught movement in the distance.

A transport van was turning onto the far end of the Market Street Bridge, headlights dim, rolling toward the checkpoint in the center of the bridge.

As she watched, the van came to a stop and the driver's window rolled down.

The dashboard light caught the side of the driver's face, highlighting the line of his jaw, the slight tilt of his head, and the shape of his mouth. Even with his face half-hidden in shadows, she knew him.

She would've known him anywhere.

"Will," she breathed.

Lucas appeared at her side, his eyes following her gaze across the water. "What? Is that—?"

Kira opened her mouth to scream, to call out across the water, to warn Will to turn back before it was too late. But before the sound could escape, Lucas's hand clamped down on her arm and yanked her away from the railing.

"You planned this whole thing, didn't you?" He spat the words at her. "That's why you came out here? You were waiting for him!"

Kira twisted, trying to wrench herself free, but his grip was too strong. "Let go of me!"

"I should have known. Should have seen through your innocent little act." His free hand shot to her throat, fingers digging in, pressing hard enough to make every breath a struggle. "Your father was right about you."

Black spots danced at the edges of her vision. She clawed at his hand, nails biting into his wrist, wanting only to breathe. But Lucas was much stronger than her, and the panic was making it difficult to think clearly.

"I'm done babysitting you," he growled, his face inches from hers. "I'm done playing nice. I'm not ending up in the Confines for you or anyone else."

Still choking her, he began dragging her backward toward his car. Kira fought him with everything she had left, kicking and clawing. Her bare feet skidded and slipped on the grating, scraping her heels raw.

She twisted her head just enough to free her mouth for a single moment.

"WILL!"

She screamed his name across the water, throwing every ounce of strength and hope into the sound.

And then Lucas threw her against the car... and his fist crashed into her jaw.

Pain detonated behind her eyes, bright and searing. The world pitched sideways, the bridge and the river and the distant lights smearing into a kaleidoscope of color and motion.

Her last clear thought was of Will—of whether he'd heard her.

And then there was nothing but darkness.

Chapter Forty-One

Ghost crouched in the cramped space behind the driver's seat, his shotgun balanced across his knees. The disposal van reeked of disinfectant and death—a nauseating combination that would have made most men sick—but Ghost had breathed worse air.

Will sat in the driver's seat wearing a black neck gaiter that Ghost had packed for him. It covered the lower half of his face. It wasn't much of a disguise, but it would hopefully be enough to keep the Guards at the checkpoint from looking too closely.

He felt the van turn onto the Market Street Bridge. Now the only thing separating Ghost from Vita Nova was a quarter mile of asphalt and a couple of poorly trained Guards.

The plan was simple, which in Ghost's experience usually meant it would fall apart within the first few seconds.

He'd stay hidden in the back while Will did all the talking. According to Will, it wasn't unusual for disposal drivers to wear bandanas or neck gaiters to block the smell, and if God was on their side, the Guards wouldn't be familiar enough with Will to recognize him by his eyes alone. If they were distracted—which they probably would be, especially if news of the hanging had reached them—they might just wave the van through without a second glance.

But if something went wrong, Ghost would be ready with the shotgun.

He would do whatever was necessary.

Will muttered something under his breath.

"What?"

"I see four Guards." Will's voice was muffled by the fabric covering his mouth. "There should only be two."

Ghost shifted as much as he could, his knees banging into the back of the driver's seat as he peered through the gap between Will's shoulder and the headrest. Sure enough, four figures moved around the checkpoint, their rifles slung over their shoulders, their SUV parked on the opposite side of the barrier.

It made sense that Devlin would double the number of Guards the night before Kira's execution. He was probably expecting trouble. He hadn't held onto power this long by being careless.

"Doesn't matter," Ghost whispered. "The plan hasn't changed."

"Okay."

Even if there had been two dozen Guards at the checkpoint, he would not have turned back.

Never again.

The van came to a stop, and Will rolled down his window. One of the Guards approached the vehicle, squinting at Will.

"You the last disposal run tonight?" the Guard asked.

"I'm the last." Will's voice held just the right combination of exhaustion and resignation. "I hate these nighttime runs, you know? Freaks me out, being at the pit after dark. Give me daylight runs any day."

Ghost listened from his hiding spot, marveling at Will's performance. He sounded completely at ease, just another weary disposal worker grumbling about his shift. There wasn't a hint of the anguish that had to be tearing him apart inside at the loss of Jonesy. No tremor in his voice. Nothing to suggest he was anyone other than exactly who he appeared to be.

The kid could've been an actor.

The Guard chuckled, using his hand to wipe his nose. "Can't say as I blame you, although you couldn't pay me enough to drive out there during the day, either." He leaned closer to the window. "You wearing that mask because of the smell?"

Ghost remembered a line from one of Madison's favorite movies.

People in masks cannot be trusted.

"Yeah. Real bad batch tonight. One must've been dead for a while before they loaded him up. It's a mess back there. Going to spray down the cargo area when I get back to the lot."

The Guard practically jumped away from the van, disgust wrinkling his features. "Nasty, man." He waved at another Guard who was manning the boom barrier. "Alright, go on through and—"

A scream tore through the air.

"WILL!"

The blood in Ghost's veins turned to ice. He pushed himself up just enough to see through the windshield. Three of the four Guards had abandoned their posts, their attention focused not on the van but on the bridge leading to City Island.

The Guard who had been talking to Will had left the side of the van and was jogging toward the railing with his rifle raised.

Across the water, two figures were illuminated by the soft blue lights of the pedestrian bridge. One was small and blonde, wearing what looked like a yellow dress—bright against the bleak, metallic span of the bridge. Even at this distance, the color was vivid, like a beacon, impossible to miss.

Kira.

The other was larger, broader, and dressed in either a dark suit or tuxedo. Ghost could do nothing but watch, his hands clenching the shotgun, as the man threw Kira against a black vehicle idling nearby and punched her in the face.

Will's hand shot toward the door handle. "That's Kira!"

Ghost lunged forward, his hand closing around the kid's shoulder like a vise, yanking him back into his seat before he could do something stupid.

"This is our chance," he spoke through gritted teeth. "Drive."

The boom barrier stretched across their path like a red and white striped arm, still lowered, still blocking their way into the city. But that didn't matter anymore. They had one shot at this, one moment while the Guards were distracted.

"But she's—"

"Drive!"

The Guards were still focused on the other bridge, pointing and shouting to each other, trying to make sense of what they were seeing. Only one remained in front of the boom barrier, but his attention was elsewhere.

Ghost vaulted over the seat divider and landed hard beside Will. He brought his boot down hard on top of the kid's foot, jamming the accelerator to the floor.

The van lurched forward, the diesel engine roaring as the vehicle headed straight for the metal barrier. The Guard spun around just in time to see three tons of government vehicle bearing down on him.

He threw himself sideways, rolling across the ground as the van's front bumper connected with the barrier in an explosion of twisted metal and shattered plastic. It snapped like a toothpick, one half spinning away into the darkness while the other half scraped along the van's roof like claws.

Ghost twisted in his seat to check the status of the Guards through the rearview mirror.

All four were raising their rifles.

The first shot took out their rear window. Ghost couldn't see it, but he heard it: safety glass shattering inside the van's empty cargo area. The second punched through the van's back doors with a metallic thunk, the bullet embedding itself somewhere in the bulkhead behind Ghost's back.

"Go, go, go!" he yelled.

Will didn't need encouragement. The van's engine responded with a surge of power despite the damage, carrying them across the bridge as muzzle flashes erupted behind them. The mangled front bumper scraped against the roadway, creating a terrible screeching symphony of metal on asphalt.

"There!" Will pointed toward the Volunteer Memorial Bridge, at the black sedan pulling away from the bridge's entrance. "We can follow them."

Ghost squinted through the windshield, his heart sinking as the red dots of light turned a corner, disappearing into the maze of city streets. "We'll find her," he said, pulling his pack around to his chest. "But first you need to jackknife this van at the end of the bridge."

"What?" Will's eyes darted between Ghost and the windshield. "We're going to lose her!"

He checked the rearview mirror again. The Guards had stopped firing and were sprinting toward the SUV.

"We'll definitely lose her with those Guards on our tail. Trust me. Block the road. Stay to the middle."

Ghost reached inside the pack, his fingers closing around the plastic explosive. Two blocks of C4 and a simple timer mechanism that he'd liberated from the Ammunition Supply Point at Fort Indiantown Gap during a scavenging run three years back. He had hidden them in his cabin, wrapped in oiled cloth, waiting for a rainy day when he might need them.

Tonight definitely qualified.

"What is that?" Will's eyes widened as understanding dawned. "You're going to blow up the bridge?"

"Just a little explosion to slow them down." Ghost checked the timer. He'd give them ten seconds to get clear. Any longer, and they risked the Guards getting past the van. "No going back now, kid."

When they reached the far end of the bridge, Will yanked the wheel hard to the right, sending the van into a controlled skid. The rear wheels came around, and the vehicle jackknifed across the roadway, blocking the middle lanes with its length. Steam hissed from the damaged radiator as Will cut the engine and threw open his door.

"How long?"

"Ten seconds." Ghost ducked under the van's chassis to plant the charges against the fuel tank. He armed the detonator and rolled out from beneath the vehicle. "Run fast, kid."

They left the van behind and sprinted across Front Street. Ghost counted off the seconds in his head—ten, nine, eight— and when he got to four seconds, he grabbed Will's arm and pulled him behind a concrete traffic barrier.

"Down!"

The explosion turned night into day. Ghost watched as a column of flame erupted skyward. The van disintegrated in a ball of superheated gas and twisted metal, windows bursting, metal skin peeling back like paper. Then the blast wave hit him like a shove, rattling the barrier he crouched behind and sending a hot wind roaring past his ears. He fell to the ground as burning debris arced through the air and clattered onto the surrounding pavement, leaving small fires where it landed.

Ghost didn't move, one arm braced across Will's back to keep him down until the worst of it passed. When he finally lifted his head, he saw a crater where the van had been, the asphalt buckled and split around the edges. But more importantly, a twenty-foot section of the roadway had collapsed entirely, concrete and rebar tumbling into the dark river below.

Through the smoke and flames, he could see the Guards' vehicle skidding to a stop at the edge of the destruction, its headlights illuminating the gaping hole. Two Guards climbed out and shouted to each other over the roar of the fire.

They could still make it across on foot.

He had bought them some time, but not much. They needed to move out now.

Will climbed to his feet, his eyes locked on the inferno they'd left behind. "A little explosion?"

Ghost only shrugged. "I've made bigger ones."

"You'll have to tell me that story sometime."

In the distance, sirens began to wail. Soon this place would be crawling with Guards, Patrol soldiers, and anyone else Devlin could muster.

"We need to go," Ghost said, shouldering his pack and checking his shotgun. "Right now."

They abandoned the street and fled into a narrow alley between two abandoned storefronts.

Behind him, the destroyed bridge marked the end of Ghost's banishment from Vita Nova. There would be no more running. No more hiding. No more allowing the people he loved to die inside these walls.

Ahead of him lay the streets of a city that had tried to erase him, and somewhere in that twisted maze waited Victor Devlin, a man who had no idea that his greatest mistake hadn't been scarring Ghost's face.

It had been letting him live.

Chapter Forty-Two

olling Meadows.

R That's what Will called it. What the entire city called it, apparently. In Ghost's day, this place had been an upscale inn and day spa on the outskirts of the city. He couldn't remember its old name. It wasn't a place he ever would've gone, even if he'd been able to afford it. A place where rich people went to relax, play golf, and get away from their city lives for a few days.

Now, people came here to die.

The front of the lodge was barely visible through the dense line of trees that ringed the property. Ghost crouched behind a maintenance shed, studying the building for signs of movement. He could sense, but not see, Will crouched a few feet away. The kid was a ball of nervous energy, a bomb ready to explode.

The lodge was quiet. Too quiet. It felt watchful.

Like it knew they were coming.

"Two Guards positioned at the front entrance," Ghost whispered. "There could be more inside."

Will shifted closer and peered around the side of the building. "I've never seen Guards here before. That means Kira's in there, right? She has to be."

Ghost wasn't so sure. Rolling Meadows was far too obvious a spot to take her. Whoever had grabbed Kira on the bridge and sped away with her wasn't just going to bring her back to the lodge to await her execution in the morning, especially now that the city's only remaining bridge had been partially destroyed and a transport van reduced to a pile of charred wreckage. Devlin knew something was happening, even if he didn't know what it was yet.

But they had to be sure.

"Service entrance," he said, pointing toward a side door partially hidden by overgrown hedges.

Will nodded. "Let's go."

They moved across the grass, keeping low and making use of the carefully trimmed hedges for cover. Ghost kept his eyes locked on the two Guards out front, but they never even glanced in his direction. Instead, they stood close together, heads bent toward each other in conversation.

He didn't like it.

Complacent Guards meant Rolling Meadows wasn't on high alert—which probably meant Kira wasn't inside.

At the side of the building, Ghost tested the service door. It was unlocked. Another bad sign.

They slipped inside and eased the door shut behind them. Ghost waited a moment, allowing his eyes a few seconds to adjust to the darkness. The kitchen was empty, stainless steel surfaces gleaming in the darkness. How many last meals had been prepared and served in this place?

They picked their way through a maze of industrial ovens and massive refrigerators, heading toward the soft glow of light drifting into the room from two small glass windows located high on a pair of swinging doors. Ghost could only assume those doors led into the dining room.

As they approached the doors, Ghost paused, raising a hand to stop Will. He heard something coming from just outside the room.

Whispered voices. Low and urgent.

He motioned for Will to stay back as he approached the doors. He rose on his toes and peered through one of the small windows, trying to get a view of what lay beyond.

Through the glass, he could see several figures huddled around one table in the dimly lit dining room. They appeared to be staff members, judging by their identical black and blue uniforms. Four people, all women except for one young man, who kept glancing nervously toward the windows. They all looked worried. He caught only snippets of their conversation.

"...shouldn't have come in here like that."

"...tried to tell them."

"...has something to do with the hanging?"

Ghost scanned the room one more time through the glass, checking the corners and doorways. He didn't see any Guards lurking around, and he doubted these people would talk openly if there were. When he was satisfied the people gathered around the table were alone, he pushed the swinging door open and stepped into the dining room, his weapon raised but not aimed directly at the group.

"Nobody move."

The group let out a collective gasp, their chairs scraping against the hardwood floor as they instinctively recoiled from the armed stranger who had turned up in their midst. The worry on their faces morphed into fear at the sight of the shotgun.

All except for one.

An older woman with salt-and-pepper hair pulled back into

a bun slowly rose from her seat, her hands gripping the edge of the table for support. Unlike the others, she didn't appear to be afraid of Ghost or his shotgun.

The woman looked him straight in the eye. "Who are you?" she demanded. "What are you doing sneaking around my kitchen?"

Ghost lowered his weapon slightly, trying to appear less threatening. "I'm not here to hurt anyone, ma'am. I'm just looking for Kira Liebert. Do you know where she is?"

"Are you with the Patrols?"

"I'd rather be dead, ma'am."

"Good answer. Are you a Guard?"

"No, ma'am. Just a friend of Kira's."

Some of the tension bled out of the woman's body. "Well, if you find her, please let me know," she said, crossing her arms. "She hasn't returned from the Volunteer Ball. A group of Guards blew through here about an hour ago, tearing everything apart. I tried to tell them she wasn't here, but they destroyed several of my rooms looking for her."

Will appeared next to Ghost, his rifle slung over his shoulder. "Mrs. Fleming? Do you remember me?"

The woman's eyes widened, and she moved closer, as if unable to believe what she was seeing. "Of course I remember you, Will Foster. I never forget any of my Volunteers. And you better call me Adeline if you know what's good for you."

Ghost shouldered his weapon. "Ma'am, we saw Kira earlier on the bridge to City Island. She tried to call out to Will, but someone in a dark vehicle grabbed her and sped off with her. He was pretty far away, but I think the guy had blond hair... and he was wearing a suit."

"Lucas Pine," Adeline said right away. "That sounds like her advocate, Lucas Pine. You say he grabbed her?"

"Yes. Where can we find him?"

Adeline shook her head, her hand going to her throat. She looked genuinely distressed. "I have no idea. I don't know anything about him beyond his name. The advocates rarely spend much time at Rolling Meadows, but Lucas showed up here often to drive her places." She glanced at Will. "He drove her to the Ball tonight, which I thought was a little strange, but everything seemed fine between them."

"Is he working for her father?" Will asked. "This advocate of hers?"

"I don't know," Adeline shrugged. "I suppose it's possible. I've never seen him around here before this week, but I just assumed—"

The door leading into the lobby blew inward with a crash that sent splinters of wood flying across the floor. A dozen armed figures in matte-black tactical gear stormed through the opening, assault rifles raised. A cluster of red laser dots bloomed in the center of Ghost's chest. Instinct took over. He shoved himself in front of Will, blocking as many of the dots as he could.

He edged backwards, moving them both toward the swinging doors. Ready to shove Will through and make a break for it. But a glance over his shoulder stopped him cold. Through the small windows, he saw the beams made by tactical flashlights. The Patrols were coming from that direction too. Not advancing but waiting. Probably hoping he tried to escape.

They were surrounded.

"Drop your weapons!" barked one of the Patrol soldiers, his features obscured by the bright light coming from the flashlight attached to his rifle.

Ghost's mind raced through their options. They could fight. His shotgun would easily cut down half of them before they even squeezed off a shot, and Will could turn his rifle on the ones trying to flank them in the kitchen.

But the civilians.

He looked at the cowering staff huddled against the walls. Innocent people who would be caught in the crossfire. He couldn't take that chance.

He dropped his shotgun onto the floor. "Put the rifle down, Will."

"What? No, we can't. What about Kira?"

"Give this one to God, kid," he said, lifting his hands in surrender and stepping away from the shotgun. "That's all we can do."

After a brief hesitation, Will did the same with his rifle.

"Get on your knees!" one of the Patrol soldiers ordered. "Hands behind your heads!"

The cold marble floor bit into Ghost's arthritic knees as he hit the deck. He forced himself to remain still, every instinct screaming at him to fight, to reach for the shotgun he'd abandoned on the floor. Will went down beside him, breathing hard. Ghost didn't dare turn to reassure him. There was nothing to say.

He thought of Kira. She was out there somewhere, depending on him, and he couldn't help her now. Not with guns in his face and his hands empty. *Give this one to God, kid.*

That's what he'd said to Will.

Now he'd have to do it himself.

Ghost laced his fingers behind his head and stared straight ahead as the circle of rifles closed in around them.

Chapter Forty-Three

Consciousness returned slowly, dragging Kira with it. Her jaw throbbed, the pain spreading through her skull. She blinked as the artificially bright world around her swam into focus. White walls. Fluorescent lights. The sharp, sterile smell of disinfectant.

Hospital, she thought. *I'm in a hospital.*

She tried to lift her head for a better look, but the world shifted sideways in a nauseating spiral that forced her to collapse back against the pillow. Her eyelids were impossibly heavy. She wanted so badly to go back to sleep. But she knew, in some deep, survival-focused part of her brain, that she needed to stay awake. Now more than ever.

She heard Teddy's voice in her mind: *Let's stay awake together, Kira.*

As her vision cleared, she took in more details. The walls were bare and colorless, institutional white. There was no medical equipment in sight. No monitors. No IV stands. None of the items that belonged in a hospital room.

Because this isn't a hospital.

She looked down at herself, expecting to see a hospital gown. Instead, the yellow gown still clung to her body. The silk was wrinkled, torn in places, and filthy. Dark stains smudged the golden fabric, although she couldn't tell if the stains were dirt or blood.

She looked like a broken doll.

The sight of the dress brought everything back in a rush. Being hauled across the concrete. Lucas's hand around her throat, cutting off her air supply. The explosion of pain when his fist connected with her jaw, and the darkness that followed.

"You awake?" a voice asked from somewhere to her left.

Kira turned her head slowly, fighting through the fog that seemed determined to curl itself around her brain.

Lucas sat in a plastic chair beside the bed, still wearing his tuxedo from the Ball, though the bow tie now hung loose around his neck and his wrinkled jacket was folded and hanging over the back of the chair. In his hands was a magazine. Something glossy that had once been colorful but now looked impossibly old, the edges yellowed with age.

He smiled, all charm and white teeth. As if the fight on the bridge had never happened. "Hey, beautiful. How are you feeling?"

She tried again to sit up, but the movement brought on another wave of dizziness, forcing her to lie back down.

"You hit me."

He crossed his legs and flipped to the next page in the magazine. "You gave me no choice. You kept fighting. I gave you a little something to help you relax." He gestured to her left arm, where she could now see a tiny red dot in the crook of her elbow. "This has been a hard week for you, Kira. Your father and I think maybe the stress has become too much for you. And as your advocate, it's my job to keep you calm."

That explained the fog in her head, the way her thoughts

moved like honey through her brain. He'd injected her with some kind of sedative. Probably the same drug they used to keep Compulsories compliant before their executions.

She still felt as if she were forgetting something.

Something important.

"I was trying to give you the best night of your life," Lucas continued. "It's important to me that you know that. Yes, I was keeping an eye on you for your father this week, but I really wanted to distract you from what was coming. Distract myself too, I guess. That's why I tried to kiss you back in the hallway. You weren't supposed to see the hanging. We were supposed to be gone before it started. But you had to go and ruin everything."

The hanging.

It came rushing back in a flash of devastating images, breaking her heart all over again. Jonesy standing on the makeshift gallows, defiant until the very end. The trapdoor opening beneath him. The sickening sound his body had made when it reached the end of the rope.

Tears slipped down her cheeks. "You murdered him."

Lucas laughed. "You think I have that kind of power? The whole spectacle was your father's idea. He thinks death has become too easy in this city. Too comfortable. People have forgotten what real death looks and sounds like, and they aren't afraid of it anymore. Anyone thinking about working against the city needs to understand that their death doesn't have to be pleasant."

"So... what?" Kira swallowed past the dry lump in her throat. "He's starting public hangings now?"

Lucas closed the magazine and leaned forward in his seat. "I don't know whether you've noticed or not, but things have been different lately. Your little rebellion is spreading to the general population. Right now, we only have two Volunteers scheduled for next week, and both of them are begging their advocates to get them out of it."

Despite the pain in her jaw, Kira felt a jolt of satisfaction at the news. Two Volunteers instead of the usual dozen or more. People were questioning the system for the first time in years. Even if she died in this room, she had accomplished something her father had never expected. She had put the first crack in his perfect, beautiful wall.

And cracks had a way of spreading.

"So, your father wanted to ratchet up the pressure a bit," Lucas continued, scratching the back of his neck. "Remind the citizens what happens when they cause problems. No more peaceful Somnumbutal deaths for prisoners and traitors. Now it's the gallows."

"And what about me? Is he going to hang me, too?"

"Even if he wanted to—which wouldn't surprise me—he knows he can't get away with hanging a Volunteer. Not even a troublemaker like you." Lucas stretched his long legs out in front of him, settling back into the plastic chair. "Then again, if he finds out that you had something to do with the chaos on the Market Street Bridge tonight—"

"Chaos?"

And then it came back to her.

The white van approaching the distant checkpoint on the other bridge, the driver's window rolling down, the unmistakable silhouette of the man behind the wheel.

Will.

He had come for her.

She tried again to push herself up in bed, and this time, her body cooperated enough that she could prop herself up on her elbows. "I saw a white transport van at the checkpoint on the other bridge. What happened to it?"

Lucas grinned. "Incinerated. Blown up."

The hope that had flared so briefly inside her chest wilted and died like the yellow dahlias in the old church in Emmitsburg, leaving behind a hollow ache that made her earlier despair at Jonesy's death seem like nothing in comparison. She pressed a shaking hand to her mouth to muffle the sob that escaped, her whole body trembling.

Will had come for her, even though she'd asked him not to. And now he was dead. Burned alive in that van. Probably right after watching her get dragged away.

"Oh, calm down," Lucas said with a chuckle, clearly enjoying watching her fall apart. "Don't start freaking out on me. The two men inside the van blew it up themselves. They must've been carrying some kind of explosives. Took out a good section of the Market Street Bridge in the process."

She stared at him, the tears cold on her cheeks. "You mean they're alive?"

"For now. But don't expect some dramatic rescue. Both men were captured after breaking into Rolling Meadows and taken to the Confines. They'll both hang as terrorists in the morning."

So this was it. Will was going to die. Whoever was with him—either Ghost or Brack—was going to die, too. And so would she. It was inevitable now. Her father would survive it all. He'd win.

The last of her defiance slipped away, and she lay there, staring at nothing, the yellow silk of her ruined dress pooling around her like a costume she couldn't take off.

"I'm sorry, Kira."

Lucas leaned forward to touch her hand, but she jerked it away. His expression tightened, the darkness edging back into his features. "You know," he said, "I was thinking that it's somewhat fitting for your life to end in this room."

"What are you talking about?"

"Don't you know where you are?"

She looked around, finally noticing details that had been hovering at the edge of her awareness. The position of the bed against the wall. The window behind Lucas, offering a view of the parking lot where she'd once sat in her car for hours, sobbing after her mother's death. And the clock above the door —its hands at just past three a.m.—the very same clock she'd watched as it ticked away the last minutes of her mother's life.

"Room 317," she whispered.

Lucas nodded. "Very good. All these rooms look the same. I wasn't sure you'd notice."

The walls seemed to close in around her, the sterile white surfaces pressing closer, suffocating her. She could almost see herself in that chair where Lucas sat now, gripping the arms until her fingers ached, trying not to vomit while the doctor calmly explained how her mother's death would happen.

Of course Lucas would bring her here.

Of course her father had told him about this room.

It wasn't enough to kill her. He wanted to break her first.

"We're going to do your injection tonight," Lucas said, glancing at his watch. "There's no point waiting until dawn, not after the incident at the bridge. There aren't any doctors or nurses on duty right now, but you don't exactly need medical training to give someone Somnumbutal. I mean, what's the worst that could happen? You kill them?" He grinned at his own joke. "Anyway, I offered to do it myself, but someone else wanted the honor. He'll be here soon."

"Who?" Kira asked, though she already knew the answer. "Who's coming to kill me?"

Lucas's smile widened, the features she'd once mistaken for handsome turning almost demonic.

"Your father."

Chapter Forty-Four

The cell was a tomb he couldn't escape, the proof of his failure.

Ghost sat on the edge of the cot, cuffed hands useless and numb behind his back. Shackles secured his ankles to a chain anchored deep in the wall beneath the bed. They'd left him just enough slack to sit up, but not enough to stand, pace, or even reach the filthy toilet in the corner.

He touched the empty pocket where Madison's picture should have been. After the Patrols dragged him into the Confines, they had stripped him of everything but his clothes. His weapons, his radio, his pack—all gone. So was the wrinkled photograph he fell asleep holding every night.

He could still see the Patrol soldier's face as he held it up, turning it in his fingers, a slow, lecherous smile creeping across his mouth. "Who's the woman?"

Ghost had said nothing as he watched his most precious possession handled by someone who would never understand its worth. The soldier had left the room with the photograph, and it had probably been stuffed in an evidence box or thrown in the trash without a second thought.

Now he had nothing left of Madison but memories, and soon those would be gone, too.

Death was what he deserved. He'd failed again. Failed Madison. Failed her daughter. Failed the promise he'd made to himself that long-ago night when he'd been beaten, cut up, and left for dead on the other side of the barricade. For twelve years he'd imagined this moment, prepared for it. He'd trained his body, hardened his heart, and gathered weapons, allies, and the will to do whatever it took to avenge what had been stolen from him. But it had all been for nothing.

He leaned back against the concrete wall and closed his eyes. He wasn't afraid of the death he knew was coming. It would be a bad death, no question. Devlin would see to that. Probably something far worse than the gallows. But that didn't bother him.

Was there even such a thing as a good death?

When the end finally came, he'd face it without fear. Most people spent their lives running from death, but Ghost had spent the last twelve years chasing it. Praying for it every day, if only to finally be free of the pain.

He will wipe every tear from their eyes. There will be no more death or mourning or crying or pain, for the old order of things has passed away.

He wasn't afraid of hell, either. Even with all his failures, his battered soul clung to the hope that perhaps God's grace was bigger than his terrible sins. That redemption could reach even a broken soldier who had failed far too many people.

No, it wasn't his death he feared, but Kira's.

She wasn't his daughter by blood, but he loved her as if she were. He loved her because she was a piece of Madison that still existed in this world. Because when she smiled, he saw

Madison reflected in her eyes. And because she carried that same quiet steel her mother had—a hidden strength that stayed buried until the moment it was needed most.

He would trade his life for hers without hesitation, but he knew that wasn't a deal Devlin would accept.

"The Lord is my shepherd; I shall not want," he said quietly, reciting his mother's favorite Psalm. He could hear her voice even now, reading Scripture to him before the cancer took her and left him alone with a father who saw weakness in everything—especially prayer.

"He makes me lie down in green pastures. He leads me beside still waters."

A father who hadn't known what to do with his own sorrow and anger, so he'd used his fists and taken it out on his only son. A father who had only ever shown pride once: the day his son enlisted in the Army.

"He leads me in paths of righteousness for His name's sake."

It struck him how often fathers failed their children, in big ways and small. How many kids grew up learning fear instead of love? How easy it was to break something you were supposed to protect.

"Even though I walk through the valley of the shadow of death, I will fear no evil, for you are with me. Your rod and your staff, they comfort me."

He wondered if the cycle could be broken or if some men were doomed to repeat their fathers' failures. Maybe it was easier to pass on pain than to try to heal it. Maybe some men never learned how to do anything else.

"You prepare a table before me in the presence of my—"

Three loud raps on the cell door interrupted his prayer.

Through the small window in his cell door, a face appeared —one Ghost would have recognized anywhere, even after twelve years. The overhead light in the corridor lit up features that were older but no less cruel.

"Enemy," he finished.

The lock clicked and the door swung open. And there, after twelve years of exile and rage, stood Victor Devlin—the man who had carved Ghost's face and destroyed everything he'd ever loved.

Chapter Forty-Five

Devlin stepped into the cell, his suit perfectly pressed despite the early hour. But Ghost could see the hairline fractures in the man's polished facade. There were dark shadows under his eyes, his tie sat a fraction off-center, and his hair was slightly rumpled at the temples, as if he'd been running his fingers through it.

He looked like a man struggling to maintain control over something that was slowly slipping through his fingers.

"Noah Hale. I assumed you'd be long dead by now."

The muscles of Ghost's legs strained against the shackles bolted to the wall. He wanted to launch himself at Devlin, to get his hands around that little throat and squeeze until the life drained from his eyes. It would be murder, ugly and brutal—but it would be justified. No one else would have to die at Victor Devlin's hands.

But the chains held him fast, forcing him to sit and watch while his enemy stood just out of reach.

"Still angry with me after all these years?" Devlin said, slipping his hands inside the pockets of his slacks. "I thought living in the wilderness might have mellowed you out. Taught you some perspective."

Ghost leaned forward as far as the chains would allow. "The wilderness didn't mellow me out. It just gave lots of time to think about all the different ways I'd hurt you if I ever got the chance."

Devlin tilted his head to the side. "You act like you're the only one who's lost something. The only one who's suffered. But that's your problem, Hale. You've never been capable of seeing through your rage to appreciate the bigger picture."

Ghost stared at the man he'd imagined killing in a thousand different ways over more than a decade. Whenever the Lord inevitably convicted him for those thoughts, he'd try to refocus on something else—a hunting expedition, a fence that needed repaired—but the rage never really left. It was always there beneath the surface, smoldering in his chest like a fire that refused to go out.

"My daughter is similarly short-sighted." Devlin shook his head, genuine frustration creeping into his voice. "She made quite a mess of things tonight. I should've known better than to give her this entire week. It has never taken her long to mess everything up."

He paused, watching Ghost closely, as if expecting a reaction or an argument, but Ghost gave him neither.

"Kira doesn't understand that I've dedicated my life to creating something lasting here," he continued. "People can live in Vita Nova without fear, protected from the broken world that exists beyond these walls. But keeping a place like this running requires sacrifice. That's what my daughter doesn't understand. Keeping people alive requires tough decisions that weaker men couldn't make. Surely you can understand that."

The bitter irony wasn't lost on Ghost. Both of them had spent the last twelve years building refuges, but Ghost had fought to preserve life while Devlin had perfected the art of taking it.

"Not much for conversation, are you?" Devlin moved closer, staying just out of reach of the chains. "I suppose living like a hermit in the wilderness doesn't do much for one's social skills. Either way, I thought you should know that your rescue attempt came at the perfect time. Watching the old man hang made the citizens of Vita Nova... uncomfortable. Perhaps it was a step too far on my part. But now that the Lawless have broken into our city and destroyed part of our vital infrastructure, the next two public hangings will be much easier for everyone to stomach. They'll finally understand that while death isn't pretty, it's necessary to preserve our way of life."

Ghost couldn't hold the words back any longer. They came out flat and hard, forged from years of grief. "Is that what you told yourself when you murdered Madison?"

One of Devlin's pockmarked cheeks twitched, almost imperceptibly.

But Ghost saw it.

"Your girlfriend was sick." Devlin's tone was soft, almost patronizing, like he was explaining something to a stubborn child. "She had terminal lung cancer. Like many others in this city, she died because we don't have the resources to care for people who can't be saved. Her death, while unfortunate, couldn't be helped."

Ghost's jaw tightened until his teeth ached, the chains rattling as he strained against them. "Tell me the truth," he growled. "Just tell me why. You're going to kill me anyway, right? So just tell me why you killed her."

Devlin's eyes shone with something close to amusement. "I already told you. She was sick. Dying. There was nothing else to be done." He leaned in closer, staying just out of reach. "I know what you want—a confession. You want to hear me admit it so you can justify the righteous hatred burning you up inside. But I won't give it to you. Besides, you're in no position to judge me. You and I—we're the same type of men. Both of us have blood on our hands. The only difference is I don't pretend I'm some vigilante hero. I'm just a man willing to do what needs to be done."

"What needs to be done?" Ghost repeated the words through gritted teeth. "How many others? How many innocent people like Madison are dead because you needed them gone?"

At that, a cold smile spread across Devlin's face. "Innocent? That's rather generous when it comes to our dear Madison, don't you think?"

Ghost surged forward as far as the chains would allow, the shackles cutting deep into his ankles. *"Don't you dare talk about her like that."*

Devlin didn't even flinch. He didn't step back. He knew he was safe.

"You want the truth? Madison was a convenience to me, Hale. A distraction. Nothing more. There were many before her, and there have been many since. Fortunately, most of them didn't produce any offspring."

Ghost's fury was so pure, so visceral, that he could barely see through it. His vision narrowed to a tunnel with Devlin's face at the center. He pulled hard against the chains until he felt warm blood running down his wrists.

But the shackles held.

Eventually, he sagged back onto the cot, breathing hard.

"That's better," Devlin said. "You really shouldn't let yourself get so worked up, Hale. It's terrible for your blood pressure. And you don't want to know what happens to people with high blood pressure around here."

Ghost squeezed his eyes shut, forcing himself to breathe. To think. He needed to stop allowing Devlin to distract him and remember why he had returned to this city at all.

"Where's Kira?"

Devlin visibly brightened, as if he'd been waiting for the question. "She's at the Compulsory Clinic. I'm heading there next to administer her injection myself. I thought it fitting, since I'm her father. Remember the adage, 'I brought you into this world; I can take you out of it?' Well, I happen to agree with that one."

Ghost's stomach twisted. He tried to speak, but no words came out.

"Oh, don't look so upset, Hale. Somnumbutal offers a very peaceful death. Far more humane than what you and your friend will receive in the morning."

Ghost felt the fight drain out of him. "Your own daughter?"

"She's no daughter of mine," Devlin snapped, the first real flash of anger breaking through his control. "Kira is a mistake. An inconvenience that never should've been allowed to happen. She's a living, breathing reminder of my poor judgment and nothing more."

He leaned forward, lowering his voice to almost a conspiratorial whisper. "I won't shed a single tear for that girl. And if we're being honest, neither will you. You don't have it in you."

Ghost stared at this man who could speak so casually about killing his own child and felt something break open inside his chest. This time, it was not rage, but something deeper. Something that reached down to the very core of what it meant to be a man. A protector. A father.

"You're right."

Devlin tipped his head to the side. "About what?"

Ghost didn't look away. He held that cold, unblinking gaze

with his own. "She's not your daughter," he muttered. "She's mine. Kira has always been mine."

"Yours?" He let out a short, brittle laugh. "You think a few days in the wilderness with her makes you her father?"

"No. I think nineteen years of you abandoning her does."

Ghost leaned back against the wall, chains rattling, and for the first time in years felt something like peace settle over him. The rage was still there, coiled beneath the surface, but something stronger had taken root inside him now. "Tell me, Devlin," he asked. "Which of us do you think she'd choose?"

The man stared at him for a long moment, his face flushing red. Ghost prepared himself, expecting Devlin to finally surrender the control he prized so much. To make a critical mistake.

A mistake Ghost had waited years to exploit.

But Devlin's mouth twisted into a smile, and he wagged a finger at Ghost. "Nice try, Hale. But baiting me will not work."

He turned toward the door but paused at the threshold. "You came here to pay a ransom for something that was never yours. You should have stayed in the wilderness. I was generous in letting you live. You should have accepted exile and lived out your miserable days in peace. But you couldn't stay away. You just had to come back."

He shook his head.

"And now you'll get nothing but death from me. *Your daughter*, as you call her, will be dead within the hour. And you'll follow her before sunrise. Enjoy your last few hours."

The door closed behind Devlin with a final click. The man's footsteps echoed down the corridor, fading away as he walked—toward the exit, toward the Compulsory Clinic, toward the murder of an innocent girl who had never asked for any of this.

"Surely goodness and mercy shall follow me all the days of

my life," he whispered, falling back on Scripture, as he so often did, the words surfacing from some deep place in his shattered soul. "And I will dwell in the house of the Lord forever."

But even those familiar verses couldn't soften the brutal truth. Somewhere in this city, his daughter was about to die, and he was powerless to stop it.

Unless heaven itself intervened.

Chapter Forty-Six

Kira lay silent and still on the hospital bed, eyes half-closed, her breathing settling into the slow rhythm of someone under sedation. She could feel her heartbeat in her skull, heavy and uneven, each pulse echoing through her head. It blended with the remnants of the sedative, leaving a hazy throb behind her eyes. The drug Lucas had injected into her arm back on the bridge still coursed through her veins, making her thoughts thick and sluggish.

But not as much as she was pretending.

She'd fought through worse than this before. She'd fought the terror of jumping from a bridge with a child in her arms, the shock of icy water closing over her head, and the searing pain in her chest as her lungs ran out of air.

She'd fought through days of exhaustion, hauling a heavy pack through the wilderness, her feet blistered and bleeding, her lips cracked from dehydration.

She'd fought three knife-wielding men who saw her as nothing but prey.

And she'd fought an armed Patrol soldier—a man twice her size, with both weapons and training.

She'd fought him... and she'd won.

Now it was time to fight again.

Lucas sat slumped in the chair beside her bed, the magazine lying open in his lap. He wasn't even pretending to read it anymore. He'd been on the same page for nearly twenty minutes, his blond hair falling across his forehead now that the expensive product he'd used had given up holding it back.

She could see the exhaustion written in every line of his face. Twice she'd watched his head nod forward before he jerked it back up, his eyes darting to hers—but not before she shut them tight. The adrenaline from their fight on the bridge had burned out long ago, leaving only the heavy, bone-deep fatigue he wouldn't be able to fight off much longer.

Through the small window behind Lucas, she caught the first pale hints of dawn creeping across the horizon. Or maybe it was just her imagination—her mind's desperate need to see one more sunrise before everything ended. The view was partly blocked by another wing of the clinic, but she could see just enough of the sky to know her final night was slipping away, minute by precious minute.

My father is coming to kill me.

Her father—the man who had given her life—was coming to take it all away. And he would do it right here, in room 317, the same sterile white space where her mother had drawn her final breaths. What better way to close the chapter on his inconvenient daughter than to end her story exactly where her mother's had ended? There was a sick poetry to it that she was sure appealed to Victor Devlin's twisted sense of justice.

But she wouldn't let it happen.

Wouldn't give him the satisfaction.

For you, Momma, she thought. *I'm going to fight for you, like I should've back then.*

Lucas's breathing grew deeper and more regular, the magazine trembling in his grip. His head tilted back against the chair, and his mouth fell slightly open.

Kira could see his consciousness slipping. *Come on,* she thought, watching him through her lashes. *I'm no threat to you. Just let go.*

Finally, she heard it—a soft, barely audible snore.

Kira waited two more full minutes, eyes locked on his face. Watching for any sign he was pretending, as she had been. But his chest kept rising and falling, the magazine now hanging loosely from his fingers, ready to drop at any second.

Now.

She shifted on the bed, easing herself upright. The world tilted slightly—the sedative was still doing its job—but she shut her eyes until the spinning settled. When she opened them again, her vision had cleared, the buzzing fluorescents less sharp against her ears. Her jaw throbbed from where he'd punched her, but it was manageable. The pain meant she was still alive.

The silk of her gown rustled as she swung her legs over the side of the bed, lowering her bare feet onto the cold floor. She felt something tug at her back and reached around, her fingers brushing the intricate dahlia that had come partially undone. Its delicate petals hung limp, like a wilted flower.

Behind her, Lucas kept snoring.

Walking on her tiptoes, she crept toward the door, arms extended for balance. Every sound was painfully loud in the silent room. The whisper of silk brushing her legs, the soft pad of her bare feet. Even her own breathing roared in her ears as if it were determined to give her away.

Almost there, she told herself. *Keep going.*

Her fingers had just closed around the door handle when she heard it.

The soft thump of something hitting the floor behind her.

The snores cut off all at once.

Kira risked a glance back. The magazine lay on the floor, pages splayed open to a faded advertisement featuring a woman laughing in a bikini on some distant beach.

Slowly, she lifted her gaze from the magazine to Lucas.

He was staring at her.

For a split second, they locked eyes across the small room—hunter and hunted—both knowing the chase was about to begin.

Then Lucas exploded into motion, launching himself off the chair toward her with a rage-filled curse.

Kira bolted.

She yanked the door open and stumbled into the hallway, slamming it shut behind her. A loud crash echoed from inside, followed by a string of angry curses. She couldn't see him, but from the sound of it, he'd fallen hard—and it had hurt.

Good.

The corridor stretched out empty before her, the nurse's station ahead bathed in dim light, unmanned and silent. Identical doors lined both sides of the hall, all closed tight. This wasn't a hospital on the night shift. There were no other patients, no nurses making their rounds, no soft beeping of monitors or hushed conversations.

Just silence.

She remembered the stairwell was to her left, past the nurses' station and through the double doors at the end of the hall. She ran in that direction.

Behind her, the door to room 317 slammed open, and Lucas's voice ripped through the silence.

"Kira!"

She didn't stop. Didn't look back.

The double doors loomed ahead, the glowing red EXIT sign over the stairwell flickering in the dark corridor. She sprinted for it, legs finally obeying her, the sedative's fog burning away with every desperate step.

She was going to make it.

She could already feel the heavy crash bar under her palms. Could almost taste the cool air on her face as she burst into the street. In her mind, she was already outside and free, with every step taking her closer to Will and Ghost.

Please, God. Please—

She was ten feet from the stairwell when Lucas tackled her.

They crashed to the ground hard, her gown tearing further as they skidded across the floor. She tried to scramble out from under him, but he used his weight to pin her, driving one knee onto her arm while his hands fought to control the other.

"You stupid girl," he snarled into her face. "You're going to regret that."

Kira thrashed beneath him, her free hand clawing desperately at his face, leaving angry red scratches that immediately welled with blood. He jerked his head back with a curse, but she didn't stop. She kept scratching at his neck, his jaw—anywhere she could reach.

Panic gave her strength she didn't know she had. She twisted partially onto her side, just enough to drive her elbow into his ribs.

Lucas grunted in pain, rage flashing across his features. He drew back his fist, aiming for her head just like he had on the bridge.

But at the last second, Kira turned away. Lucas's fist, meant for her face, slammed into the floor with a sickening crunch.

The sound of breaking bones echoed in her ears, followed by his high-pitched, agonized screams.

Lucas rolled off her, clutching his shattered hand to his chest. Blood seeped between his fingers where the impact had split his knuckles open.

Now. Go. Now!

Kira scrambled to her feet, the gown tangling around her legs. The stairwell was so close—but as she turned toward it, she realized Lucas was still between her and the doors. Even injured, he was already trying to push himself to his feet.

The elevator.

She spun around and ran in the opposite direction, racing back down the hallway, past her room, toward the elevator she remembered was at the other end.

"KIRA!" Lucas screamed. "GET BACK HERE!"

She could hear him coming after her. Even hurt, he was faster than she was. Stronger. And the drugs were still clouding her vision, making it hard to keep her balance.

The elevator doors came into view at the end of the hall— two silver panels gleaming under the fluorescent lights. She sprinted for them, slamming her palm against the down button again and again. She heard the mechanical whir of the elevator car somewhere above, grinding its way upward.

"Hurry," she whispered hoarsely. "Please, hurry."

She turned and looked back down the hallway. Lucas was coming for her, but he wasn't even rushing anymore. He moved with the steady confidence of a predator who knew his prey was trapped, his broken hand cradled against his chest. Blood dripped steadily from his shattered knuckles, leaving a grotesque trail of crimson dots on the pristine white floor.

"There's nowhere to run, Kira," he called out. "Even if you make it out of this building, what then? Everyone in the city knows your face. You're the mayor's daughter, remember?"

The elevator dinged behind her. She heard the soft whoosh of the doors sliding open.

Thank God, she breathed, spinning toward the open doors.

But what she saw inside drained every bit of warmth from her body.

Victor Devlin stood in the center of the elevator car, his expression a mix of irritation and disgust, as if this whole scene was nothing more than another inconvenient mess he'd have to clean up before moving on to more important things. His eyes swept over her torn gown and disheveled hair with the detached appraisal of someone assessing damage to property.

But he wasn't alone.

Beside him, small and fragile in pale blue pajamas, stood Teddy Easton.

Chapter Forty-Seven

Ghost had been drifting in and out of sleep for hours, his body exhausted but his brain too restless to fully shut down. Thoughts of Kira filled every dark corner of his mind.

Was it done?

Was she already gone?

"Hale?"

Why hadn't he done more for her? He should've fought harder. Planned better. Offered to die in her place.

"Hale, look at me."

Ghost sat up slowly, his body protesting the movement. His muscles ached, and his joints were stiff and throbbing. He tried to stretch out his legs but met resistance—the cold metal of the shackles biting into his ankles. He rolled his shoulders, wincing as the movement sent fresh waves of pain radiating down his back. He blinked into the darkness, trying to orient himself.

Only then did he realize someone was standing inside his cell.

A whispered voice: "Hale?"

Madison.

He knew it was impossible. Madison was dead. But his desperate, broken heart refused to listen to logic.

For a moment, he could see every detail of her face, those beautiful eyes, the soft curve of her lips. The fantasy was so vivid that when the woman stepped forward and revealed herself to be one of the Guards, Ghost felt something inside of him crumble.

"Don't move," she spoke in a low voice, her fingers drumming a nervous rhythm against her leather duty belt. "Don't talk. Just listen to me."

She moved farther into the cell. She was young—mid- to late twenties, maybe—with short brown hair cropped close to her skull in the practical style worn by most of the Guards, including the females. Her eyes darted between Ghost and the corridor behind her as if she expected to be caught at any moment.

"Who are you?" he asked.

It seemed like the most pertinent question, given the circumstances.

"Officer Lambo," she said, clearing her throat. "Donna Lambo. I'm one of the Guards on duty tonight. I need to ask you something."

Ghost remained perfectly still, studying her face in the dim light. Trying to decide if she was friend or foe. "Go ahead."

Her eyes lifted to meet his. "People are saying you're one of the Lawless, and that you came here from the Unregulated Zone for Kira Liebert, the Volunteer. They're saying you blew up the bridge and attacked Rolling Meadows trying to find her." She paused for a beat. "Is that true?"

There was no point in lying. "I didn't *attack* Rolling Meadows. But otherwise... yes."

Donna nodded as if she'd expected that answer. "You had

to know you'd be caught. That this was a suicide mission. So why do it?"

He didn't even have to think about his answer. "Because she's my daughter."

Her eyes widened. "Your daughter? But Devlin said—"

"Devlin says a lot of things," Ghost interrupted. "Most of them are lies. But I knew Kira's mother. I *loved* her. That makes Kira my daughter in all the ways that count."

Something in his answer—or maybe the truth of it—seemed to satisfy Donna. She moved closer, kneeling beside his shackles. "I was on duty the night she surrendered. She walked up to us with her hands in the air. I've never seen anything like it. I was the one who drove her to the Confines. And the next time I saw her, she was standing in the middle of the field at the Reverence Ceremony, volunteering to die to save Theodore Easton. She came back for the little boy, didn't she?"

Ghost nodded. "She did."

Donna's expression crumpled, her face contorting as if she'd just tasted something bitter. For a moment, Ghost thought he'd misread the entire situation. That his honesty had been a mistake. But then a single tear slipped from her right eye, and he realized she was fighting not to break down completely.

"My little sister was put to death as a Compulsory," she said, choking out the words. "My mother followed two months later as a Volunteer. She couldn't take losing a child. Said there was no worse pain in the world. I didn't get to bury either of them. My sister went to the burial pits, and my mother... went into the sky."

"I'm sorry for your loss."

"Me too."

Donna pulled a key ring from her belt and slid it into the shackles at his ankles. They clicked open, and he felt the blood rush back into his feet. Then she moved behind him and reached for the cuffs at his wrists.

"I've been thinking about this all week. Ever since Kira showed up on that bridge. People give up their lives every week in this city, but what she did was different. I realized I hadn't seen a real sacrifice until the moment she stepped out on that field."

"So you're letting me go? This could get you killed, Officer Lambo."

She unlocked his wrists from the shackles and looked up at him. "Maybe. But I don't want to be a part of this city. Not anymore. And please call me Donna."

Ghost tested his hands, flexing his fingers as the circulation returned. After hours of confinement, the simple act of moving freely felt like a small miracle. He rose from the cot and stretched out his legs, trying to shake off the stiffness. He wasn't anywhere near full strength, but he was no longer confined.

Donna stepped into the hallway and bent down to retrieve something from the floor. She returned holding the item in her hands. "Figured you might want this back."

His shotgun.

Ghost took it from her, the cold steel against his palm grounding him in a way nothing else could. It wasn't just a weapon—it was an extension of himself. The thing that had kept him alive all these years.

He checked to make sure it was loaded. It was.

"I couldn't find the rest of your stuff, but these were with the shotgun," Donna said, passing him several extra shells, which he pocketed. "We've got a skeleton crew working tonight. With everything happening downtown, Command pulled most of the Guards out of here. There are only seven of us left on the grounds. I'm one of them, and four others are with me on this."

"What about the other two?"

"I'd appreciate it if you didn't kill them. They're not bad men." Donna glanced at her watch. "Shift change is at three. That's in eighteen minutes. That's our window, so we need to move fast."

Ghost shifted the shotgun in his grip. "Window for what?"

"Getting as many prisoners out of here as we can."

Chapter Forty-Eight

Teddy Easton's small hand was swallowed by Victor Devlin's grip, his pale fingers nearly disappearing in the mayor's much larger ones. The boy's face was blotchy and swollen from crying, tear tracks still fresh on his cheeks, his nose red and running.

"Hello, daughter," Victor said. "Having trouble sleeping?"

Kira stood frozen in the hallway, caught between Lucas—limping toward her from behind—and her father blocking the elevator, her only remaining escape route.

But even if the path had been clear, even if she could have darted past her father and into the elevator, she wouldn't have tried.

She would never abandon Teddy to her father.

Behind her, Lucas stopped his limping pursuit, one shoulder pressed against the wall for support. "Sir," he panted, still cradling his broken hand like it might fall off. "She tried to escape. I had everything under control, but somehow she—"

"I can see exactly what happened, Mr. Pine," Victor interrupted, stepping out of the elevator and tugging Teddy along beside him. "Though I find it difficult to believe that you couldn't restrain one sedated girl."

Kira ignored them both, her attention focused on the small figure at her father's side. She crouched down, bringing herself to eye level with him.

"Teddy? Are you okay, buddy?"

The little boy had been staring at the floor, his small brow furrowed, lost in whatever dark thoughts had taken root in his mind. It was understandable, considering everything he had endured. But the moment he heard her voice, his head snapped up. His wide eyes locked onto hers, and for a moment, he just stared, like he couldn't quite trust what he was seeing.

Then his entire face lit up. It was like watching the sun emerge from behind storm clouds.

"Kira!"

He tore his hand from Devlin's grasp and launched himself at her, colliding with enough force to nearly knock her over. Her legs were still shaky from the sedative, but she caught herself on the edge of the elevator frame and folded the boy into her arms. He clung to her so tightly she could barely breathe.

"Teddy," she whispered. "I missed you so much."

"What happened to you, Kira?" The questions tumbled out of him in that familiar rapid-fire way that used to drive Brack half-mad during their long trek through the wilderness. "Where's Will? Are you sick? Why are you in the hospital? What happened to your dress?"

"I'm okay," she managed, forcing herself to smile as she wiped away the tears that had escaped her eyes. "I'm not sick. I just missed you so much it made my heart hurt. That's why they brought me here. To fix my heart and make me all better."

Teddy's arms tightened around her neck, his fingers twisting into the torn silk of her dress. "Are you going away soon? Momma told me you were. She said you were going to be a superhero, and I wouldn't see you anymore. But I don't want you to go."

She lifted her eyes to look at her father over Teddy's shoulder, and the satisfied smile on Devlin's face made her nauseous. She hated him more in that moment than she ever had before. Even more than when his wife had confirmed the unthinkable—that Devlin himself had ordered the death of Kira's mother.

Could he see the disgust in her eyes? The revulsion she felt at the very sight of him? Did he even care?

"But she has to go, Theodore," Devlin said in a gentle voice. "Superheroes never run away or back down from a challenge. They always stand tall and do what's right, even when it's hard. She isn't just trying to save the whole city... she's trying to save you. Isn't that right, Kira?"

She saw the challenge in her father's eyes, the threat beneath the smile. If she agreed, she'd be taking part in a lie that would soften her death for Teddy. Make it easier to understand.

But if she refused... Teddy would pay the price.

She tightened her arms around him. "That's right," she whispered. "I'm going to save you, buddy. I promise."

***

Room 317 felt smaller with four people crammed inside. Teddy remained glued to Kira's side as she settled back onto the hospital bed. His small hand clutched hers and refused to let go, as if he could keep her from leaving simply by holding on tight enough.

The two men positioned themselves at the foot of her bed. Devlin—calm, unreadable, and as polished as ever. And Lucas

—red-faced, fists clenched, and looking like he wanted to kill her on the spot.

She watched as her father leaned toward Lucas and muttered something under his breath.

Whatever he'd said made Lucas's eyes light up. "Yes, sir," he replied, and slipped out into the hallway.

The door had barely clicked shut when Devlin turned his attention back to Teddy, his expression softening into the same warm, paternal look Kira had seen him wear with the twins at dinner. "Theodore," he said, circling the side of the bed, "I need you to say goodbye to Kira now. It's time for her big moment to be a superhero."

Teddy's grip on her hand tightened, and he shifted his body, positioning himself between her and her father. "No. I don't want her to go anywhere."

Devlin crouched a little. "I understand. It's never easy to watch the people we care about leave us, even when they have important work to do. But sometimes we have to be brave and let them go."

"I said no!" Tears welled in his eyes. "I don't want her to be a superhero anymore!"

"Theodore..."

"I want to go with her. Can I do that? Can I be a superhero with Kira? Please, Mr. Devlin?"

Kira's entire body went cold. "Teddy, no. That's not how this works."

But Devlin tipped his head to the side as if considering Teddy's request. "You want to be a superhero too, Theodore? That shows remarkable courage. You're a very noble boy, aren't you?"

Teddy nodded, hope lighting up his face. "Yes! I'll help Kira save everyone. We did it before when we jumped off the bridge. We can do it again!"

Devlin's smile widened.

He's actually considering it, Kira realized.

Two deaths instead of one. The mayor's brave daughter and the innocent boy she'd given her life to protect.

"Absolutely not," she said, staring up at her father. "I'm doing this alone. That's my choice."

"But I don't want to be without you again," Teddy insisted, his grip on her hand becoming almost painful. "I want to stay with you forever."

The door opened, and Lucas stepped back inside, a small metal tray in his good hand. He crossed the room without speaking and handed it to Devlin.

On the tray lay a syringe and a glass vial filled with a clear liquid that looked no more threatening than water. The same combination that had stolen her mother's life in this very room.

Her own death snapped into focus.

This is actually happening. I'm going to die today.

Her gaze flicked to Teddy. She couldn't let him see this. Couldn't let him carry the weight of watching someone he loved die right in front of him.

"Teddy?"

"Yeah?"

She stared at him, determined to memorize every detail of his sweet face. The constellation of freckles scattered across the bridge of his nose. The tiny gap between his front teeth. The way his lower lip always seemed a little fuller when he was about to cry. All the little imperfections that made him perfect.

"I need you to go outside with Mr. Pine for a few minutes," she said. "Please wait in the hallway while I talk to Mayor Devlin, and I'll see you again soon. I promise."

The lie burned her tongue. She would never see him again. Never feel his little hand wrapped in hers. Never watch him grow up into the incredible man she already knew he was meant to be. And if someone tried to hurt him again, she wouldn't be there to stop it.

All she could do now was to place him in God's hands.

"You promise?" His eyes searched hers, as if looking for the lie behind her words. "You promise we'll always stay awake together? Just like when we jumped?"

The bridge. In that split second of pure faith, she had stepped into empty air, trusting that she and Teddy would somehow both survive. She'd lost him in the churning current, but Will had been there. Will had pulled them both to safety.

But this time, there would be no rescue.

"I promise."

God, forgive me for lying to him.

Lucas stepped forward and rested his unbroken hand on Teddy's back. "Come on, champ. I bet you're getting thirsty after all of this excitement. Let's see if we can find some juice and cookies hiding around here somewhere."

Teddy wavered, looking between Kira and Lucas as if trying to decide what to do. Then he leaned forward and pressed a kiss to Kira's cheek. "I love you," he said. "Stay awake until I come back."

"I love you too, buddy." The words came out steady despite the grief threatening to bury her. "More than you'll ever know."

This is for him. This is how he gets to live.

She blinked away tears as Lucas guided him toward the door. She couldn't let Teddy see her cry.

At the threshold, he turned and waved—small fingers wiggling in a final goodbye. She forced herself to smile and lifted her hand, giving him one last image of her alive and whole.

Then the door clicked shut.

And she was alone with the man who had created her—not to love her, but to destroy her.

Chapter Forty-Nine

Ghost followed Donna down the corridor, moving through air thick with despair and the stench of unwashed bodies. The concrete walls did little to block out the terrible sounds. He could still hear every muffled sob, every scream, and every rhythmic thud of someone banging their head against a cell door.

This wasn't a detention center. It was a warehouse for the forgotten. A place where people were stored until they could be disposed of.

They wound through the maze of concrete and steel, passing row after row of heavy metal doors. Behind each one was a human being—someone's child, someone's parent, or someone's sibling. Someone who had dared to challenge Victor Devlin's authority. Ghost counted doors as they passed, gauging the numbers. There were at least a dozen prisoners in this wing alone.

They could not save them all. Not in eighteen minutes.

But they could save some.

As they neared the central hub, Ghost tensed. Two

Guards sat behind the main desk, eyes lifting as he and Donna entered. But instead of shouting and reaching for their weapons, the men merely nodded and turned back to their paperwork.

"It's okay," Donna whispered. "They're on our side. The two who aren't with us are outside right now, walking the perimeter."

She stopped at a heavy security door and swiped a keycard. The lock disengaged with a soft click.

"This is Cell Block D. Your friend's in cell seven. Let as many others out as you can, but only the ones who can walk."

Ghost glanced at her. "What are you going to do?"

Donna pressed the keycard into his hand. "I'll take the other cell blocks." She unholstered the service pistol from her belt and passed it to him, along with a spare magazine. "Give this to your friend. We'll meet at the loading dock. Take the stairs at the end of the cell block to the basement, then follow the green line on the floor."

"Copy."

She paused, staring at him. "You've only got ten minutes, Hale. Then I'm leaving with or without you."

Ghost nodded, tucking the pistol into his waistband and slipping the magazine into his pocket. He hurried down the corridor, scanning each cell number stenciled in white paint. Seven was halfway down the block. He reached the door and peered through the reinforced glass.

Will was slumped against the wall, alert but battered. A deep bruise bloomed along his cheekbone, and dried blood crusted the corner of his mouth. When he saw Ghost through the window, he lifted his head from the wall, confusion quickly giving way to recognition and relief.

Ghost swiped the keycard and opened the door. "Time to go, son."

Will pushed himself to his feet, wincing at some unseen pain. "Kira?"

"We're going to get her." Ghost handed him Donna's pistol and the magazine. "But first we need to get out of here."

Ghost was already moving to the next cell, using Donna's keycard to unlock door after door. Most of the prisoners weren't restrained as he had been, and they crept from their cells hesitantly, pale and blinking, like creatures that had lived in the darkness for far too long.

Some didn't move from their cots, even with their cell door hanging open. Some were too weak or broken to process what was happening. But others understood. You could see it in their eyes—the flicker of urgency, of life coming back.

"Stay together," Ghost muttered to each one as they emerged into the corridor. "Take the stairs to the basement. Follow the green line to the loading dock. We'll meet you there. Stay quiet."

A woman with dark hair caught his attention. She was young and pretty, her gray uniform hanging loose on her emaciated frame. She wasn't heading for the stairwell like the others. Instead, she walked toward Ghost on unsteady legs, staring at him as if she knew him.

"Get to the loading dock," he repeated as he opened another cell. "We've got no time left."

"You're him." Her voice emerged hoarse and scratchy. She cleared her throat and tried again. "That scar on your face. You're Noah Hale, aren't you? Kira told me about you."

Ghost paused, studying her more carefully. "You know Kira?"

"I'm Emma Castile, her best friend." Her eyes drifted to Will, who had just appeared next to him. "And you must be the boyfriend. I recognize you from the Volunteer Ball. You look a little rough."

Will moved to steady her as she swayed. "You don't look so great yourself. Can you walk?"

"If it gets me out of this hole, I can run."

Emma's voice was rough, but there was steel beneath it.

Ghost liked her immediately.

They freed eight more prisoners before time ran out. As the last door clanged open, Ghost paused, his eyes sweeping the corridor. So many doors still locked, so many lives left behind. Each one was a person with a name, a story, and a reason they didn't belong here.

But they had no time left.

They had only a few minutes until the next shift, and they'd need every second to get clear of the building and off the grounds.

"We have to go," he said, turning to Will and Emma. "Now."

They moved fast, feet pounding down the stairwell and into the underground service tunnel. They followed the green line painted along the floor to the loading dock, a cavernous space with massive bay doors and concrete ramps that sloped up to the outer service road. Stacks of crates and broken pallets lined the walls.

Donna was already there with at least two dozen other prisoners, her face flushed from running. She raised a hand, signaling them to get lower. "Keep quiet," she whispered. "Just another minute or two."

One of the bay doors was halfway open, just enough to see the tops of two Guards' heads as they passed by outside, their flashlight beams sweeping in slow arcs across the pavement.

"The Guard in the shack at the bottom of the hill is with us," Donna whispered to Ghost as he crouched beside her. "But those two aren't. We have to wait until they finish their round and head toward the back of the building. That's our window."

Ghost gave a sharp nod, eyes fixed on the gap in the door, the pressure coiling in his chest like a spring. They were close. So close. But one mistake, one wrong move—and the entire operation would unravel.

Ghost watched the Guards' slow progress, counting their steps. The nearest one was maybe twenty-five yards away, his rifle slung over his shoulder. In thirty more seconds, both would be out of sight around the corner of the building.

"Stay calm," he hissed to the cluster of prisoners behind him, feeling their tension like static prickling at the back of his neck. "Almost there."

But one of them was breaking.

A kid barely out of his teens, more bones than muscle, started trembling uncontrollably. His breaths became fast and shallow, panic threatening to overtake him completely.

"I can't—I can't do this," he gasped.

Too loud.

"Shut up," Emma snapped. "You're going to get us all killed."

But it was too late.

The kid broke free from the group, bolting up the ramp like a spooked animal, half-limping on legs too thin to carry him far. An older man with a bushy gray beard scrambled after him, both of them slipping beneath the half-raised bay door and stumbling into the glow of a streetlight.

"Hey!" one of the Guards shouted. "Hey! Stop!"

A flashlight beam cut across the asphalt, landing on the two figures, pinning them like insects under glass.

The air around the loading dock went still, every prisoner frozen in place.

"Oh no," Donna breathed. "No, no, no—"

The younger man raised his hands, trembling.

But the older one ran.

The sharp crack of rifle fire split the night air.

The bullet hit the prisoner mid-back, a brutal, unforgiving impact. He pitched forward, hit the pavement hard, and didn't move.

That's when the dam broke.

The remaining prisoners panicked. A few pressed further back into the shadows, but others surged forward in a desperate rush for freedom, their survival instincts overriding all reason.

"Go, go, go!" Ghost roared.

He tore up the ramp with the prisoners, beating most of them to the top and bringing his shotgun up. At the top of the ramp, he aimed high and fired. A warning shot that passed just over the nearest Guard's head. The blast thundered through the night, echoing off the walls of the prison.

The Guards dove for cover behind a nearby barrier, swearing, scrambling for position.

Ghost didn't wait. He spun, waving the others forward. "Move! Now!"

More prisoners poured outside, a chaotic flood of gray uniforms scattering into the darkness. The Guards returned fire from behind their covered positions, muzzle flashes lighting up the night.

The world exploded into chaos and gunfire. Ghost saw an older female prisoner cry out and fall, clutching her shoulder. A middle-aged man took a bullet to the thigh and collapsed, his legs tangling beneath him. Others dropped around him—some crying out, some falling silent—but Ghost forced himself to keep running.

Gunfire cracked to his right—Will, returning fire, forcing the Guards to duck behind the barrier.

As Ghost began to sprint down the hill, he heard one of the Guards yelling into a radio. "Requesting immediate assistance at the Confines! We've got a prison break in progress! Repeat, prison break in progress. Multiple prisoners, armed and dangerous!"

Ghost pumped his legs harder, his boots pounding against the pavement. Behind him, he could hear the wounded calling for help—voices that would haunt him later, if he lived long enough. But right now, survival meant moving forward. It meant getting as many people out alive as possible, even if it meant leaving some behind.

At the base of the hill, a lone figure stood outside the Guard shack—an older man with gray hair and kind eyes. He waved them past, his pistol untouched on his hip as the stream of escapees rushed by.

"Thank you," Ghost said as he passed, their eyes meeting for just a second.

The man nodded. "Just keep moving. Don't stop."

Will caught up to him, supporting a limping prisoner. It was the man who'd taken a bullet to the thigh. "What now?"

Before Ghost could answer, Emma appeared at his side and grabbed his arm. "There—look!"

A city bus sat at a transit stop a block away, its lights on, engine running. The driver had probably just finished his route and was taking a break before heading back to the depot.

Some prisoners peeled off in different directions, vanishing into alleys and side streets. But a group of ten or twelve stuck close to Ghost, following him as if, during the mad sprint down the hill, they'd silently agreed he was their leader.

"Hurry!" Emma shouted. "Before he drives away!"

Through the windshield, Ghost saw the driver glance up. He took one look at the scarred man with the shotgun and the prisoners streaming toward the bus, and his face went pale.

The bus lurched as the driver shifted it into gear and pulled away from the curb.

Ghost sprinted ahead of the group, cutting straight into the vehicle's path. He raised his shotgun and aimed it directly at the windshield.

The driver slammed on the brakes.

The tires shrieked as the bus jerked to a halt, stopping just feet from where Ghost stood. For a long moment, the driver stared at him, frozen, as if weighing whether to hit the gas and plow through him anyway.

Then his shoulders slumped, and he shook his head, reaching for the lever beside his seat.

The pneumatic doors hissed open.

The driver was a heavyset man in his fifties, dressed in a stained transit authority uniform. His voice shook as he spoke. "Please. I've got grandkids. I don't want any trouble."

"You won't get any trouble from us," Ghost assured him, lowering the shotgun. "But we need your bus. You can just walk away."

The man didn't wait for a second offer. He grabbed his thermos and lunch bag from the dashboard, clutching them against his chest, and hurried down the steps as fast as his stocky frame would allow. He jogged away from the bus, casting a single nervous glance over his shoulder before disappearing around the corner.

Ghost stepped onto the bus, his eyes sweeping over the rows of scuffed vinyl seats, torn in places and patched with duct tape. The floor was sticky beneath his boots, and the air smelled of industrial cleaner mixed with years of accumulated sweat and exhaust fumes.

How long had it been since he'd ridden on a city bus? More than a decade. He'd certainly never driven one. The steering wheel looked massive and foreign, surrounded by gauges and switches he could only guess at.

Behind him, the group of prisoners climbed aboard—some limping, some helping others who were too weak or wounded to walk on their own. Will and Emma were the last to enter, both breathless and pale.

Ghost moved toward the driver's seat.

But Emma pushed past him, sliding behind the wheel like she'd been waiting her whole life for this moment.

For the first time since Ghost had met her, the young woman smiled.

"I'll drive."

Chapter Fifty

Devlin settled on the edge of Kira's bed, placing the metal tray beside him. He removed the plastic cap from the syringe and let it fall onto the tray, then he lifted the vial, pierced the rubber stopper, and slowly drew the clear liquid into the barrel.

There was no emotion on his face. No conflict. No hesitation.

Kira watched the syringe fill, watched the poison that would end her life slide silently into the chamber. "You're really going to kill me."

It wasn't a question.

Devlin held the syringe up to the overhead light. "Yes, I am. I decided I should handle this personally after your little act of heroism on Sunday night." His voice remained calm and conversational, like he was discussing a business deal instead of his daughter's execution. "And should you attempt any form of resistance, Theodore Easton will join you. Not peacefully, as your death will be, but violently. In front of you. Not by my hand, of course. I have associates who would take genuine pleasure in that sort of thing."

He glanced at her then, the corner of his mouth curling into a half-smile, clearly savoring the horror he must've seen on her face.

"Afterward, I'll release a compelling narrative about how the Lawless infiltrated the city and murdered the boy in retaliation for your betrayal. His death will rally public support. It will justify the purging of every settlement within a hundred miles of this city."

Something cracked inside her chest, like a dam giving way after too many years of pressure and silence. "You're a monster."

Devlin didn't flinch. "No, Kira. I'm practical. I do what's necessary to preserve order and protect what I've built."

"And my mother?" Her hands twisted the bedsheets into knots. "Was murdering her practical? Inventing a terminal illness and faking a Compulsory Order—how exactly did that preserve order?"

Devlin paused, as if seriously considering the question for the first time. "Your mother was a liability. A loose thread. Too many loose threads, Kira, and the whole garment comes undone. She would've caused problems as you grew older and she no longer felt the need to protect you." He lowered his voice a little. "And yes, if I'm being honest, every time I saw her, I was reminded of my own momentary lapse in judgment. She represented a mistake that should never have happened. Just as you do."

He shifted closer on the bed, raising the syringe. A single drop of the poison shimmered at the needle's tip.

"Fortunately, all mistakes can be corrected."

Kira pressed herself back against the pillows, every instinct screaming at her to run, to fight, to survive. But escape was impossible. Even if she could overpower Devlin, she would still have Lucas to contend with.

And running meant Teddy would die instead of her.

No—this was her ending. She would die as her mother had, in the same sterile white room, at the hands of the same monster.

"I want you to know," Devlin said, reaching for her arm with his free hand, "this brings me no satisfaction." His fingers were surprisingly gentle as he turned her wrist, exposing the delicate network of veins beneath her skin. "Despite everything, I am still your father."

She looked into his cold gray eyes and saw nothing. No warmth. No regret. No recognition of the life he was about to extinguish. Whatever part of him had once been human was gone—traded away long ago for power and control. All that remained was a hollow shell of a man in an expensive suit.

"You were never my father," she said, her voice steady even as her heart pounded against her ribs. "My real father doesn't live in this terrible place."

Closing her eyes, she let her mind drift away from the sterile room and the horror that was about to happen to her. Away from the monster who shared her DNA but nothing else.

She thought of Ghost, scarred and broken, yet somehow carrying more genuine paternal love in his damaged heart than Victor Devlin could ever comprehend.

She thought of Noah Hale, the handsome man on the ferry who'd bought her ice cream and loved her mother with a devotion that had endured long past her death. The man who had saved her life in more ways than one.

And then she thought of her true Father—the One Will had introduced her to back in Emmitsburg. The One the mess hall ladies in Haven sang about as they stirred pots and baked bread. The One who had walked beside her in the wilderness and never once let her go. Even when everyone else had. Even when she barely knew Him.

Perhaps when she opened her eyes, she would be in a better place.

A place where Ghost's scarred face would be beautiful again.

A place where Will would find her someday, giving her that lopsided, dimpled smile that had stolen her heart the moment she first saw it.

A place where children like Teddy were never considered expendable. Where no father ever looked at his child and saw a mistake to be corrected. Where every soul was cherished for the miracle it was and never discarded.

A place where she would finally be safe in the arms of a Father who had never seen her as anything less than beloved.

"I'm not alone," she whispered as the needle pierced her arm. "I never was."

Without opening her eyes, she lifted her free hand toward the ceiling, fingers stretching upward in the silent hope that someone might take her hand and pull her away from this place.

Toward somewhere infinitely better.

Let him reach, Aunt Reeva whispered in her memory.

"Goodbye, Kira," her father said, his voice polluting her final moments. "I wish things could've been—"

An explosion rocked the building, sending a shockwave rolling up through the structure like an earthquake. The walls groaned and shuddered around her, and the window beside her bed rattled in its frame. From somewhere below came the sound of shattering glass raining down onto the floor.

Her eyes snapped open. She glanced at the window and saw thin gray tendrils of smoke curling past the edges of the frame.

Whatever had just happened, it was big.

The overhead fluorescent lights flickered—once, twice— then died, plunging the room into near darkness. For a terrifying moment, the only sounds were the groans of the building's stressed infrastructure and her father's sharp intake of breath.

Then the emergency power kicked in. Cold LED lights snapped on with a stuttering intensity that was more unsettling than the darkness.

The syringe slipped from Devlin's hand, pulling free from Kira's arm and clattering to the floor. He shot to his feet and rushed to the window, pressing his face to the glass and staring at the parking lot three stories below.

"What in the name of—"

The words died in Devlin's throat as he took in whatever destruction lay beneath them.

Whatever he was seeing... it scared him.

"Sir!" Lucas's voice rang from the hallway, muffled by the closed door. "Sir, there are people in the building! I can hear them!"

But Devlin didn't move. He remained frozen at the window, his palms pressed flat against the glass, staring down at whatever destruction lay beneath them.

Then he said a single word, and Kira's heart jolted as hope —and not poison—spread through her body.

"Hale."

She slipped off the bed and crossed to the window, her breath fogging the surface as she leaned closer, trying to make sense of what she was seeing.

A city bus had plowed straight through the clinic's main entrance like a battering ram, its front half buried in what had once been the lobby. The collision had torn a gaping wound in the clinic. Chunks of concrete, bricks, and shattered glass littered the ground around the impact site. Steam hissed from the engine compartment, curling into the air like smoke from a battlefield.

There was movement everywhere.

Stick-thin figures in ragged gray clothing clambered out of the wreckage, climbing through emergency exits and open windows.

Prisoners, she realized, recognizing her clothing from the Confines.

One or two fled barefoot into the shadows beyond the parking lot, while others charged straight ahead, vanishing into the massive hole the bus had torn in the building.

And there, standing in the center of it all, was Ghost.

He held his shotgun in his hands, his scarred face turned upward as his eyes scanned the building's upper floors. Two gray-clad figures rushed past him, and he shouted something at them, his voice too faint to hear through the glass.

But Kira didn't need to hear it.

She saw his lips form the words.

Find her!

Behind Ghost, a woman hauled herself out of the bus's rear emergency exit. Blood streaked down the side of her face from a gash on her forehead, but she barely seemed to notice.

Emma.

She was laughing.

Kira remembered one of their lunch dates when Emma had leaned across the table and told Kira what her one request would be if she ever became a Volunteer.

"I want to get behind the wheel of a bus just one time, and I want it to be loaded with passengers, and I want to give them the ride of their lives."

Kira's throat tightened, and then, unexpectedly, she

laughed. She pounded on the glass with both fists, the sound muffled by the window.

"Emma!" she shouted. "You did it!"

Her shouts seemed to snap Devlin out of his stupor. He spun from the window, eyes wild as they landed on her.

"You!" he snarled. "You did this!"

He lunged, but Kira was already moving, her torn gown tangling around her legs, nearly sending her sprawling as she bolted for the door.

"Lucas!" Devlin roared from behind her. "Call for backup! All units to the clinic!"

Kira reached the door just as it swung inward, crashing into her and sending her stumbling back into the room.

Lucas filled the doorway, the radio clutched in his one usable hand. Just behind him, Teddy stood frozen in the corridor, eyes wide with terror as the sound of gunfire erupted from the first floor of the building.

Kira glanced back.

Devlin was on his knees beside the bed, one arm stretched beneath the frame, groping for something.

The syringe, she realized. *It must've rolled under the bed when he dropped it.*

"Kira!" Teddy's voice cut through the noise. "What's happening?"

Lucas turned his head slightly, glancing back at the boy.

It was all she needed.

Kira launched forward, slamming her shoulder into his chest—and his injured hand—with every ounce of strength she possessed. The impact caught his hand between their two bodies, and he let out a strangled scream before doubling over and collapsing to the floor.

"Teddy, come here!"

The little boy didn't hesitate. He ran to her, his small body crashing into hers as she caught him and scooped him up. His arms wrapped tight around her neck, holding on like he never meant to let go.

Then she was flying down the corridor, Teddy's grip on her neck growing tighter with each step.

Behind them, she could hear Lucas struggling to his feet. "All units converge on the Compulsory Clinic," he barked into the radio. "We're under attack!"

But Kira kept running.

Not away from danger—but into it.

Into the fight.

Toward Ghost.

Toward freedom.

Chapter Fifty-One

The stairwell looked like a direct path to hell.

Red emergency lights bathed the concrete walls in a blood-like hue, each flicker threatening to plunge the stairwell into total darkness. The air was thick with smoke clawing its way upward from the floors below, burning Kira's throat and stinging her eyes until they watered.

Teddy whimpered against her shoulder, his small body trembling, and buried his face in the crook of her neck.

"It's okay, buddy," she assured him, cradling the back of his head with one hand. "We're getting out of this place."

She pressed her other hand to the rough concrete, using it to steady herself as they began the descent. The sounds of fighting intensified—sharp bursts of gunfire, angry shouting, the crash of something heavy slamming into a wall.

Outside, sirens wailed, overlapping one another, and the screech of tires signaled more vehicles skidding to a stop. Reinforcements. More Patrol soldiers and Guards were arriving on the scene.

Kira had no idea what awaited them below, but there was no going back.

The only way out was down.

She had just reached the second-floor landing when the door one flight below burst open, the metallic bang echoing up the stairwell like a gunshot.

Teddy let out a strangled whimper.

"Shh," she whispered, shifting his weight as she pressed herself flat against the wall, trying to disappear into the shadows. "Quiet, buddy."

Retreating up the stairwell was impossible. Lucas and her father might still be up there. But going down wasn't an option either. Even if she slipped past whoever had come through the door, there was no way she could outrun them. Not with a child in her arms.

A shadow moved into view below—tall, broad-shouldered, holding what looked like a pistol. He wasn't climbing, just scanning the stairwell, searching. A Guard, maybe. Someone alerted to her location by Lucas.

Kira held her breath, every muscle coiled, ready to bolt back up the stairs the moment he moved in her direction. If he saw her—if he started to climb—she would have no choice but to run.

Go away, she silently begged. *There's no one here. Please... just go away.*

But then... footsteps.

He was climbing the stairs.

She pushed off the wall and turned to flee, the dress snagging around her legs with every step. She stumbled twice as her foot caught the hem but didn't stop. Up was better than down. She would rather take her chances with Lucas, who she knew was unarmed and injured, than whoever was barreling up behind her.

The footsteps halted, and a voice echoed up the stairwell.

"Kira?"

She froze, her foot hovering above the next step. That voice. She knew that voice. But her mind pushed back, warning her not to believe it. Not now. It had to be a trick, her terrified brain manufacturing a voice that she desperately wanted to hear.

Then the voice came again, a little louder, a little closer.

"I came a long way to get here. Please don't make me chase you up the stairs."

The tension drained from her shoulders all at once. Her legs wobbled beneath her, and she slumped back against the wall, clutching Teddy tighter as relief washed over her. She felt her lips curve into a smile. A real one. The first in what felt like years.

Some things never changed... like Will Foster, making light of danger like it was his job.

"Took you long enough," she called down, her vision blurring.

He came into view just below. Those unmistakable blue eyes. That beautiful face she'd memorized and kissed and fallen in love with more times than she could count.

He slipped the pistol into his waistband and took the stairs two at a time. In seconds, he was there, closing the distance between them and sweeping both her and Teddy into his arms. His embrace was crushing, as if he believed that by holding them tight enough, he could somehow shield them from everything that was still to come.

She could feel the frantic rhythm of his heart through the torn fabric of his shirt, could smell him—smoke, sweat, and that grounding, woodsy scent that was just... Will.

"You're alive," he whispered into her hair. "When I saw you on that bridge—when that guy grabbed you—"

He pulled back and examined her face. The warmth

drained from his eyes, leaving them a darker shade of blue than she'd ever seen. He reached up, his fingertips grazing the tender spot just below her left temple, careful as if the touch itself might hurt her. "He hit you," he muttered, voice low and dangerous. "I saw him hit you."

"I'm okay," she said, though it wasn't true. Not really. She wasn't okay. She would not be okay until they were far away from this place. "I thought I'd never see you again."

Will pulled back just enough to cup her face in his hands, his thumbs brushing away tears she hadn't even realized were falling. Then his lips met hers, and for one perfect moment, everything around them vanished. There was only the saltiness of tears—hers or his, she couldn't tell—his calloused hands against her cheeks, and the staggering relief that he was alive and he was here.

"Someone had to rescue you from your own heroic ideas," he whispered, and despite everything, she laughed softly against his lips.

When they finally pulled apart, Teddy lifted his head from her shoulder and blinked at Will like he was just noticing him for the first time.

"Hi, Will."

"Hey, little man. You doing okay?"

Teddy nodded but kept his arms tightly wrapped around Kira's neck. "I protected Kira until you got here."

"I know you did." Will reached out to ruffle his hair. "Thanks, bud. She's a real handful, isn't she? Always getting herself into trouble."

"You shouldn't have kissed her," Teddy said seriously. "You'll probably get cooties."

Will laughed. "Probably. But I'm willing to risk it."

Kira shifted Teddy higher on her hip. "How did you even get here? Lucas said you were captured."

"One of the Guards let Ghost out of his cell," Will said, glancing back down the stairwell. "She gave him his weapon back. Said she was tired of watching people die."

Kira whispered, "Donna."

The female Guard who had escorted her to the Confines. The one who'd looked her in the eye and given her hope when no one else had.

They won't break you. Not if you don't let them.

"She and Ghost freed the rest of us—or at least as many as they could before things went sideways and we had to get out of there. Ghost knew where you were. Your father told him."

Another burst of gunfire erupted from below, the sharp staccato sound followed by fresh screams.

Will's hand found her back. "We need to get you two out of here. Now."

They descended the stairs quickly, with Kira carrying Teddy tightly and Will leading the way with his pistol. On the first-floor landing, Will paused and eased the stairwell door open just a crack, peering through.

"The exit's about thirty feet to the left," he said over his shoulder. "We're going to stay low and move fast. Okay?"

Kira nodded. "Okay."

The hallway leading to the front lobby stretched before them like a war zone—overturned chairs, shattered glass, and debris littered the floor. Smoke hung in the air, catching the light and casting everything in a dreamlike haze. Several bodies lay sprawled across the floor, dark stains spreading beneath them. They all wore the tattered gray of Confines prisoners.

Kira instinctively turned Teddy's face into her shoulder, shielding him, but her own eyes locked on one of the bodies. A young man slumped against the wall near the nurses' station, a bullet hole in the center of his forehead.

He couldn't have been much older than she was.

Beside her, Will muttered something under his breath.

"What?" she asked. "What is it?"

He pointed toward the shattered front windows.

Kira followed his gaze... and her heart sank.

Guard vehicles lined the road outside, forming a makeshift barricade around the abandoned bus. Dozens of uniformed figures moved between the cars, weapons drawn, spreading out into tactical positions.

There was no way out.

Chapter Fifty-Two

"Will? What are we—"

"Out of my way!"

Two hands grabbed Kira from behind and shoved her hard against the wall. Will reacted instantly, stepping between them and raising his pistol, but the man was already staggering toward the ruined front entrance. A prisoner clutching a bleeding shoulder, his eyes wild and unfocused. Like an animal that had been caged for far too long.

Outside, the Patrol soldiers saw him coming and shouted.

"Get down!"

"On the ground! Now!"

He ignored their warnings and kept going.

"Wait!" she yelled, trying to get his attention.

But Will grabbed her arm and pulled her away from the lobby just as a fresh volley of gunfire shredded the air where they'd been standing.

Over her shoulder, Kira caught one last glimpse of the prisoner, his body jerking as a barrage of bullets tore through him.

This isn't a rescue, Kira realized. *It's a massacre.*

People were going to die today. Many already had. And when the dust finally settled, many more would be hunted down and killed as punishment for the uprising.

And it was all because of her.

Every drop of blood spilled tonight could be traced back to her decision to defy Victor Devlin.

If there was ever going to be an end to this—

She had to be the one to end it.

Kira turned away from the carnage just in time to see a familiar figure emerge from the empty waiting room just ahead, her face smeared with dirt or ash or a combination of the two.

"Emma?"

The anger and hostility was gone from her best friend's eyes. Emma crossed the debris-strewn hallway in three quick steps and wrapped her arms around Kira and Teddy, holding them as if she never planned to let them go.

Kira shook her head, unable to process that Emma was not only alive but free. "I can't believe you're here."

"Of course, I'm here. Where else would I be?" Emma pulled back to look at her, one eyebrow raised. "Wow. You look terrible."

"Thanks. You've never looked better."

Emma ran her hands over her narrow hips. "Best diet I've ever been on. Did you see what I did with that bus?"

Kira laughed. "You gave those people the ride of their lives."

"I sure did."

Will appeared beside them. "Emma, is there any other way out of here?"

She wiped a smear of dirt from under her eyes. "There's an emergency exit in the back, just past the bathroom. It leads into an alley. We might be able to get out that way, as long as it's not crawling with Patrol soldiers. Otherwise..." She shook her head.

"I didn't exactly plan much past the whole ramming-the-bus-through-the-front-door thing."

Kira adjusted Teddy's weight in her arms, her muscles aching from the strain. The boy seemed to get heavier by the minute. And every time she tried to reposition him, he clung tighter, his arms like a vise around her neck, his legs locked around her waist.

"What about Ghost?" Kira asked. "Where is he?"

Emma blinked at her. "Who?"

"The man with the scar on his face. He was on the bus with you."

"Oh... you mean Hale? I have no idea. I saw him right after I got off the bus, but then I ran inside, and I haven't seen him since."

Will took her arm, his eyes scanning the surrounding corridors. "Ghost can handle himself. Trust me. But we've got to get out of here before more reinforcements show up."

But as the carnage continued around them—more gunfire thundering from the upper floors, followed by sharp screams of pain—Kira wasn't so certain.

This has to end here, a quiet voice whispered inside her head. *You have to stop this.*

And she realized... she knew how.

"No," she said, pulling back against Will's grip. "I can't go."

"What?"

Kira knelt and set Teddy on his feet. His arms immediately went around her legs, and she had to pry his fingers loose one by one. "You're going to go with Emma now, okay, buddy? She's my best friend in the whole world, and she's going to take you someplace safe."

His lower lip trembled. "Where are you going?"

She gave him the strongest smile she could muster. "I have to be a superhero, remember?"

"But I don't want you to be a superhero anymore. I just want you to stay with me."

Kira pulled him into a fierce hug, holding him close for longer than she should have, just in case she never got another chance. "This won't be for long, I promise. But I need you to be brave for me one more time. Can you do that?"

Teddy nodded against her shoulder. "I can be brave."

Kira glanced over his head at Emma. "Get him out of here safely. I don't care what it takes, but don't let anything happen to him."

"Of course. What are you going to do?"

"I'm going to stop this." She turned to Will. "Go with them. Help Emma get him somewhere safe."

"No." Will's voice was flat. Unyielding. "I'm not leaving you."

"Will, please—"

He closed the distance between them, his expression harder than she'd ever seen it. He looked like he was ready to fight the entire world for her if he had to. "You're not going without me. Whatever you're planning, we're doing it together."

Before she could stop herself, Kira grabbed the front of his shirt, yanking him toward her. The kiss was quick but desperate, the scrape of stubble against her skin, the taste of smoke and adrenaline on his lips. His hand found the back of her neck, holding her there for half a second longer than she'd intended.

"Love is beautiful and all." Emma's voice cut through the moment. "But can you stop making out until we're not actively being shot at?"

They broke apart as another burst of gunfire rattled from the lobby, a chunk of plaster dropping from the ceiling as if to drive her point home.

Will turned to Emma. "Get Teddy out of here. We'll catch up with you."

Emma shifted the boy higher on her hip, but before she could move, Kira caught her wrist.

"The building's public address system—where is it?"

Chapter Fifty-Three

They climbed the stairs to the second floor, Will in the lead with the pistol and Kira following behind, one hand on his back. The sounds of fighting and death swirled around them, the stairwell seeming to amplify the noise until it was coming from all directions—in front, behind, and even overhead.

When they reached the second floor, Will pushed open the stairwell door, and Kira leaned around him, peering into the corridor beyond. This part of the building had fared no better than the first. Two more frail bodies in gray prison uniforms lay sprawled across the floor, dark stains expanding beneath them.

Muzzle flashes lit up the far end of the hallway where the two Patrol soldiers had taken defensive positions behind two overturned filing cabinets, firing at something Kira couldn't see. Their backs were mercifully turned, so they didn't see the two people emerging from the stairwell behind them.

"This way," Will whispered, pulling her away from the main corridor. They hurried down a short hallway lined with administrative offices—Human Resources, Accounting, Medical Records. A few of the names on the doors were familiar. She remembered them as people who'd introduced themselves to her at the Volunteer Ball the previous evening.

Emma's word repeated in her mind. *You can access the PA system in the control room. Take the stairs to the second floor and turn left. It's at the end of the hallway.*

But would the PA system still work when the building was operating on emergency power? Kira could only pray it would.

The door to the control room was slightly ajar. Will pushed it open and did a quick sweep of the room.

Empty.

The office had no emergency lighting, but the harsh LED light spilling in from the hallway illuminated a cramped space with a bank of security monitors mounted on one wall. The day-shift security officer had clearly left in a hurry when his shift ended. A coffee mug sat on the desk with dried residue in the bottom, next to a dog-eared paperback book. A large security jacket hung over the back of the chair.

On the corner of the desk, Kira saw a rectangular black box with various buttons and switches. A microphone on a flexible stem emerged from the center of the device like a flower.

Will positioned himself in the doorway. "Do you know what you're doing?"

"Not really."

Most of the buttons were small and unlabeled, but there was a large toggle switch on the left side of the panel. It looked important, so she flipped it up, silently praying the PA system was set up to run on emergency power.

A burst of static crackled through the speakers, echoing through the building.

"Hurry." Will shifted his body further into the room, his

eyes still on the corridor. "The gunfire sounds closer. We don't have much time."

Kira's fingers shook as she pressed the large rectangular button below the microphone and held it down. "Hello?"

Her voice echoed from every speaker in the building, amplified through the corridors, patient rooms, and the destroyed front lobby. The effect was immediate and unsettling. The gunfire coming from the other corridor stopped abruptly, the sharp cracks cutting off as if someone had thrown a switch, and the shouting that had been constant since the bus had crashed into the building cut off mid-sentence.

Somewhere in the maze of corridors below, dozens of people—Guards and prisoners alike—had all stopped killing one another at the sound of her voice. In her mind, she saw their hesitation, their fingers easing off the triggers of their weapons. She had their attention.

Now she had to decide what to do with it.

This has to end here.

"My name is Kira Liebert. I'm this week's Volunteer."

She realized she had no idea what to say or how to use this moment to end the bloodshed that had come to define Vita Nova. She could feel the moment slipping away from her, could almost see guns being raised again in the building's hallways. If the gunfire resumed, all hope would be lost.

Give me the words, she prayed. *Show me what to say.*

Her free hand moved to the hidden pocket in her torn dress, fingers finding the folded paper Chandra had given her. The one she'd stuffed into her pocket before leaving for the Volunteer Ball. It was the list of names. The proof of her father's many crimes.

"To any Guards and Patrol soldiers in this building or stationed outside, I know you've been told that you're fighting to protect your city, but that's a lie. You're fighting to protect one man. You're fighting to protect Victor Devlin, and he has been lying to you—to all of us—for years."

Will glanced back at her, and as their eyes met, she remembered that first day in her office in the Governmental Sector. Those few awkward moments when he'd offended her by asking if the doctors had done any additional tests or performed a biopsy to confirm her mother's cancer diagnosis.

Will had known, even then. Even before the full extent of her father's crimes had been revealed.

He had known... and he'd tried to tell her.

"The Compulsory Orders you've been enforcing?" Kira continued, her voice growing stronger. "Many of them were lies. Hundreds of perfectly healthy people have been sentenced to death in this city because they knew too much, or asked too many questions, or caused problems for the wrong people."

She unfolded the paper with trembling hands, her eyes scanning the list. So many names. So many lives wasted. So many futures destroyed.

She began to read.

"Henry Kaiser, age thirty-seven. The official diagnosis was pancreatic cancer, but he wasn't sick. He died because he'd witnessed a Patrol soldier physically assault a female in an alley near the Tenements and tried to report it."

Chandra's careful handwriting filled the page, documenting years of Victor Devlin's systematic elimination of any threats to his power. Each entry was a life, reduced to a few lines of text. Chandra had loved her husband, mothered his children, shared his bed, and all the while she had been watching, recording, and building a case against him.

"Thomas Bradshaw, age twenty-two. False diagnosis: brain tumor. The real reason for his elimination: Thomas had discovered discrepancies in the city's food distribution records that proved the elite were hoarding supplies."

A harsh sob echoed from the next corridor—the kind of sound that tore itself from someone's throat before they could stop it.

A soldier? Someone who knew Thomas?

Buoyed by the sound, Kira leaned closer to the microphone. "Thomas was someone's son. Someone's brother. He didn't have to die. None of these people had to die." Her eyes continued to scan the paper. "Sarah Martinez, forty-two. Official reason: Early onset Alzheimer's Disease. The real reason: she worked in the Agricultural Sector and was caught sneaking food to families in the Tenements."

She could hear conversations in the hallway, soldiers talking to each other, their voices quiet and angry. The paper trembled in her hands as she continued down the list, the reading of each name a small act of liberation. She was setting these people free from the lies that had buried them. They deserved to be remembered as more than statistics on a piece of paper, more than casualties in her father's war against the truth.

And then she found it.

Her mother's name.

"Madison Liebert, age forty-seven." Kira's voice broke, the sound traveling to every speaker in the clinic. "False diagnosis: terminal lung cancer." She had to stop, take a breath, and force the rest of the words out. "The real reason: Considered a security risk."

The silence that followed was absolute. Even the sounds from the street outside—sirens, shouting, the rumble of Patrol and Guard vehicles—had faded to nothing.

"My mother," Kira whispered into the microphone, "wasn't a security risk. Victor Devlin murdered her because she knew who he really was. Because she'd loved a man Devlin had left for dead outside the barricade, and he couldn't stand the thought that one day she might tell her story. So he murdered her, just like he murdered all the others who stood against him."

Something broke loose inside of her. She had actually done it. She had told the truth about her mother and about so many others, and no one—not even her father—was powerful enough to take her words back.

"Please stop fighting each other for him. Please stop killing each other for a man who sees all of us, including his own daughter, as expendable."

Her head dropped forward over the microphone, her tears falling onto the desk. Years of pent-up grief poured out of her, her soft cries echoing through the building.

Will left his position at the door and crossed to her side, his arms closing around her and pulling her away from the control panel. Her face pressed against his chest, her tears dampening his shirt.

"I'm so proud of you," he said.

She felt Will's hand shift away from her back, his fingers trembling as he reached down to pull something out of his pocket. She pulled away and looked down at his palm. Nestled there was a simple gold band with a small diamond, the stone glinting like a shard of ice.

"Ghost gave this to me," Will said, resting his forehead against hers. "He bought it for your mother, but he never got the chance to give it to her. I know this isn't the most romantic place to do this, but I don't want to wait another second."

He took her left hand in both of his and slipped the ring onto her finger. It fit perfectly, as if it had been made for her.

"Will you marry me, Kira?" His thumb traced her knuckles, and she could hear the vulnerability in his voice, as if her answer could possibly be anything apart from yes. "Will you be my wife?"

"Yes." The word burst from her lips before he even finished asking. "Yes, of course, yes—"

She framed his face with her hands and pulled his lips down to hers, kissing him with everything she had. The ring on her finger had been meant for her mother, and she would wear it as a promise. Not just to Will, but to the love story that Madison and Ghost had begun but never got to live.

"I love you," she whispered.

"I love you, t—"

The words cut off as his whole body stiffened against hers. A sharp, strangled gasp tore from his throat, and his arms cinched tighter around her, almost crushing, like he was bracing for something or trying to shield her from an unseen threat.

"Will? What's—"

Over his shoulder, Lucas Pine stepped out of the shadows, moving with the confidence of someone who already knew he had won. An empty syringe dangled from his good hand, the tip of the needle gleaming as he turned it lazily between his fingers. His gaze lingered on her, his lips stretching into thin, knowing smile.

"*No!*" The scream tore from Kira's throat as she saw the small bead of blood on the side of Will's neck where the needle had pierced his skin.

Will released her, his hand flying to his neck to press against the injection site, but it was too late. The damage was done.

The syringe clattered to the floor, empty.

"No, no, no..." She repeated the word over and over, grabbing Will as his legs gave out and lowering him to the floor as gently as she could. She looked into his eyes and saw they were already losing focus, recognizing the same glazed look she'd seen in her mother's eyes during those final moments in room 317.

She looked up as Lucas stepped around her to silence the PA system with a flick of his finger. He leaned back against the desk, his gaze settling on Will.

"*That's* your boyfriend?" Lucas shook his head. "I have to say, Kira, I'm disappointed. I was expecting someone with a little more fight in him. He went down way too easy."

She ignored him and pressed a hand against Will's chest, feeling his heart beating too fast, then too slow. Just like her mother. The same poison spreading through his veins, shutting down his organs one by one.

"I'm sorry," Will whispered. "I'm so sorry—"

"Don't," she said, pushing on his chest as if she could somehow hold the life inside him. Tears streamed down her face, dripping onto his shirt. "Don't you dare leave me, Will Foster. You're not allowed to go. You have to fight this, okay? You have to fight. Please stay with me."

But his eyes were already rolling back. Those brilliant blue eyes that had looked at her with such love during their dance at Avery's wedding were now fading to something distant and unreachable. The warmth inside them was slipping away, like the last light at the end of the day.

Death is a horrible thing.

Each breath became a struggle. She could feel his chest rising and falling beneath her palm in an irregular rhythm. This was the same terrible progression she'd witnessed with her mother, the slow shutting down of a body that could no longer fight the poison coursing through its veins.

Will was dying in her arms.

The man who had walked into her life planning to deceive her had instead fallen so completely in love that he'd given up everything for her. The man who had taken her out of the city and shown her the truth of what it was—of who *she* was. The man who had pulled her out of the river twice and carried her when she could no longer walk.

That man was slipping away from her now, one breath at a time, and there was nothing she could do but hold him and whisper his name over and over.

And pray that wherever he was going, he knew how much she loved him.

Chapter Fifty-Four

*"R*ob Huston, age twenty-four. False diagnosis: kidney failure. Rob refused to serve in the Patrols after he witnessed the execution of an unarmed Lawless woman in the Unregulated Zone."*

Kira's voice filled the empty hospital room as Ghost knelt beside a wounded prisoner, pressing both hands against the man's abdomen to stem the flow of blood. The bullet had carved a ragged path through the prisoner's stomach. Painful and messy, but from the location, probably not fatal.

Ghost had been methodically searching the second floor for Kira when he'd found a young man, no more than twenty-five, dragging himself down the corridor and painting a crimson trail on the floor. Every instinct told Ghost to keep moving, to find Kira before it was too late. But he couldn't leave a wounded man to bleed out alone.

His training wouldn't allow it.

Besides, he could hear her voice flowing through the PA system, reading that damning list of names. As long as she kept talking, she was alive.

The young prisoner stared up at him, his face pale and slick with sweat. "Am I going to die?"

Ghost maintained pressure on the wound with one hand while using his teeth and free hand to tear a long strip from the bedsheet. "Not a chance, brother. This is barely a scratch."

"Jennifer Walsh, age twenty-nine. False diagnosis: cervical cancer. Jennifer organized a small group outside the Executive Mansion to protest the Compulsory Program."

Ghost tore another strip from the bedsheet, the cotton coming away in long white ribbons. "I'm going to wrap this around you," he told the wounded kid. "It's going to hurt a lot, but it'll help stop the bleeding."

The kid nodded weakly, then gritted his teeth in pain as Ghost lifted his torso enough to wind the makeshift bandage around his midsection. Blood seeped through the white fabric, but not as quickly as before.

"What's your name?" Ghost asked him.

"Marcus Wolfe."

"How long were you in the Confines, Marcus?"

"Two years." The kid closed his eyes and breathed through his nose, some of the color returning to his face. "I tried to save a kid."

"They imprison people for that now?"

The kid opened his eyes and looked at Ghost. "They do when you work at the Compulsory Clinic."

Ghost kept his expression neutral, his hands still applying pressure to the bandaged wound. "What happened?"

"I trained as a nurse's aide." Marcus bared his teeth as a wave of fresh pain washed over him. He waited it out, then continued. "I was here every day. Saw what they did to people. Most of the time, it wasn't so bad. Everyone was older; a lot of them were sick. But then I saw them taking this little girl into a room."

Ghost felt something cold settle in his stomach. "How old was she?"

"Seven. Maybe eight." Marcus struggled to sit up, wincing as the movement pulled at his wound. "The doctor said she had leukemia, but she looked fine to me. Scared, but healthy. There were no parents with her. I think she was an orphan."

"Andrew Mitchell, age thirty-six..."

"They gave her the injection. Somnumbutal. Standard procedure. Everyone else left the room, but I stayed. I didn't think it was right for her to be alone. She just lay there, breathing slower and slower, her little chest barely moving. She kept asking for her momma."

Ghost closed his eyes, his hands clenching into fists. Even in a world full of cruelty, there were still depths of evil that surprised him.

"I couldn't stand it," Marcus whispered, tears shimmering in his eyes. "Watching her slip away like that, alone and scared. So I tried to save her, even though I had no idea what I was doing. It didn't work. She didn't come back. Then the doctor came back into the room and started screaming at me. He called the Guards to take me away, but not before I watched that poor little girl take her last breath."

Ghost felt something break apart inside him. Not just anger, but a grief so profound it threatened to crush him. He'd seen enough death to last a dozen lifetimes, but this was different. He lowered his head, his scarred cheek burning with phantom pain.

"Madison Liebert, age forty-seven. False diagnosis: terminal lung cancer. The real reason: Considered a security risk."

At the sound of her name, memories flooded his mind, each more painful than the last. Madison at the grocery store, looking as beautiful as he remembered from high school. Madison's hand in his as they walked beside the river. Madison's tears when he'd finally shown up at her door that awful day. The last time he would ever see her.

"My mother wasn't a security risk. Victor Devlin murdered her because she knew who he really was. Because she'd loved a man Devlin had left for dead outside the barricade, and he couldn't stand the thought that one day she might tell that story. So he had her killed, just like all the others who knew too much."

Ghost pressed a hand to his forehead as twelve years of grief came roaring to the surface. The pain in Kira's voice was *his* pain, Madison's loss like a wound that had never properly healed. For over a decade, he'd forced himself to push her memory deeper, not because he wanted to forget her, but because forgetting was the only way to survive each day without her.

But Madison would not let him forget.

He knew her spirit wasn't in the room with him. She was in heaven, where she belonged, far beyond Devlin's reach. Yet in that moment, Ghost felt closer to Madison than he had since the day he'd been exiled from the city.

"What is it?" Marcus asked.

Ghost shook his head. He couldn't even begin to explain.

"Please stop fighting each other for him. Please stop killing each other for a man who sees all of us, including his own daughter, as expendable."

Kira's words cut through the air, followed by the sound of her muffled cries. And then he heard another voice, one that sounded an awful lot like Will's.

Some of the tension left his body. *Good. The kid found her.*

Will would protect her until Ghost found them both.

He turned back to Marcus. "Think you can walk? They're not shooting out there right now. We could make a break for it."

"I think so. Just might need a little—"

A scream exploded through the PA system: *"No!"*

Ghost's blood went cold. That wasn't just fear in Kira's voice—it was total devastation. The sound of someone watching their world collapse in front of their eyes.

"No, no, no," her voice continued through the speakers, each word more broken than the last.

"Where is she?" he demanded, turning to Marcus. "Where is she broadcasting from?"

Marcus struggled to focus through his pain. "Control room, probably. Administrative wing. It's... on this floor, but... on the opposite side of the building."

"Take me there." Ghost was already moving, helping Marcus to his feet. "Now!"

They moved toward the door, with Ghost half-carrying, half-dragging the kid along with him. He carried his shotgun in his free hand, prepared to fire a round of buckshot into anyone who got in his way. But when they moved into the corridor, something had shifted. The gunfire that had echoed through the building for the past half-hour had stopped completely, leaving behind an eerie silence.

Three Guards clustered near the elevator bank, their assault rifles hanging forgotten at their sides, their faces drained of color. When they spotted Ghost and Marcus hobbling down the corridor, they made no move for their weapons.

They simply parted like water, pressing themselves against the walls to let them pass.

In the next corridor, a female Guard knelt beside an escaped prisoner, her hands working frantically to apply a tourniquet to stop the bleeding from his shattered leg. A Patrol soldier sat slumped against the wall, his rifle lying at his side, staring at nothing while tears streamed down his face.

Marcus tightened his grip on Ghost's shoulder. "Why aren't they killing us right now?"

Ghost studied their faces. These were men and women

who—until today—had seen themselves as protectors. Only to learn they'd been complicit in the slaughter of hundreds of innocents. Their rifles lay forgotten, their beliefs dismantled by the voice of a nineteen-year-old girl.

"Because of Kira," he said. "She just burned down their entire world with the truth."

Chapter Fifty-Five

Kira knelt on the floor of the control room, cradling Will's head in her lap. His eyes were closed now, and he looked so peaceful, as if he were only sleeping. Except he wasn't sleeping. His breathing was becoming more shallow, his body growing noticeably cooler in her arms.

The poison Lucas had injected into his neck was doing exactly what it was designed to do, and she could do nothing to stop it.

She stared down at him, the tears drying on her cheeks. The numbness creeping through her chest was different from the grief she'd felt watching her mother die. At least then, she'd known it was going to happen. They'd shared a last meal together, held each other, and talked about what was to come.

But with Will, there had been no time. No chance to tell him goodbye and let him know how much she loved him. Just Lucas stealing away the man she loved before she could tell him how grateful she was that God had brought him into her life. Before she could thank him for showing her what real love looked like.

Kira's eyes shifted from his face to the ring on her finger.

Another promise unfulfilled.

Another dream broken.

She touched the gold band with her thumb, thinking of all the things they would never share. The marriage they would never have. The children who would never be born. The future she'd imagined long before he'd slipped the ring on her finger. All of it was fading away with Will on the dirty floor of the control room.

Please, God. I'm ready to go. Please let them kill me, too.

Will's breathing hitched, a horrible rattling sound that made her heart skip a beat. She'd heard that same sound come from her mother. It was the body's final, desperate attempt to hold on to life.

Kira leaned down to press her lips to his forehead. "You promised you'd never leave me," she whispered to him. "Don't you remember? That night at the wedding. You promised. So, I need you to keep fighting for me now. For us. You're so strong, Will. I know you can fight this."

Lucas laughed from his spot at the desk where he'd been watching her. "You actually think your Lawless boyfriend is going to wake up, don't you? You're even more of an idiot than I thought you were. Do you even realize how ridiculous you look, sitting there in your ugly yellow dress, whispering sweet nothings to a corpse?"

His voice was like pouring lemon juice on an open wound. He shouldn't be here. He shouldn't be defiling Will's last moments with his presence. How had she spent her entire Final Week with this creature? How had she ever seen him as anything but evil?

"Please leave us alone," she muttered. "Please just go away."

"I hate to break it to you, Kira," Lucas said, "but he isn't taking a nap. I injected him with an entire syringe of Somnumbutal. He's not resting. He's dying. And the dead don't come back to life."

"That's where you're wrong, son."

Lucas spun around and found himself staring into the barrel of a double-barrel shotgun.

Ghost stood just inside the doorway, one finger resting on the trigger. A wounded young man in gray prison clothes leaned against the doorframe behind him, blood leaking through a bandage around his midsection. "Get your hands up in the air where I can see them. I'm looking for a reason, so don't give me one."

Lucas obliged.

Kira blinked. "Ghost?"

Her mind wasn't working properly. She knew she was supposed to be relieved that Ghost had found his way to her, but she felt something closer to disappointment. She didn't want to be saved, not anymore.

She wanted to be with Will.

And her mother.

Ghost's eyes swept the room, taking in Lucas with his hands in the air and Will dying on the ground. When his eyes finally landed on Kira, his granite-hard expression cracked, revealing something raw and painful. The look was gone as quickly as it had appeared, his eyes snapping back to Lucas.

"I didn't mean to interrupt your little victory speech, son. Were you done?"

Lucas opened his mouth to respond, but Ghost cut him off with a slight adjustment of the shotgun's aim. "That was rhetorical. You say another word and I'll turn you into abstract art on that wall behind you."

Lucas's mouth snapped shut.

The wounded man pushed himself off the doorframe with

obvious effort, wincing at the pain. He moved around Ghost and limped over to Will.

"How long ago was he injected?"

The words seemed to come from underwater, jumbled and distant in Kira's mind. She stared at this stranger, unable to process what was happening or what he wanted from her.

"Kira?" Ghost's sharp voice cut through the fog. "How long has Will been down?"

She forced herself to focus. "Five minutes? Maybe ten. I don't know."

The man turned to Ghost. "I might be able to bring him back."

Ghost grabbed his shoulder. "How?"

"Naloximate. It's a reversal agent for the Somnumbutal. It hasn't been tested much, obviously, so I have no idea how effective it is. But when I worked here, we always kept it on hand in case of an accidental staff exposure. It's the same stuff I gave to that little girl." He exchanged a look with Ghost before turning back to Kira. "Check his pulse for me, please. I can't bend down that far. Is his heart still beating?"

When she remained frozen, Ghost barked an order like the soldier he'd once been. "Kira! Check his pulse!"

She jumped and pressed her hand against Will's neck, searching his cold skin for any sign of life. Then—faint but unmistakable—she found it. A weak, irregular pulse fluttered beneath her fingertips like a trapped bird.

"He's still alive."

"Barely." The young man shuddered in pain and pressed a hand against his stomach. "I need the antidote."

"Where is it?" Ghost asked.

"There should be some in a cabinet down the hall, near the nurse's station."

Ghost nodded and turned toward the door. "Can you walk?"

"I can manage." He pushed himself off the wall and took a few unsteady steps toward the doorway, but before he could step into the hallway, he let out a sharp gasp of pain and grabbed the edge of the doorframe for support.

Ghost lowered his shotgun and reached out to steady the wounded man. "You good, brother?"

"I'm fine," he breathed, clutching his wounded side. "Just need to rest a second."

After a few moments, he straightened his back, took a deep breath, and pushed away from the doorframe. Despite his obvious pain, he exited the room, his uneven footsteps echoing down the corridor as he headed for the nurse's station.

That's when Kira heard a faint click from behind them.

She turned to see Lucas aiming a small pistol at Ghost's back.

The weapon had appeared from somewhere. An ankle holster, maybe? Or tucked into his waistband beneath his jacket. Lucas gripped it awkwardly with his good hand while his broken one hung useless against his chest, but at this distance it would be just as deadly as Ghost's shotgun.

"Drop the shotgun," Lucas muttered. "Now."

Ghost turned slowly, his scarred face showing nothing but mild irritation as he took in the small pistol in Lucas's hand. As if Lucas were a child who'd interrupted the adults with some foolish demand.

"You know what separates soldiers from pretenders?" Ghost asked, his voice calm. "Soldiers don't announce their intentions. They don't threaten. They just act. But you? Well, if you had the guts to shoot me, I would already be dead. You don't have the spine for this, son."

"You think I won't do it?" Lucas's voice cracked slightly.

"You think I'm some kind of coward? I've done worse things than you can—"

Ghost closed the distance between himself and Lucas, moving with the fluid precision of a man who had successfully disarmed dozens of enemies over the years. Before Lucas could even think about pulling the trigger, Ghost's hand shot out and clamped down on his wrist, twisting it at an impossible angle.

Lucas cried out—a high-pitched, childlike wail—and the pistol clattered to the floor at his feet.

"Sit down," Ghost growled, shoving Lucas back into the desk chair with enough force to send it rolling. "And shut up."

He grabbed a length of Ethernet cable from behind the control panel and went to work, winding it around Lucas's chest and arms, securing him to the chair.

"That's too tight—"

"I told you to shut up."

As Ghost pulled the wire even tighter against Lucas's chest, the wounded man reappeared in the doorway, a small medical bag in his hands. His face was paler than before, and more blood had seeped through his bandage, but he was still on his feet.

"Got it," he said, breathing hard from the exertion. "I found three vials in the cabinet."

Kira looked down at Will. His face was so pale it was almost gray, and his lips had taken on a bluish tinge. "Will it work?"

"No promises." The man limped over and lowered himself to the floor with Ghost's help. He pressed two fingers against Will's neck. "His pulse is still there, but just barely. It's been too long since the injection. But I'll try."

The man began preparing a syringe with clear liquid from one of the small vials. He found a vein in Will's arm, inserted the needle, and pushed the plunger down slowly.

The antidote disappeared into Will's bloodstream.

Ghost bowed his head slightly and closed his eyes. "Lord, this boy's got more good in him than most men see in a lifetime. If You're willing to spare his life..."

"That's your plan?" Lucas sneered from his chair. "Tough guy thinks he's going to pray his boyfriend back to life. What's next, crossing your fingers and hoping real hard?"

Without opening his eyes, Ghost lifted his boot and gave Lucas's chair a sharp kick. The chair tipped backward with a crash, leaving Lucas staring helplessly at the ceiling, his legs flailing.

"Please, Lord," Ghost continued, opening his eyes and meeting Kira's gaze. "This boy has got people here who still need him. Please give him back to us."

Kira pressed her hand against Will's neck again, searching for his heartbeat. She couldn't find it anymore. "Come on, baby. Please."

The wounded man glanced at the clock on the wall, his face grim.

"Come on," Kira whispered, her hand gripping Will's. "Come back to me."

A full minute passed.

Nothing.

The antidote wasn't working.

She felt her hope beginning to crumble, that familiar crushing weight settling back onto her chest. She'd been a fool to allow herself to hope, even for a moment, that God would bring Will back to her. Life didn't work that way. She loved him with all of her heart and soul, but even love wasn't enough to bring someone back from the—

Will's eyelids fluttered.

Just barely, the movement so slight she might have imagined it. But then she saw it again. A tiny whisper of movement that caused her heart to leap into her throat.

"Will?" she whispered.

His eyes opened, unfocused at first, then gradually finding her face. "Kira?"

His voice was little more than a whisper, but it was the most beautiful sound she'd ever heard.

"I'm here," she said, laughing through her tears. "I'm right here."

Will tried to sit up, but Ghost gently pressed him back to the floor. "Easy, son. You've been through hell. Just lie still for a minute."

"What happened?" Will's gaze shifted around the room, taking in Ghost and the wounded prisoner before finally returning to Kira.

"You almost died," Kira said, wiping the tears from her cheeks. "But God brought you back."

Will managed a weak smile. "That's... good." He reached for her hand, his fingers intertwining with hers, still cold but growing warmer. "Can't... miss... our wedding."

"You're not getting out of it that easy," Kira said, squeezing his hand.

Will's eyes shifted to something behind her, and his smile faded. The relief on his face drained away, replaced by something that looked like pure terror. His grip on her hand tightened until it was almost painful.

"Kira," Will croaked, his voice failing as he tried to force out the words. "Behind..."

Before she could react, a pair of hands seized her, yanking her to her feet. An arm wrapped around her waist, pulling her back into the doorway, and she felt the sharp prick of a needle against the side of her throat.

"Hello, daughter," Victor Devlin spoke softly into her ear. "It seems we need to have a little talk."

Chapter Fifty-Six

Ghost could do nothing but watch as Victor Devlin held a syringe to Kira's throat, the shotgun heavy and useless in his grip. After twelve years of exile and imagining this moment, Ghost finally had Victor Devlin in his sights. He was close enough that Ghost could smell his cologne along with the unmistakable stench of sweat and fear that clung to his body. But he couldn't take the shot because the man was using Kira as a human shield.

"You just keep racking up the charges, Hale. First the bridge, and now you've destroyed one of our medical clinics. Plus, you facilitated the escape of dozens of dangerous prisoners. That's a lot for one night, even for you."

Ghost kept his weapon trained on the man, waiting for an opening, a mistake. It would take only one. "You inject her with that garbage, and you'll be dead before she hits the ground."

Devlin's grip tightened around Kira's waist, pulling her more firmly against him. "That would really destroy you, wouldn't it? Watching her die in the same way as her mother?" His lips expanded into a cruel grin. "You know, Madison was always expendable to me. I discarded her like an old toy because that's what she was to me. An old, broken toy. And you picked her up and played with her. How pathetic."

Ghost bit down on his tongue hard enough to taste blood. He could feel the fury rising in his chest, and he sat with it for a moment. Allowed it to flow through his blood like poison. Then he forced it back down. He had no use for it now.

Not with Kira's life on the line.

His vision narrowed to a single, critical point of focus: the tip of the syringe against her neck and the thin trickle of blood where the needle had already broken her skin.

If he injects her, you still have the antidote. The drug brought Will back. It might bring Kira back, too. So let him inject her... and then you pull the trigger and blow him straight to hell.

But Marcus had tried and failed to save the little girl with the same antidote.

It didn't work, he'd said. *She didn't come back.*

Could he take that chance with Kira?

He already knew the answer.

"Isn't that the defector you ran off with?" Devlin nodded at Will, who was trying unsuccessfully to push himself off the floor, beads of sweat clinging to his forehead. He collapsed back onto the ground, gasping. "What happened to him?"

Lucas twisted on the floor, still attached to the chair but moving it enough to draw Devlin's attention. "I injected him with the Somnumbutal, sir," he said in a strained voice. "But they used some kind of antidote to bring him back. There are more vials in that bag right there."

Devlin's eyes shifted to the medical kit on the floor beside Marcus. "Is that so? Well, we can't have that, can we, Hale?"

"Have what?"

"A way to reverse the effects of the drug. That makes me

nervous. If there's an antidote, and I inject my daughter, you might bring her back. That's not fair. If we're going to make some sort of deal tonight—a gentleman's agreement, if you will —it should be a fair one, don't you think?"

Ghost had no intention of making any deals with Devlin. Not ones he intended to keep, anyway. But he would do anything necessary to get that needle away from Kira's throat. "What kind of deal are you looking for?"

"First, I want you to take those extra vials my associate mentioned out of the bag and crush them under your boot. All of them. Right now."

"Yeah, that's not happening."

Devlin pressed the needle deeper into Kira's skin. "You think I won't do it? My daughter has systematically destroyed everything I've built, and now she's destroyed my life. Did you hear what she just said over the intercom? There's no coming back from that. Half the people in this city want me dead right now. You'd be doing me a favor by blowing me away."

Ghost saw it then. The desperation beneath Devlin's calculated facade. The man was cornered, his own city turning against him. He needed Ghost as much as Ghost needed him.

"This doesn't have to end like the last time," Devlin continued. "We can all walk out of here. We'll cross the river together and go our separate ways. But you have to break the vials so I know you're willing to negotiate in good faith. Otherwise, I will kill my daughter right now, right in front of you, and you can take your chances that the antidote will actually work on her."

The offer hovered in the air between them. Ghost could see the twisted logic. Devlin knew he was finished in Vita Nova. His lies had been exposed to the entire city. His own Guards were laying down their weapons. He needed an escape route, and he was willing to trade Kira's life for safe passage out of a city he could no longer control.

Ghost shifted his gaze to Kira. She couldn't shake her head because the needle was pressed against her neck, but he knew what she wanted from the look in her eyes. She didn't want him to go along with any deals her father proposed. She had the same fighter spirit as her mother, and she would rather die than give Devlin what he wanted.

But Ghost couldn't do it.

He couldn't watch another woman he loved die in Victor Devlin's hands. Not if he had the chance to save her.

He nodded at the medical kit, his jaw clenched. "Marcus," he said, never taking his eyes off Devlin. "Take the vials out of the bag."

Marcus looked up at him, his eyes growing wide. "No, you can't—"

"Do it. Now."

The prisoner reached into the medical kit and withdrew the three remaining vials of Naloximate, placing them carefully on the floor. Each vial contained a liquid that could bring someone back from the edge of death. The same antidote that had saved Will's life just minutes earlier.

Ghost raised his boot over the vials, the leather sole hovering inches above what might be Kira's only chance at survival. It was the sort of psychological warfare Devlin did best. He wasn't just threatening Kira's life; he was forcing Ghost to participate in her death. To become the one who ensured that if negotiations collapsed, if the syringe struck its target, there would be no antidote. No resurrection. No second chances.

But if destroying the vials was the price of keeping her alive long enough to get them all across that river, then it was a bargain he had to make.

The glass crunched like bones underneath his boot.

Chapter Fifty-Seven

Ghost stared at the shattered remains of the antidote. The liquid leaked across the floor, the tiny fragments of glass reflecting the uncertainty on his face. There was no going back now.

No second chances.

Devlin grinned at him, the tip of the needle still digging into Kira's neck. "You see that, daughter? Even after I carved up his face and ordered the death of his lover, he still bends the knee whenever I snap my fingers. He's a good soldier, and good soldiers always follow orders. Isn't that right, Hale?"

Ghost gave him nothing, kept his face as hard as stone. Let Devlin think he'd won. Let him gloat. The man had always been too fond of his own voice, and that weakness would eventually be his undoing.

But Kira's entire body was trembling. Not from fear, but from pure, concentrated fury. Her hands had curled into fists at her sides, and Ghost could see the muscles in her jaw working as she fought to contain the rage building inside her.

"You're pathetic," she muttered, her voice as deadly as the

poison in the syringe. "You've slaughtered hundreds of innocent people, and now... what? You're just going to slink out of the city like a coward. What's the matter? Too terrified to face the same gallows you built for Jonesy? At least my mother had the courage to die with dignity."

"Dignity?" Devlin laughed. "If surrendering without a shred of resistance is dignified, then yes—your mother had that in spades. Your mother didn't die brave, Kira. She died easy."

Ghost saw the exact moment when something fundamental snapped inside Kira. Her shoulders went rigid, her breathing stopped, and then every muscle in her body coiled like a spring under pressure.

The next three seconds unfolded in slow-motion horror.

Kira drove her elbow back with bone-crushing force, the impact landing in the center of Devlin's stomach. His body folded around the blow, a grunt of surprise tearing loose from his throat. She twisted free and lunged for the door, bare feet skidding in the liquid and broken glass. But Devlin grabbed a fistful of her hair, yanking her backward. She screamed as the torn hem of her dress tangled around her legs like a snare, dragging her down.

Will clawed at the floor, trying to drag his unresponsive body toward her, but his limbs wouldn't obey.

Ghost's would.

He hit Devlin like a freight train, driving his shoulder into the man's ribs with twelve years of pent-up aggression. All three of them went down hard, with Devlin crashing into the base of the desk. The syringe spun away into the shadows, and Ghost heard the satisfying crack of something breaking.

Hopefully, Devlin's spine.

He was vaguely aware of Kira rolling away from the fight, crawling toward Will on her hands and knees.

And then his hands found Devlin's throat, fingers digging

into the soft flesh of the man's windpipe as he pinned him to the floor and squeezed. Devlin's face turned red, his eyes bulging. Ghost could have crushed the life out of him in a second. One sharp twist, one application of pressure in exactly the right spot. But he didn't.

He wanted this to last.

"How does it feel?" Ghost brought his face within inches of Devlin's. "How does it feel to be the one dying?"

Madison's face flashed through his mind. Beautiful. Haunted. She wouldn't want this. She'd always been better than him. She'd believed in mercy, forgiveness, and finding another way. Madison would never have wanted Ghost to become a killer, not even to avenge her death.

His grip loosened just a little.

It was all Devlin needed.

He drove his knee into Ghost's stomach, breaking the chokehold and scrambling to his feet. Ghost registered the impact as pain, but only distantly. He rolled off the man and shot up onto his feet. When Devlin swung wildly at his head, Ghost caught the man's wrist and twisted it until he heard something pop. Devlin screamed and tried to pull away, but Ghost held on, applying just enough pressure to keep the bones grinding together.

"Does that hurt? I bet it does."

He released Devlin's wrist and stepped back, savoring the look of terror that crossed the man's face as he realized he was being toyed with.

Good. Let him think he has a chance. Let him grab whatever pathetic weapon he can find.

Which is precisely what he did. Devlin picked the coffee cup off the desk and launched it at Ghost's head, but Ghost ducked easily and charged at him again, lifting him off his feet and slamming him against the wall. His feet kicked uselessly in the air as Ghost held him there, watching the panic bloom in the man's gray eyes.

"Twelve years," Ghost said. "I've spent twelve years thinking about this moment. And you know what the sad thing is? It's not even enjoyable. You're even more pathetic than I remembered."

He dropped Devlin, who collapsed to his knees in the corner of the room, gasping. Ghost circled him slowly, savoring the moment.

This was justice.

This was what Madison deserved.

The once-powerful mayor of Vita Nova cowered against the wall, his expensive suit torn and filthy, his silver hair matted with sweat. He looked like what he'd always been beneath the polish—a weak, frightened man who'd built his power on the suffering of others.

"Please," Devlin begged without turning around, his voice gruff from the pressure Ghost had put on his windpipe. "Look at my daughter. She's watching you. Do you want her to see you murder her father?"

Anger flared in Ghost's chest at hearing Devlin claim her. Even now, even beaten and defeated, the scumbag was still trying to use Kira as a weapon.

"She's not your daughter," Ghost said, moving closer to the man huddled in the corner. "Not anymore."

Devlin struggled to his feet, still facing the wall, his movements slow and pained. He put one hand against the wall for support, head sagging on his shoulders, looking like a man who could barely stand.

"Turn around and face me, Devlin."

The man obeyed, turning slowly and deliberately, and Ghost caught a glimpse of black metal. The dull gleam of a gun barrel. But his mind stuttered, unable to track where it had come from or how Devlin had gotten his hands on it. The image registered, but too late. Far too late.

Kira screamed, "Look out!"

He had time to realize: *That's Lucas's gun.*

And then the muzzle flash lit up Devlin's face, the gunshot like thunder in the windowless room.

Ghost's hands instinctively went to his chest, checking for blood, for pain, for the burning sensation of torn flesh. Nothing. He was still standing, still breathing. His eyes swept the room, searching for the bullet's impact, trying to understand what had happened.

In the opposite corner of the room, Lucas jerked and gurgled, blood bubbling from a hole in his throat where Devlin's wild shot had found an unintended target.

"Oops," Devlin muttered. "Sorry, Lucas."

Ghost's head snapped back around.

Devlin still held the pistol—steady now—and had it aimed squarely at Ghost.

The second shot punched through his chest like a sledgehammer.

Chapter Fifty-Eight

Fire exploded through Ghost's torso as the bullet tore through muscle and bone, flesh and ribs, right through the spot on the left side of his chest where he'd kept Madison's photograph all these years.

Kira's scream tore through the room, and Will's voice soon joined hers, both of them crying out Ghost's name as he collapsed backward onto the floor.

But all he could think about—not the pain, not the warm rush of blood soaking through his shirt, not his daughter's screams—was whether Madison's picture had survived the bullet.

They took it from you, he remembered distantly, the thought surfacing like a half-forgotten scene from a movie. Not real. Not something that had just happened to him. *They took it at the Confines.*

Devlin straightened his jacket and walked across the room. He stopped just close enough that his shadow fell across Ghost's face, casting him in near darkness.

"You should have stayed on your side of the wall, Hale. I was too generous when I allowed you to live. I won't make the same mistake again."

He raised the pistol and aimed it at Ghost's head, then paused, seeming to savor the moment. "You know what's funny about this? All these years, you probably saw yourself as some kind of victim. A noble soldier, ripped away from his one true love. But do you know what you really are? You're a broken man clinging to the memory of a woman who was never yours to begin with. She never loved you the way she loved me, Hale. You know that, right? That's why she didn't go with you. That's why she stayed behind."

Wrong, Ghost thought, the bullet wound in his chest sending waves of fire through his torso with each breath. Madison's love had been the one pure thing in his life. Devlin could manipulate everything else, but he could not distort Madison's love. *She stayed for her daughter.*

"Give my regards to Madison if you see her on the other side. Tell her I said that being with her was entertaining while it lasted. And tell her not to worry; I'll be sending our daughter along to see her very—"

Devlin's words cut off abruptly, his smirk faltering. The satisfaction drained from his eyes, replaced by a flicker of confusion. His face blanched, and a tremor ran through him. Then his hands flew to his throat, clawing at the syringe buried deep in his neck.

The same syringe he had held to his daughter's neck only minutes earlier.

Over her father's shoulder, Kira stood frozen, her hand still gripping the plunger she'd just depressed.

"That was for my mother," she whispered.

Devlin's mouth opened and closed like a dying fish, his

fingers pulling at the needle, ripping it from his neck. But it was no use. The Somnumbutal was already spreading through his bloodstream. His legs buckled, and he went down beside Ghost, his body going limp as the poison did its terrible work.

Ghost turned his head. The simple movement drained what little strength he had left. On the floor beside him lay the shattered remains of the antidote vials, traces of liquid still glimmering on the floor. There would be no reversal this time, no miraculous recovery.

Devlin had forced him to destroy the only thing that could have saved his life.

Kira stepped over Devlin's dying form and dropped to her knees beside Ghost. Her hands pressed against his chest, applying pressure to the bullet wound. He could feel the warmth spreading everywhere, soaking through his shirt, pooling beneath him, and seeping through her fingers. It was no use. She didn't need to bother.

"Hey..." Her tearful voice seemed to come from very far away. "Hey. Don't do that. Don't close your eyes. You need to stay with me."

He wanted to say something meaningful, something she could remember and hold in her heart. He wanted to say perfect final words that would comfort her long after he was gone. But the searing pain in his chest made it hard to think, hard to form the right words. It was unlike anything he'd ever felt before.

Except for the day he'd walked away from Madison.

"It's... okay..." He had to fight for every word. "I'll get... to see... your mother... now."

Kira's hand found his, her fingers intertwining with his blood-stained ones. She kissed the back of his hand, his blood leaving a stain on her lips. "You're my father, Noah," she said, her voice breaking. "I finally found you. You can't leave me now."

Those words filled him with more happiness than he would've thought possible. Even if he only got to be her father for a few moments, those moments would be precious to him. He reached up to touch her tear-stained face. "Will... take care... of her."

Ghost's vision was growing dim, but he could see Will struggling to stand, with Marcus trying to help him.

"Do you... hear me?" He tried to raise his voice. "Take care... of my daughter."

Will nodded through his tears. "I will."

Ghost closed his eyes and let himself drift away. The pain in his abdomen was fading, replaced by something that felt almost like sleep. Maybe if he was lucky, Madison would be waiting for him wherever he was going. Maybe she'd greet him with that same beautiful smile that had lit up his world and fractured his heart into a million pieces, all at the same time.

Maybe after twelve years of exile and guilt and loneliness and sleepless nights, he could finally go home.

He could hear Kira calling to him from somewhere far away, the words seeming to come through water, distant and muffled. The darkness was pulling him down, and he didn't have the strength to fight it anymore. Didn't want to fight it anymore.

For the first time in years, he wasn't afraid. He was finally going home. Not just to the love of his life, but to his Father in heaven. The one who had never abandoned him. The one who had never let him die, even when he'd desperately wanted to. The one who had always been there, waiting patiently for him to come home.

Take me home, Father.

The last thing he heard was Kira's voice, strong and clear and so much like her mother's.

"I love you, Daddy."

Then there was nothing else.

Only peace.

Chapter 59

Epilogue

Kira sat on a folding chair, still as a statue, while Grace worked behind her, wrestling another section of blonde hair into place with a frustrated huff.

"Sorry," Grace muttered around the bobby pins between her lips as her belly bumped against Kira's back for the third time. "I swear this little one is determined to get in the way of everything I do these days."

Kira smiled at Grace's reflection in the small, cracked mirror propped against the windowsill. "Give it a few months, and she'll really be getting in your way."

"No kidding." Grace moved around to Kira's side, her hands on her hips as she studied her work. "By golly, I think I did it. Considering I have no idea how to style hair, I've impressed myself. Maybe I found a new career."

"I think you have."

Through the window facing the mess hall, Kira could hear singing and the distant clatter of pots. The ladies were hard at work, singing hymns while preparing what would undoubtedly be a feast for later.

The other window overlooked the open field where Nic and Avery's reception had been held a few months earlier. That night had burned itself into her memory like a photograph—the lanterns swaying in the evening breeze, the sounds of laughter mixing with guitar music, and Will's arms around her as they danced in the clearing. She could still remember the joy on Avery's face, the way she'd glowed in her simple wedding dress just before tragedy struck.

But the events that followed—the gunshots shattering the celebration, the church erupting in flames, and Avery's blood soaking into her wedding dress—had also burned themselves into the field's history.

Yet, looking at it now, the field held no remnant of either celebration or tragedy. Clusters of purple asters had bloomed where blood once stained the earth, their color vivid and defiant against the late-autumn landscape. It was as beautiful as she remembered. Maybe more so for having endured.

Places didn't hold on to memories the way people did, and that was a mercy.

"I still can't believe they rebuilt the church so quickly," Kira said, running her fingers along the smooth windowsill. "And it's even more beautiful than before."

"These people know how to build, that's for sure." Grace bit her lip and adjusted one of the pins in Kira's hair. "Just last week, I watched them put up a two-bedroom cabin in three days. But we need the room. More people keep arriving every week. Gosh, can you imagine if Aunt Reeva were alive to see this? She would say something like, 'Lord, have mercy, it's like Noah's ark around here now. Two of every kind of fool from here to kingdom come!'"

They both laughed, and for a moment it felt like Aunt

Reeva was right there in the room with them, fingers linked into the pockets of her overalls, shaking her head at all the fuss.

"Are most of the new arrivals coming from the city?" Kira asked.

"Some of them are, but many are just finding their way to us. Since Brack put up those signs along the old highway, it's like the floodgates have opened." Grace smiled, a hint of pride finding its way into her voice. "He's found his calling. My man was born to lead, even if it took him thirty years to figure it out."

"I'm so glad he's happy here. It's a good place for you to raise your baby."

The past six weeks had brought so many changes, it was hard to believe such a short time had passed since that terrible night at the Compulsory Clinic. October had vanished in a blur of color—the greens fading into a blaze of red, gold, and orange, like a final celebration only God could have orchestrated. And now November had arrived, cloaked in unseasonably warm air, as if the world were trying to hold on to its fragile beauty just a little longer.

"What about the city?" Grace asked. "You went back again last week, right?"

Kira nodded. "I wanted to visit my little brother and sister. They made me promise to come at least every other month. Their mother has been incredible. Last week, she stood up in front of the newly elected city council members and read an official statement about everything her husband had done. She also gave them access to his office and personal records, which they will make public. Hundreds of arrests have been made, including Patrol soldiers, some Guards, and many of the people who were frequently seen at the Volunteer Ball. Most people are finally starting to see the truth."

"Most?" Grace raised her eyebrows. "Not all?"

"There are people who will always believe in the

Compulsory and Volunteer programs, no matter what they learn about Devlin." Kira shook her head. "They will never see any life as precious except for their own. Most of them have left the city in small groups, heading out to start their own settlements where they can keep doing things the old way."

"You mean killing each other?" Grace visibly shuddered. "That's terrible."

"It won't last," Kira said, feeling the truth of it in her soul. "Vita Nova fell, and so will any community like it. It's inevitable. You can't build a future by killing your own people."

Through the window, Kira could see people moving between the cabins of Haven, heading toward the church. Some wore their finest clothes, while others dressed in simple, homemade clothing. It was exactly the kind of mixed gathering she'd hoped for—city people and village people, all coming together. Something she could never have imagined a few months earlier.

"We're stronger together, you know?" Kira said, rising from the chair. "The city and Haven, I mean. We're no longer enemies, we're sharing resources... I never thought any of this would be possible. The wall is coming down soon. Hopefully, by Christmas. According to Emma's father, the next step will be rebuilding the bridges."

Grace ran her fingers through her long red curls. "Someone who came in from the city yesterday said they're going to start baseball games in the Stadium next spring. If that happens, I expect you to tell me. Baseball's the only sport I can stomach."

"Will do."

Kira turned away from Grace to look in the mirror. The white dress she wore was simple but elegant, with long sleeves and a flowing skirt that fell just below her knees. Nothing like the dresses she'd worn to her Volunteer Balls. Grace had woven small wildflowers into her hair—late-blooming purple asters that were still growing in the fields.

This is my wedding day.

The realization hit her all at once—the weight of everything gained and lost. The journey from the terrified girl who had jumped off a bridge to save a little boy to a woman about to marry the love of her life. The faces waiting for her in the church, and the faces she would never see again. Tears sprang to her eyes.

"I wish my mom were here."

Grace came up from behind and wrapped her arms around Kira. "Oh, honey. She is here. Can't you feel her?"

Kira leaned into the embrace, letting herself cry for a moment. She didn't have to worry about her makeup because she wasn't wearing any. "I wish she could see this. I wish she knew that I've found someone who loves me."

"She knows," Grace whispered. "She knows, and she's so proud of you. We all are."

A knock on the door interrupted them, followed by Brack's impatient, grumbling voice. "You ladies going to bawl around all day, or are we having ourselves a wedding?"

Grace laughed through her tears. "Give us five minutes, you big oaf!"

"Five minutes, or I'm telling Will she's having second thoughts," Brack called back.

"I better get out there," Kira said. "Your husband's patience is wearing thin."

"Wait. I have a surprise for you." Grace crossed the room and dug into a small cardboard box near the doorway. She pulled out a bouquet of flowers: yellow dahlias tied together with a simple white ribbon. "I salvaged these from the church in Emmitsburg," she explained. "I'm trying to grow some new ones, too, in Aunt Reeva's honor."

Kira accepted the bouquet and wiped the fresh tears from her eyes. "They're perfect, Grace. Thank you."

"You're welcome." Grace's hand squeezed her arm. "You ready to marry this boy?"

"So ready."

Kira stepped out of the small room and into the vestibule of the church. The smell of fresh wood and pine sap filled the air, mixed with the scent of the wildflowers Grace had used to decorate for the ceremony. The walls were bare except for a single wooden cross Brack had carved himself, hanging above the doors that led into the sanctuary. It was nothing like the elaborate churches from before the virus—no stained glass windows or ornate altars, no sound systems or coffee bars.

It was simple. And it was perfect.

A man stood with his back to her, peering through a gap in the doors at the gathering crowd. His dark suit was slightly wrinkled, clearly past its prime—probably borrowed from someone in the village—but it still framed his broad shoulders well. He fidgeted, shifting his weight from one foot to the other in a way that suggested he was nervous.

She couldn't help but smile.

"Hey, Dad."

When he turned, she saw his scarred face, every line and mark telling the story of a man who understood the true meaning of sacrifice, and her heart filled with more love than she would've thought possible for this man who had chosen to be her father.

Ghost smiled at her. A smile that made her understand why her mother had loved him so deeply. "You look beautiful, Kira."

She remembered the frantic hours after he'd been shot, when Marcus had limped from the room and found Sarah Whitman among the freed prisoners. Sarah was a doctor who'd been imprisoned for refusing to take part in the Compulsory program. Working together with one of Guards, they'd stabilized him long enough to get him to the hospital. The bullet had somehow missed his heart and lungs. The doctor would say later that it was a miracle. Surgery had taken six hours, and there had been moments when they'd thought they might lose him.

But God had provided. He always did.

"How are you feeling?" she asked, studying his face for any signs of pain. She still worried about him, and she supposed she always would. It was funny how love worked between a parent and a child. First, they protected you, and then one day you found yourself protecting them.

"Like a man who gets to walk his little girl down the aisle," he said, offering her his arm with a slight grin. "Though I have to ask—are you sure about this Will character? You don't think you can do better?"

He was only teasing her. He loved Will almost as much as she did. "Yeah, I'm pretty sure he'll do."

Brack pulled open the doors to the sanctuary, giving her a quick wink before stepping aside.

Her breath caught in her throat.

The small church was packed with people, the light streaming through the windows illuminating the faces of all the people she loved. People from both Haven and Vita Nova.

She saw Emma seated in the third row, fully recovered from her ordeal in the Confines. Marcus sat beside her, his hand clasped with hers. They had started dating soon after that night, when Emma had volunteered to help at the hospital and Marcus—who was recovering from his stomach wound—had been one of her patients. Kira didn't think it would be long before she got to watch her best friend walk down the aisle.

On the right side of the church, in one of the middle pews,

a little girl with dark hair sat next to an older man. Maisie and Edward Brannigan, the father and daughter who had traveled hundreds of miles to be here. The radio silence that had worried Ghost so much had been because Maisie had fallen critically ill. She had recovered, but it had been touch and go for weeks. When Brannigan finally made contact, he insisted on bringing his people south to help rebuild what the Patrols had destroyed. He and Ghost had finally embraced in person.

Neither man had walked away from it dry-eyed.

Next to Maisie sat a little boy with blond hair and freckles. Kira's favorite little boy in the world. Teddy and Maisie had become best friends since the Brannigans' arrival, bonding over their shared love of animals and mischief. Teddy lived with Brack and Grace now. His mother had left the city without him, choosing life in one of the new settlements—one run by Sienna Graves—over her son. But the little boy was thriving in Haven. He was excited about becoming a big brother to Brack and Grace's baby, and he and Kira still spent many evenings staying awake together, lying in the grass and watching the stars come out.

Chandra Devlin and the twins were seated in the front row. That didn't surprise Kira—old habits died hard, and the Devlins were still adjusting to a world where their last name didn't automatically put them at the center of everything. But Vance and Violet waved excitedly when they spotted her, and she lifted her bouquet in response, genuinely happy to see them.

Kira closed her eyes briefly and imagined her mother sitting in the front of the church with Aunt Reeva, both women alive and joyful and smiling.

She didn't need to imagine her father because he was right there beside her, his arm strong beneath her hand.

When she opened her eyes, she was looking at Will. His

hair was still unruly despite his obvious attempt to tame it, and his borrowed suit was a size too large, the sleeves rolled up slightly at the cuffs. But he was smiling at her, and he'd never looked more handsome to her than he did in that moment.

He stood at the front of the church beside Pastor Coleman, a man who had only found his way to Haven two days earlier, thanks to Brack's roadside signs. One of the first things Ghost had asked him upon his arrival was if he would mind performing a wedding ceremony. The man had laughed and said he'd been wondering what God had led him there for. Now, it seemed, he had his answer.

An old man in a worn leather motorcycle jacket sat on a little wooden stool next to Will, his weathered hands cradling an Appalachian dulcimer that looked almost as old as he was. When Pastor Coleman leaned forward and gave him a nod, he struck up "Here Comes the Bride" on the instrument, his fingers moving deftly across the strings.

As they walked down the aisle together, Ghost leaned over and whispered, "She would love this, you know. Every single second of it."

"I know she would," she whispered back. "She'd want to dance with you all night long."

When they reached the front of the church, Pastor Coleman looked up from his open Bible, his kind eyes crinkling at the corners as he smiled at her. The old preacher looked exactly like what Kira had always imagined a minister should look like, his face lined with years of laughter and tears, of funerals and weddings and everything in between.

"Who gives this woman to this man?"

Ghost straightened beside her, his hand clutching hers with the grip of a man who wanted to hold on forever but knew he had to let go. With his other hand, he reached into his jacket pocket and pulled out the small, worn photograph of Kira's mother on the ferry—the one taken from him at the Confines. Kira had gone back to retrieve it days later, after the facility had been shut down. After hours of searching, she'd spotted it lying at the top of a trashcan in a forgotten office and brought it to him in the hospital. When he'd seen it, he'd wept.

Now, he pressed the photograph against his chest, his pride-filled voice carrying through the sanctuary.

"Her mother and I do."

Letter to Readers

I hope you enjoyed *Ransom*! If you haven't read my first series, *The Subversive Trilogy*, you can find those books online at Amazon or Barnes and Noble.

I'm currently working on my next series, and I hope to be able to share it with you very soon. My newsletter readers will be notified when my next novel is ready. Click here to sign up!

Also, if you've enjoyed this series, please consider leaving a review on Amazon, Goodreads, BookBub, your book blog, or wherever you wish. Reviews are so important for indie authors, and I truly appreciate each and every one!

Acknowledgments

To my editors, Kimberly Murphree and Lori Werni: You are the unsung heroes who catch my plot holes, grammatical errors, and strange word choices. I am forever grateful for your talent, dedication, and friendship!

To my husband: Thank you for being my best friend and the one who keeps me from completely losing it on a daily basis. God gave you your calm and patient nature for a very good reason, and I'm pretty sure that reason is me. Thank you for loving (and putting up with) me!

To my boys: You are incredible young men, and I am so blessed to be your mother. I love you so much, and I can't wait to see what God has planned for you. Whatever path you choose in life, walk it for Him.

To my readers: Thank you for taking a chance on my books. All I've ever wanted to do is tell stories, and by reading them, you've made that dream come true. I pray that in some way, this story has blessed you.

On a separate note, as I wrote this series, it began to take on a life of its own, as books often do. I noticed during *Rebellion* that this story—which was originally about the value and sanctity of human life—was also becoming a story about the complicated relationships between fathers and their children. Not all of those relationships are good or healthy, because all fathers are human, and humans make mistakes.

Some, like Victor Devlin, make much bigger ones than others.

So, if you were blessed to have a good father in your life, thank God for him every day. And if your father is still alive, give him a call and thank him for all he's done for you. A phone call, not a text. I promise, he will appreciate it.

And if your earthly father failed you—in big ways or small—I'm so sorry. But please remember that you have a Father in heaven who loves you more than you can imagine. Give your life to Him, because He knows your worth, and He will never fail you.

Finally, to my Lord and Savior, Jesus Christ, and my Father in heaven: Thank You for loving me unconditionally. Thank You for sacrificing Yourself so that I would not be forever imprisoned by my own sins. And thank You for being the truest example of selfless, sacrificial love.

You alone are worthy of reverence.

— Raena Rood
    August 2025

About the Author

Raena lives in Pennsylvania with her husband and three children. When she's not writing, she enjoys exploring historic battlefields (her kids always drag her up the tallest lookout towers), family movie nights that feature cheesy 80's and 90's action films, and daydreaming of expanding her backyard farm (goats are still under discussion). Her goal is to write stories that challenge, encourage, and remind readers that even in the darkness, when all hope seems lost, God is always in control.

Books by Raena Rood

The Subversive Trilogy
Subversive: Book 1 of the Subversive Trilogy
Sanctuary: Book 2 of the Subversive Trilogy
Salvation: Book 3 of the Subversive Trilogy

The Reverence Trilogy
Reverence: Book 1 of the Reverence Trilogy
Rebellion: Book 2 of the Reverence Trilogy
Ransom: Book 3 of the Reverence Trilogy